THE SICILIAN DAUGHTER

THE SICILIAN DAUGHTER

A NOVEL

Carolynn Pietrangeli

Radius Book Group
New York

Radius Book Group
A Division of Diversion Publishing Corp.
www.radiusbookgroup.com

For more information, email info@radiusbookgroup.com

First Radius Book Group Edition: June 2026
Trade Paperback ISBN: 9798895150764
eBook ISBN: 9798895150825

Cover design by Jen Huppert
Interior design by Westchester Publishing Services

Printed in the United States of America
10 9 8 7 6 5 4 3 2 1

For Angelina, my mother and mentor.

Contents

Principal Characters

Gaby Pecorero—main character, narrator; thirty-five years old

Ana Pecorero—Gaby's mother

Arturo Pecorero—Ana's husband

Nani / Grandma—Nunzia Raspanti—Ana's mother; Gaby's grandmother

Nonno / Grandpa—Carlo Raspanti—Nani's husband; Gaby's grandfather

Russ—Gaby's partner

- Noah—Russ's brother

Zia / Aunt Maria—Ana's sister; Gaby's aunt

- Salvatore—Maria's husband; Gaby's uncle
- Claire—Maria and Salvatore's daughter; Gaby's cousin
- Josh—Claire's husband

Giuseppe Bianchi—Grandpa's / Nonno's cousin

- Concetta—Giuseppe's wife

Secondary Characters

Matteo—Bronx textile merchant

Paolo—owner of Paolo's—favorite Bronx neighborhood restaurant

Father Bernadin—priest at Gaby's Church, St. Benedict

Rabbi Rosen—rabbi at Gaby's and Russ's wedding

Dr. Miller—Ana's respirologist

Dr. Fleming—Ana's oncologist

Sicilian Family

Giulia—Arturo's mother

Fantino—Arturo's father

Graciela—Giulia's sister

THE SICILIAN DAUGHTER

CHAPTER 1

Coming Home

I have been here many times. Rays of understanding piercing dark thoughts. The darkness is born from growing up as someone not quite me. Pure feeling always lost in *shoulds* and *musts* and *must nots*.

I drive up to the house where I was raised, still the same after all these decades save the short wrought-iron fence around the postage stamp front of the property. The two strips of pavement are meant to accommodate the wheels of a car. A long concrete flight of stairs is topped by a wide porch. Red brick saltbox structure, white-painted wood bunting hugging the roofline. The house is warm and welcoming. I park in front, my antennae tuned for judgment and unsolicited advice.

I meet my mother inside the screen door and melt into a huge bear hug, one of her specialties. She holds me at arm's length, inspects my eyes, tests the sincerity of my smile. She once told a much younger daughter: *I never know what you're thinking—you never talk to me!*

I smell braciola, the thin slices of beef rolled with garlic, simmering in spaghetti sauce. I make my way inside, run the water from the tap until it's cold and fill a glass. I tip it toward my mother, in silent query. She shakes her head.

She reaches for my hand as we settle ourselves at the table. Morgan's eight unexpected puppies frolic, challenging our footing. Reaching down, I lift the soft-furred Black Velvet to my face. His littermate Cinnamon Toast nuzzles my ankle.

"Your trip was good? You hungry I bet. It'll be ready in about ten minutes. What kind of macaroni you want? Not too much. You got to be good for the wedding." Strike one. I ignore it.

"Smells great, Ma. Penne?"

"Sure." She has the pot of water on the stove and the penne out of the cupboard in seconds.

"You still like Boston?" she asks. "Any plans to move back?" I've been in Boston fifteen years. I'm not moving back.

"I'm good. Not looking to relocate."

"Russell?"

"He's pretty happy too."

"He should be! You living together before you marry. Why you doing that?" Strike two.

She insists. "I didn't raise you that way." I want to ask: "What way?" but I have lots of experience down the maternal rabbit hole. I refrain also from reminding her that she started raising me—whatever way—some thirty-five years ago.

"Ah! The water's boiling. Sure you want penne? I have rigatoni, spaghetti."

"What do *you* want, Ma?"

"Me?" She smiles, pretends to be easygoing. "You know me: I'm good with anything."

Stirring the pasta, she shows me the back of her neatly tied apron. "How long you staying? Russell coming down?"

"Three days, Ma. Russ is working." She knows this.

Waves of disappointment move toward me. "Oh."

She sets the plates out and wipes her hands on her apron. I'm standing at the small kitchenette table, weighing the price of escape.

Criticism and displeasure are essential ingredients of Ana's mothering. Right now, I long to shut them out.

My mother points her pasta spoon toward a kitchen chair. "Sit down," she tells me. She has placed me where she can see me as she talks.

Only Ana can make braciola. I melt back to my childhood, surrounded by cousins and aunts, the men inside sharing some joke not for our ears.

"Tell me about school." I'm a university professor.

"About the same all the time—different students, same courses, some good, some bad things happen."

My mother teaches home economics at a local Catholic high school. "How's school by you, Ma?"

"I think the kids don't really want to run a home—planning, budgeting, money-saving, cooking, cleaning. All the stuff I learned the hard way. I do know that they like sewing and needlework a lot more."

"Do you feel frustrated that they don't like the 'home' part?"

"Not really—it's just the generation and what they learn at home. We learned how to care for a home before we learned anything else."

I like to hear my mother talk about her work. She enjoys talking about it, and it gives us both a break from her criticizing me and my life.

"They're learning quilt-making—they love picking out the material. The actual sewing and quilting I'm not too sure about. That's work."

Unbelievably, we make small talk for over an hour. Even as a kid, I could never see the point of small talk. But it's where I'm most comfortable with my mother.

I can't remember when I started to be careful around my mother. Careful for her? For me? So far, safe ground. But it won't last.

"I'll do the dishes, then I'm going for a short run."

Ana folds her arms in front of her. She never has been a fan of my running. She organizes the used dishes and cutlery. One eyebrow shoots up. "Suit yourself. Go. I'll clean up. It'll take less time."

Already in running tights, I lace up my shoes and grab the hi-vis shell from my travel bag. I'm glad I kept my feedbag light. I call to her as I'm headed out the door.

"Don't be long," my mother yells back.

The city hasn't been good to these streets. The sidewalk is cracked where it's always been cracked. Only more deeply. The trees planted near the curb are tired; pockmarked roots push at the surrounding concrete, competing for space and air. My feet plant where I deliberately set them. Ana will be really put out if I fall.

A bad habit, I heel strike the square of concrete that brought an end to my Roll Capades career.

CHAPTER 2

Roll Capades

Debra and I sashayed down the block in front of my house on our roller skates, choreographing and singing as we went along as a unit. Roll Capades was a collaborative invention of ours. A game we played often. Debra strapped her hands around my waist. We reached one arm up and twisted to the right. It would have worked, too, if it hadn't been for the fractured sidewalk. I tripped, grunted and went down with a sickening thud. My right wrist, on fire, was trapped under my legs. Debra bounced back up, found me splayed on the sidewalk and announced that I'd better show my mother. She carefully removed her skates, then mine, and asked if I wanted her to come with me.

"No. She'll be mad. You better go." Her relief was palpable.

Amazed, I watched my wrist grow to twice its normal size as I opened the front door to my house.

"What's wrong?"

"I fell playing Roll Capades with Debra."

"Playing *what*?" She glared past me. "Debra okay?" She was drying her hands as she propped the screen door open.

"Maddone!" She took my arm in her hand and poked at the wrist.

"Can you move it?" In a game of Simon Sez, she instructed me to move my own wrist side to side, up and down. My wrist complied. Painfully. But it completed the moves.

"We'll watch it. Maybe the swelling will go down on its own."

I turned to go upstairs. She grabbed my upper arm.

"What's *Roll Capades*?"

I described our game of dancing and singing on roller skates, knowing, too late, how she would react. Realizing at the same time that at fifteen years old, we were too old for this kids' game.

My mother's eyes turned to steel. She spit "Stupida!" through clenched teeth and slapped my upper arm. Hard. A magnitude 6.0 earthquake radiated to my wrist.

She let me go. "Wash and dry your arm and get a large clean rag out of the linen closet. We'll make a sling." Shaking her head, she waved me away. "What if you had cracked your head? At least Debra's not hurt. I'll call her mother."

The next morning, the swelling was down and I could move my wrist. I wouldn't tell her that it still hurt. I was determined not to draw her attention.

My homework handwriting was choppy. At school, I did not want the sling or any questions. At my school desk, the pencil delivered a sawtooth script. Sister Edward and her rosary beads swished down the aisle. She asked what was wrong. She didn't forget to tell me that my penmanship was awful.

A week later, my wrist had returned to the twice-as-large-as-normal size. Just as it had been after the accident. My fingers, inserted into fluffy mashed potatoes, had become fat Oscar

Mayer hot dogs. My knuckles had melted away to baby-doll-sized dimples.

"Now we have to go," my mother announced. She asked if it hurt.

I told her it did not hurt. Which wasn't true, but I couldn't risk her railing at me.

We visited our family doctor, my mother's cousin—Dr. Salvi. Smiling, my mother passed him an oil-stained, brown-bagged care package of her homemade, and his favorite, broccoli rabe—Italian broccoli sautéed in olive oil and garlic.

"Tell him!" my mother commanded, and I reluctantly recounted the humiliation of my short Roll Capades career. He asked a few questions, and, when they were ready, he looked over the X-rays of my wrist. Frowning, Dr. Salvi removed his glasses and wrote a referral to an orthopedic surgeon. For us to follow up on. Immediately.

"Surgeon," my mother said. Gritting her teeth in disapproval, she shot a menacing look my way. "She's going to need surgery." Ana asked these questions as if they were facts.

"I don't know, Ana, but she's got to see him. It's already been over a week. Not good. And I don't like the X-ray."

It was three days before we could get an appointment. Dr. Metzger was a strangely shaped man. Unremarkable to his waist, a huge pumpkin propped on skinny legs protruded below. I kept wondering if his fly would pop open. If it was about to, I was pretty sure I didn't want to be there.

Looking over his own set of my X-rays, Dr. Metzger told us I had a greenstick fracture in my wrist. He assured us that it's not uncommon for these to produce swelling that comes, then goes, then, of course, comes again. I wanted to ask if the pain was like that, too, but glancing at my mother, I thought better of it.

I had checked out, wondering how much of what he had in mind was going to hurt. My mother had her antennae up, wondering how much this was going to cost. I steeled myself for more of her teeth grinding and eye action.

Dr. Metzger was definitely pushing for orthopedic surgery. My mother was resisting.

"What happens if she doesn't have surgery?"

"I can reset her wrist, and we can hope for the best. But the longer you delay surgery, the worse it will be. She'll probably never have full function in her wrist."

I was only fifteen years old. That meant when I was old like my mother, I wouldn't be able to use my wrist. And this was my *right hand*. The one I really needed. Gulping hard, I wondered if it was too late to be left-handed.

I looked at my mother. I could see her thinking: *It's only a wrist. We'll get it reset and maybe it will be okay. There's no money for this.*

Shaking his head, Dr. Metzger led me to a stretcher. Once I was on my back, he grabbed my wrist and demonstrated the size breath I should inhale. And that I should look away.

His instructions were followed by a sickening crack and a wash of nausea that threatened to launch me from the stretcher. I didn't cry out. But I wanted to.

"She's very brave," Dr. Metzger remarked.

My mother nodded her head. "She hardly ever feels pain," she said.

Sporting a bright white plaster cast, I was ready to leave Dr. Metzger's office. Underneath the cast, a white sock swaddled my swollen fingers and my arm peeked beneath the plaster. I understood for the first time what an opposable thumb is. I had lost one of mine.

* * *

I'm at the turnaround point in my run. All my familiar haunts. The bakery featuring my favorite Italian bread, fresh rolls and jelly doughnuts on Sundays. The fancy restaurant with the red-draped ceiling-to-floor windows where we never ate—it was too expensive. You couldn't see inside—the long drapes hid the tables and the diners. Across the street sat McDonald's Golden Arches. When it opened, we ate Big Macs three nights in a row.

The grocery store, where my mother was the first customer every Saturday morning. Next door, John's Deli. I can smell soppressata dried sausage, pecorino Romano cheese and the pickled eggplant as I run past. The photo place where my Communion portrait stood in the window for two years. So weird for a little Italian kid to have blond hair. John's Bargain Store selling shiny pots and pans, potholders with patterns I loved, serving spoons, dinner dishes. I always liked these much more than ours. I run past Frank's Five and Ten. We used to sneak through the narrow aisles to avoid Mr. Frank—till we got caught: "If yer not gonna buy nothin', get *out*!" he would yell. For someone who hated kids, 90 percent of what he sold was for us.

* * *

Seven weeks after the collapse of the Roll Capades, I found myself again in Dr. Metzger's office, smelling of plaster and rubbing alcohol laced with pipe tobacco. The cast was no longer white, and the sock was a distressing shade of gray. I was aware of a sweet-rancid odor emanating from the cast. I was afraid of what lay beneath.

I turned my head away as Dr. Metzger fired up his saw. Chips of plaster and dust floated through the air, some landing in my hair. Snapping the plaster in two, he was down to the sock. The smell was nauseating. I steeled myself. After all, this was cast-off day, and I'd been promised ice cream.

From his stainless-steel tray, Dr. Metzger selected an odd-looking pair of scissors, the blades at an angle to the finger holes. A small, thin spatula was perched on the end of one of the blades. He clipped the sock carefully, releasing a fine spray of gray and white fibers. I was terrified. I knew, somehow, that my wrist would not look normal.

By my estimation, my arm, casted just below the elbow and decorated with flakes of dead white and gray skin, had shrunk to half its precast size. The sickly sweet stench was overpowering. I was grateful when the nurse walked me to the huge porcelain sink, soaped my arm, and rinsed and dried it. Gingerly, she supported my arm into a fresh, clean muslin sling, fixing it around my neck and shoulder.

In the next room, my mother and Dr. Metzger consulted in low tones. I saw my mother shake her head, her mouth set in disagreement. Dr. Metzger invited me to join them, explaining that he wanted to get another set of X-rays.

Examining the films, he said, "It's improved with the resetting but there is still damage here and here." His thick finger jabbed at the negative image as he spoke. "I understand you don't want surgery." He looked hopefully at my mother, who nodded her assent. Snapping the X-rays from the light box, he remarked, "We'll see how it goes, then."

We both thanked him. Dr. Metzger advised, "Call my office if there are any problems. Swelling, pain, if you can't use your wrist, okay?"

We walked to the ice cream parlor down the block. My mother ordered butter pecan; I had my favorite, soft vanilla and chocolate swirl in a cone. We tasted each other's ice cream and laughed, happy that it was over. My mother inspected my arm. "It's thin," she remarked. "You'll have to use it to get it strong again." To me, it was ugly and weird, and the wrist was bent sideways. I hated it.

CHAPTER 3

The Wedding Suit

Coming into the house after my run, I'm setting my shoes aside when I spy Ana at the top of the stairs, ready to go.

"He's not open all night, you know," she reminds me. "Get a move on."

I don't dare shower. Instead, I take a soapy washcloth to all my strategic body parts, grateful for my very short hair, and take the stairs down two at a time.

My mother is lurking at the front door. She has always designed and tailored all her clothes. She's wearing a nicely fitted below-the-knee brown wool skirt and a floral top, lipstick, and a subtle bit of eye makeup. Her ear-length brown hair is smartly styled. What's she dressed for?

"We are going to Matteo's. For the material for your wedding dress. Did you forget?" she asks.

"No, Ma. I'm ready." Naturally, I had no recollection of this date at Matteo's. Matteo is the owner of the shop who has sold her virtually all the fabric she's used for her entire wardrobe and mine.

At 2 P.M., we head to Westchester Square, site of Matteo's shop, the local elevated train and the city bus hub close to home. I have always been electrified and terrified by the activity in this part of town.

Food-stained sidewalks smelling of gasoline, stagnant water and urine creating rainbow-rippled pools along the weed-infested asphalt.

The streets and paths around Westchester Square are paved with discarded food wrappers, flattened dead cigarette butts and spent pizza crusts along with their boxes. Competing with this is the irresistible aroma of the pizza place on the corner. The park is inhabited by creatures I dare not make eye contact with. Baseball caps perched the wrong way on tight beaded braids or on long heads of hair. Gold chains over sweatshirts and blingy T-shirts. Rings on every finger. Earrings dangling from the ears of people of both sexes. Lots of black eye makeup and teased hair on girls sporting tight jeans and dangerously high heels.

* * *

Traveling to my high school through Westchester Square, I was always certain I would board the wrong bus and wind up lost. While I couldn't confess this to anyone, I dreamed about it, wondering how I would get home. Traveling with my friend Jane made it better—she always knew where we were going and how to get there, but I felt humiliated and defeated by my lack of directional resourcefulness.

Traveling from home, as the bus turned into the Square, we had to finish talking before we arrived. The steel-on-steel crunch of train wheels against rails and the belching of crowded buses as they approached their stops was all our hearing could take. We did this twice a day. I was always disoriented by the back-home direction.

But, on the way home, I relaxed when we switched to the Tremont Avenue bus that would deliver us close to my street, just down the hill from the bus stop. This was the last leg of the day's travel, and as we approached my street I felt encouraged by the landmarks along the route. I began to anticipate sitting at my desk near the window in the upstairs hallway where I would tackle my homework every day.

I remember a day when Jane and I made fun of our schoolmate Annetta as we bounced along in the back of the Tremont Avenue bus.

Jane instigated the discussion. "Hey, did she give you a sweaty mint?! Did she say: *Would you like a peppermint?!*"

We stared at each other full on—"Eww!"—and twittered behind our hands.

Jane nodded as I offered my opinion. "She is *sooo* weird."

Feeling a bit guilty, Jane observed, "I think she's lonely too. I mean, nobody hangs out with her." I was deservedly ashamed.

Halfway home, I spied something moving on the floor of the bus, near our shoes. "Oh!"

"What?" demanded my friend.

"I'm sure I just saw a cockroach run across the floor!"

"A what? That's disgusting!"

"We have to get off the bus before it gets into our schoolbags!"

"Don't they hang around in packs." I'm not asking. Panicked at the thought of carrying even one live cockroach into my mother's house, I shivered at the thought of a colony. I knew they had no self-respect—they would reproduce in my schoolbag for sure.

All buses for the next half hour would be full. We didn't ask each other if we were prepared to wait or to walk the rest of the way. Exposure to vermin is a true emergency. We decided to exit the bus.

Queasy with the swaying of the vehicle, we staggered our way to the front door. "You have to let us out," Jane demanded.

Heroically supporting my friend, I echoed a resounding, "Yes! We just saw a *cockroach*!"

Glancing in the rearview mirror and mouthing a toothpick across his lower lip as he ignored us, the driver continued along Tremont

Avenue. A soft snigger emerged. "Y'don't say." He clearly failed to appreciate the seriousness of the situation. If I carried just one of these things home, my mother would evict me.

We grabbed the bar next to the driver's seat and planted our feet. "If y'wanna get out, y'gotta wait till the next stop. I'm not stoppin' in between."

Tacitly, we agreed to wait, lifting our schoolbags high above the floor as we struggled to remain upright.

Brakes screeching, at the next stop, the driver adjusted his cap and stopped, half laughing, half sneering as we shrieked down the steps, recounting our brush with disaster. We stopped to inspect our schoolbags. Clear. But I was still anxious. Weren't cockroaches good at hiding?

I told my mother about our adventure. "What? *Cockroaches!* Don't you dare bring that schoolbag in here till you empty it out! We get one roach in here, in a week we'll have a million."

I didn't bother to tell her that I had already checked the bag. I checked again. I wanted to be sure, and I didn't want her to hover.

Jane and I had successfully avoided *The Invasion of the Killer Cockroaches.*

* * *

I wish I'd had a shower. Grimy and still damp with sweat, I follow my mother obediently into Matteo's fabric shop. The place is a shotgun closet, bolts of fabric piled high on ancient shelves reaching up on either side of a scarred central wooden table and crowding the floor. I find myself estimating the size of the fire hazard. The ancient cash register sits in a corner of the bench that measures fabric and elastic, lace and ribbon. The yardstick is imprinted right into the bench, the numbers worn, the font vintage 1940s and faded over time.

Sunlight punctuated with lint dust filters through the single battered door and trestle window. Despite the openings, stale air scented with cotton and polyester is permanently settled over the shop. Matteo ignites his broadest smile and rubs his hands together when he sees us. Truth be told, when he sees my mother.

"Ah! Ana! Ah'm-a so happy see you!" He holds both her hands and plants the alternating triple kiss on both cheeks.

Is she blushing?

"Yes, Matteo! This is my daughter Gaby—she's getting married."

"Oh, so nice-a see you all grow up, signorina! Congratulazioni!"

"Grazie, Matteo!" My mother is strapped tight into the driver's seat. She produces an impressive set of wedding dress photos collected from magazines.

"So you need a material fer vestito de sposa—for a wedding dress—no?" Matteo sizes me up. He registers that at thirty-five years old, I'm no blushing bride.

"You marry before, signorina?"

"No!" my mother insists. I manage to control my sense of humor.

"Mi scusi! Ovviamente! Ovviamente!" Of course not, for sure not!

"So we want to look at white satin and white lace."

"Okay. Raso e pizzo bianca. No problem!"

"Matteo," I cut in. My mother shoots me a look. I soldier on.

"I'd like to see fabric in a pale coral or peach color to have a suit—a jacket and pants."

"But, signorina! You no marry before! You got to have-a dress—bianca."

I'm treated to my mother's smug nod as Matteo looks back at her, smiling. A few beads of sweat have formed on his forehead.

"You see? You mama, she want this too."

She sets her mouth and crosses her arms. "I won't sew a suit," she declares.

"That's okay, Ma. I'll buy one." Her face hits the ground.

"I mean, I don't *want* to, but I *do* want a suit. In pale coral or peach, not white."

I pull a sketch out of my bag. My friend Margaret's handiwork.

They put their heads together and take a long look.

Matteo inclines his head to one side in shy query. "It's-a nice, no?"

"If you're a man, sì." My mother is clearly on a campaign to kill my wedding suit.

Matteo is eyeing his shelves. "Coral like pale pink, sì?"

"More like orange and pink mixed together Matteo," I tell him. My mother grits her teeth at me.

"Ah! Sì."

Matteo slides a battered wooden shelf-mounted ladder toward him and, climbing up, stops at a tower of silk and satin bolts of fabric in every conceivable color. Scaling the rungs, he selects three bolts of fabric without disrupting the others and climbs down single-handedly.

"Ana, signorina, what you think?"

Raw silk in pale peach catches my eye immediately. I can feel the comfort of the pants and the ease of the jacket across my shoulders. "Ma?"

"Well, white is out, and that's what I want." She doesn't mean to be, but she's pretty funny when she pouts. I control my impulse to smile.

"Signora Ana, is Gaby wedding, no?" Bald and stubble-cheeked, he's not an appealing-looking little man, but suddenly I want to plant a huge kiss on his gray scratchy cheek.

For his trouble, he is treated to my mother's raised eyebrow and a warning. "She'll look ridiculous!"

He smiles. "Maybe no. Maybe she look bellissima!"

Determined to be tough but surprised by Matteo's mild defiance, my mother stares at the textile merchant in disbelief. Matteo and I hold our collective breath.

After what feels like an hour, she speaks. "Yes, Matteo—remember who's paying, but, yes, the raw silk looks good. Show me some patterns for dresses *and* ladies' pantsuits." Her truce tells me that this is part of my wedding present.

After appraising me—front, back, up and down—Matteo takes my measurements and collects several patterns from the ancient wood drawers standing behind his table. My mother reminds him/me that I'll be losing weight before the wedding.

Mopping his forehead with a withered handkerchief and smiling, he nods and spreads the patterns before us. He presents high-waisted broad bell-shaped pants beneath a peplum jacket. Next, he showcases a double-breasted square-shouldered jacket over straight-legged pants. Another pattern of the same over wide pants. Several others sport bows in the front or ruffles around the jacket neckline. I ignore the dress patterns. All are poorly disguised first cousins to wedding dresses.

I pull out the single-breasted jacket over slim-fit ankle-length pants. Suddenly, I feel optimistic about balancing on high heels. I'll carry flats with me for the reception.

My mother is focused on the ruffled jacket. She's turning the pattern over, calculating the amount of fabric, lining and trim we need. I place myself between her and Matteo's line of sight. Diplomatically, he is unrolling and stomping the bolt of peach raw silk across the table, preparing to cut.

"Matteo?" I pull the pattern from the pile and turn it toward him. "This is the one I like. Ma, have a look. I know you'll like it."

"Ugh. So plain. And these pants—you gonna lose that much weight? And what kind of shoes? Remember, you can't walk in high heels. And you can't wear running shoes."

Matteo gently rescues the pattern with his free hand. "Ana, guarda! Va bene, no? Look, it will be good, no?" My mother dismisses his compliment of my choice with the wave of a hand as she flashes him the most disappointed look she can muster.

"Signorina Gaby, a nice white blouse?" He strokes his own wrinkled shirt sitting beneath an ancient threadbare jacket. "Satin, maybe? Ana, you like, no?"

My mother adjusts her line of sight. "Maybe, sì."

I struggle to curb my enthusiasm. Can I actually be winning?

"But," she continues—I hold my breath—"I get to pick the pattern and the material for the blouse."

"Okay, signorina?"

"Yes, okay!"

Matteo turns back to his wooden drawers, extracting five blouse patterns. He sets them out, then swings the ladder back his way to pull bolts of fabric. White. Satin floral jacquard. Embossed jacquard. Feather fan. Plain ivory raw silk.

It's a good assortment of patterns. Simple boat neck with long sleeves. Cowl neck. Ruffled sweetheart neckline. Plain sweetheart fitted with pearl buttons.

Another virtual year passes as my mother examines the patterns. She holds each one up to each fabric. I swear she sees me in every combination as she judges.

"Remember," she reminds me, "I get to pick."

Sweetheart with buttons. Plain ivory raw silk. I exhale.

"Looks great, Ma."

"Yeah, I know." She smiles and places the pattern on top of the ivory fabric.

Matteo is beaming. "Everything very nice, no?" He glances hopefully at my mother. She rewards him with her smile. "Bella sposa"—*beautiful bride*—he declares.

They gossip in Italian as Matteo measures, cuts and tallies. I don't press my luck as buttons are selected for the jacket and blouse. Matteo adds using a pencil stub sharpened with a kitchen knife, licking the tip of the pencil as he completes his calculation. As usual, he includes extra fabric to my mother's order without charge.

"Grazie, Matteo." He nods a huge smile. I smile back; Matteo and I have been worthy allies.

I carry a large brown paper package tied with string as we exit Matteo's shop.

"Ma—Matteo—how long you been coming to him for material?"

"Since you were little. He helped me get my job in the dress factory after your father died."

"You like him, Ma?"

"Sure. What's not to like? He's polite, a good businessman."

"Good looking, Ma?" There's easily more than a half foot between them, in my mother's favor.

She tries to glare at me, but the corners of her mouth turn up and her neck reddens.

"What? I don't care about that."

"You ever think about spending time with him? Like for a movie or dinner?"

"Ach. Never. Non mi piace. I wouldn't like that. That stuffy shop. I'd wind up with emphysema or something."

"But, Ma, there'd be more than the shop, right?"

She shrugs but doesn't answer. We make our way back from Westchester Square.

Walking into the living room when we arrive home, Ana immediately spreads the fabrics on the sofa and nods her approval. "Bellissimo!"

I run upstairs, shouting back, "I'll be back down—got to clean up." Recalling my teenage years, my bedroom ceiling still features a yellowed, dog-eared and somewhat outdated periodic table. I take a running leap at my twin bed dressed in its light pink chenille bedspread, worrying that my mother has heard from downstairs. I exhale when she doesn't call up to me.

Convinced that all is calm, I channel a well of immaturity, letting out a low laugh as I punch my fists at the ceiling. I've won the battle of the wedding suit. Worth celebrating because it is rare for me to win a standoff with my mother. I have to remind myself that I am thirty-five years old.

I shower for a long time, still chuckling to myself as I smooth the hot water over me and take my time drying and dressing. I seek out my mother in the kitchen.

Much of my soul belongs to my mother's kitchen. Outdated, it is a repository of our family history and home to my childhood images. The immaculate distressed gas stovetop. The scrubbed, scratched countertops. *You're not finished doing the dishes*, my mother would say, *until you scrub the stove, the sink and the countertops.*

When I was a kid, my mother painted a realistic brick wall backsplash that still looks real. The ancient nested cast-iron frying pans and pots that gleam with years of steel wool scrubbing sit in the cabinets below the stovetop. These keep company with the two-footed wobbly colander and the dented set of aluminum pots in sizes from single-serving soup pot to gigantic pasta-worthy cauldron. Outside the stove area, a small table accommodates breakfast and cups of espresso. With biscotti.

The window above the pitted porcelain sink admits, in this heart of the Bronx, a world of trees and Italian postage stamp backyards stuffed with tomatoes, carrots, lettuce, radishes, basil, oregano and mint. I can still see Mr. Paccino—I called him Pop—his slow walk up and down his rows of vegetables, inspecting, pruning, debugging, harvesting, wearing his scrappy straw hat ally against the sun. To my mother's delight, he would ring our doorbell, hat in hand, to deliver zucchini, tomatoes and spinach. Ma's magic would make them supper.

Hard to believe, but I am hungry for dinner.

"Ma, you have rice?"

"Of course, I have arborio. Why?"

"I'll make risotto for supper."

"You?"

"Ma."

"Okay." She extracts the rice from the cabinet above the stove and separates the medium cast-iron pan from the nest of three below the stove. I pull out onions and garlic and fresh basil, oregano and parsley. Of course, there's pancetta—cured Italian-style bacon—in the fridge and a rectangular tin gallon of imported olive oil in the pantry.

I love making risotto. The gentle discipline of heating and stirring. Aromas maturing in the pan. I toss a salad of arugula and shaved Parmesan. I easily locate my mother's huge jug of balsamic vinegar to finish off the dressing and decide on veal in my mother's fridge for this risotto.

The dish is almost cooked through. Onions, garlic, olive oil and veal join forces. I shave some more Parmesan into the pan. Cream and a bit of milk. I grind pepper over the top of the greens.

My mother comes back downstairs. She says she's been preparing the pattern for cutting.

"Smells good," she affirms. "I'm hungry."

I finish slicing the bread. Salad, olives, pickled eggplant are already on the table. I bring out the casserole dish containing the risotto and release the aroma in a cloud of steam.

We eat and talk with no criticism of my risotto. Then I remember: She taught me to cook—she would be critiquing herself.

* * *

She had always encouraged me to cook. The training intensified when I got caught in a teenage lie. My supermarket job made me fast friends with Tanya. When I was sixteen, Tanya was the girl I wanted to be. She was eighteen, thin and shapely and tall and wore great clothes and shoes. She had gorgeous hazel eyes. An enthralling single beauty mark just below her left lower eyelid. A ready smile, infectious giggle, smart.

Unbelievably, she considered me a work friend. At sixteen, I was short for my age and clumsy. My once-blond hair had long darkened to an unruly thick, wavy brown mane. Attempts to style it failed repeatedly. But I didn't want to cut it. That and my father's bushy eyebrows gave me a serious, studious look. I had inherited my mother's mouth—a thin upper lip complemented by a full lower lip. I wasn't fat, but a paunchy stomach constantly tormented me. When not in my school uniform, I wore baggy shirts that reached below my thighs. As a rule, I didn't laugh very much. But I did with Tanya.

On Friday nights, we would retreat to her beat-up Dodge to talk and share a bottle of cheap sparkling rosé wine and cherry turnovers that I bought in the supermarket checkout aisle. I understood I was not welcome to her inner circle the rest of the time.

Tanya helped me understand that my sixteen-year-old angst was normal. That I'd come through. That I was funny and smart. At two years younger, I had to believe her. But I knew my mother would never approve of my Friday night wine fests. So I did what many sixteen-year-olds do: I lied. I congratulated myself for my creative and credible lie—I worked late on Fridays to help prepare for Saturdays in the supermarket.

In my experience, every lie has its reckoning. One Friday, our neighbor Mr. Bowles was walking through the parking lot when he witnessed the wine bottle pass from Tanya to me. He did what any parent would do. He ratted me out.

My mother was ready when I came home. Too sweetly, she asked me how it went. Anticipating trouble, I barely answered.

"Oh, good," she said. But she had my attention. Her body language screamed, *I've got you.*

She told me that Mr. Bowles had busted me, and then, hands on her hips, she laced in. "When did you get the idea that it's okay to drink at your age, and *in the back of a car*?" She pointed a long, overworked index finger a half inch from my nose. I gasped for air. "When did I give you permission to behave like *trash*?" Then she went for the jugular. "I'm just glad your father isn't here to see this. You know exactly how disappointed he would be."

I couldn't explain, only try to apologize. But I never got the chance. A dismissive gesture of her hand shut me down.

"I'm going inside. You go upstairs. I can't see you right now."

Later, I heard her on the phone with Zia Maria. "I *have* to be a terrible mother! Why would she do this? I know, I *know*, Claire has never done a bad thing in her life, right? I'm talking about Gaby right now."

Hearing my mother say she was bad at anything clued me in to her vulnerability. I had never before associated the word *vulnerable* with my mother.

I imagined my mother rolling her eyes. I rolled my own, remembering how Claire hounded the confessional because she had stolen eye shadow from the drugstore. I winced, knowing my own time in confession was coming. It would be my luck to draw Father Adolf. His specialty was making me sweat. I'd be saying Hail Marys until I was twenty-five.

I was grounded for a month. And was ordered to the kitchen to cook all our dinners. That was the month I learned how to cook.

CHAPTER 4

Family and Movie Night

We're washing the dinner dishes when Ma tells me that Nani—my grandmother Nunzia—will be visiting along with Zia—my aunt, Maria, my mother's sister—the following day. I've always been close to Nani—she's my most steadfast supporter, and, I'm sure, the source of my sense of humor. Zia Maria, my mother's sister, is the most sympathetic soul I know. My mother takes good care of Zia, but, always, beneath her smile, I feel my aunt's strong undercurrent of pathos and sorrow. I'm reminded that we were all young when the men, my father, Arturo, and my uncle Salvatore, passed within three years of each other. Claire and I were teenagers. Our mothers were still settling into the end of their thirties.

I return to my room to get some work done. I pull out a sheaf of articles to support my next lecture, and, as usual, I'm lost in minutes. Controversial information and conclusions—my specialty—a chance to rank the quality of the research. I see the lecture take shape and feel myself nodding. A challenging but instructional lecture for the students. A study in learning for me. Many more student dartboards with my photo in the middle to be hung and targeted.

I call Russ when I take a break. I rub a corner of the vintage childhood chenille bedspread between my thumb and forefinger while I wait for him to pick up.

When he hears my voice, Russ is cheerful and upbeat. I remind myself that I have a right to be cheerful too.

"Well, what's happening out there that's good?"

I tell him about my winning the pantsuit and peach raw silk battle, and he laughs. I brighten as I tell him about the visit tomorrow. I guess I've interrupted his work. He has become distracted. My reaction is self-blame. I'm not interesting.

I realize halfway through that I haven't asked about him. So I do.

He inhales through his teeth. "This project's a bear. Team's at each other's throats. And the deadline doesn't change."

"What about management?"

"The only thing they care about is getting it submitted on time to the FDA. Naturally, we don't want to wait for the next review cycle."

"Are you taking care of yourself? Basketball? Watching sports?" I ask.

"I am. I'll be happy when you're back." Russ clues into my mood. "You sound spent. What are you doing for yourself?"

"Running some, not enough, actually enjoying my old neighborhood."

"I'm glad you're enjoying your time there. I like both our Bronx stomping grounds. You're home in, what, two more days?"

"Leaving on the third morning."

"Call me again—I miss you."

"I miss you too. Good luck with the project." The line disconnects.

I feel the familiar nagging that I don't live up to Russ. I love him. I want to be married to him, but I fall short. Often, I place myself first, just like he places me. I resolve to be more aware. Can I do it? Disquieted by Russ's work stress and my self-insights, I retreat to the go-to-work prescription. As always, my preferred remedy.

Eventually, my mother calls up the stairs with a welcome invitation. "I'm watching a great movie. Come down—I'll make popcorn."

I join her in the kitchen, where she's pouring olive oil into an ancient kettle-shaped pot. The lid sits nearby as the battered pot wobbles on the cast-iron stove grate. Adding the popcorn, she turns to me. "How is Russell—you called him, no?"

I perceive a level of intrusion in her question, but I plaster a smile on my face. "He's good, Ma."

She counters with: "I need to know him better before the wedding."

"You will, Ma, I promise."

Shaking the kettle as it wobbles on the burner, she nods. The heat is doing its job, sending staccato bullets to the inside of the lid. Same pot, same protocol from when I was a kid. The comforting sound anticipates the welcome sharing of a movie with my mother.

"You want salt or butter?"

"Just salt for me, thanks."

She divides the popcorn into two large bowls and sprinkles a generous helping of salt into each one. Then she places a small amount of butter into a miniature pan. When it melts, she pours it into her own bowl. I follow her back into the living room. Fold my legs under me, draw up a throw for both of us and dig into the popcorn.

My mother loves vintage films. Especially from the forties and fifties. *Mildred Pierce* is one of her favorites, and one of mine too. I watch her carefully as the opening credits roll. She's as relaxed as I ever see her. I exhale and settle back.

Of course, everyone is *supposed* to, but I discover a renewed dislike for the Veda character. So entitled! So greedy and dismissive. And

I always feel sorry for Mildred Pierce, trying desperately to satisfy her offspring's insatiable selfishness.

"Oh! What a nasty daughter!" my mother exclaims, as she always does, when Veda unpacks the dress her mother has mail-ordered for her. Out of sight of Mildred Pierce, but within hidden earshot, Veda turns to her sister, condemning the styling and quality of the dress. And criticizes the mother for failing to provide better.

Ana and I converse lightly as we anticipate our favorite scenes.

My mother says, "Oh, I love when Mildred works so hard at the restaurant and then opens her own. You remember? She'll be RICH in this scene!" We graduate to ice cream and brownies. I'll *really* have to run tomorrow.

I comment on Mildred Pierce's marital status. "Ma—in that time—the thirties—I didn't think divorce really happened."

She thinks for a moment before she responds. "It didn't—even in my day. LOTS of women, for sure, were miserable. They didn't know they'd be doing so much dirty work. Hard work. For no pay. Worse, no acknowledgment. Just criticism all the time. I knew lots of girls like this. They just put up and shut up—they had kids. No real choice."

"What about you and Papa, Ma?"

Her face softens. "Ahh, your father; he was different. He always wanted to know what I was thinking and what I wanted. He was always taking care of me, and you—at first, I had to redo your diapers. He caught me once and made me give him a lesson. Yeah . . . your father was a good one."

She places her ice cream bowl on the coffee table and reaches over to pat my knee. "You, you live in a better time. Look at your job. There weren't many girl university professors. Now, girls can do whatever they want! It's wonderful—but I still feel bad for the wives I knew back then."

"I'm grateful, Ma, believe me! Hey, great brownies."

"Of course—from scratch."

We wash up. I kiss her on each cheek and wish her good night.

"You too—sleep tight. God keep you."

This night, my head hits the pillow beneath my periodic table in the sky and I forget to dream.

CHAPTER 5

All of Us Immigrants

"Gaby! You plan to sleep all morning? Come on down—I want to get breakfast going."

I wake disoriented, immediately feeling Russ's absence. I remember where I am.

The clock reads 6:40 A.M. Lots of morning left, by my estimation.

I grab the ancient, immaculately clean bathrobe from the back of the bedroom door and swing it over my shoulders. I pull on worn but impeccably clean slippers, also left for me. I buy myself time by using the bathroom. I emerge with a clean face and clean teeth, but I REALLY need a shower. And a run. Not in that order.

I meet my mother in the kitchen. "Ma, I've really got to get in a short run before I eat. I don't wear popcorn, ice cream and brownies real well." Not to mention today's feasts.

"Your grandmother and your aunt will be here soon." They will arrive at 2 P.M.

She pulls her apron off and pours herself a cup of stovetop espresso into a delicate blue-and-white porcelain cup sent from Italy as a wedding gift for my parents.

"You want before you go?" She nods at the pot on the stove.

My answer trails behind me as I bound up the stairs to change.

"No, Ma—later. You have roasted red peppers?"

"Sure. And good fresh bread too."

"Ooh," I yell down. "Can I have an egg-in-the-bread when I come back?"

"Of course." She chuckles. "Still your favorite, huh?"

I start out anticipating a side of spicy Italian sausage.

This time I head left out of my childhood home, toward Brinsmade Avenue and the Throgs Neck Expressway. From four blocks away, the truck and car noise is deafening.

I make it through the neighborhoods of my grade school friends, remembering Laura and Bianca, whose parents had arrived in New York from Calabria only two years before we all started high school together.

* * *

Bianca was shy and always looked stunned. Early on, I had the feeling that her family life was on one planet and her school life on another. When I'd ask if she wanted to do something after school—go for pizza, wander into the discount clothing store on Tremont Avenue—she'd look down at the sidewalk and respond, "My parents are old-fashioned." So we just hung out together.

One day after school, Bianca unexpectedly invited me into her home. It was an attached house, three stories, typical of our mixed ethnic neighborhood. I was dying to see how Bianca lived—she'd been in my home many times.

A long concrete staircase led to a white-lacquered front door. A ferocious wolf's head knocker made anyone think twice before asking to be admitted. Ignoring the knocker, Bianca extracted her key from her bag.

"They won't hear, so they keep the door locked."

"Everyone in the Bronx keeps the door locked." A short laugh betrayed my nerves.

The house was home to at least three families. Inside Bianca's apartment, we headed up an endless carpeted staircase as Bianca chirped, "Ciao, Mama."

She introduced me as we entered her family's living space. "Questa è Gaby, il mia amica." This is my friend Gaby.

With a wide smile on her face and smoothing her bun, Signora Piazzi emerged from the kitchen. "Ciao! Benvenuta, Gaby!"

"Ma," Bianca interrupted, "English—remember?"

Mrs. Piazzi corrected herself. "Welcome, Gaby." She searched her daughter's face for repentance.

"Ah just make biscotti—"

Bianca cut in again. "Ma, we just wanna—"

I couldn't help trying to rescue Signora's crestfallen expression.

"I'd love some! I haven't had biscotti in ages." Well, since last weekend.

Signora's face lit up. "Ah, you mama, she no make biscotti?"

"Not too often."

Bianca blew steam as her mother headed to the kitchen.

"Oh, she always interferes!"

I let her tirade, then spoke. "Look, Bianca, she loves you. She's like my family, in a strange land. Let's face it, the Bronx is just about as strange as you can get. Let's cut her some slack, huh?" Bianca inclined her head and cast her eyes downward.

Signora Piazzi reemerged with a large tray laden with biscotti, a milk pitcher and glasses. Waddling from side to side, she shimmied past the gargantuan claw-footed Italian brocade sofa and rested the tray on the huge glass coffee table. Bianca was five foot five. Her mom was a few inches shy of five feet. She wore her light brown hair in a meticulous bun. Good linen blouse with a long bow tied at the collar. Below-the-knee tweed skirt. Both cocooned under a full-body apron. Impeccable silk stockings and sensible Italian leather pumps. She picked up her daughter's cue to decline my invitation to stay. I felt Bianca exhale when her mother left us.

The biscotti were delicious. We chatted about school, homework. I told her how happy I was that she invited me to her home.

I looked around. Ornate, oversized furniture everywhere. The regulation custom clear plastic slipcovers on the sofa. I estimated that the entire space was only marginally bigger than our kitchen. I couldn't imagine why the room was so stuffed.

Tentatively, unbelievingly, I told Bianca, "Your apartment is nice." She cocked her head and waited for the "*But . . .*"

I chose my transparent words very carefully. "Do you find you have enough room?"

Bianca laughed without humor, swept the room with her right hand. "Does it look like it? My parents bought all this stuff after we moved from Italy. They keep saying we're leaving here and buying a big house, and we'll need all this."

I was panicked at the thought that Bianca might move.

As usual, she read me perfectly. "Oh, we're not going anywhere. My dad works on the Long Island Railroad. He doesn't make enough money for us to buy a house. Sooner or later, they'll see it. But it's hard. They're very proud.

"They're immigrants," she said, like it was an affliction.

"We are all immigrants," I told her.

CHAPTER 6

Did Somebody Say Food Is Just a Meal?

I come back to the present as I round the corner to my mother's house. I climb the concrete staircase slowly, desperate for a few more seconds alone. I realize, suddenly, that this has nothing to do with my mother. I feel like this at home too.

I sit down to the strong aroma of espresso and Italian sausage. My mother serves up the egg-in-the-bread crowned by a generous slice of roasted red pepper. She retrieves her own cup and sits beside me, brushing away an imaginary stray hair from her cheek.

"Ma, thank you! This is perfect!"

She smiles broadly. "Sure."

After I eat breakfast, she insists she doesn't need help in the kitchen, motioning instead toward the floor and the place she stores the vacuum cleaner. I tell her I'm on it after I shower.

"You'll change after, right?" I roll my eyes and head up the stairs. How old am I?

I start upstairs because vacuuming means the whole house, no matter where people will be. It also means *clean the bathrooms—properly*. So I do that too.

By now, the house smells like an Italian feast. Sauce—I'm guessing she'll make lasagna and dough for stromboli. Wafting from the kitchen, the fragrances of garlic and Parmesan cheese mingle with olive oil, basil and oregano. Good wine vinegar and salami are also on deck. Some people, including me, dream in color. I also dream in smells, these prime among them.

When I'm finished cleaning, I take stock of the kitchen. My mother points a flour-encrusted finger toward the refrigerator. "Antipast' and the caprese," she orders. I obey.

"Ma, just you, Nani, Zia Maria and me, right?"

"Sì."

"A lot of food, no?"

"You know how much Nani and Zia eat. And we'll have leftovers maybe."

She continues layering salami, provolone, mozzarella, sun-dried tomatoes and pancetta onto freshly rolled dough. "Go, get ready—they'll be here soon . . ."

"Ma, I can do it—you get ready."

"Okay, you finish this? Roll it tight, remember, and seal the ends—otherwise, everything spills out."

Even though I've made stromboli at least twenty times, I feel chastised, apprehensive and threatened should I mess up.

She hands me her apron. The stairs creak under her step as I roll the strombolis and place them on wobbly ancient baking sheets. I set the oven temperature and scan the dining room table.

I retrieve the nice tablecloth, the good dishes—the best the supermarket up on Tremont sold over the years with a minimum purchase of groceries—cutlery, napkins, salt and pepper and lay out the table. Laying a table always reminds me of my childhood Christmases, offering up nostalgia, joy and melancholy in equal measure.

I hear my mother wander through the dining room on her way to the kitchen. "You set the table—good!" Her eye passes critically over the settings. She moves in to adjust the placement of knives and forks. Tells me to put out the antipasto plates.

She focuses on the oven. "You didn't put the stromboli in the oven yet. Why not?"

"They'll be here in three hours."

"So you want to do it last minute? Put them in."

No use arguing. I know enough to tiptoe as I do her bidding.

We organize the antipasto—my mother's homemade pickled eggplant, hot red peppers, squares of aged provolone cheese, slices of fresh sun-dried tomatoes, pepperoncini, bruschetta, discs of crisp Italian bread on the side, bocconcini in olive oil and lemon, prosciutto.

I retreat upstairs to wash up and read as my mother settles into fussy last-minute quality control.

It's no good. Waiting for Zia and my grandmother, I can't settle down. I've always suffered high anxiety when visiting anyone, especially family, and also before people visit my space. I am bootstrapped by the feeling that I must be *someone*. Someone else. Someone people expect to see. I disappoint people because I can't meet their expectation, whatever it is. It exhausts me.

It's 1 P.M. One hour to showtime. I peek into my mother's sewing room before I head downstairs. Material neatly folded and laid out on her long wood table for the suit and the blouse. Two patterns side by side. My mother's body form, I notice, is already adjusted for me—she'll verify on the real body form before she cuts the fabric. My mouth goes dry. I know she'll have a conference with my grandmother and my aunt. Over the disgrace of my exceptional bridal gown.

In the kitchen, my mother stands at the stove assembling the espresso, laying out biscotti on one of her good plates. Nani and Zia Maria are supplying dessert.

Finally, the knocker sounds, my mother smooths her hair and wipes her hands on her apron. The door bursts open. Nani first, Zia Maria following behind. At four feet ten inches and shrinking, Nani is small but mighty. I have no recollection of her without a tight bun wound at the nape of her neck. Her hair, once black, is now shot with wide gray streaks. As always, she wears a black dress and black wool stockings. Short black leather pumps. She carries her "pocketbook" in the crook of one arm. On her other arm, she balances a package wrapped in brown paper.

Behind her mother, Zia tentatively guides herself over our threshold. She is burdened with a tray of cannoli shells covered in waxed paper. At five feet eight inches Zia is noticeably shorter than my mother. For color and shape, the sisters share the same brown eyes. Zia's mouth is softer than Ana's, her hair longer, also tamed into a modest bun. Maria dresses for her middle-aged spread in a wide floral top and comfortable black twill pants with, I know, an elastic waistband. She wears sensible black flats.

I'm surprised and delighted to find my cousin Claire, offering a bowl containing the cannoli filling, in their wake. Zia presents her daughter as if she is the gift of jewelry on Christmas Day. Claire and I had always been close, but we've lost that in recent years.

My mother, jubilant, greets everyone. Kissing, hugging, holding my cousin, patting her cheeks and her hair. She is laughing and smiling, a mother I love to see—even if she's rarely directed my way.

"Entra! Entra! Claire, what a great surprise!" I hug and kiss all of them as they file into the kitchen. Nani hands over her package of homemade sweet ravioli. They will be drizzled with honey before we eat them. Zia finds counter space for her cannoli. She'll fill the shells while the espresso is percolating. My mouth waters.

I follow my grandmother into the kitchen to retrieve another place setting. Nani peruses our late lunch–early dinner, lifting the cover on the pot of tomato sauce, nodding sagely, adjusting an errant crust on one of the stromboli, using the palm of her hand to waft the aroma of the lasagna her way. Watching Nani closely, Ana places the baked stromboli and the lasagna in the oven to heat them and to keep them warm. Nunzia staunchly refuses to use a microwave.

After my aunt effuses about how happy she is that I'm going to be married: "Claire just loves being married! Of course, you and Russ—"

My mother shoots her sister one of her sternest warning looks.

Through the small talk, my grandmother, one eyebrow raised, burns a look my way. At some point, she'll draw me aside to find out what's going on with Russ and me.

We start off in the living room. It is full of Italian and English conversation and laughter. Claire and I settle into glad mutual interrogation. Josh, her husband, is well and happy in his lawyering with a Manhattan firm.

"Lots of work; interesting, he says. I find it overwhelming. He's up for partner, so he's really pushing."

"How about you?"

"Banking is banking. Corporate loans is a big deal for the bank; lots of critical decisions! It's like doing a huge puzzle. Got to make sure you don't miss placing any pieces."

She doesn't ask about Russ. I don't offer. Claire and I have always engaged in subtle competition. She's married. I'm still living with Russ. Her husband is a high-powered lawyer. Russ works as a consultant to clients preparing submissions to the FDA. She's a banker. She works with money. Lots of money. I'm a university professor. I work with mice. Lots of mice.

We start exchanging versions of the past, remembering who we were to each other. This is the first taste of comfort I've had since I came home.

My mother decides it's time for stromboli and antipasti. "Maybe you girls can bring it to the table?"

"Sure, Zia," Claire pipes up.

I place my arm around Nani's middle as she trundles to the table. She laces her arm around my back. We smile at each other as I hold the chair for her.

My mother's stromboli is greeted with deserving oohs and aahs. Pretending there is no main course, we all eat too much.

Claire and I switch to the past. "Remember the nosebleed?"

"How could I ever forget?!"

* * *

We plotted to go upstairs to escape the extended family gathering raging below. Facial hair and moles were an unhappy genetic trait among the women in our family. We compared the number of old aunts we could avoid kissing.

Our stomachs were already full and complaining from the antipasti. I pushed for a visit to my bedroom.

We shot up the stairs and raced into my room, the twin bed neatly made, sneakers tucked underneath, my schoolwork organized in the schoolbag on the floor, even with the placement of my pillow.

"Let's go!" shouted Claire, already doffing her shoes and setting her hair free from her barrette.

We were bouncing so high, I saw only Claire's wild mane of long, thick black hair and arms reaching for the ceiling-bound periodic table. I cautioned her not to pull it down. Her eyes, I noticed, were closed. What I didn't notice happened next.

She didn't see the edge of the narrow bed and mis-stepped.

Shock prevented us from calling out. Was that blood? From Claire's nose. A lot of blood.

Automatically, I mobilized my mother's instructions. *Put your head all the way back and pinch the top of your nose.*

That done, we heard my mother and my aunt herding up the stairs. When they reached us, Claire was sitting on the floor at the side of my bed, one leg curled beneath her, her head obediently pitched backward, her thumb and forefinger grasping the top of her nose. I sat next to her, my arm wrapped around her shoulders. Her blood stained my bedspread and the wood floor, as well as my fingers and blouse.

My mother glared at me. The promise of punishment to come.

Zia was beside her daughter, asking me to bring towels. "Take a couple clean ones, but not new ones," my mother ordered. "What were you two up to? How did this happen?"

My mother commanded Claire to stop speaking as she tried to choke out a muffled reply. "Gaby will tell us if she ever gets back here with the towels."

I had trouble choosing the towels—if they were too new, I would be sent back with another strike against me. Too threadbare and my mother would be embarrassed in front of her sister. Picturing Claire bleeding onto my bed and floor, I pulled myself together and grabbed two middle-of-the-road towels. And cleaning supplies from the bathroom.

I had chosen well. The towels earned no remark.

My mother demanded, "Now, what happened here?"

I avoided our mothers' eyes and focused instead on the floor. "We were jumping on the bed."

"*Jumping?* On the *bed*! And who will buy you a new bed?"

My mother issued her orders. "Clean up the floor! Later, I'll figure out how to get the blood out of the bedspread."

Deliberately ignoring my mother's tirade, I began cleaning. And continued my story. "Then Claire fell off the bed and she got a nosebleed."

Zia nodded at my explanation and refocused her attention on my cousin. "Is it hurting? Take the towel away. I want to see if it's still bleeding."

Claire responded in squishy nasal tones. "I amb fine, Momb." As she removed the towel from her nose, beyond the crust of red circling her nostrils, we could see that the bleeding had slowed. I started to relax.

After my mother barked instructions for us to rest quietly in my room, the women headed out, arguing about our behavior. I heard my mother spit, "Gaby's *really* in for it!"

Crisis passed, Claire and I stayed in my room, our heads touching as we lay on my bed. We both started giggling. Afraid of a new bleed, I reminded her to take it easy. She lifted the bloody towel to her nose.

Claire was curious. "What do you think your mom will do?"

"I don't know. Probably no television."

Claire moaned, "I'm sorry!"

"For what? It was worth it, right?" We held each other as we nodded our agreement.

OKAY. No television for two weeks, and cleaning the house, including meal dishes and pots and pans, for one month. Also grounded.

* * *

Around the dinner table, Claire and I are called back to the present. With a break after the stromboli, I know what's coming.

"Come on, Ma, Maria. I'll show you the material and the patterns for the wedding. Claire, you come too."

Claire consults me with a cautious look. I shrug and nod at the same time. Up to her.

Everyone heads upstairs to my mother's sewing room. I stay behind and clean up. I don't want to see their expressions—a coral pantsuit instead of the imagined fluffy white dress.

I hear my aunt speak first. "What, no dress?" My mother describes her valiant effort to change my mind. "What was I supposed to do? Let her *buy* a suit? But I got the blouse!" she triumphs.

"It's good," pronounces Nani.

Claire says, "It's Gaby, for sure."

My aunt delivers the zinger. "Ah, what would Arturo say?"

Her mention of my father catches my breath.

My grandmother has me exhaling. "Arturo's no here." I can see her nailing my aunt with her steel hazel gaze.

I'm placing the lasagna on the table as they file back into the dining room. Fresh garlic bread. The caprese salad.

Lead cheerleader Claire. "It's gorgeous, Gaby! It's just you." I nod my thanks Claire's way.

Head bowed, the matriarch of our family says grace for us. My mother serves up her trademark generous portions.

Zia Maria dips a chunk of garlic bread into her lasagna sauce.

Nani squeezes my forearm and makes sure I'm looking directly at her. "Ah'm-a think you papa, he like it a lot."

"Grazie mille, Nani."

My aunt's silence says everything she won't.

Again, my grandmother speaks. "You no worry a Zia Maria. She like it too, later on."

Zia finds her voice. "But, Claire! She had such a beautiful dress. A real wedding dress."

"Dress no make the bride or wedding. Gaby e Russ, they make these." Her final tone caps the discussion.

We finish supper sharing impressions of changes in the neighborhood and the city. We carry light laughter into the living room, where Claire and I serve dessert.

Cannoli and sweet ravioli to wash down with strong espresso. We sit contentedly on the sofa, my mother's legs crossed at the shins, my grandmother's at the ankles. We're all smiling, layering our collective happy memories and anticipating those to come. I relax as our interaction approaches its natural resolution.

My grandmother speaks briefly to Zia and smooths the lap of her dress.

Claire follows their lead when the two women rise at once.

Bathroom visits and many hugs, many kisses at the door. My mother distributes care packages of lasagna and dessert.

Nani pulls me aside, asking for help with her jacket.

"You love him? Russ? We no see him too much."

"We're good together, Nani."

"I no ask you this. I ask if you love him."

Only Russ and my grandmother can get to me by locking their eyes with mine.

"I guess."

Gently, she grabs both my hands in her worn fingers.

"You no guess with this. Sì o no. That's all. No answer for me. Answer for you and Russ. You marry—sì o no. Only you answer. Talk to him about what you feel, bene?"

I hold her jacket open as she struggles arthritic hands and arms into the sleeves. She never complains, but I know pain is a regular companion in her day. I adjust her collar and fasten her buttons, holding both her hands as I hug and kiss her. Nani, my touchstone.

I save my last hug for Claire.

And they're off.

CHAPTER 7

The Mass Pike

Dressed for running, I prepare the espresso and swipe half a leftover dessert ravioli for breakfast.

"You need a real breakfast." Ma pivots to the refrigerator, extracting eggs, provolone and last night's garlic bread.

"Go, run," she commands. "I'll make breakfast for when you get back."

"Thanks, Ma." I resolve a short run. Anxiety mounts; I'm leaving her later today.

When I return, my senses make it barely two steps into the vestibule. Espresso, garlic, cheese.

My breakfast is already on the table. She hands me a napkin as she pours my coffee and returns to the kitchen to retrieve her own plate. Twice as much food on mine.

We talk lightly about the visit. My mother softens Zia Maria's reaction to my wedding suit. Shakes her head and smiles. "Zia is old in her thinking, and for her, Claire must always be better than you."

She agrees to let me know when she's made progress on the suit so I can come for a fitting.

"You watch what you eat—not a lot of extra material to work with . . ."

Showered and packed, I strip the bed and walk the linens to the laundry downstairs. I start the washing machine, remembering that as a kid I stood on a step stool to load it.

I sweep out my bedroom, deposit my bag and computer case by the door and visit my mother in the kitchen. She's beat me with the dishes, wipes her hands on a fresh apron and turns toward me.

"Drive safe! God be with you." We embrace and kiss each other.

When I thank her, she becomes stern. "You don't thank. I'm your mother. I do this for you."

She bends, returns with an oil-stained paper bag and presses it into my hand. A flashback to the broccoli and eggs of my childhood to accompany me home.

"Sandwich for you and lasagna and sweet ravioli for Russ. Don't drive and eat."

No way—I would have to struggle with both hands just to fit the sandwich in my mouth.

She watches me start the car and, I know, waits by the door until I'm out of sight.

I finally breathe, inhaling the sorrow of leaving her and the happy anticipation of being home.

I turn onto the highway, shaking off the spell of my childhood home. Wondering why I always feel closer to my mother as soon as I am away from her.

I like the monotony of the drive to and from the Bronx. The road back to Boston brings me face-to-face with the worn, scalded neighborhoods of my home borough. Not so much farther north, I drink in green gentle foothills before the route carves through its monotonous personality, via I-84 and I-90, the Massachusetts Turnpike. I know I'm on the Turnpike thanks to the black colonists' hats sitting on field signs along the way. Road-weary shrubs and trees, their leaves edged in brittle brown, line the road. Weeds flourish. Each mile resembles the last.

The wedding fabric intrudes on my thoughts. Uncomfortably. I will certainly not be dressed to my mother's specifications. Ana associates my clothing choice with the choice to live with Russ before being married.

* * *

I had deliberately told my mother about our living arrangements over the phone. "What?! I didn't raise you that way! What did I do wrong?"

"Ma, it's got nothing to do with you—it's my decision. With Russ."

"But your 'decision' is sinful. Go to confession. And then make it right and move on your own until you're married. We can't do anything about, you know, being ruined."

I held the receiver away from my ear. That ship had sailed long before Russ. But I didn't tell her. She was already raging mad.

"You know, Claire—she never did that! She and Josh lived together only after her wedding. Proper Catholics."

She was working herself into a rant. No point cutting in. I didn't let on that Claire and Josh went to great lengths to hide the fact that they lived together for three years before they married—post office boxes, hijinks with telephones and meeting Zia Maria in borrowed Ithaca apartments while they were both in school at Cornell. Living together the whole time.

"Oh," she moaned, "I'm glad your father isn't here to see this—it would kill him. You know that." I had anticipated this, but my heart still contracted.

"Ma, calm down."

"Calm? My only daughter behaves like a puttana—a loose woman—and I should be *calm*?!"

"Ma, I have only ever lived with Russ."

"Oh, so this makes it okay? Is it because of two apartments? I'll give you money for rent."

"No, it's not about rent. Russ and I have been living together for three years. We want to see that we really are compatible, to live together."

"Three years, and you're just telling me. You need three years to know this? Hah! Your father and me—we found out after we were married. We made a promise to be compatible. We were married—that was our duty. We had backbone!"

I checked out and let her continue. Rolled my eyes at Russ every once in a while. When I hung up, the receiver and the left side of my face were slick with sweat. Russ poured me a club soda, and I gave him the Cliff Notes version.

He nodded, rested his beer bottle on the counter, and took my hand.

"So let's tell her we're getting married. And set a date. What do you think?"

"I don't want her to be in charge of my marriage. To anyone."

"Say, are you mad at me or your mom?"

I smiled. "Not at you—that's for sure!"

"So let me try again: You want to marry me?"

Mid-lift, I returned my glass of soda to the counter. Russ's eyes were smiling.

"Yes!" I said, and we moved into a kiss and hug that dissolved the sting of the phone call.

I turned to face him. "But we pick the time and place!"

"Of course!"

* * *

I've settled into enjoying the ride. Hungry, I register the next service stop in twenty miles. Gas. For me and the car.

Entering the food court, I buy a Diet Pepsi and find a table that I hope is far enough away from everyone else. Open the brown paper bag and inhale the unmistakable penetrating aroma of broccoli and garlic. With eggs. Someone two tables away turns my way and scowls. Sorry. This is too great to leave in the bag.

The ride is almost four hours. I'll be back in Boston soon. I feel disconnected from my Boston life. From Russ. I thought I had done it, but I am still struggling to shake off the Bronx. My mother. One foot in her life, one in mine. I have been living like this since I went away to college.

* * *

I was seventeen when I went away to college. Excited and anxious, I perched on my bed upstairs to fit the last items into my suitcase. A gift from Zia.

I eavesdropped on Ma's and Nani's downstairs conversation.

My mother was agonizing. "Arturo always wanted her to go away to college. But she can't go alone."

"What you mean, alone? She got friends who go, too, no?"

"But, Mama. She's . . . There's no man with her. What will happen? Disgrazia."

"She no need the man right now. You raise her good, no?"

Through my imaginary hole in the wood floor, I saw my mother glaring at Nani. "Of course. How can you ask me that?"

"Ah, okay, then she be good at the college." Nani chuckled. "An' maybe she come back with the husband. Arturo, he's happy with this, trust me."

Nani rocks! I stopped listening and finished packing.

Next day, I'm off to study biochemistry at Northeastern University. Hardest four years of my life. Until graduate school.

* * *

Four hours after my mother's blessing to go with God, I am home. At the door, Russ hugs me with one arm, plants a kiss and treats me to a wide smile. A glass sits ready for some Sanpellegrino.

When we're apart, I forget Russ's height. Standing at six feet four inches in stocking feet, he is slim and athletic. His fingers constantly tame a great shock of curly brown hair. Light brown eyes that smile easily as he gives in to laughter. I have missed the two o'clock stubble that shades the deep dimple on the left side of his face.

"Glad you're home," he says, and I smile as he draws me close. I cradle his neck and return his kiss. He smells of soap and freshly ironed cotton. I'm also glad I'm home.

I lift the bag with the lasagna and dessert ravioli from the doorway and hand it to Russ. His eyes go wide as he peeks inside the bag.

"Wow! I think you need to go to your mother's more often!"

I pantomime holding a gun to my head as we settle at the kitchen island.

I tell him about my wedding outfit and the visit with Nani and Zia—and Claire.

"I like Claire," he says thoughtfully, "and your nani is much younger than your mom, you know that, right?"

"What about Zia?" I ask.

"Never could warm up to Maria. She's always got an agenda—comparing you and Claire, mostly. Claire does not do that, and neither do you, come to think of it."

"We were always sisters and great friends—we always understood our mothers and we still do. But under the surface, we are competitive."

He raises both eyebrows in surprise. "I didn't know! You wear it well, I'll say that."

"Not always. Don't you want to know what happens now?"

He nods and slips his hand into a terry cloth mitt as he turns to rescue a tray of stuffed mushrooms from the oven.

"My mother has the dress form fitted to me. You know, on one of those dress model dummies. She's ordered me not to gain weight. And, naturally, she hates the pants. Anyway, she'll let me know when she's ready for a fitting."

Russ considers this, then says, "You think I should come?"

Knowing that Russ does not enjoy my mother's criticism of me piques my guilt at the way I talk about her and the stories I tell. I can't quite figure why I am surprised that Russ's dislike of my mother's criticism has transitioned into his dislike of her. Do I really think he wants to hang around with a woman I often describe as intolerant, strict and harsh?

Every time I go to the Bronx, it takes longer for me to settle back into my life. This time, I am reliving and rewriting conversations and the visit to the fabric store. Time spent with Nani and Zia and Claire. I float on the edges of reality, waiting for real life to land from the cloud above me. Three days after my return home I remain suspended.

I don't discuss this with Russ or with any of my friends because I can't find the words. I feel unhinged and I don't want anyone to see it. Can they?

The image of my father before he died captures my thoughts. Big, rough hands, kind eyes, smile lopsided by the V-shaped chips in his two front teeth. Wispy tufts of curly black hair behind his ears. A wide bald area in between. He stood six feet four inches tall. Warmed by his closeness and the affectionate smoothing of the back of my head, I always saw him towering above everyone. I've inherited his two bottom teeth, leaning away from each other, two Bronx towers of Pisa. I loved when he'd tell stories from his life. Practical jokes. Adventures with his friends. Rebelliousness. Always, his thoughts and actions placing my mother first.

Skimming reality, I feel my father asking me to make a better effort with his wife. But I'm defiant and exhausted by the effort I'm sure it will take. I would have to reexamine all my recollections and perceptions. Revise them to account for her point of view. Retell them to Russ and everyone who knows me. And, what, ask for forgiveness? It's easier, less embarrassing—and I convince myself to nurse my resentment. But I'm conflicted: I want Russ to like her. To like being with her.

Naggingly, I hear my father asking me to understand what it was like for her to lose him so young. I argue back that it's enough for me to understand what it was like for *me* to lose him so young.

CHAPTER 8

Sailing to America

I asked Nani to fill me in on how my parents met. Nani (Nunzia) and Nonno (Carlo) came over long after the immigration flood of the early 1900s, drawn by the promise of L'America and opportunity. Nani stressed that she came along, defiant and unwilling, hauling my mother, Ana, in tow. Because she associated airplanes with military attacks, Nunzia couldn't bring herself to board one. She insisted they travel by ocean liner instead.

"I was so sorry we leave. I love la famiglia in Sicilia. After we go, I never see my sister Ercilia o my papa again.

"When we prepare, Fantino, who own the farm next to us, ask to speak with Carlo. When Carlo come back, he convince me." She traces a wide circle in the air. "Fantino son, Arturo, come with us a L'America.

"This now make four—Ana, Arturo, Carlo, e me. Giulia, mama di Arturo, hold him very close on the dock before we go up the ship. Then we see her cry when the boat she start to move. Fantino reach out to her but she too angry and she push him away. I feel bad. But we go."

* * *

Nani wipes her hands on her napkin and stirs her espresso. "Ana e Arturo, they with each other all the time. Chasing, making games, fooling with they food."

"How old were they, Nani?"

"Lessee—Ana, she twelve. Arturo fifteen. I tell Carlo: 'Maybe we watch close. They young. Maybe like each other too much?'

"You grandfather, he laugh. He say: 'Why you worry? What they supposed to do every day on a boring ship?'

"But I'm worry what they find to do on a boring ship. I no ask, I just watch."

I smile at my grandmother conspiratorially. "So did they behave?"

She chuckles, brings the delicate cup to her lips and shrugs. "Who knows? But I think so."

Nani asserted that Arturo was missing his family. Ana didn't know what she'd do if she'd been forced to come to America without her parents. She strapped her much shorter arm around Arturo's shoulder and listened to him talk.

I had lots of photos of my teenaged mother but not of my father. My grandmother described her son-in-law as he was on the ship. His eyes were hazel, changing color with his clothes and his mood. When happy and relaxed, they brightened his face. But, as I remembered him, when he was upset or angry, steel was the order of the day. I was surprised to hear that he had thick curly hair. When he was my papa, he had very little hair. Nani said he had a square jaw, shadowed by the beginning of the dark stubble he would wear into manhood.

He already stood six feet tall. Long legs, the wide barrel chest in development. He was comfortable in his skin, unhurried. He smiled easily. Especially when Ana was near. As Nani told her story, I welcomed the memory of my parents softening in each other's presence.

"Arturo grow a lot on the boat." Halfway over, Carlo had to buy Arturo new clothes and teach him how to shave. Nani told me she gave his outgrown clothes to other travelers with growing teenagers.

Nani continued, "I see Ana go into herself." Arturo's changes made Ana uncomfortable; she wasn't sure he'd want to be her friend anymore. She didn't know if she felt like his friend anymore.

"Ana—she growing up too. I see her change. She know she changing." In the mirror, Ana saw a little girl with long, thick, wavy black hair and bangs. She tried taming it by holding it in a ponytail at the back of her neck. Large dark brown eyes. Olive skin. Bushy eyebrows borrowed from her father. Her mother's thin upper lip and full lower lip. She was skinny. Her legs were short. She was a great swimmer, but awkward around kids her own age.

"She nervous with Arturo now." They still laughed, but she avoided touching him. Nani said, "I watch her. She embarrass easy." For his part, Carlo studied Arturo. At meals, they talked one-on-one, adding to Ana's isolation. The ease between them contributed to her discomfort. Ana knew her father was, in fact, interrogating Arturo, but the younger man bathed in the attention of his surrogate father.

"The boat stop Roma, Marseille, Lisbon. We love go into the cities." Nani told me that at these times, her anxiety over stepping off the ship in America was manageable.

Nani described their family picnics in local parks. Spreads of bread, cheese, olives and local meats, fish and fruit on a worn, repurposed bedspread.

In Lisbon, they were all on edge again. A literal ocean full of space to navigate before they saw New York Harbor and the Statue of Liberty. No turning back. I felt Nani's anxiety as she filled me in.

Buildings, bathrooms, neighbors, expenses, school and friends. Language, conversation, clothes. Ana sensed everything she had would make her a laughingstock. Nunzia wondered about available fabrics, parts for her sewing machine.

Carlo would join his cousin's construction business. Having family and security for his family was everything. He thought of meals around his dinner table and holidays and traveling together during the summers. First, English lessons and a home.

CHAPTER 9

Growing Pains

When I return home from the Bronx, I'm withdrawn for the better part of two weeks. Something about my visit remains with me. It's affecting Russ and me, but I can't identify it. He can tell I'm working through something. He asks me how work is, thinking I'm puzzling through the design or results of an experiment.

I feel guilty letting him think so. When I look at him, when he's not looking, I think what a great man he is. How really blessed I am that with all my baggage, he wants to be with me. I assume we will always be as we are now. I'm uncomfortable, knowing I am withholding and anxious.

Nani has cornered my thoughts. *Do you love him?* I assume I do. But I couldn't commit an answer to her scrutiny. Do I know? How do I tell? Before Russ, I had two boyfriends—one in college, one in graduate school. I didn't like being a girlfriend; I was always confused by the label and never seemed to know the rules. I was never Russ's girlfriend. I am more like a puzzle piece that fits.

Do I love him? Russ wants to marry me; isn't that enough? Isn't asking and saying yes proof of love?

I extract the tried-and-true remedy out of my toolbox. Work. I'm relentless. Extra tutorials for students. Perfectly good lectures reworked. I launch a new series of experiments and map out three manuscripts. I convene long lab meetings, trainees side-watching each other when they think I'm not paying attention. I make out soft groaning and rumbling as they exit the room. "*Did she say Wednesday?*"

I'm in early and I leave late. I'm anxious as I approach home and walk through the door.

"What's going on, Gaby?"

"Just work . . . I'm really okay."

"All right. You've been like this since you got back."

Over dinner I am oddly quiet, a person I'm meeting for the first time. My home belongs to someone else. I'm here visiting.

* * *

My flagship—school—hit the rocks my first semester at college. I was frantic. I had no place to go and I couldn't hide from myself. I largely avoided people because I knew how fragile I was—likely to burst into tears for any reason. And for no reason.

My high school go-to strategies did not work anymore. I spent long hours attending extra lectures, studying, completing additional assignments. Only to earn C's on the first set of science exams. Science! My brain was slow. I could not see the science clearly. I could not see anything clearly.

I punched and I fought until points of light pierced the waxed paper around my brain. I needed to change my strategy, to study differently, learn differently. Do a few experiments with myself. Concentrate on problem-solving; use the textbooks to find the facts I needed to apply.

Changing was torture. And my time was short. I wouldn't keep my scholarship if I didn't do better. I had to do better. Now. And I could not fail. My anxiety soared along with my determination.

I had always defined successful learning as a repetition of facts. I would memorize information from textbooks, write it down several times and quiz myself to ensure I had learned it verbatim. This system had worked well through high school. Not so in college.

Real learning finally dawned on me when I encouraged myself to stretch beyond my textbooks and find out why the information was important. How would it apply to a real-life situation? If the facts I was trying to grasp steered away from normal, what would happen? How could we get *back* to normal?

I anxiously tested my new method at the midterm. Searching for my student number on the sheet that posted the chemistry exam results, I traced my index finger along the row four times before it sank in. *A? A.* I jumped, pumping my fist into the air. I soon found out my new method was working in my other courses too. When I became a professor, I shared it with students.

Rapidly, I realized that my learning would extend beyond books. I needed to connect with people. Hiding myself away was suffocating me. So, shyly at first, I found people to talk to—to do nonacademic things with. People from different backgrounds. Some from the same background.

In the dormitory where I lived during college, I became friendly with Rosanna. Rosanna's parents had come over from Calabria. Dead set against her going to college, they cut her off, pouted, and waited for her to come home to Brooklyn to get married. It was her destiny, her duty, and she was depriving her parents of it. She dug her heels in at school and worked two part-time jobs in addition to babysitting.

Like me, Ro carried a scholarship on her back. She was always working and always laughing and joking. When she discovered that her boyfriend, Joey Zabatino, had bedded another woman living in the dorm, she shrugged. "That guy is fucked up from J to Z." She laughed that time, but not the time after that or the time after that. Their on-again, off-again relationship gave me whiplash. And it was hard for me to witness Ro's pain.

Her parents refused to attend her graduation. Her mother told her she was happy because she would finally come home and marry.

Instead, she enrolled in graduate school. Psychology. "I love my parents," she told me. "I just hate that they live back in Italy—sometime in the 1800s. I'm going to graduate school."

Rosanna had earned an undergraduate degree in English. "Why psych?" I asked. "To connect with your parents?"

Blowing smoke from the deep drag on her cigarette, she flicked the ash onto the quad. She squinted my way through a thick blue plume and regarded me in a rare show of seriousness. "No, to connect with me."

I was completely humbled by Rosanna. No support, emotional or financial, from her parents. Only ancient intolerance and parental punishment. But Ro was committed to her path, and to her parents. She inspired me. Her courage in making her own success was contagious—a role model.

I had grown up in a diverse neighborhood, but for the first time, at college, I listened to conversations in Yiddish, Spanish, Chinese. I understood nothing, but I realized that our differences did not stop at our birth languages. I started to learn how each of us defined culture. Clothes and hair. Food. Dance. Music. Movies. TV. We lived our preferences, without rank or judgment. I watched an Irish dorm-mate help me make spaghetti sauce by squeezing half a bottle of ketchup into the pot. My stomach lurched, but I stayed quiet and didn't try to stop her. It wasn't spaghetti sauce, but it was tasty.

Maybe my right way / wrong way was not the bottom line on how to be. I'd always struggled to fit in. And I was always the wrong key for the right lock. It occurred to me for the first but not the last time that my mother had been scared, too, to color outside the lines. She also had not fit in. Like her, I had learned that not following the rules was a sure recipe for disaster. My experience challenged that conviction.

I left my high school academic performance in the rearview and took stock. I learned to breathe and started to really enjoy the learning—all of it—even the professors and the assignments. I was startled to realize that the first turn of the wheel had come by oiling, not tightening the axle.

* * *

Weeks after my return home, I am still troubled by my visit to the Bronx. Russ and I weigh all the permutations and combinations. His advice is sage and considered. I decide to get a second opinion.

Claire's surprise is matched by her pleasure when she hears my voice. "Yes. Everyone's fine. Really great to see you too. Glad you like the wedding suit."

Claire sighs. "You know not to pay any attention to my mother, right? She lives in another century, even in a different century from Zia Ana."

"My mother doesn't understand me," I whine. I sound like a man about to cheat on his wife.

"She always wants things her way. Whatever I want isn't good enough. Whatever I do isn't good enough. I'm always on the receiving end of that frown that starts at her neck and finishes at her hairline. You know that look."

Claire laughs. "Thing is, you don't understand your mother, either. And you always want your own way too. Even more, you're always keeping score, needing to win against her. I pretend to understand my mother. I even pretend to agree with her. Avoid stuff that sets her off. She still thinks I don't know anything about birth control."

"I can't separate my mother from marrying Russ. I can't figure out if I'm marrying him against her, for her or for me." I tell her about Nani's million-dollar question that I have yet to answer.

"Well, do you, love Russ, I mean?"

"Love. Whenever I think about it, I run into trouble. I think I don't deserve to love him. But I can't bear the thought of being without him."

"Maybe having to think about it is your real trouble."

I go mute.

Claire picks up the slack. "Look, Gaby, you always choose anxious over relaxed; you always dig until you're past the sting of the shovel against your shoulder. And then you keep digging—harder. I think Nani is trying to tell you that when it's right, it's easy. There's no need to dig. You've mixed your mother into your feelings for Russ. Does she belong there? Does she like Russ?"

I pull at the lint on my sweater. "Yeah. I mean, I guess so. She never said she doesn't like him. But, come to think of it, she doesn't know him."

Claire waits a few seconds before responding. "Oh."

"Gaby, you've got a bunch of things all tangled up. First, *you've* got to decide if you want to marry Russ. Whether it's got to do with love or not, some people *do* get married without loving their partner, right?"

"But I don't want to be one of them. And I don't want to wait until I'm sure."

"Okay, then you've got to understand that you don't have to leave Russ behind in the event that Zia Ana doesn't like him. Actually, you might want to think about why, just maybe, you don't want your mother to get to know Russ—maybe you don't want her to tarnish him for you?"

"Ouch! How'd you pick up on all that?"

"You know, we've always been sisters for each other. You always say more with the emotion in your words than with the words you say."

We drift off into discussing life in general, annoying people at work, funny management politics that are anything but funny.

"Thanks, Claire."

"Hey," she closes, "what are sisters for?"

* * *

In my first clear memory of Claire we were five years old. Both in school for the first time. Zia Maria and Zio Salvatore were visiting for Sunday dinner. Nani had been invited to join her friend Luisa's family. Close to Halloween. Jack-o'-lanterns and multicolored maize adorned our front door. Inside, huge black fabric spiders climbed the banister on filmy spiderwebs.

My mother and father exchanged kisses with Zia and Zio to the sounds of cheerful laughter and half conversations in the vestibule. My father gathered jackets. The strong aroma of lamb and garlic had permeated the house. The adults settled on the sofa. I watched my father go to the kitchen for drinks, my mother for the antipasti.

"You'll have something to drink with dinner," my father assured Claire and me. "Have some antipasti, but not too much. You don't want to ruin your supper."

Avoiding the cubes of hard, bitter cheese and the wormlike pickled eggplant swimming in olive oil, I grabbed a fistful of salami and a hunk of my favorite crusty bread dotted with sesame seeds. Claire went for the bread and fresh mozzarella. The olives looked good, but I knew I would get oil all over my dress.

The adults were in heavy conversation. I asked Claire if she wanted to see my room. "Don't run," I warned. "Stay quiet."

When we closed my bedroom door, we bounced on my bed, threw our heads toward the ceiling and erupted into giggles. We tried, unsuccessfully, to stifle our laughter. We scrambled off the bed and put our ears to the floor, eavesdropping on the adults below. We couldn't hear anything, but we pretended we could. Mostly, we listened for footsteps on the stairs.

No footsteps. Growing tired of this, we dressed up in old blouses and skirts from my mother's done file. I proudly produced my special molded-plastic high heels. Shiny pink, with a shocking ruff of fuchsia fur on top. No toes. We took turns walking around in them, pairing them with different outfits. Claire was better at walking in them. I tasted jealousy and suggested ditching the high heels for a game in skirts and blouses and playing with my Barbies.

"Supper's ready," Zia Maria announced, summoning us from the bottom of the stairs.

Even though there wasn't much Italian spoken, I couldn't figure out what the adults were talking about. Why bother having Claire and me at the table? We weren't allowed to ask questions or talk to each other or to anyone else at supper. As far as I could tell, we were invisible. I had a passing thought to give in and pick my nose, but I didn't dare.

A reprieve. Claire and I were excused to my room again until dessert. Cannoli (Zia's specialty) and biscotti—one end dipped in chocolate and almonds (from my mother's kitchen).

When we were called downstairs a second time, the adults were sipping espresso, my father offering anisette. Claire and I were given glasses of chocolate milk, a special treat.

But dessert went on forever. I was tired and ready to be by myself. And I had to tough it out.

Finally, Zia Maria reminded everyone that tomorrow, Monday, was a school day and a workday. There was a big fuss at the front door while they got ready to leave. Claire and I hugged and kissed each other. The front door was open, and I felt cold, but I remained at my father's side. He stroked the back of my head gently until he followed our family downstairs to Zio Salvatore's car.

Back upstairs, tucking me in, he assured me, "You were a good girl tonight. I'm very proud of you." I earned a kiss on top of my head. I caught my mother standing outside the bedroom door, smiling at us.

I always got excited when I knew I'd be seeing Claire. We understood each other. We liked doing the same things—even the ones that got us into trouble. And we had each other's backs. We would learn to depend on that.

* * *

After I speak with Claire, I muster the courage to call my mother.

"What's wrong, Ma?" I know I've waited too long to pick up the phone.

"What's wrong? My daughter doesn't call me for a month. What's wrong by you?"

"Just working a lot, Ma—and thinking of you a lot too." Have I, though?

"Hmpf. I'm almost done with your, uh, 'wedding suit.' When will you come to try it on?"

"It'll be a little while. I'll get back to you."

"Will Russ come?"

"Ma, I'll get back to you, okay?"

"Okay. Not too long. And don't gain any weight."

We continue small talking. Changes in her neighborhood. The Tadlines have sold their home. What will the new neighbors be like? Zia Maria visits a lot. They shop together. Cook together. Drive each other crazy together. They wouldn't have it any other way.

My mother visits Nani almost every day and picks her up once or twice a week to do her shopping and to have her home for dinner with Zia. I can feel Zia's high anxiety at these dinners. My mother is Nani's favorite. Nani always defers to her. If Zia offers an opinion, Nani shoots Zia down and searches my mother for agreement. Zia tries in futility to anticipate her sister's pronouncements and to support them. I've seen it backfire. Badly.

A recent example springs to mind as I promise my mother I'll call her back within the week and we say goodbye.

"This espresso no good. Non mi piace." I don't like it.

The face around my aunt's anxious smile went pale.

"But you told me to change! Last time, you didn't like the regular one."

"Yeah, well, this no good." Even in her dissatisfaction, Nani carefully minded the clean tablecloth as she pushed the elegant cup and saucer away. Folded her arms under her breasts—the Sicilian shelf—and frowned at Zia. She shook her head gently from side to side.

I sidestepped into the kitchen, rummaging for a leftover supply of the "good" espresso.

"I found some of the other espresso, Nani. It's coming."

Nani's face broke into her consolation smile. Zia Maria had retreated to the kitchen.

"Ah, Gaby, grazie!"

When Zia rejoined us, she was crushed, but she managed a cautious smile.

I wanted to pull Zia aside and say, *Sometimes Nani can be mean*, but I opted, as always, for silence.

Having revisited the recent memory of the women's interaction, I review my phone conversation with my mother for the to-tell-the-truth factor. I never score high. Either by fact revision or omission, I'm always measuring what she'll accept without unleashing her disappointment on me. At the same time, I dabble in wondering if she's truthful with me. But my childhood experience stands in testament to how very honest she is.

I can't afford her visiting in my head for too long. Besides, I need to have the come-with-me-to-my-mother's-for-a-fitting conversation with Russ.

He's at his desk, flannel cuffs rolled up, jeans torn at the knees. Impressive scruffs of curly brown hair peek from his wrists and knees. I can tell he's struggling. Standing in three directions directly from his scalp, his hair tells me he's been scrubbing his eyes with his fingers, then trying to tame his mane. I come behind his chair. He reaches around.

"You okay?" he asks, his eyes fixed to the screen.

"Just got off the phone with my mother." Immediately, he stops and swivels in his chair to face me head-on.

"Sure you're okay?"

I laugh a little too lightly. "Yeah."

"What's up?"

"She's finished my suit. Wants me to visit for a fitting. Will you come?"

Russ exhales slowly.

"You want me to, right? But it never goes well, does it? I'm missing something for your mother."

"That's because I'm missing something for my mother. I constantly disappoint her. I always make the wrong choices. Not her choices. I frustrate her ambitions. You know that."

Russ and Ana have met each other on only a handful of holiday and family celebrations. I have never witnessed them in private conversation. I *have* witnessed my mother's close surveillance as he interacts with other people in the room. And how he interacts with me. While she registers finding no fault with Russ on these occasions, she remains suspicious and critical.

"Look, I'll come because you want me to. But I have a condition."

I hate conditions.

Russ explains, "Go easy on Ana. And that will go easy on both of us. Convince yourself you like her for the time we're there."

He pulls me down gently and plants a very welcome kiss.

"I do love her, you know. She just makes me crazy. So I can let her know we'll come—together—next month? She'll torture me till I deliver a when."

CHAPTER 10

On the Road Again

I decide to wait two days before I call my mother again.

But she beats me to it.

After dinner I answer the phone to her anxiety and disquiet.

Suddenly gripped with fear, I master delivery of the questions.

"Are you okay? What happened?"

"It's your grandmother."

Am I being forced to live the nightmare of losing Nani? I wait.

"She fell." Hip surgery and a wheelchair come to mind.

"Where, at home?"

"No. She's so stubborn, you know. She went to the negozio di alimentari. She loves to go to that Italian grocer's to gossip and share espresso with the ladies."

My stomach churns as I wait.

"You know how bad those sidewalks are where she lives. She just had to buy some groceries—she loves their soppressata and their olive oil. So she bought too much, and she tripped on the sidewalk on her way home. The jar of olives she picked up—smashed. Also, her wrist."

"Oh *God* . . . where is she?"

"She's in Misericordia. She's in a lot of pain and she's confused. Zia and I went up there when the ambulance came. She was crying and begging us to bring her home."

"Oh, Ma. This is awful! But she's in a great place, right? Misericordia is a fantastic hospital. I'm sure her wrist is set and they're managing her pain. Pain medication is probably adding to her confusion. How are you and Zia doing?"

"Zia and me, we're upset, but we're okay. We go back tomorrow morning. I'll make her something decent to eat and bring a thermos of espresso. Zia will make her something sweet." Sicilian mantra: Feed a fever. Feed a cold. Feed a broken wrist.

"I'll come down, Ma. Tomorrow."

"No. No. I need you here after she comes home. To sit with her and cook for her—just keep it simple." For my mother, I can't be trusted to cook anything that's not "simple."

"Ma. You really okay?"

"Sure. I mean, I don't like it, but she's so stubborn. I always tell her I'll take her there, but she just has to walk there by herself. And then buy bags of stuff. I'm just glad she didn't break her hip or hit her head when she fell."

She sends a deep sigh over the line. "My mother can't be still. She's always so busy. And now she has to stay quiet for a while.

And Zia, she's so upset. I don't have a clue how to manage her with this. And Nani will not tolerate her emotions."

"She'll settle down, Ma. You know Zia. She's got to let it all go up front. Then espresso and a few biscotti, and she'll be all fixed up!"

My mother treats me to a rare genuine laugh. I can see her head leaning back as she cups the receiver to her mouth.

"You're right about that, Gaby!"

A short pause as I get my own blood pressure under control. Nani. In Misericordia. I imagine her holding a tutorial for the staff on proper room cleaning.

"So you'll let me know when you want me to come. I'll fly. And I'll rent a car—you don't have to come get me."

"Of course I'll come. I can't have you renting a car."

My mother hates LaGuardia Airport. And she will be most distressed to give up her car so I can get around.

"Why can't I rent a car? I've decided." I wince as I imagine the snide twist of her mouth over the telephone.

I tell an astonished Russ what has happened. He agrees I should go as soon as I hear from my mother.

It's a bad break for an older woman who has never had enough calcium in her diet. My mother cannibalized her bones in utero and she still eats very little dairy.

Five days later, having decided to drive after all, I arrive in the Bronx at Nani's apartment.

I come bearing bags of her favorite groceries. Meat—she favors chicken and veal—eggplant, zucchini, cured Italian meats, good hard provolone cheese. Italian bacon, mozzarella, an assortment of breads. Salad fixings. Fresh tomatoes, her go-to brand of canned tomatoes and tomato paste. Cured Sicilian olives, roasted red peppers, and her S cookies. She loves dunking them in tea.

I use my key, and looking in on her, I find her tired and drawn. I kiss her as she greets me from a reclining position in bed. The offending arm is propped beside her, encased in a cast that extends above her elbow. When I prompt her, she tries half-heartedly to wiggle her fingers-turned-Italian-sausages. She snorts, making it clear that she's had enough of this exercise.

"Nani, how are you?" I ask.

"Bah." She waves her good hand at me. The yellow traffic-light warning.

I can tell she's glad to be home. I see that my mother has supplied four extra pillows so she can see everything around her. This Nani-eyed view is not without peril.

"Ach." Heavy sigh.

"What, Nani? You have pain?"

"Pain? No. But I got to see the floor with dust all over! An' I can't do nothing."

An invitation to get the dust mop and get to work. My grandmother has never used a vacuum cleaner.

I accept the invitation, first wiping imaginary dust from her bedroom armoire and bureau. Her bedroom has a screened storm door that leads to her backyard, graced with an impressive vegetable garden and two now-towering fig trees transported from Sicily. Close to the end of each summer, these trees provide a bounty of sweet fruit. Once her family and friends are satisfied, my grandmother always invites neighbors to pick and enjoy. As fall arrives, she enlists the same four burly men to wrap the trees for the winter, capping each tree with a smart pail that reminds me of the Tin Man in *The Wizard of Oz*. For their work, the men are treated annually to the best of Nani's kitchen.

My grandmother owns her custom-built brick home, commissioned by my grandfather when they moved from Arthur Avenue. Years ago, the main house had been separated into two apartments, one of which she rented out.

Nani's bedroom features her ancient pedal-operated sewing machine, famous for its ocean voyage when the family traveled to New York. On the wall above the armoire hangs an invasive sepia-toned photograph of my grandmother's parents.

Stern and unsmiling, they stare wide-eyed into the camera. Nani's mother is stocky and tough-looking. The hair at her forehead is stretched by what must have been a tight bun fixed at the nape of her neck. She wears a brooch at the throat of a punishing collar topping a closely pleated blouse. She wears a mutely flowered shawl wrapped around her shoulders.

Her husband's slicked hair is parted in the middle. He sits proudly, sporting a smart jacket that partially conceals a vest and the chain of his pocket watch. On his upper lip is a waxed mustache and at his neck sits a tight high shirt collar that I'm sure had been brutally starched. This was surrounded by a soft-looking ascot, fashioned into a tie resting on the front of his shirt.

I would not willingly have spent time with these people.

Despite her complaint, my grandmother's home is spotless. To ease her restlessness, I go through the motions, dusting immaculate furniture and mopping clean floors, treating the bathroom and the small kitchen to a needless thorough cleaning.

The living room is outfitted with the sofa wrapped in requisite permanent plastic slipcovers. The backs of my thighs tingle just looking at it. A sprawling print of a Venetian gondolier on one of the canals hangs above the sofa. My grandmother loves this painting.

On the side table sits an Italian candy dish. Opening it, I score three squares of individually wrapped torrone nougat.

To finish, I give all the furniture a careful lemon oil rub.

Nani coos lazily from her bed. "Oh. Ah'm-a love this smells."

She turns her head and falls back asleep before I can get to her. I actually get some work done on my computer while she snoozes.

An hour later, she wakes with a muffled moan and pain etched across her forehead.

"Nani? You want some medicine for pain?"

She opens her eyes slowly.

"Wha'? No. Ah'm-a no drug addic'!"

I control my impulse to laugh.

"Of course you're not a drug addict! But you are in pain, and it will help."

I earn her signature frown of disapproval and the accompanying shake of her head from side to side. Thankfully, I am a rare recipient.

"Beyack! Ah'm-a no take the pills! Ah'm-a okay."

And that's that.

I anticipate my mother's query as I hear her at the front door.

"No, Ma. She wouldn't take it."

"So you just let her go without?! What's wrong with you? She's in pain."

"Look at it this way. She won't get confused if she doesn't take medication, and every hour that goes by, she's in less pain."

I thank myself silently for not sharing that Nani woke in pain.

My mother stays awhile. In the bedroom, she and my grandmother have a private chat in Italian. I check out what my mother's brought with her.

Biscotti ai pignoli—my absolute favorite!

Selfishly, I don't offer to make espresso while my mother's here. I want to bring a nice tray into Nani's room later.

My mom emerges from Nani's room about fifteen minutes later. Smiling, she tells me Nani looks good. "And she sure hasn't lost her spirit!"

Doused in guilt, I half-heartedly ask her if I should make some espresso for us, to go with the cookies.

"What? You think those are the only ones I made? When you come home, we'll have the biscotti and espresso together. Right now, take good care of your grandmother."

When I peek into her room, Nani is dozing, lightly enough to open one eye and launch a grin my way.

Inviting me to sit, she pats the edge of her bed with her good hand. She remembers to smooth the bedspread. I'm guessing it's a relic from her "hope-a chess." Smoothing it is a sign of her favor and trust.

"How are you?"

"Bah, all this for just a little fall. Ah'm-a old lady! Ah'm-a supposed to fall sometime."

Laughing in spite of myself, I shake my head.

"Nani, you want some espresso?"

"Sure."

The tray enters before I do. It is fully adorned with her fine espresso set, silver spoons and a plateful of my mother's biscotti.

"Ah'm-a tell you mama make the biscotti ai pignoli! Belli!"

I secure her bed tray, serve her and settle on the chair next to her bed. I balance the cup and saucer on one palm as I grab a cookie from the plate.

In a family-historical mood I ask her: "Why don't you like Zia Maria?"

Her eyes go wide. "Who says I no like Maria?" Abruptly, she now focuses on me through thin slits. "She my daughter."

I'm determined to remain upright in the chair under her gaze. "You always seem mad at her, no matter what she does."

"No! I love her. Ah'm-a no anger. But she no like you mama. You mama strong. She just get things done. Even when you papa he die. She no spend time in bed, o cry, o make you take care like Claire do for Maria.

"I love her. But she weak. She need to be strong. But she follow too much an' she afraid. I ask her, 'Why you afraid? The worst, she happen—you husban', he gone.'"

She takes a delicate sip from the cup and shrugs hopelessly. "But she just cry. Ah'm-a no happy to see this." I feel my eyebrow rise on its own. She delivers a short humorless snort. "Ah'm-a anger too! I tell her be more like Ana, but she can't." Her head wags from side to side as if to say, *What do you do with this?*

She drinks her espresso and continues, diagnosing Zia's anomaly. Some women, she insists, always need a man to live. Others live with or without a man. And still others cannot live with a man.

Zia has been living with Nani all of Zia's life. I don't presume to offer a remedy. So I adopt my default position when I can't bear to go head-to-head with my grandmother.

"Nani, tell me about when you and Nonno and my parents started living in New York. I'll go make more espresso."

I plump her pillows and straighten her sheets on my way out. I'm treated to a grin, her good hand reaching up to smooth my hair. "Ah, cara! Bene, bene!"

When I come back, she's ready. I hand her a fresh cup of coffee, offer the plate of pignoli nut cookies—she takes two—and sink into her bedside chair, my legs tucked beneath me.

CHAPTER 11

Living in America

"First," she begins, "everything very different. Everything."

Her story draws strong mental images for me.

My grandfather Nonno Carlo's cousin Giuseppe met the ship, waving his fedora to attract the attention of Carlo and my grandmother Nunzia. Ana and Arturo scanned the crowd, their anxiety rising at they witnessed the number of people waiting at the dock. Relying on photos he had seen, Arturo rested his hand on Carlo's shoulder and pointed. Giuseppe reacted at almost the same moment.

Carlo gave the signal to head into the sea of people. Nunzia grabbed her daughter's hand on her left. Arturo gently squeezed Nunzia's free hand and hung on.

Hugging and kissing, the adults went hoarse as they shouted above the din. Ana and Arturo stood back until they were introduced by Ana's father. Giuseppe knew that Arturo was a plus-one to the family. He raised his eyebrows at the young man, wondering about him and Ana.

Giuseppe and his wife, Concetta, owned a pizzeria-delicatessen on Arthur Avenue in the Bronx. They lived in the apartment above the store. The awning of the shop was adorned in Italian flags. The blended aromas of pizza, Parmesan, olive oil and vinegar bathed the sidewalk outside the small grocery.

Inside, sparkling cases behind the counter displayed marinated stuffed olives, sun-dried tomatoes, four different kinds of pasta sauce, deli meats, homemade meatballs, artichoke hearts, fresh pasta, an array of cheeses including fresh mozzarella and homemade ricotta. Homemade ravioli and manicotti also beckoned. Soppressata, Genoa salami, long logs of Parmesan and pinched links of salsiccia—small dried sausage—were suspended from the ceiling. The aroma was intoxicating.

Pizza ovens and storage cases stood to one side of the shop with lengths of pepperoni and chubs of mozzarella ready to be cut, grated and baked onto fresh dough covered with cloth, waiting to be kneaded.

The shop was loud with the business of customers querying their servers and employees satisfying their requests. They weighed slices and chunks of Italian cured meats, cheeses, salads, olives and pickled vegetables.

Bakers assembled an endless parade of pizza. Men expertly inserted paddles under partially baked pizzas, turning them for even baking. Clerks sliced the pies into triangular portions, joking with patrons and offering the final product across the counter.

As they approached, Giuseppe's wife, Concetta, greeted everyone at the entrance to the shop. She broke into wide dimples and exclamations, reaching for Nunzia and then Carlo. Once again, Ana and Arturo waited to be introduced before falling under Concetta's spell.

Following their hosts into the store, the newly arrived party was introduced to several customers and employees as Giuseppe and Concetta stopped to greet their patrons and workers. They continued while Concetta checked in with her staff, asking questions and providing instructions.

They hurried past the lure of freshly baked bread as they walked through an immaculate storage room to a doorway leading up to the apartment.

Both washrooms welcomed Carlo and his family before the guests followed their hosts into the dining room and settled into comfortably cushioned chairs.

Nunzia placed the box of Sicilian candied orange peel and blood orange confections into Concetta's open hands. Concetta admonished her guest, who hushed her host in return.

A vintage crocheted ecru tablecloth coddled an antique set of delicate lace-patterned dinner plates accompanied by appetizer plates and bowls. Linen napkins with crocheted edges wrapped entire sets of gleaming silverware at each place. Ana watched Arturo's eyes widen as she gestured subtly toward the ceiling.

An immaculate, graceful baroque-style crystal chandelier glittered from above. The older men and women exchanged information as Ana started to silently count the number of crystals. Arturo retreated into examining his hands, safely stored in his lap.

Giuseppe invited everyone to be comfortable. "Sei a casa adesso!" This is your home.

"Ah'm-a think will L'America ever be home," Nani confided.

"Nonno remind me we here to make the better life."

Naturally, I am most curious. "What were my mother and father doing, Nani?"

"Well, that first night we all have the dinner together," Nani continues.

Refusing help from Nunzia and Ana, Concetta began marching a feast to the table. Antipasti: Prosciutto. Genoa salami. Rolled spinach bread. Pickled eggplant, provolone cheese and fresh mozzarella. Roasted red peppers and olives swimming in marinade. Seafood antipasti. Caprese salad. Breads. Bread with chunks of pork baked in, affectionately dubbed "fat bread" as I grew older. Bread with chewy crusts and soft, tender insides. Bread spotted with sesame seeds. Small dishes of olive oil and herbs scattered about the table.

Ana was mortified when her stomach announced itself. She knew Arturo was also hungry, but they both waited for Nunzia's signal after Carlo delivered a solemn grace at Giuseppe's invitation.

Conversation lightened as everyone reached for the antipasti. Laughter and jokes were shared around the table, along with reminiscences of Italy. Ana and Arturo answered questions, but offered no conversation on their own. Ana wondered if she was destined to have a home like this someday. Beautiful, yes. But it made her anxious.

The meal was spectacularly endless. Ignoring Concetta's protests, Nunzia pressed Ana into action to clear antipasti dishes and to deliver soup, homemade gnocchi and homemade ravioli, fish grilled in olive oil, garlic and lemon and slow-roasted veal stewed with onions, white wine and eggplant on polenta, in succession. The meal was served slowly, under Concetta's direction. Nerello Mascalese wine punctuated each course for the adults. Ana and Arturo shared bottles of Sanpellegrino sparkling water.

Full to bursting, the party retired to the sitting room featuring ornate velvet-flocked wallpaper and plastic-smothered sofas and wing chairs. Lush area rugs. A corner curio cabinet gleaming of lemon oil was stuffed with crystal that dazzled under a mini chandelier. Handmade lace doilies covered tables, footstools and armrests.

Ana turned to her mother, seeking approval as she chatted with Concetta. Carlo and Giuseppe leaned toward each other, arms propped on their knees as the two men engrossed themselves in discussion. Carlo unbuttoned his jacket and smoothed his tie against his midsection. He nodded repeatedly as Giuseppe drove his message home with a thick index finger poked in Carlo's direction.

Concetta stood, folded her hands over her apron and announced dessert. Nunzia motioned to her daughter to follow Concetta into the kitchen.

For Ana, her newly introduced older cousin Concetta was an easy conversationalist. She asked insightful questions and listened to answers. She laughed easily, showing off her dimple and smooth complexion. Ana started to believe that she might manage living here after all. The young girl felt herself exhale.

Along with Nunzia's candied gifts from Sicily, espresso, anisette, ricotta cake, sweet ravioli and cannoli were placed on a huge tray. A second tray bore Concetta's porcelain dessert set, a perfect complement to the dinner service.

Ana, terrified she would drop the tray with the dessert set, followed Concetta's lead back to the sitting room. Ana stepped carefully and as she placed the tray safely on the coffee table. Giuseppe had carefully showcased the crystal liquor glasses from the curio cabinet. Along with amaretto, limoncello, Campari and sambuca were offered.

Ana was full. Really full. But she didn't resist the sweet ravioli, smothered in honey. Arturo snagged a slice of ricotta cake, followed by a cannoli. They split a ravioli.

Concetta further burdened the table with bowls of nuts and assorted fruit. Stomach near bursting, Ana reached for a blood orange and a handful of walnuts. She and Arturo shared her score.

Giuseppe and Carlo indulged in digestifs and tales of the past. Carlo's folded jacket and tie now hung neatly on the back of the wing chair. He reclined against the chair as he fondled a tiny crystal glass of anisette.

The cousins were born a month apart and raised in Camastra in northern Sicily. At twelve years of age, Ana's current age, they were thick as thieves as they dreamed up and plotted practical jokes directed at their parents and friends. They attended school together and played soldiers—Allied soldiers, of course—when classes let out.

As a schoolboy, Giuseppe was fascinated by the political studies of America in their classes.

"I will live there when I can go myself," he assured Carlo. Who planted a phony punch to his cousin's stomach.

"You're crazy. You'll always live here. Like me."

"No. I'm really going." By the time he was twenty-two years old, Giuseppe had saved enough money for his passage. Despite the fact that he broke his mother's heart, he was determined to start a new life.

He had written to a friend already living in New York for advice about emigrating. His friend, Paulo, did better. He gave Giuseppe a home and recommended him for a job in an Arthur Avenue delicatessen. Eventually, he opened his own shop.

Ana was relieved when her mother motioned for her to begin cleaning up. Working efficiently and carefully and minding Nunzia's direction, she ignored Concetta's protests.

When Ana and Concetta reemerged from the kitchen, Concetta reviewed the sleeping arrangements. Linens and toiletries would be found in our assigned rooms. Ana would have a fold-out sofa in her parents' room. Arturo would take another fold-out in Giuseppe's office.

Buona notte and grazie all around and everyone finally retired.

The family stayed with Concetta and Giuseppe for two weeks. For many of those nights, Ana did not sleep. But those weeks provided enough time to ready the apartment waiting for Nani and her family.

"It was big place," Nani explained. "Lots of cleaning before we go in. And we do lots for Giuseppe and Concetta. So we busy. You mama e papa, they go to school too, first time in English. They no complain, just help."

Their new apartment was sprawling and generous. Like Giuseppe's and Concetta's, it was located in the Arthur Avenue area, above a business selling imported pasta and olive oil, dried beans, spices, cookies and chocolates packaged in Italy. Three bedrooms, a spacious kitchen with a large porcelain sink with antique faucets. Not too much cabinet space, but an area that could easily host a standalone pantry. In the bathroom stood a claw-foot tub with a retrofitted shower and a calcium-stained vintage shower curtain.

Ana and Nunzia scrubbed the kitchen, bathroom, bedrooms, cabinets and walls. They replaced the shower curtain and inspected and cleaned the mattresses. Carlo and Arturo made repairs, refinished the wood floors and painted the walls, baseboards and moldings. Nunzia assigned bedrooms to Ana and Arturo. Either one of them would be required to pass hers and Carlo's room to get to the other.

By day, all hands were at Concetta's disposal. Nunzia cared for the home above the pizzeria-delicatessen, prepared meals each day, cleaned and did laundry. Despite her young age, Ana served customers in the shop. Arturo also manned the counter, hauling stock from the basement, cutting wheels of cheese, replenishing the cases with fresh salads, fish, meat, baked goods and desserts.

Gradually, life fell into a routine. In addition to school, Ana signed on for evening English classes along with Arturo and her father. She put her talent for language to work for herself and for her family. Smart and hardworking, she joined the debate team, earned A's and B's in her courses, and continued to work in the pizzeria-delicatessen after school and on weekends.

"You mama, she good at school. But she sad sometimes with other kids. She Italian and they know she different. Hard for her, but she strong. Good because I'm pregnant with Maria three months after we get here."

Ana's social transition was rocky. Her clothes and style identified her as an immigrant. Her strong, dark Sicilian features drew comments from other girls. Walking from her locker one afternoon, she caught, as she was meant to, an exchange among a small group of classmates: "Guess no one told her we pluck our eyebrows." "And wear makeup." "And shave our legs." Chased by giggling and laughter, she walked off at an unhurried pace, glad to be showing them her back.

Her hair was black, long, thick and wavy in several different directions at the same time. Conceding defeat, she fastened it back into a ponytail with an industrial-sized barrette. At lunch one day, she was ambushed in the cafeteria by two classmates. They robbed her barrette, forcing her hair to flow freely down her back. Running, they lifted their trophy high. She smoothed her hair as best she could, tucking it precariously behind her ears. She had lost her appetite, but resolved to slowly finish her lunch. The next morning in homeroom, her barrette was nestled into the ancient unused inkwell in her desk.

Having passed the hazing, shortly after the barrette incident, Ana was approached by the leader of the group to join them for pizza after school. "On Friday," announced Rina, "you should come."

Shocked, Ana controlled a smile and said yes. But she made it clear she had to check with her cousin Concetta. Because of work.

Over time, Rina and Ana became close friends. Rina's parents had emigrated from Calabria before Rina's birth. They compared notes about their families and having lived in America only versus having lived in both Sicily and America. Rina was rebellious and mischievous, experimented with cigarettes, borrowed high-heeled shoes, dark red lipstick and low-cut blouses. She laughed at Ana, who was scandalized by her friend's daring forays into womanhood.

Ana was serious, rule conscious. A punctual perfectionist, she delivered an excellent product of everything asked for, on time. When one of the ovens in the delicatessen was placed in her responsibility with Concetta's instruction to give it "a good cleaning," Ana decided that steel wool and elbow grease were the weapons of choice. Wetting down the inside of the oven, she slathered it with a scouring powder and forced herself into the claustrophobic space. She scrubbed for over two hours.

A loud gasp announced Concetta's return from the shop out front. "What are you doing!"

Ana's eyes went wide. What had she done wrong? "I'm cleaning the oven. Isn't this what you asked me to do?"

Wiping a scar of scouring powder from Ana's cheek, Concetta embraced her. Turning to the cabinet under the wide sink, Concetta produced a tall yellow aerosol can. "*This* is what we use. Next time, you will have a much easier time cleaning the oven. I am so sorry."

Ana was humiliated, but determined to finish her job. And she would always recognize the label on a can of Easy-Off oven cleaner.

Concetta praised her, and later to Nunzia, for her work. She wrapped a ring of Ana's favorite fat bread and a container of hot cherry peppers and pressed the package into her hands. "This is just for you, okay?" When the bell summoned Concetta back to the front, Ana, salivating, ripped into the ring of bread, knowing that Arturo also loved it. It hurt to give up any of her prize, but in the end she shared her gift with him.

She adored her parents and loved Giuseppe and Concetta. She looked forward to serving their neighbors in the delicatessen, enjoyed the freedom of temporarily living in the language and the mannerisms of her native skin. Customers treated her like a cherished daughter, asked about school and plans for the future. And bragged and complained about their own families.

Every Friday, Concetta was pleased to see Ana go off with a group of friends after school. Though, secretly, she scorned the pizza place they preferred to her own. Reasoning that the young people need their own space, she let it go.

Nunzia and Carlo decided that America was strange, but good to them. Nunzia continued managing Giuseppe's and Concetta's household and her own. She provided breaks for Concetta in the shop, working alongside Ana and Arturo. And agonized quietly over the danger in Carlo's work in construction. She prepared for the new baby, the first of the family to be born in America.

With Giuseppe's connections, Carlo had taken on a position in a construction company. He studied English and qualified as a building inspector. He decided to take on, in addition, hands-on construction, returning home each night exhausted but upbeat, happy to be providing for his family and building a future. Nunzia ministered to him constantly, unquestioningly. He admired his wife's dedication. Wildly excited about the new baby, he vowed that Nunzia should not work after the birth of their second child. "An' do *what*?"

It took little time for Nunzia to recognize the deepening relationship between Ana and Arturo. Quiet and reserved in the presence of the two older adults, when alone they could be found on the sofa, sharing popcorn as they watched a show, laughing and exchanging observations. Nunzia noted that though they sat well apart, Arturo's arm eventually crept to the back of the sofa, as if to draw Ana closer. Many times, Nunzia watched Arturo's eyes as he reacted to Ana as she joked, told a story about her day or shared an insight on politics, so different from Italy's.

Nunzia confronted Carlo with her impressions one night as she sat on the edge of their bed, waiting for him as he buttoned his pajama top.

Carlo's head snapped to attention. "What you say? They brother e sister, no?"

"No, they not."

Carlo shrugged. "So what you want to do? Send him back home?"

"Ridicolo. No. Ah'm-a just want to watch, make sure we see everything."

Madonna mia! You got nothing a worry about!" Chuckling, Carlo planted a chaste kiss on Ana's cheek, patted her stomach and rolled onto his side. But it took him over an hour to fall asleep, wondering how he could have missed it all.

* * *

This is more than Nani has ever shared with me about early life in America. I wonder about the moment Ana realized she loved my father. I wonder if Nani and my mother had been scared. Or had been just tough enough to take it in stride.

I have fabricated an imagined story from Nani's descriptions. Speaking English for such an extended period of time had tested her reserve. She had fallen more deeply into broken English over the course of her narrative. A few times, I reminded her that she was not speaking English at all.

Nani is exhausted by the time she finishes. Going back has taken her away, temporarily, from the present. Both hands had flown as she had continued her story. I am sure her pain has peaked.

She refuses medication again. So I help her to the bathroom, tuck her back into bed and kiss her forehead. With a tired smile, she motions me out of the bedroom and closes her eyes.

I head back to the dinette table, making a mental note to record her stories in the future.

I flip the cover of my laptop just as the phone trills in the kitchen. I dive for it before it wakes my grandmother. It's my mother, suggesting that she and I go out to dinner—she has gotten Zia to stay with Nani for the evening.

I agree. My anxiety is piqued, all too common in the world I share with Ana.

From her bedroom, my grandmother's voice is an exaggerated yawn.

"Who's this?" she wants to know. I tell her that my mother and Maria are on their way.

"Good," she says. She has closed her eyes by the time I get to the bedroom door.

My mother and Maria appear in the apartment ten minutes later. Nani is already asleep. Zia nods from my grandmother's bedside chair that she is ready to take charge. Ana and I make for the door, but not until my mother tucks the covers under Nani's arms.

"Madonna! She's so frail! I don't know how she'll recover—this is taking all her strength."

"Ma, you're catching her late in the day. She's actually pretty good. I do wish her appetite was better, though." *Did I really say that out loud?*

"What? She not eating? What are you making for her? Why didn't you tell me? *I'll* cook for her!"

"Ma! She's eating; she just gets full really fast."

Forced into a rundown of the food I've brought for my grandmother's daily meals, I hear the defensiveness in my voice as my mother presses her advantage.

Ana issues her orders.

"You will make breakfast and lunch for your grandmother. Make sure she gets protein. You know she doesn't eat cheese or drink milk."

Knowing my effort is futile, I lodge my formal protest. "Ma," I begin, "I can cook for her. She likes what I cook."

"Then how come she's losing weight? No. I will bring her dinners. That's final. She can't be losing weight. She'll disappear."

We go to our favorite neighborhood Italian place, Paolo's. Naturally, Paolo greets us by clasping his hands together as if in prayer and plants the triple kisses on my mother's cheeks. She smiles, reaching for his hands as they exchange greetings in Italian.

Noticing me, Paolo exclaims at how long it's been since I've come to the restaurant. Asks how I've been, slyly slipping in a subtle prompt about marriage and kids.

As he floats a set of linen napkins across our laps, my mother fills him in. "She's getting married soon. I'm making her, uh, wedding suit."

"Bene, bene!" He laughs. "What joy! Ah'm-a so happy for you! Congratulazioni!" With that, Paolo leaves us with menus as he returns to the bar for my mother's wine.

Ana pretends to be engrossed in the meal choices, but she always orders the same thing.

I ask for a bottle of Sanpellegrino. She thanks Paolo for the wine and for my benefit she orders for us in English.

"Antipasti per due; eggplant parmigiana with spicy sausage. And olive oil with balsamic for the bread, please."

He returns with a huge bottle of Sanpellegrino and glasses. Disappears briefly and returns, bearing bread and the olive oil and balsamic dipping dishes.

My mother sips from her glass and nods in my direction. "You know? I think I'll move her in with me. We can rent out her apartment. I will ask Zia's nephew Antonio to manage the house. She'll be with me if anything else happens. I'll sleep better."

I have a million questions, and just as many comments, all squelched by the weight of her made-up mind. I run my ring finger around the rim of my glass. Say nothing and wait for it.

She throws a preemptive scowl my way. "Sì. She will come with me. Why not? It makes good sense." She turns her attention to pulling her bread apart and wipes her hands on her napkin.

If you're the daughter, yes, it makes good sense. If you're my mother's mother, Nunzia, not so much. Fiercely independent. The carer, never the care-ee. Uncomfortable, out of sorts when out of her own space. If it's going to work, my mother will have to convince my grandmother that she, Ana, needs her to move in. Nani will do almost anything for her daughter.

I'm not meant to answer. I pick at the salami and olives and dip another piece of bread in the olive oil / balsamic.

My mother's left eyebrow signals impending argument. I remain busy chewing.

"What?" she demands. "You think she won't come, right? She's too proud, right? Too stubborn."

"Well," I try, "you got it from somewhere." I try a shallow grin.

"Bah!"

"Ma, you'll have to convince her it's good for *you* that she moves in with you. Then she'll come. Maybe."

"What? Why?"

I incline my head and wait.

"I should say I'm lonely? She'll never believe me, you know this."

"Are you?"

"Am I what? Lonely?"

"I miss your father, but I'm not lonely anymore."

"Why don't you visit Sicily, Ma?"

"Ach! Just over the phone they get all weepy because of your father. For them, it's a scandal that I don't wear black. Besides, a lot of people are gone now."

"It's a big world, Ma. Maybe you and Zia can go on a cruise. That's really fun because you pack and unpack once, and you get to see all these great places. Great food—not as good as yours, but still good—and lots of activities. You guys should do it."

I note something like interest lurking behind my mother's eyes.

As always, the meal is excellent. Next to my mother, Paolo makes the best eggplant parmigiana with sausage. Already planning tomorrow's run, I concede that I have no willpower here.

My anxiety is piqued as my mother introduces the topic that brings us here.

"With Nani like this, you got to know where her papers are and where my papers are. Your father left some money and some investments—not so big, but you need to know. Next visit, I'll have everything ready for you to look at. I'll let you know what I want."

My supper churns, but I know she's right. "Okay, Ma. It's good to do this before we need to."

She raises the napkin to the corners of her mouth and nods.

I exhale. I hope she's just confirmed that she *doesn't* need to do this now.

I stay three more days, heartened by Nani's recovery and the return of her appetite. My mother's plan works. Ana's evening meals for her mother are restorative.

I witness a familiar drama acted by Nani and Zia. When Zia visits, my grandmother's mouth stretches into a taut line. Her eyes harden and her voice, laced with scorn, reports in at a stern octave higher than normal.

Cowed but not vanquished, Zia takes tentative steps toward her mother, planting her cheeks with ritual kisses.

Maria always brings sweets, which my grandmother loves, but never gives Zia the satisfaction of letting her know. When my mother's there, the two sisters make things light and draw Nunzia into their circle. Almost always, Nani laughs along. This is one of my mother's talents. Zia makes espresso, and we all enjoy the sweets.

Ma takes a first pass at introducing her own home as Nani's permanent residence. Too smart to be sideswiped, my grandmother has anticipated this chapter of my mother's playbook. And has summarily shut it down. For now.

"I been thinking, Ma . . ."

"What? What's wrong?"

"Nothing, really."

"You know, with this happening"—my mother points to Nani's arm—"I think maybe we're both lonely."

"And what? You want to move here? Too small, no?" She pretends to understand finally. "*Oh*, you want I move with you."

"Well, we're both lonely, and we could help each other."

"Lone-ly? My arm no make me lonely. Ah'm-a without you father forty years. You without Arturo, what, twenty?"

She doesn't wait for Ana's response. "No," she concludes. "Ah'm-a no move. Ah'm-a happy here."

I know how this will play out over the coming months. I smile, knowing that Nani has won this round. I am sure she will not move in with my mother.

Ma makes arrangements for Zia to be with their mother the next day. I will have a fitting of my wedding suit before I head back to Boston.

I wake early and run in my old neighborhood, again both comforted and stunned at how little it has changed over the years. I am almost dreaming as I pace myself. Flooded with inadequacy, a need to hide, a need to be someone better, someone smarter, someone—*anyone*—else.

I come in, sweaty and out of sorts. My mother has breakfast on the table. Espresso, a huge omelet with prosciutto and sun-dried tomatoes. Blood oranges and biscotti.

I am dreading following her upstairs. My weight. The no-wedding-dress wedding suit. The color. The heels I'll never be able to walk in.

"Hurry and shower. You shouldn't stain the material. I'll get it dry-cleaned anyway, but, just the same."

Add sloppy and sweaty to my list of charms.

After my shower, I join Ana in her sewing room.

She has dressed the sewing mannequin in the suit. Blouse. Jacket. Pants. The final seams have been impatiently waiting for this fitting.

I button the pants.

Talking around a mouthful of straight pins, she complains, "These don't flatter your figure at all." She pulls on the waist.

Hard. Pins the hem on the pant legs after she lets some room in the hips.

"I told you not to gain weight!"

Blouse next. Blessedly, it fits perfectly. I have high hopes, suddenly, for the jacket.

Dashed in the next twenty seconds.

"Look at this. The arms are too tight, and you won't be able to button it! I have lots of work on this piece!"

I know better than to respond. My mother's performance is a thinly veiled disapproval of my choice of wedding clothes. Best to bear it and get on the road.

"You have enough material, Ma?"

She glares at me. "Since when don't I know my way around material? Of course I have enough! But you have to go on a diet, for sure."

Finally, she releases me from bondage.

My bag, computer and briefcase are already in the car. She is poised at the front door, arms crossed under her bosom, mouth fixed between smile and disappointment at watching me go.

"You have enough gas?"

"I'll get some, Ma."

"Get it here—it'll be cheaper than on the highway.

"Here, wait." She returns from the kitchen with a care package. Veal with polenta. Pickled eggplant and artichoke hearts. Fruit. Prosciutto. And good Italian bread. Napkins. Plastic utensils. Bottle of water. Despite my command to diet, she can't help feeding me.

I step up, kiss her, deliver a huge hug and I'm on my way.

As usual, I see her wave from the porch, then watch from inside the storm door until we're out of each other's visual field. As usual, my heart aches as I pull away. My heart aches as I navigate my way out of the Bronx. By the time I reach the highway, I've shaken myself into the present, grateful that my grandmother is recovering. Wondering how many conversations it will take before my mother gives up trying to get Nunzia to move in with her.

I don't feel like calling Russ while I'm on the road. I'm not sure if I'm ready for my own life again. That's odd, right?

As I drive, I review my last discussion with Nani before leaving. I travel into my grandmother's insights of Nani and Maria.

"Nani," I started. Best to probe gently before asking. In this family, we ignite like a pile of dry straw when the conditions are right. Or wrong, as the case may be.

Nani released the rim of her glass of apple juice. "Che cosa—what's up—cara?"

I'm deliberately cautious. "Why, when Zia comes over?"

She offered me a disappointed frown.

"I get mad, no?" She shook her head from side to side, then sadly clucked her tongue.

Confident that she would continue, I waited. Nani loves to talk when she's forced to stay put.

One more sip of apple juice and she was ready.

"She's a-kids, she no strong. You grandfather tease. Take-a her—what—the soft candy."

"Marshmallow?" I offer.

She nods. "Yeah, yeah, he take it away an' she cry like crazy kids! I tell her, 'Go get from you father.' But, no, she go away very sad."

"Nani, you really expected her to do that as a kid?"

"Sì, certo—of course. You mother, she do! You grandfather, he laugh. Ana, she go to Maria, hug her, talk to her. But Maria? She just upset, then calm down with Ana."

"She have-a hard time with the other kids. They make fun. But Ana, she always there. She not afraid. I watch one time in the schoolyard when Ana and me, we go to meet Maria after school. Maria, she play with some girls. Two girls, they come along an' play with Maria braids—make-a mustache with the braids. I see Maria start to cry an' I almost rush in.

"But you mama Ana very calm, go in an' pull Maria behind her. I hear her say to the girls: 'You try this with me? Why you bother her? She no bother you. Next time, you make sure you come to me. Okay?' The girls, they run off. Maria? She happy for her sister. But she no want to go in the schoolyard no more. Fffft!"

As Nani related the events in Maria's life, I saw that a lack of resilience was my aunt's only crime. And she soldiered through it. While my grandmother scorned her, I was developing a newfound respect for my mother's younger sister.

It was hard to be Maria. She was indecisive. She agonized over every event, her pregnancy delivering newfound terror. How would she carry her baby for nine whole months? If she did, how would she take care of the child? How would her husband, Salvatore, react if it wasn't a boy? What if she did something wrong?

My grandmother had no tolerance for these neurotic musings. I could hear her saying: *What you mean, do something wrong? What? You no feed? You no watch? You let her go off somewhere alone?*

CHAPTER 12

The Gun Lesson

Ana told me that Zia was a great mother, but hesitant and unsure of herself. As she grew, Claire guided Maria's parenting. She had a way of communicating what her mother should do when she had trouble with schoolwork or wanted to join friends on class trips. Claire stepped up big-time after her dad, Salvatore, died. He was imposing. He stood over six feet five inches tall and he was strong. I realized later that he was the archetypal New York City detective. He had exchanged his strong Italian accent for the accent spoken by his blue-uniformed brothers.

* * *

Salvatore's hair stuck straight up off his scalp in a stiff black steel wool pad. His green eyes were soft and kind. He loved to laugh and he made us laugh. He took charge of his family in every way. Claire was always the apple of his eye. He was security and happiness, and the love of Maria's and Claire's lives.

Being with Zio Salvatore was joy. He would step gingerly into the house after his shift, bending for the doorjamb. When we were together, Claire and I would rush toward him, progress abruptly halted as he splayed his huge hand in a must-be-obeyed stop sign.

We followed behind him as he checked his gun, placing it on top of the high china cabinet.

Hugs and scratchy cheek kisses, both of us giggling. "Can we see it, Zio?" Suddenly serious, his eyes turned to steel, his jaw square, his smile saved in his pocket.

"My gun?"

Claire scolded me with her eyes, her head moving from side to side in a slow warning.

I was in it now. "Well, I mean, I'm curious. Claire too?" She searched her father's face for the correct response.

He reached back up, pointed the gun toward the wall, made sure he had removed the ammunition. Checked the safety again. Gave us firm instructions not to touch it, and started to teach us.

"Lesson one: If you ever see a gun anywhere, never touch it. You'll never see this one anywhere that you can touch it."

We listened in rapt silence.

"This is a lethal weapon. You know what that means?"

"It can kill," Claire announced. Her father nodded his approval.

"Lesson two: Never point a gun—even a phony gun—at a person, even one that you absolutely know has no bullets. Never." I swallowed hard.

"Lesson three: An officer or detective is allowed to fire his gun only to stop someone from harming someone else or himself. An' he better try to talk that someone down before he uses it.

"If we have to fire our gun, there's an investigation to let everyone know if it was a legal, proper use of the gun or not."

"You mean you can be blamed if you use your gun?" I was astounded. I always figured a policeman could use his gun whenever he wanted to.

"Of course. We have to follow rules and be responsible—just like you."

Transfixed by my uncle's discussion, Claire and I nodded in unison.

"Lesson four: Never touch or surprise a police officer or detective when he's wearing his gun."

Foolishly, I asked, "Why not?"

"Well, why do you think?"

"An accident, maybe?"

"Good girl!"

At this, hands wringing a mappina—a tea towel—Zia approached from the kitchen.

"Salvatore!" she demanded.

I was shocked because I had only seen Zia subordinate and smiling when it came to Zio. When it came to anyone, really. I had never seen her take charge.

He looked up, his eyes softening again. Gauged her expression. Knew already what was coming.

Playful shrug as he teased her. "What, Maria?"

"You crazy, showing the girls your gun? What if something happen?"

"You think I'd let anything happen? No bullets, safety on. They have been very good—not touching the gun, just learning."

"Learning? It's a bad idea."

"So they're not curious anymore. Maybe a little afraid. They won't go near a gun if they see one." Checking it yet again, Zio Salvatore returned the gun to the top of the china cabinet.

"Where they see a gun?"

He looked around the room, incredulous. "Maria! We live in the Bronx!" He started to chuckle, stood, then grabbed my aunt and drew her near.

She made a feeble attempt to push him away, draped the mappina over her shoulder and dissolved into laughter.

Then she went back to dinner simmering on the stove.

The four lessons scared me for a long time.

Zia Maria taught Claire all the housekeeping necessities. Like my mother, Maria was an Italian maestro in the kitchen. The sisters were obsessively clean. Claire and I would describe things as "Ana-Clean" or "Maria-Clean."

But my aunt didn't know how to handle Claire growing up. As I grew older, I understood that Zia wanted her daughter to remain a child. So Claire would consult with me to learn how my mother would manage clothes, part-time jobs, makeup, curfews, boys.

When Zio died, Maria insisted that the house be ablaze with light. Claire and I ran through the rooms, turning on every switch. Zia stared blankly from the wing chair in the living room. My mother took charge of the kitchen, forcing Maria to drink water and tea. Toasted thick slices of Italian bread. Slathered them with Sicilian wild berry jam. It was the only thing Maria would eat for a long time. And only if my mother prepared it for her.

She couldn't focus. She couldn't cry. My grandmother sat next to her, compassionate, worried. I wondered if it frightened her that Maria did not cry. It frightened me. Claire and I cried a lot.

I wondered how Zio must have felt as he headed up the tenement building stairs to arrest what my mother explained were the members of a human trafficking ring. She had to explain what that was to us. We'd never heard that term before. People forced into prostitution, forced labor, threatened with violence and worse. I shivered through a mental image of the manacled and force-marched slave coffles we learned about in school.

I pictured Zio's bulk bursting through the door blasted with graffiti, gun drawn, three criminals with guns pointed his way. He was shot instantly. Other members of the ring pumped three more bullets into my uncle.

He was gone before the rest of the detectives and police reached him.

Claire and I occupied the same cocoon. I didn't know what she needed, but I was in it with her. We both missed her dad. Mostly, though, we worried about her mother.

She had barely made it through the police department funeral and our family funeral. When they gave her the folded US flag, she leaned on my mother and handed it to her. Did she think it might burn in her hands?

Zia appeared briefly at the funerals but could not attend either reception. Her doctor prescribed sleeping pills to give her some rest and comfort. Then she would wake, unrefreshed and in pain, losing Salvatore all over again.

She lived in her bedroom. My mother cooked and delivered meals, with stern instructions that Claire and I must tell her if Zia did not eat. We were detailed to clean and respond to Zia's needs. We changed Zia's bed linens every few days and administered sponge baths.

This went on for weeks.

When Zia emerged, she was confused and more tentative than ever. Her eyes were rimmed in red liner. Her mouth was pinched, creating deep creases in her upper lip, turned down at the corners. A huge shock of white hair was emerging over the left side of her forehead. Maria had always been stocky, verging on overweight. Now we saw that she had lost a worrisome amount of weight and that her hands suffered from a slight nervous tremor. When she looked up, it seemed she was expecting another unspeakable blow. She was so brittle that everything, even someone's sneeze, startled her.

As Maria slowly regained a childlike ability to care for her home and herself, my mother and Nani decided that the first page of the next chapter should be turned.

When Ana introduced the idea that Zia and Claire should live with us for a while, Maria resisted. She had to be assured that she wouldn't lose her home. Salvatore was there. Their house was one of the few ways she could stay close to him.

Claire and I were ecstatic.

Nani was with us on Friday nights. She taught us to make Sicilian pizza. Huge doormats of garlic, basil, oregano and olive oil–infused tomato sauce slathered onto thick dough. Pizza nights came and went in a continuous stream of intoxication for the entire week.

Saturday mornings, Claire and I would stretch out the sofa cushions, get on the floor in pajama'd legs and slippered feet. We watched our television shows and shared leftover pizza stolen from the cold oven. We silently signaled our private joke when my mother asked us why we weren't hungry for breakfast.

My mother and Nani were firmly convinced that Maria would improve. My mother worked at gradually increasing Maria's self-sufficiency. Her love, friendship and compassion worked its magic. Zia's commitment to get better for Claire helped. But it took a year.

Of course, Claire was happy her mother was better. I was happy Zia was better. But they moved back home. Claire and I missed our dinner and nighttime rituals, exchanging food from our plates while my mother wasn't looking. Giggling in whispers under the covers, sharing the eerie light under the tent to illuminate our books after curfew. Talking after lights out until one of us realized the other was already asleep. Something told me my mother was aware of it all.

Once they had moved back home, Claire and I called each other almost every day. Claire talked a lot about her mom, who got together with my mother several times a week, over espresso and Maria's sweets in each other's kitchens. Nani joined them. The triumvirate could be found once a week in Nani's favorite Sicilian grocery store, scoring the best of what they loved to eat.

CHAPTER 13

Stomachaches Are Not Created Equal

I autodial Russ when I'm about halfway home. I'm always out of sorts when I get to this point. I don't belong in the Bronx anymore, but I'm not home yet. Desperately missing Russ, I resist the urge to depress the accelerator and soldier on.

I feel both of us smiling as he answers the phone.

"So," he says, laughing, "you really are coming home!"

"I'm about two hours away. You want me to pick up dinner? What do you want?"

"I'm highly insulted!" he answers. "I made my famous chili and garlic bread—Italian bread from the North End. Tell me that's not worth comin' home to!"

We both laugh as we finish our call.

I start to prioritize tomorrow's work. I'm coming back to a now-rushed deadline for a grant submission and final changes on three manuscripts for publication. The two sets of deliverables depend on each other. The grant can't fly without submission of the publications. Securing the grant, in turn, ensures future publications.

The team I work with has left the lab and me in good shape. But not relaxed. To score the next grant will take a near-perfect research grant proposal and showing the agency that we've achieved our goals with the current grant.

Funny. I had always believed that I wasn't competitive by nature. And here I am, always, competing for journal e-print / actual print space for completed research. Competing for funds to continue the work in the lab. Competing for my salary. I chose this profession of research investigation and high-level teaching. Couldn't congratulate myself when it went well. It had to keep going better and better.

The month brings high productivity at the cost of long hours writing, consulting with colleagues and lab members, leading to constant critique and revision. A fresh grant to fund the research and the salaries of the lab members is the goal. The uncertainty of achieving that goal gnaws at me like a colony of termites.

Returning home, I am reminded that teaching is the prime source of my own learning. Teaching students gives me the lift I need through the stress. But I'm edgy and tired. With the grant looming, I have not called my mother. I need to speak to Claire.

Claire and I have been in close touch after having connected on the weekend Ana presented the non-wedding fabric. I am relieved when Claire reports that our grandmother is just about fully recovered. Lifting stuff, walking, shopping at the same grocery store with the same cart, hosting her friends, visiting my mother, hosting Zia. Insisting she's fine when pain settles in her arm, apparently much thinned compared to its partner.

"Have you called your mother?" Claire asks.

"Uh, no, why? She's okay, right?"

"Gaby!" Claire laughs. "I'd never take you for a coward."

"Busted!" I say.

"Hey, now that you and Russ are getting married, d'ya ever think about your dad?"

"Nothing to do with getting married. I think about my father every day. I miss him every day. I know you miss Zio Salvatore too."

"Yeah, they've both been gone such a long time."

"You know what, Claire?" I try a cough to camouflage choking up. "We lost our mothers too. They were never, well, the same. I almost said 'normal,' but they were never normal, right?"

When we hang up, I revisit my mother after my father's death.

* * *

With my father, she laughed. A smile was her default expression. She made him laugh, stepped lightly, moved from activity to activity easily, confidently. He'd watch her walk past him. She knew he liked what he saw.

I would sneak partway down the stairs on Saturday nights. My parents' TV movie night over a shared bowl of popcorn. I'd witness them on the sofa, my mother's legs accordioned under her bottom. Watching the screen, she would tuck her head against my father's chin, his fingers playing at the top of her arm. I'd run back upstairs when they started kissing. It was gross.

My father, who had always loved the delicatessen business, learned it thoroughly under Giuseppe and Concetta's guidance. In a short time, they appointed him manager, in charge of inventory and pricing. He optimized their return by outsourcing non-cost-effective goods like bread and the expertise of on-site bakers. "We have all these fantastic bakeries here! Let's scratch some backs!" He and my mother also developed a market for freshly prepared packaged foods and meals for families and schoolkids. Giuseppe and Concetta developed a deep sense of confidence in Arturo and Ana and their ironclad code of honesty.

In short order, they earned a share of the profits each month and realized the benefits of discussing family or work with customers. Which they took to naturally.

In the late afternoons and evenings, my mother fulfilled her dressmaking passion. She established a cottage industry in the house we had bought a year earlier in the northeast Bronx. Ana attracted a female clientele in our neighborhood and among women along Arthur Avenue who would take public transit to my mother's shop. At first, she confined herself to repairs and alterations. With stern instructions to avoid the fabric with the sharp seam ripper, I was placed in charge of dismantling seams that needed resewing. Ana graduated quickly to designing and sewing dresses, blouses and skirts. She refused to design or sew women's pants.

My father was never home before 9 P.M. I would wait for him; we'd share stories of our days and on Saturdays he would bring home a ring loaf of pork bread from the deli. This we would share and eat with hot cherry peppers. I'd head upstairs content and happy, hearing my mother's "What are you giving her hot peppers for before bed? She'll be up all night!" I never was.

All forgiven, my mother would then sit with him while he ate supper through gentle conversation. I fell asleep happy my parents were happy.

I knew I was blessed. Too many school friends told stories of yelling, drinking and worse between their parents. Now in my thirties I still feel close to my father when I eat pork bread with hot cherry peppers.

Friday. I headed home from work at the deli. It wasn't unusual for my father to be away from the deli, making and verifying orders with vendors, so I didn't miss him while I was working. But his car was parked in front of the house when I arrived home.

By the time I reached the top of the concrete flight of stairs, my initial uplift had given way to queasiness.

My mother wore a worried expression. Without looking at me, she ordered: "Go up and see your father."

He was propped up by several pillows, reading a book. I was shocked into the reality of seeing him in bed, in pajamas, so early. His eyes lit up and he smiled broadly as I came near to give him a kiss.

"Pa! What's wrong?!"

He waved my concern aside. "Oh, just my stomach. A lot of heartburn." He smiled again. "I can't resist your mother's cooking!" I wanted to believe him. But his face was gray and there were dark circles under his eyes. No adjustment of pillows brought him comfort.

When I found my way downstairs, my mother was on the phone with Zia. She ended the conversation when she saw me.

"Ma, shouldn't he go to the doctor?"

Her jaw tight, she continued to avoid my eyes, the potato peeler paring the vegetables into thin shards.

"We went." The wait was excruciating. I knew I'd get nothing if I pressed.

She wiped her hands on her apron and, finally, faced me.

"Your father has a heart condition."

"But, Ma, he's young, sort of, and he's not fat!"

"True," she agreed, "but he still has a heart condition. And he had a mild heart attack."

Heart attack! Wait, it's heartburn. He said so. How is that a heart attack?

I waited for her to continue.

"So now, we have to make sure he works less and we do something about his stress."

Stress? As far as I knew, my father was never stressed.

"Lots of chicken and fish from now on." I groaned. Despite his Sicilian origins, my father hated fish, and chicken was second on his list of loathed foods. I reviewed my school learning and took a quick food inventory. Olive oil—good. Pork—the way we liked it—no good. Lamb—no good. Beef—no good. Pasta—not too much and only with homemade tomato sauces. No problem. Vegetables—eggplant, this my father liked; asparagus, mushrooms, also caprese—good, but not too much fresh mozzarella, and not a lot of oil; broccoli rabe—check; zucchini—this he didn't favor, but no loud complaints.

My mother finished assembling the chicken soup on the stove, rooted around for the orzo in the cabinet. She was wound like a high-tension power line.

"What about the deli?" I tried. "Papa should retire, no?"

"He won't do it." Her jaw clenched into a hard line. "He says we don't have enough money yet for your college." My mouth went dry. Oh no. My fault.

I cleared my throat. "Ma, I'll win scholarships. I already know which ones to apply for. And I can work. Now. In college. If we want his stress down, he shouldn't work anymore."

"Okay, so you tell him. He won't listen to me." Stubborn Siciliano, my father. Like all us Siciliani.

I ran back upstairs, found him dozing, the book splayed on his lap, his breaths even and deep. Not a good time to talk about this.

Three days later, I got my chance. He brushed me off in a flurry of bravado.

"What? You think I won't send you to college?"

"Pa! I'm just saying it's my schooling—I can at least pay for part. I've got time. I'm thirteen. I already work in the deli. When I'm older, I'll make more money. And I can work in college to keep paying for it—take loans—this is America! There are lots of student loan programs."

Pa raised his left eyebrow. While he knew this, it was important to him that he relied only on himself to send his only child to college.

He smiled at me. "I'm getting better. I'm not ready to leave the deli. Dr. Maskowicz is taking good care of me, and so is Mama. I want us all to get back to normal."

"Yeah, but I wanna do something—and this college money thing I can help with."

"You're too young to worry about money for college." He treated me to a half smile as he fixed his glasses to the bridge of his nose and returned to his newspaper. I was officially dismissed.

I sought refuge in the kitchen, scents of steak, thyme and fennel rising from the cast-iron skillet on the stove. Potatoes roasting in the oven.

"Mama."

"Let me guess, he won't stop working."

"He's *infuriating*!"

"Yeah," she said, smiling, "but would you have him any other way?"

I walked on eggshells after the mild heart attack. I worried when he was at work. I worried that he was too sick to work. I lived looking over my shoulder, wondering when something would happen. I was relieved when I didn't see the car parked in front of the house after school or work.

My parents were constantly hosting our family as well as friends and concerned customers and business vendors who wanted to see for themselves that Ana and Arturo were both okay.

Always laden with food, Nani was a constant fixture. Not to be outdone, Zia Maria also provided her brand of comfort food. Together with Nani, she and Salvatore visited often. So did Claire.

Giuseppe and Concetta came always with enough food and drink for us and for any visitors.

Six months after his first heart attack, I had just started to breathe again, when he suffered a second attack. This one had him in Jacobi Hospital for two weeks. My mother and I headed there every day.

The day before Arturo was discharged, we walked through the open door of the hospital room to find Zio Salvatore and my father laughing over a joke. I ran to both of them, calmed to see my father out of danger, happy, ready to come home. I was encouraged by Zio's presence, knowing he would help if anything should happen.

My mother signaled an end to our visit when my father yawned, still squeezing her hand. He didn't object as we headed toward the door.

Zio Salvatore insisted on walking with us through the parking lot. As we approached our car, my uncle swept his long arm in front of us, placing us firmly behind him.

"What, Salvie, *what*?" my mother pleaded, jockeying to overtake him.

"*Back*, Ana!" he commanded. She instantly fell back, drawing me behind her.

Placing his left index finger across his lips, Zio pantomimed car keys with his remaining hand. He stepped lightly toward the car, inserted the key and jerked the back door open. In a single swift motion, he pulled the slumped hulk of a sleeping man, about twenty-one years old, out of the car.

The man was disheveled, his eyes bloodshot. Wearing the odor of sweat and a too-long-unwashed body, he wore a stained white wifebeater. A huge black comb was buried in his dusty matted head of hair, and he wore his once-white Adidas without socks, the laces untied and tapping against the scraped toes. Greasy black cargo pants completed his outfit.

Now fully awake, my uncle's captive was terrified. "What, man? *Wha'!* Not doin' nothing—just tired is all."

My uncle forced him out of his slouch and ordered him to splay his hands on the hood of the car. Then kicked his legs apart and patted him down, barking questions in a voice foreign to me. *He's not looking for a gun*, I hoped, my stunned awakening giving way to fear. For the man, and for my uncle.

"Zio! Zio!" I heard myself yell. "Don't hurt him! He was just sleeping."

Jaw clenched, my mother grabbed my arm and shot me a searing look. "Let your uncle do what he has to do." Salvatore nodded his agreement.

"Tell me what you were doin' in this car."

"Just sleeping, man! Nothing else—I swear it!"

"Yeah? What's *this*?" My uncle pinned the man and grabbed a half pint of liquor from the back seat of the car. He dangled the bottle in front of him. The man let go an animal sound somewhere between a moan and a sob.

"Oh man, yo! You've got to be the man! Am I right?"

Standing directly in the man's line of vision, Salvatore smiled meanly and poured the remainder of the bottle onto the asphalt.

"That is *rude*, man. Why'd you do that?"

"Get out of here," my uncle barked, "before I change my mind and get some of my guys from the precinct down here. Hurry up." He kicked him lightly in the seat of his pants and we watched the man trip and weave across the parking lot. I started to cry.

Salvatore nodded in my direction, but addressed my mother. "Ana! What's wrong with her?! Gaby! He was *in your car*! What do you think would have happened if I wasn't here?"

I couldn't answer, but I knew it wouldn't have been good. I was angry at the humiliation I had witnessed. I had been a full partner in delivering it. I loved my uncle. It didn't change that. It just showed me a side of him I never expected to see.

My father of course came home from the hospital and went back to work after his second heart attack. I was more vigilant than ever. More frightened than ever. I wanted to believe he was good as new and nothing more would happen.

It did happen. Two years after his first brush, just as I turned fifteen, my father suffered a final blow. He had returned home from the deli early on a Saturday. A car accident in front of our house produced lots of noise and two smoky car hoods belching at each other. Nobody was hurt, but for some reason, my father didn't pick up the phone. He walked up the hill to the police station and collapsed right outside. Best efforts of the police were useless. His heart had given out.

I knew when I answered the phone at the deli. "Hi."

It was our neighbor Michael. "Gaby, let me speak to your mother . . ."

I found her out in front, serving a customer. Exchanging places with her, I swallowed bile and told her about the call.

I knew what had happened. I prayed he was still alive, but I suspected he wasn't. I was sure that heart attacks were bad in threes. I was already a shell of myself. He was my support. My coconspirator in what I thought and in what I wanted to do. How would I live without that? Without him? He had to be alive.

Peering inside, I anxiously watched Ana on the phone. Her shoulders slumped as she cradled the receiver. She wouldn't look at me. Immediately, she made two more calls, shielding herself from my view.

When our last customer, Mrs. Barzini, left the deli, my mother joined me in the front, grabbed me by the shoulders and looked me in the eye.

"Your father walked up to the police station to report a car accident in front of the house. He had a heart attack. He passed. We're going home as soon as Papa's helpers get here."

Passed? *Died?* She'd just punched me. My lungs struggled to breathe, my brain to understand. I couldn't focus on my mother's eyes. I thought hills weren't good for his heart. Would he still be here if he hadn't walked up the hill to the police station?

Regaining my attention, my mother pulled me toward her and hugged me hard, for both of us. Salvatore was on his way to pick us up.

Nani was at the door when we arrived home to guests in every room. She didn't say anything. Just squeezed our hands and stood aside as we entered a house that would never be whole.

Zia Maria had taken over the kitchen. Claire stayed close, acting on her mother's instructions and shuttling espresso and food out to the people. As soon as we walked in, Zio Salvatore started managing visitors and answering questions. He dealt with the police—thanked them for trying to help Arturo, directed them to the funeral home he knew my mother would choose.

Hushed when they saw us, cousins, friends and neighbors parted into rows for us, and then made their way to my mother and me. I could hear the clicking tongues of these spectators who now had the tale of a fresh tragedy to pass along.

I was angrier than I had ever been. I wanted to scream at them all to leave us alone. I craved the company of only my father, my mother, Zia, Zio, Claire and my grandmother. I didn't want to share the story of my father's death with anyone.

The sound of conversation and even laughter swelled as people became comfortable with our being there. My mother was under Nani's protection. People would not approach Ana without my grandmother's permission. Or Zio's.

I was hollowed out. I was too angry to speak and too shocked to cry. I kept drinking water, but my mouth and throat remained stubbornly parched. At the same time, I was somehow relieved. It had happened. It couldn't happen again. I wouldn't have to wait for it anymore.

Claire escaped the kitchen and found me. As if to help me up the stairs, she placed her right arm around the back of my waist. Halfway up, I rested my head on her shoulder.

On my bed, holding each other, Claire and I cried together. I told her about feeling angry and about being hollowed out. About wanting the people downstairs out of my house. Crying for the first time, I confessed that I couldn't understand why my father would walk up the hill to the police station.

"Gaby, he was supposed to be okay," she reminded me. "Nobody could've known."

"I was always afraid that he wasn't okay. I kept waiting for him to self-destruct."

My grandmother was a wizard at getting everyone to leave. She tricked them into thinking it was their idea. It took almost thirty minutes of persistent persuasion, but she did it.

"We so glad you here," she would begin. "You see Ana—I know you wan' her go rest. You help me get her upstair. Maria, she wrap cookies for you." As much as they were all hungry for details of my father's death, they got it.

My aunt cooked us a simple supper—polenta with sole and asparagus—and the six of us sat down. Despite everything, I was hungry. Somehow, I anticipated my father coming through the front door. Then I would remember. A chorus of helplessness, rage and nausea attacked my stomach. It took five years for me to eat sole again.

After Claire and I cleaned up, Nani encouraged us upstairs to my room. I knew the adults would be plotting what to do next. "Making arrangements" is what they called it. Arranging what, exactly? The heartbreaking vision of my father with his arms immobilized across his chest, his eyes closed, looking not at all like himself, stuck to my senses.

From downstairs, muffled conversation punctuated by soft sobs. My mother's? Zia's? Nani's? All of them?

Nani slept with my mother, Claire with me. Zia and Zio went home, promising to return "very early, Ana. Sleep. We'll let ourselves in. Don't worry—we take care of everything." I knew that my mother would not sleep.

We all spent a miserable night. I stared at the periodic table, testing myself on placement of the elements and their atomic weights. I couldn't stay focused. Feeling me awake, Claire reached out. We drowned each other in tears, clawed at tissues, hugged each other, until, exhausted and sobbing, we finally fell asleep. In the morning, we woke in the same position. I balled the tissues off the floor on my way to the bathroom. My face and eyes were swollen, painful and red. Lips chapped, hair disheveled, teeth unbrushed.

I bent over and fashioned a huge sloppy bun on top of my head. Washed my face, brushed my teeth. Listened for life sounds.

Claire, hands clasped behind her back, head tilted my way in anticipation, stood at the open bathroom door. We hugged each other, no need to speak. I knew we were both listening for Nani and Zia and Zio. Wondered what time it was. I tapped my wrist. Claire whispered, "Five thirty." Well, I thought, we had made it through the night. My father had not.

I prayed my mother was asleep. I couldn't bear to see her in such pain so early in the morning.

Ahh. Two women speaking Italian in the kitchen. Nani and Zia Maria. Salvatore must have collected Nani before he and Maria had headed over to our house.

Claire and I tiptoed down to a breakfast of oatmeal, bread, cheese, espresso and orange juice. I amazed myself by eating. Everyone agreed my mother should not be disturbed.

Concetta and Giuseppe arrived later that morning, wrapping us, as they always had, in love, food and support. Having them with us was more proof that they were family.

Everyone carved out their responsibilities for the day. Giuseppe continued calling people who had not yet heard our news. Concetta, loaded with provisions from the deli, set about preparing and cooking with Nunzia. Checking in with the cemetery and the pastor at St. Benedict's, Zia Maria and Zio Salvatore finalized plans for my father's funeral.

The day before, my mother had called on her sister to help choose my father's burial clothes. Standing outside my parents' bedroom, I heard hangers click and scrape along the steel rod. "Ah," I heard my mother sigh. Composed and weary, she said, "Here's the vest I made him for our anniversary. The blue suit, right, Maria? With the red tie." I watched Maria nod her approval and then step from the bedroom, her fist silencing dry sobs.

The night before my father's burial at St. Raymond's Cemetery, I lay awake. Years before, I had also lain wide awake the night my father told me the story of the Lindbergh kidnapping, the accidental killing of the baby as he was stolen from his crib. I couldn't understand why they hadn't been more careful with the child. He could have lived. Could my father have lived if he hadn't climbed the hill?

The day of the funeral, I woke suddenly afraid of what it would be like when everyone left us. They would go home to their unchanged lives. We would remain here to greet a life unknown. We would be alone in our grief. I had learned what fear was when it came to my father's life. Now that he was gone, what would grief be like?

When I closed my eyes, I saw my father stretched out on the bed in the spare bedroom, sipping ginger ale and munching on saltines and pretzels. A heavy weight pressed my body to the bed. I could barely turn to see Claire, still half asleep, reaching out to me.

"Are you okay?" she asked. "Sorry, that's really lame. Of course you're not okay." I found a smile for her, but I could feel the tears coming.

"Do we really have to do this?" I whined. "Why do all these people have to come? Why can't the six of us just do this funeral thing alone?"

"You'll feel different when you wake up. Your mother needs you. And Nani and my parents are here for you."

My father was missing and I would be forever vigilant always looking over my shoulder. I would live my life knowing that good events would be rare. They would inevitably give way to trauma and pain. The trauma provided some relief, followed by a period of calm.

I was murky, empty, my brain full of a swirling, slimy emulsion of confused, foggy thoughts. Where to focus my attention? How to be un-angry? Who was I angry at? Papa? How could he walk up the hill and leave me? Leave my mother? Was I angry at the doctors? The police who couldn't revive him? All the answers were so many grains of sand, slipping through my fingers as I tried to puzzle them out.

I decided I wouldn't wear black. Instead, I chose the dress that Papa really liked. A gauzy beige peasant dress with embroidery around the collar and a long tasseled tie.

Claire tried hard not to be scandalized. "Gaby. I mean, I know you feel bad, but think of Zia Ana! You, like, I'm just telling you, you just can't wear that. Really."

Ignoring her, I headed for the stairs. Nani was ready to greet me on the bottom step.

"Oh, cara!" Her eyes fixed on mine as she cupped my face with her work-worn hands. She protected me in her arms, appraised me in a single long look. Soap, talcum powder, flour, toast. I breathed in her nurturing scent until she took a short step back from me.

"Ah! Arturo, he love this dress! Bellissima! Ana! Guarda tua figlia!" Come look at your daughter.

She ushered me into the kitchen, where my mother sat cradling a cup of espresso, ignoring her egg-in-the-bread, a roasted red pepper congealed in the cold yolk.

Ana looked up through weary eyes. I knew she had not slept. I heard Nani try to comfort her in the night.

"Oh, Gaby! Your father loved this dress—it's perfect!"

"Ma," I asked, "what can I do for you today?"

Taken aback for a short second, she responded, "At the reception after the funeral, just see what other people need and try to get it for them, okay?"

"Ma, you don't have to stay at the reception afterward, you know. I'll come back home with you."

"I want to go. This is the last thing I can do for your father."

My grandmother gently nudged me out of the room.

"No worry—I watch her, make sure she no too tired, okay?"

I headed back upstairs to tame my black mane.

Claire emerged from my bedroom.

"I'm sorry! I just thought. I didn't want Zia and Nani to get mad or anything. Oh, God, I'm doing everything *wrong*!"

I gathered her up as we both gave in to tears.

"Hey," I said, "help me with my hair, will you?"

Claire massaged my scalp and after a thorough brushing, she parted my hair in the middle and carefully plaited it down my back.

Perfect. It was neat and out of my way. I hugged her, let her know how much I loved it.

My mother had retired to her bedroom. Nani insisted that Claire and I eat. "Long day. You girls gotta be strong."

An egg-in-the-bread magically appeared before each of us. Normally, my favorite comfort-food breakfast. This morning, though, I wanted to gag. Instead, I forced myself to eat what tasted like sawdust.

Only an hour to go. Claire ran to Zia and Zio, disclosing my mother's whereabouts. I heard Zia mount the stairs. Muffled conversation. Steps in the hallway and downstairs traffic.

My mother appeared in a dark gray shawl-collar dress cinched at her waist with a black patent leather belt. A white camisole peeked out from the V neckline. Her black hair, now shot with a few strands of gray, was parted on the left side. She had fastened it with a clip to keep her face free of interference. She carried a black patent leather purse and wore low-heeled black leather pumps.

She took a deep breath and nodded. I knew my mother was thinking: *Just do this.*

We loaded ourselves into Zio's car and met the funeral director at the funeral home. He explained the day's events to my mother, Claire's parents and Nani. I was suffocating under the weight on my chest.

Next, Zio shepherded us to St. Benedict Church. We arranged ourselves with Giuseppe and Concetta in the front row, the collapsible stainless-steel cart facing the altar, ready to receive Papa's polished mahogany casket. Zia pressed wads of tissues into our hands. She sat close to my mother on one side. I sat close to her on the other side.

Of course, Nani linked my free arm with hers.

I was there and absent. St. Benedict's was foreign to me. As the church filled, rhythmic waves lapped through my brain. I tried to convince myself that Papa's funeral was not happening.

We got through Mass, Giuseppe and Zio delivering eulogies that I could not hear. Then, the cemetery. My father would go into the ground.

At the cemetery, as we walked to the gravesite, I nestled closer to my mother. The priest delivered the prayers at Arturo's graveside, blessed our assembly, kneeled before my mother, invited her to visit him and to accept his support and continued prayers. It was the first time I had understood anything all day.

Eyes clear and pained, my mother stepped up to the casket and placed a single white rose on top. Still facing the casket, she stepped back to my side and laced her hand with mine.

Papa was gone. I was thankful that I didn't have to witness his casket being lowered into his grave.

Reluctantly, we made our way to the reception. None of us spoke as Zio Salvatore drove.

Paolo had closed the dining room of his restaurant for us. Along with a black wreath, he had hung a sign on the front door: PRIVATE EVENT.

Subdued but emotional, Paolo greeted the six of us at the entrance, and escorted my mother and me to a tidy pocket-sized room just off the main dining area. He explained that the room was kept for his son or daughter when one of them came to assist at an event. A small table was set with an embroidered cloth and adorned with fresh flowers. It hosted a full place setting and glasses. To one side, a chenille coverlet and clean pillow waited on the love seat. "In case you need to come away, signora," he explained.

Everything was ready. The appetizers invited guests to a long narrow table. Three rows of steam tables waited to receive hot dishes from the kitchen. White-cloth-covered tables, each with a small vase of cut flowers. Soda, beer, wine, Sanpellegrino, coffee, tea. Glasses, cups, plates, utensils—wrapped, waiting on a side table.

We stood like soldiers in a line formed by my mother, then me, Nani, Zia Maria, Zio Salvatore and Claire, Giuseppe and Concetta. We greeted a somber surge of hugs and kisses, long faces tilted to one side, tongues clucking, eyes peering past us, anticipating food and drink. Reading my mind, my mother grasped my hand in a gesture of endurance.

It was excruciatingly endless. Laughter. In this place. On this day.

In harmony with his staff, Paolo had planned perfectly. Excellent food and drink, attentive, quiet service. Everyone devoted to shielding my mother. We barely saw Paolo as he quietly organized his servers and circulated among the guests.

Early on, my mother retreated to Paolo's safe room, leaving the rest of us to see everyone out. "Ana—she lie down," was Nani's message as people filed out.

Finally, we organized ourselves to leave. Palms sweaty, I knocked on the safe room door. Responding to my mother's invitation, I found her on the sofa, patting her hair into place as she swung her feet to the floor. She was dry-eyed but exhausted, stepped into her shoes and tried a weak smile.

That forced smile would pierce me many times. The video running through my mind replayed my father in bed with sunken eyes and his dark smile, agonizing about my college tuition. The scene would shift to his trudging up a hill from which he would not return. I kept answering the phone call asking for my mother. Her slumped shoulders as she cradled the phone. My world falling apart.

Paolo had prepared four shopping bags full of leftover food. This on top of the kitchen at home bursting with dishes people had prepared for us.

Nani and Claire stayed with us again. Stunned with fatigue, emotionally sore and sad, none of us could sleep. Four peas in a pod, Nani, Ana, Claire and me, swaddled in nightgowns, sitting close to each other on the sofa. The television blared to blind eyes and deaf ears.

In the morning, Claire and I woke early, certain that we would beat my grandmother to the kitchen to prepare breakfast, so she would be sure that we could manage.

The aroma of good espresso hit me first. My grandmother was lifting a pan of brioche col tuppo from the oven. I had no idea when she'd found the time to prepare the dough. The table was already set with a selection of cheeses, sun-dried tomatoes, olives and fruit brought to us by visitors.

I kissed Nani, asked her if I could help. "Ah! Water. An' bring some aspirin. Your mama might need."

I filled the water pitcher, laid the glasses and rummaged in the medicine cabinet for acetaminophen. Placed the bottle near my mother's water glass.

Half of me was upstairs, listening for running water, a flush, the creak on that fourth step down. I made myself busy when I heard the telltale signs of my mother's arrival.

She emerged on the landing in a white linen blouse with lace at the shoulders and neckline, a softly patterned light wool blue pencil skirt. The one with the short slit in the front. The funeral pumps. She announced, as she kissed me on the forehead, that in two days, Monday, I would go back to school. I was relieved, breathed a sigh of relief at the promise of something normal. Maybe the weight on my chest would lift.

Nani came in, her hands busy with her apron. "Ah!" She invited us to choose a seat, her head nodding toward the table. Standing behind her daughter, she smoothed the back of her collar and gently patted her back. My mother reached around and found her mother's hand.

We sat together. Ate and talked. This was the first day of the unwelcome new normal life.

* * *

Russ's chili is, in fact, famous. Vegetarian. Full of vegetables, spicy. It begs corn bread, which I find right next to it on the table by the time I arrive home. Glass of red wine for Russ and a glass of Sanpellegrino for me.

I breathe, organize my thoughts, summarize my trip and Nani's condition for Russ. I had spent too much time thinking about my father's death, now two decades in the past. Can't tell Russ about it yet.

We start a new Netflix series—a crime drama, naturally—and I sink into Russ's lap, later waking myself with a snore that makes us both laugh. We head to our bedroom.

In the following days, we arrive home late to share a meal of takeout or prepared food. More often than not, I am out of sorts and despite Russ's gentle nudges to connect, I am mostly quiet. I feel guilty for shutting him out. I am steeped in old events, old thoughts and emotions.

Living in two worlds unsettles me. The predictable, juvenile, loving suffocation of my mother's home and the frightening responsibilities of adult partnership and life with Russ. I'm not sure I am a fully mature adult. I often copy the moves of other people I judge to be good adults. The stresses of my profession are real. I am grateful for my mother's ignorance of science, relieved that I can escape that reservoir of criticism.

And yet. When I think of my mother, when we're not in the same room, I feel warmth and connection. The aromas of her kitchen are déjà vu that I carry with me. The small cast-iron pan studded on the outside with the acne of past olive oil encounters is familiar and constant. It is one of my favorite images. Anything I need in my mother's house comes to hand without thinking or looking.

I realize that always, when I travel from Boston, at one mile from my Bronx destination I panic. How should I be? *Who* should I be? Who does she *want* me to be? I am playing darts on a movable board. I guess, trying desperately to fit her idea of me.

The home of my childhood takes my breath away. Fulfilling expectation is always out of reach. I am constantly aware I am doing something wrong, something that disappoints.

I feel my father peering from his perch, expecting me to satisfy the love of his life. Shaking his head from side to side when I fail. I mourn not only his death, but the receding details of his face. I can no longer hear his voice. Grief is a multitiered companion.

By the time I return to my thirty-five-year-old life, I am confused, guilty. Left wondering how to walk the bridge between the turbulent child and the functional adult. I am painfully aware that the child-adult divide gets wider each time I venture to my mother's home. And the confidence that defines adulthood is the finish line I cannot cross.

I return home to a long series of lectures at the university in the following weeks. Microbiology. Immunology. Vaccine development. I feel excited, as I always do when teaching. It comes while I am preparing publications and attending immunology conferences to discuss work with colleagues face-to-face. I suck it up and keep running, flipping the switches between writing and teaching and traveling. I push everything else away.

I've been home in Boston for two weeks when I answer the phone to my mother's voice.

She launches right in. "I thought you might want to know how your grandmother's doing."

I'm swamped up to my waist in guilt.

She goes on to tell me that Nani is moving ahead as always, irrepressible, ornery, dismissive of advice. Hosting her friends, baking and cooking up a storm. I can tell from my mother's tone that she's relieved and delighted. So am I.

I wonder how Zia Maria is doing. Nani is always hardest on her when she's under the weather. Insulted by Zia's ministrations, Nani pushes her away, ignores her, blows up at her. She far prefers my mother to care for her, welcoming Ana's overtures and efforts. It always hurts me to see how Nani treats Maria.

My grandmother has trouble over the phone, but when my mother and I finish, I call her anyway. I keep it short to avoid tiring her from the effort to speak English. This time, she surprises me by peppering me with questions.

"You work hard, no? You think about you an' Russ? You mama, she almos' finish you wedding suit. So you come home soon, eh?"

I deflect her questions, resort to making her laugh, assure her that I love her and that I'll be home soon. I'm clammy with sweat when our conversation ends.

Home. I realize I have and have had many homes. Even in college and especially in graduate school. But my mother's home is the mother ship.

I am reminded of my relationship with Russ by my grandmother. With her trademark tenacity, she has re-asked the sixty-four-thousand-dollar question, prompting me to think with my heart.

In the movie *The Big Easy*, Ellen Barkin's character tells Dennis Quaid's that she's never had luck in love. He tells her that her luck is about to change. One of the top three most seductive scenes in any movie.

Before Russ, I had been unlucky. I learned to shrink, convinced it would never end well. A race from myself to avoid humiliation.

I discard the thought and turn my mind to our upcoming vacation.

My mother calls regularly. She wants me to come home.

"You're working too hard—don't bother telling me no. Nani and Zia want to see you."

She couldn't say that *she* wanted to see me.

CHAPTER 14

A Break on the Cape and the Boston Visit

Teaching finished for now, my last article submitted and lab responsibilities organized, I burst into our apartment, ready for camping on Cape Cod.

Homemade hamburgers and fries. "Last civilized meal for a while," proclaims Russ.

We clown with each other, pack, invite Eric Clapton to join us. Tent, sleeping bags, pads and pillows. Coleman stove. Cooler. Dishes. Cutlery. Pots and frying pan. French press coffeepot. Coffee. Kitchen towels, washcloths, SOS pads, dish liquid and scrub brushes. Collapsible water containers. Very few items of clothing and toiletries, but we remember the rain gear.

We load the car that night and head off early the next morning, the sun greeting us on our journey. Robert Johnson, Pink Floyd, Led Zeppelin, k.d. lang, Tracy Chapman and Joni Mitchell are a few of our companions.

We head for one of our favorite destinations—Truro on Cape Cod. When we arrive, I treat myself to a short run to shake out my legs before we assemble the tent and set up camp.

When we finish, we splash each other, feast on barbecued sausages and welcome drowsiness in front of a mesmerizing fire.

We rise early the next morning. Complementing each other, I get the bacon into the pan as Russ scrambles eggs and pan-toasts slices of the sourdough brought from home. Hiking, talking, connecting has me warm and grateful by the end of the day. By the end of each day.

We join a fishing excursion and catch too much cod. So the family in the next campsite joins us for supper. Their kids—a boy, seven, and a girl, eleven—are great company with many adventures to tell.

Legs swinging from a too-tall picnic table seat, Jake tells us how he has defeated several frogs. "I trapped them, but I didn't hurt them." He finishes his tale by assuring us that "I let them go," after showing them off to his family. His dad ruffles Jake's crop of cowlicky hair.

Flipping her gorgeous silky brown ponytail, Cathy demonstrates how she manages to stay upright greeting the waves. Their parents smile, the mom a bit nervous that her children are speaking too much. I can't get enough. I keep prodding them with questions.

"What do you think about going home?"

Vigorously shaking their heads from side to side, the sister-brother chorus sings out a resounding "Noooooo!"

Wine for Russ and our guests. Sparkling water for me. A delicious berry crisp donated to the mix by our camping guests.

Totally relaxed by day three, I don't want to leave. Naturally, as soon as I realize this, I flip the switch and start to organize my time back in the city, back in the lab.

Reading me as he always does, Russ reminds me where we are. "We've still got four more days. Enjoy them, okay?"

I do.

I come back renewed. I work with the team to design a new series of experiments. I'm focused, calm—for me—happy and expectant.

As good as my mood ever gets when I have a lot to do.

Too comfortable, I bite the bullet and set a date to visit my mother. Time for a fitting.

Time to see Zia and Nani.

In the end, Ana beats me to the phone.

"I'd like to come out and see you and Russ."

My understated surprise emerges as hard-imitated delight and a query for dates.

She has never come to Boston. She'll be here a month from now. A month to agonize. I'd always defined my Boston emigration as my safe zone. I'd always told myself that my mother didn't touch me here. A no-judgment space. I simply could not imagine my mother in the home Russ and I share.

Now she is coming. I wonder how she will react to Russ and me together, in one bedroom. She will cook for us, for sure. I will take a few days completely off work, but what will she do with the parts of the days I will be working?

I plunge into a deep cleaning before she comes. Grocery shop for all her staples. Set the kitchen and pantry up into territory familiar to her in her home. I purge and clean the fridge, turn the second bedroom into her haven.

I am relentlessly hypercritical, seeing everything through a mask of clutter and disorganization. I deep-clean the guest bedroom twice. Scrub the bathroom—with Comet—each time either one of us uses it. Saw away with the scrub brush under the rim of the commode and banish every ring before it appears.

I fit twice-washed brand-new sheets and fresh pillows to her bed. Place the fluffiest towels, good soap, shampoo and conditioner on the dresser. Make ready two drawers and space in the closet for her clothes.

On Friday evening at Boston South Station, my mother picks up her pace when she recognizes us walking toward her. Russ plants three generous kisses on her cheeks as he commandeers her satchel and sends her my way.

I am genuinely happy to see her. She treats me to a huge hug while we greet each other.

"Ma, I'm so glad you're here! First time you visit us."

"It was time. If I waited for an invitation, who knows?"

Steady now. "I know you don't like us living together."

"You're still my daughter. I have to see where you live. I can't always imagine. And the two of you work too much. And I love Boston. Was here years ago with your father."

I link my arm in hers and we exchange smiles. Russ dutifully brings up the rear.

"Oh!" my mother remembers, "I need to get a map; one that's got the subway system on it."

Russ points out a newsstand ahead, jokes with the agent as he pays, hands my mother the map and we carry on to the car.

When we arrive at our home, my mother and I lock arms as I lead her up the short flight of stairs. Her eyes grow wide as Russ ushers her inside. He points down, alerting her to the three steps just inside the foyer. Takes her jacket as I guide her toward the bathroom and her bedroom. She nods, heading for the bath. Opening the bedroom door, Russ places the satchel next to her closet.

When she emerges, humid commas of hair punctuate either side of her forehead. She finds a place on the love seat. I extend my neck out of the kitchen, let her know dinner is just heating and we'll be eating in ten minutes. Russ takes care of getting her a glass of water and setting wine on the table.

I slice thick chunks of Calabrese bread to accommodate the accent dish brimming with olive oil, herbs and balsamic vinegar and place the olives and pickled eggplant on the table. Next to the arugula with lemon, olive oil and shaved Parmigiano-Reggiano.

I call out that supper is ready and ladle the Sicilian fish soup into my favorite pottery tureen.

"Oh!" my mother says. "This is so nice! I haven't had stufato di pesce in ages! I love it, but Nani and Zia don't, so I never make it just for me."

Did I just do something good?

"Ma! You're worth it!" She chuckles, becomes serious as she folds her hands in her lap, focuses her gaze down and waits.

"Go ahead, Ma, you say grace."

Lighthearted chatter as I serve the fish stew and salad. We pass the bread and olives.

I ask about Nani's health. My mother's hands animate our conversation.

"Feisty as ever. She scared Zia and me one day—we couldn't get her on the phone."

"Nani not at home? Supermarket?"

"Unusual day and time for her. So I go over there. Her apartment is neat, but her jacket and pocketbook are gone."

Building suspense, my mother spoons some soup and dips a chunk of bread in the broth.

"Zia searches the supermarkets she likes. She's not there. I cover a few nearby parks and call her friend Luisa and a few more of her cronies. No luck. Now Zia and me, we're starting to get worried."

"No kidding," I remark.

"Late afternoon, your grandmother appears at her apartment. She has a basket of blackberries in her arms and her lips are black and blue. When we ask her where she's been, she tells us that she went for a walk with her friend Aurora. They found blackberry bushes. So they went back to Nani's, picked up two baskets and went picking. And eating."

"I've got to laugh, imagining Nani telling the story and your reaction, Ma! Did you scold her?"

"Of course! But when she went to wash up, Zia and me, we both laughed."

"What did you bake?"

"Oh yeah! Nani gave us lots of the berries! Muffins for all of us. They were wonderful. I even saved a few berries for my morning oatmeal—delicious! Imagine finding blackberry bushes near where we live."

I put on a pot of espresso and arrange fruit and cantuccini on plates. Vin santo in a decanter with two of the small delicate glasses I never use. A wineglass for me, for the Sanpellegrino. Russ carries the tray into the living space while I retrieve water and glasses.

My mother, I notice, is different here. She smiles and laughs easily. She's not thinking about what's next. She's simply here. Free of responsibility, planning. Ana in Boston has exchanged relaxation for duty.

In the living area, my mother claims the love seat. Russ and I take the sofa, his arm propped across my shoulder, my legs tucked beneath me. Russ and my mother sip their wine slowly. I savor my Sanpellegrino in its fancy wineglass.

"You'll live here after?"

Russ and I look at each other, a short shrug from my fiancé. "We're not sure, Ma. I guess we'll decide later."

She looks around carefully, critically. Our condo is open and simple. Beige walls, spartan furnishings, cushy sofa and love seat—no plastic slipcovers. A modern reclining armchair and ottoman and a big-screen television mounted on the opposite wall. The dining area, just off the kitchen, accommodates our antique wood table with seating for six. Surprisingly, for the size of the condo, the kitchen generously fits a six-burner gas stovetop and a large oven. The microwave sits perched above. We have lots of cabinet space.

"I like this," she admits, more to herself than to us. She nods as Russ offers more wine, pinches off a cluster of grapes and settles back.

I ask her about what books she's reading. Unlike Zia, Ana is a voracious reader—a taste she says she shared with Arturo. I know she likes Holocaust historical fiction. She's just finished *The Boy in the Striped Pajamas*, her voice thick with emotion as she describes the two little boys, one a prisoner, the other the privileged son of the commandant, as they enter the gas chamber.

I realize that this visit is for her, about her. It gives me pleasure to see her relax, soak in our company and hospitality and feel wanted. My anxiety abates a notch, but only because I am furiously planning. Tomorrow, Saturday, we'll tour Boston and eat dinner at a North End restaurant. Sunday Mass and maybe a walk out by the Charles River and a visit to Cambridge.

Ana has had a big day. When she tires, I make sure she is settled and head to bed, but I don't fall asleep for a long time. I run through several checklists. Worried now because there is no tension. Worried that when it settles in, my anxiety will soar.

Russ asks how I'm doing.

"Anxious," I confess.

"I can tell," he says, wrapping his arm around my back and drawing me to him.

"It's good. Ana is in a great mood," he reassures me.

"I know. That's what's got me anxious." He chuckles and draws me more closely.

Just as I fall asleep, I ask myself whether or not she's brought my suit.

In the morning, over breakfast, we discuss the coming day. She likes the bus tour idea. "We can see what we like and get off and on, right?"

I feel excited. I've never done anything like this with my mother. Russ catches my eye over the rim of his coffee cup. *See*, his look seems to say.

I rule that we will clean up later. No comment from my mother—she is vibe-free. *Who* is this woman and what has she done with my mother?

As she heads to her room, I remind her to wear comfortable shoes as I stuff water bottles, a few sandwiches, apples and granola bars into my backpack. I'm grateful when Russ claims the bag.

My mother emerges in a muted plaid light wool skirt, low brown wedge shoes, a beige challis long-sleeved blouse with a high collar and long cuffs, and a sweater draped over her arm. Russ retrieves the sweater, finds it a plastic bag and adds it to the pack.

We walk to the bus stop three abreast, Ana linking her arm in mine, a broad smile on her face. I feel one of my own creeping up. I catch Russ's eye as we board the bus. His hand presses my waist as he helps me climb the steps. We produce a hat trick of smiles.

We ride a good part of the route so we can get the lay of the land. My mother is amazed at the city, the people, the shops. She struggles to hear the tour bus commentary as we approach Boston Common. "The city was important in the Revolution, right? But I didn't know it was still so—alive! New York is, too, but this is different!"

Russ fills her in between descriptions of the sights. I notice, as if for the first time, my mother's face. Fine lines in the corners of her eyes. Thick, wavy almost-black hair, eyebrows to match, soulful brown eyes, intelligent and strong but sad. The bangs swept across her forehead try to conceal what I know is a deep widow's peak. Wiry gray hair sprouts along her hairline. Strong jaw, high cheekbones, rounded nose and chin. Full lower lip, slightly protruding upper teeth. She wears lipstick—a muted orange—that always winds up on her teeth.

We exit the bus to walk the Freedom Trail, my mother once again owning my arm. As we find the telltale double-brick markings in the pavement, she motions behind us, her free hand inviting Russ to join us. Russ smiles as he accepts her invitation, linking his arm to her free elbow.

We stop at a small park to share the sandwiches—chicken cutlet on crusty sesame seed Italian bread. We are happy to find Faneuil Hall and Quincy Market when we continue our tour.

I wait for my mother's reaction as we enter the market. "Really?" she exclaims. "Right in the middle of the city?" She searches both our faces. "Do you shop here? You *should*."

Russ assures her that we do. She burrows among the fishmongers, butchers, delicatessens and bakeries. The sharply aromatic cheesemongers' stalls draw her particular attention. She gravitates toward the kiosks stocked with Italian foods, ordering a pound of Illy espresso beans. She falls into a brief Italian discussion with the owner, who turns her head from side to side, sizing up and nodding her approval of Russ and me. With my mother distracted, the woman slips two sample bottles of extra virgin olive oil into the bag with the coffee. Russ stashes my mother's purchase in the backpack.

"You have a grinder?" she asks. "If no, we'll get one."

"Yeah, Ma, we have one."

The day is perfect. Blue sky, a few high scudding clouds, temperature designed for walking, a light breeze keeping us comfortable and cool. Russ suggests we stop at one of the outdoor pubs; my mother agrees but insists on first visiting all the market wagons to inspect their offerings.

Jewelry, leather goods, scarves, mosaic-encrusted lanterns that bend the light with color when fitted with a lit candle. Exotic Indian clothing. Shoes, sandals, jackets. Boston-branded hoodies, sweatpants and T-shirts. Miniature statues of Paul Revere, the State House, Faneuil Hall, the USS *Constitution*.

My mother is efficient in her observations, quickly sorting wheat from chaff. She smiles finally at Russ, asking which pub he's chosen for us.

Russ leading the way, we soon find out. The pub is a 1950s study in cushioned mahogany booths, rich wainscotting and tin ceiling tiles. Miniature black-and-white ceramic tiles lay on the floors, some of them chipped. The wraparound bar, distressed by years of use, is immaculately polished walnut with welcoming red-cushioned high-backed stools. The walls are adorned with photographs of celebrities popular over several decades. Singers, comedians, television personalities, news anchors, sports greats.

Ana nods as she takes in the scene. “I like this,” she says simply.

A glass of red wine with a water chaser for my mother, a Samuel Adams for Russ. Perrier for me. A plate of fried calamari and a small pizza to share. Russ follows the server with instructions for the bill.

We finish and decide to taxi to Boston Harbor, where we board a relatively brief historical sightseeing tour. Full stomachs, rested legs, relaxed conversation. I can’t remember when I’ve experienced this in my mother’s company. How to share it more often?

Evening finds us, by design, in the North End. Carmelina’s is our destination. We walk in to an explosion of aromas that makes my stomach rumble. My mother is in critical mode. This is proudly announced as the Best Sicilian Restaurant in Boston.

Menus. Bread with olive oil. Water. A bottle of red wine for Russ and my mother. My usual Sanpellegrino—I ask for a wineglass.

We order family style. Mussels in garlic marinara, caprese salad, capellini with frutti di mare—seafood—risotto with braised beef ribs.

We go through two more baskets of bread to accompany our meal. My mother is animated, responding to Russ’s questions with stories about her journey from Sicily to New York, describing how she and Arturo learned to trust each other early on. She talks about her parents and how she realized how scared they really were, but how they didn’t want the kids to see.

"My parents came because they saw doors closing in Italy. Services shrinking. All the professions being squeezed. Nani was a seamstress. Ready-to-wear was taking off. Nonno worked in the building trades. But these were drying up. The writing was on the wall. They contacted cousins and friends in America. Became convinced that they would find opportunity across the ocean, so they came. But they were still scared."

She talks about her confusion as they started their lives in New York, so crowded, so foreign, no one and nothing familiar. How she fell in love with Giuseppe and Concetta. "I would have done anything for them."

Mildly teasing, Russ dares to ask her when she knew she was in love with Arturo. She peers at him over a shard of bread, sets it down, dabs her lips and smiles.

"Ah. I was very young when we came over on the ship. Nani and Nonno kept trying to keep us apart, but it was impossible. We ate all our meals together; my father had us in English lessons together every day on the ship. In our free time, we explored together, and he told me all about his family. He was very homesick. He didn't know why he had to leave."

A sip of wine fuels the story ahead. "I knew I loved Arturo after two weeks. I also knew I couldn't tell Nani and Nonno. I was so young. They were already afraid. I knew Arturo loved me too. We never talked about it on the ship. To me, it felt like a giant balloon that would pop if we showed it to each other."

Emboldened, Russ forks a portion of beef and asks, "So when did you tell each other?"

My mother looks up, as if unlocking a memory she will never forget.

"Arturo waited until I was seventeen." She shakes her head. "I was beginning to think it would never happen. But I knew I only wanted to be with him. I dated, but I was disappointed because I kept waiting for him.

"So that's it!" she concluded. "We married when I was eighteen, my mother and father paralyzed with worry about a scandal until we did."

I see the playfulness around Russ's eyes as he enjoys a sip of wine. "So, did they need to worry when you were on the ship and after?"

I want to stuff my fingers in my ears to a chorus of "la-la-la."

My mother gives as good as she's gotten: "I'll never tell!"

Is this her being coy?

I'm pretty sure I've just found out that my mother and father had sex before they were married. Can it be?

Russ settles the bill and we stroll the streets of the North End, my mother clearly enjoying the ambiance and activity. I suggest we stop at Modern Pastry Shop to pick up cannoli, and we head home.

A long, satisfying day. I have never enjoyed my mother's company as I have today. She reminds me of Nani, all the good sides of Zia. And, if I'm honest with myself, me.

Happy to be home, I slip the key into the lock. I make espresso for my mother—it is never too late in the day for her. Milk for Russ and me. Cannoli for everyone. "Delizioso!" my mother pronounces as we nod in agreement.

I clean the morning dishes and announce that I am heading to bed. "Got to get up early—some work to do, not much, but I want to finish before lunch."

"I'll be in in a little while," says Russ, kissing me on the forehead and smoothing back my hair. I kiss my mother, who strokes the back of my neck and pats my arm as I turn.

I hear Russ rummaging in the kitchen, the telltale clink of glasses as he emerges.

"Sambuca?" he asks.

"Ah," I hear her say.

Russ pours the clear liquid into what I know are two small glasses.

"Ah, Russ bring in the coffee, the beans, I brought home today, hey?"

I smile. My mother will add a single bean to each glass.

"Oh," says Russ, "I didn't know you were supposed to do that."

"We do it often."

My mother starts by asking about Russ's early life, his parents, brothers and sisters.

Confident that they can't see me, I stop before the bedroom door and slide to the floor.

"I'm the oldest—three brothers, three sisters. I was thirteen when my youngest sister, Lottie, was born. Lots of activity in our house."

"You help with the kids?"

"Lucky for me, my oldest sister, Rima, was just a year younger, so she got that duty. She was a surrogate mom to the other kids. I would help her sometimes."

"Where'd you grow up?"

"In the Bronx, and in Monticello, a small town in upstate New York. My dad owned a Jewish delicatessen."

"So did you go to shul with your family?"

"Not too much. My dad kept the deli open on Saturdays—there was always a lot of non-Jewish traffic. My brothers and I did Bar Mitzvah, though, and we celebrated my sisters' Bat Mitzvahs."

"Your mom?"

I could hear Russ's intake of breath. "She kept everything together. I never saw her sleeping when one of us was awake, and she was always the last to bed. We'd tell her to quit and she'd always say, 'I'm just about done,' usually as she snipped a darning thread with her teeth. She was a great woman."

"I'm sorry she's gone—you can only lose your parents too early. Your dad?"

"He's alive, still owns the deli, but he goes in only part-time. Very sad since my mom died."

"I know how that feels. Not like your dad, of course, but just because of Arturo." I hear the second splash of sambuca fill the delicate hourglass-shaped glasses. "Nieces and nephews for you?" she asks.

I know how much Russ cherishes his siblings' children. "Oh, sure! From everybody but Rima. She and her husband couldn't have children, and it has broken her heart. Her spirit, I think."

"That's very hard . . ."

I'm stunned. I've never heard my mother come close to validating such a specific personal feeling. I'm much more accustomed to her trying to convince a person, me, what they should or shouldn't be feeling.

Intrigued, I quietly settle into serious eavesdropping. This is far too interesting to miss, and I won't risk curdling it by showing myself.

"I never really thought about it. She couldn't have kids. End of story, in my mind."

"And now?"

"I think it's shaped her life. It's like she carries around a question mark: What would life be like if I had kids?"

"Hmmm," my mother muses. "Good description."

"Is there someone in your family who couldn't have kids? You sound like you know about it."

"Yes, for a long time I thought I couldn't have children."

I clamp my hand over my mouth to stifle my reaction.

"Arturo and me, we started trying right after we married. We wanted lots of kids."

My mother pauses and I realize suddenly how difficult this is for her. I realize also that I'm about to become jealous because she isn't telling *me* this story. I set that second reality on the back burner as I listen, more and more unhinged by what I'm hearing.

"But?" prompts Russ.

"Well, I was pregnant right away. We were over the moon. I was a month in when I started rubbing my stomach and talking to the baby—in English and Italian. We waited another month before we told Nani and Zia. They were so happy! Zia cried—started calling herself 'Zia Maria.' My mother said: 'Ah, Ana, now you really are a woman.'

"We named her Rosa. We didn't have ultrasound or anything like that. I just knew she was a girl. We rolled her name over and over again, talking to my belly as if she was already here. It was magical."

My mother pauses. What do I do if she cries? I'm not supposed to be hearing this. Can I say I heard part of it on my way to use the bathroom? Both Russ and my mother are too sharp for that.

It's the soundtrack to a horror movie. I can't listen completely, but I can't turn away. I continue to listen as if I have one index finger in my ear, afraid of what's to come. Miscarriage? Sudden infant death syndrome? Some tragic accident in infancy?

As he always does with me, Russ grants my mother the time she needs. The no-pressure-patience-and-compassion routine that can drive me crazy sometimes.

A strong intake of breath and my mother is ready to continue. "Yeah, so, at three months I start to feel, well, funny. Of course, I figure it's just normal—the third month. I have no way of knowing, and, as it turned out, there was nothing to do for it.

"We were out to dinner with Nani and Nonno and a coworker of my father's. It was just about time to leave when I felt a pull in my stomach, strong cramping. Nothing happened in the bathroom, but I knew I had to get home. I signaled Arturo. My mother gave us a worried look. When the cramping started again, I grabbed my purse and Arturo's arm.

"Arturo drove directly to the hospital. When we got there, the doctor told us, 'This might not be a healthy pregnancy.'

"Emergency ultrasound told us that Rosa was not in my womb, but halfway down one of my tubes. The doctor, he showed her to me on the ultrasound. He said, 'Signora, your baby is dead.' They wouldn't let Arturo in with me. I was devastated and alone."

"Oh, Ana, I am so sorry! I wonder why Gaby never told me."

"Because Gaby doesn't know. I made my mother and Zia promise never to tell her. Now I'm asking you not to tell her."

I know Russ wanted to ask why, but I sense he's holding back to allow her to finish. Tears are rolling down the sides of my face. I continue to clamp my hand over my mouth. I want to run to her, to hold her, but I'm not supposed to know any of this. Worse, Russ had just been sworn to secrecy. Sicilians live in a world of secrets. Come to think of it, doesn't everyone?

"So they got me into emergency surgery. They told me they would remove the tube and Rosa, no longer alive. I was in the hospital for a week. Arturo was there every day before and after work. He kept encouraging me that we would try again. At first, I don't want to try again," my mother says. "Too hard. But Arturo could always talk to me, and so I came around. Month after month, I was excited, but scared. Month after month, nothing happened, and then, about a year and a half later, I was pregnant again."

Pregnant with me? A quick calculation tells me it couldn't have been. My mother would have been nineteen or twenty years old. She didn't deliver me until she was twenty-five.

Not figuring the math, Russ offers an enthusiastic, "That's great."

The only thing pregnant in this apartment is the pause in their conversation.

"No, Russ, not so great. Same pain, same hospital, even the same doctor, saying the same thing: 'This might not be a healthy pregnancy.'

Another ultrasound with the same result. "Another girl—I was sure of it—but we didn't name her. We never did.

"This time, they gave me a drug so I wouldn't lose the tube. And it worked. I didn't lose the tube, but, of course, I lost the baby. Our second baby."

Unbelievably, my mother continues her history. It seemed that everyone she knew was pregnant at that time.

"I made a list of all the women who became pregnant and had children at that time. There were twenty-eight women on my list. And no one remembered what had happened to Arturo and me."

She continued, "Once, Arturo and me, we went to a party. There were eight or nine kids there, playing, running around. One new mother, proudly showing off her son to everyone. I became hysterical. Arturo rushed me out of there.

"For a long time, I couldn't go down store aisles with kids' clothes, diapers, toys."

By this time, she explains, she was convinced she could not bear children. I know my mother well enough to realize that she would have been planning a childless future. And that she would not have been able to forgive herself for making Arturo share her fate.

I couldn't imagine her sadness. But now I knew something of the remote desolation always in her eyes. I had always sensed it was different from her sadness over my father's death.

Eventually, she came around to the surprising reality of carrying my father's third baby.

"That day," my mother said, "I knew God was real, and I did not worry. I told Him that I couldn't do it again, lose another baby, and He answered me. I couldn't believe it at first—that He was really talking to me. He told me that just as I was carrying the baby, He was carrying me."

Conversation lapsed. I heard Russ clear his throat. I knew he was composing himself.

"Can I ask you, Ana," he started, "why you never told Gaby?"

Why not? I was about to hear why she had cut me out of such an important chapter in her life.

"We thought about it for a long time—until I was sure she would be old enough to understand. Arturo wanted to. But I decided no." Collecting her thoughts, she paused.

"I wanted her to know she was enough for us. That we weren't always missing her sisters who weren't with us. I didn't want her to try to make up for those girls."

Once again, I stifle a gasp around my tears.

"Can I ask you one more question?"

"Of course. Of course."

"Why are you telling me?"

"Because you need to know Gaby's whole family, love us, I hope, before you have your own. When that happens, I hope you'll tell her."

But, Ana, this is yours to tell. I knew Russ would agree with me, but he did not press her.

I raised myself carefully from the hallway floor, resisted using the bathroom, softly closed the door to our bedroom and changed in the dark. I slipped between the sheets and lay trying to control my well-honed Sicilian anger.

In the morning, I had to have the last word with Russ. I turned toward him ready to launch my quietest whisper.

He knew the minute he looked at me.

"Uh, yeah, so what are you thinking?"

"What do you mean?" My intended whisper had morphed into a raspy hiss. "I'm feeling she should have told *me*. Me. She put you in a lousy spot!"

"Why? You heard it firsthand for yourself. She wanted me to know because she knows I'll tell you no matter how—I'm already working on it."

"What am I supposed to do now? How do I even look at her?"

"What's different? It's sad, but these sisters never were part of your family life. You heard what she said about why she didn't tell you. She's been carrying that love for you all these years. You know what I think?" he said.

I waited.

"I think she really has wanted to tell you, but she buried it for so long, she doesn't know how to dig it up." He shrugged in resignation. "She's afraid."

"My mother? *Afraid?* Have you met my mother?"

"Yeah, I know, not an Ana trait, for sure. But think about it for a minute. What if you gave her the silent treatment? You've told me yourself that Sicilians are famous for that. What if she relived the experience again, trying to tell you?"

"She didn't seem to relive it when she told *you*. I wouldn't do that to her." Just like that, I realized I wanted to go along. All I had to do was rewind to the day before yesterday.

Russ says, "I know you wouldn't do that."

He moves in close to me.

I get out of bed and start working. Energized, I put my mother's secret aside and, checking my watch, I bounce into the kitchen to make pancakes.

Ana has beaten me to it. Russ raises a cup of Ma's espresso and plants a kiss as I walk around the island. I meet Ana at the stovetop and we exchange cheek kisses.

Ana is fully dressed, her usual ration of makeup applied. White linen blouse and soft lightweight tweed skirt. Her six-foot frame straight and businesslike as she multitasks breakfast.

"You're just in time," she says. She instinctively dries her hands on an apron. She serves up a Russ-sized portion of frittata with toast. Clearly impressed, he grabs his utensils. My mother fills his espresso cup and taps his wrist.

She frowns. "What? You're not waiting for us?"

Russ decides to behave.

Work was the morning plan for Russ and me. We suggest we'll do something fun together later in the afternoon.

"Good," my mother responds. "I'm going back to the market. I want to have another look. I'll be back by one."

"Great," I say. "You know how to get there, right?"

"Of course." She inclines her head Russ's way. "I have my map. Gaby, before we do anything this afternoon, you'll have a fitting."

I bite into a hot pepper and wince at the thought of the fitting. "Sure."

My house. Her rules.

Russ and I work till noon. When I finish my run at one, my mother is opening the door with her key. I kiss her and help her inside with enough grocery bags to feed an entire neighborhood. Has she decided to stay?

"Ma. What did you buy?"

"Never mind. I can't believe you don't go there every day. Produce, fish, meat—never mind cheeses, spices, olive oils."

"Don't forget pastries, Ma."

"I didn't," she assures me. I walk in behind her.

I kiss Russ, shower, and round back to the kitchen to find Genoa salami sandwiches on crusty Italian bread dressed with pickled eggplant and sun-dried tomatoes. Cured olives, cubes of tart, crumbly provolone on the side. More bread. Spiced olive oil for dipping.

I pick up my sandwich.

"No," she scolds. "You have your fitting first! You shouldn't be bloated."

"Ma, I'm hungry."

"Don't argue with me."

I drink tea and drool. Russ and my mother chow down.

She motions toward her bedroom, following behind me. I wonder if she fears an escape attempt.

Already adorning the bed are the jacket, the pants and the blouse. She's also sewn an elegant brocade vest. Just the right style and colors for the suit.

"Ma, the vest is wonderful!"

She smiles. "It is, isn't it? Zia and Nani both love it too!"

I grin to myself, imagining her extra trip to Matteo's to select the fabric for the vest.

I obey her command to get undressed and try the blouse first. She fits it more closely to my waist. "Now that there's a vest." She points to the pants.

Thankfully, I have no trouble pulling them up. The buttons are perfect. High waist. Skinny legs. They feel great.

"Did you lose weight?" my mother wonders, rolling the pins between her lips. When I was a kid, I was always afraid she'd choke, but she never did. I came to see it as just another part of the seamstress in her.

"Okay," she says. "Now the vest. Tuck the shirt in."

The pins go to work, fitting the vest snugly, but not too tightly. The sleeves of the blouse cascade in natural pleats, the cuffs long, pearl buttons already in place. The mirror doesn't lie. Everything looks great. I admit something I rarely do: *I* look great.

Last step, the jacket. After I slip it over my back, Ma has me hug my arms in front of me. Walk around. She tugs on the lining to be sure it won't sag beyond the outside of the jacket. She rummages in her overnight bag and removes an antique square leather box. She plants this firmly in my hand. I am about to ask what it is when she hushes me, closing my fingers around the corners of the box.

"From your father's mother. She never liked me, but Arturo forced her to make peace. It's from your papa's family to have for your wedding."

The pin is gold. That pink-tinged eighteen-karat gold identifies it as Italian. Forged in the shape of two rosy-faced lovebirds, beaks touching, plumage ruffled. Unbelievably intricate and delicate. It takes my breath away.

"Ma, save it for the day; then I can return it to you right away."

"Gaby. I saved it all these years for you. It's yours. Keep it. Think of me when you wear it."

She draws me in for a solid hug and smooths my hair.

"Good!" she says, passing her hand over my outfit in a motion instructing me to return the suit to her.

"Go!" she barks. "Have your lunch."

Russ is drying his hands on the dishtowel as I appear in the kitchen.

"So, how'd it go?"

"I think it's good. Apparently I might have lost weight."

He smirks. "I know."

"Want to stay here this afternoon," my mother announces when she joins us. "I want to make a special dinner with the food from the market."

It's music to my ears. I have a lot to get through before I return to the lab. I read relief on Russ's face too.

"Ma? What will you make?"

"Of course, antipasti. Then, I got some fresh farfalle pasta—bow ties." She nods at Russ.

"I'll make these in fresh tomato sauce. And then Sicilian pork Milanese."

"Should we pick up dessert, Ana?" Dessert is Russ's favorite part of supper.

She smiles. "Don't worry. I'm making sweet ravioli. I got fresh dough and nice ricotta. Some local honey too. To drizzle on top. Just leave me the kitchen and go about your business." The apron already around her waist, she gestures to Russ in recognition of the clean kitchen. Shooing us both away. "Good," she says.

CHAPTER 15

The Market Supper

Ana gets to work. First, the sauce. She inhales deeply as she removes the Roma tomatoes from the string bag. Just the right degree of ripeness. She puts up water to boil as she washes and scores them, removing the remnants of the stems. The tomatoes are simmered in water until the skins are wrinkled. Then she throws ice on the scalded fruit. She peels the tomatoes, mashes the pulp and sets them aside.

In a separate pot, she sautés onions, garlic, basil, oregano, pepper, salt and tomato paste in olive oil. She throws in a bay leaf and adds the tomatoes, fixes the lowest stovetop setting and stirs.

Satisfied, she turns to the sweet ravioli. Raids Russ's liquor cabinet for rum, finds the coarse brown sugar in the cabinet. Mixes the ricotta with the rum and sugar. Adds lemon zest, cinnamon and egg yolk.

I take a break to check on my mother's progress.

I find her far away in thought, shaking her head as she continues preparing the food.

"Ma?" She jolts herself back into the present.

"You need something, Gaby?" She's clearly in charge of my home.

She has prepared the ravioli. She is now focused on the antipasti of prosciutto, salami and buns stuffed with pancetta—the salt-cured pork belly that serves as Italian bacon. Cured and pickled olives, onions and eggplant. The aroma of roasted red peppers engulfs the kitchen. On my favorite platter, she arranges the giardiniera—a mixture of olives, carrots, pepperoncini, celery, peppers and onions in olive oil, vinegar and brine.

She gets me to unwrap the provolone and the fresh mozzarella. Tells me to carve the giant Oxheart tomatoes for the caprese salad.

"Put that aside. You can finish making the caprese later. Now, I need that provolone in cubes. You've got time?"

I assure her that I do.

After I finish, I tell her that I'm heading back to work.

Her eyes on the countertop and the stove, she acknowledges me and I go back to my computer.

I don't last long. I want to be with her as she works in the kitchen, so I go back and ask what I can do.

"Those pork chops. You have a mallet, yes? Pound them with the spikey side."

Ana protects the fresh farfalle—the bow tie pasta—in a damp dish towel and turns back momentarily to me.

"Oh. And don't forget you have to finish the caprese."

While I assemble the caprese salad, she prepares the pork on the stovetop and inserts the garlic bread into the oven. She then revisits the dining area, setting out the antipasti and making sure plates, salt and pepper and flatware as well as serving pieces are in order.

Still in the dining area, my mother warns, "Fifteen minutes. Go get Russ. He needs to open some wine."

"Ma, it smells amazing." I stay with her as she fusses over the final details of the Milanese.

Ana balances the platter of pork and delivers it to the table. She notes that Russ is opening the wine for Ana and him. He chooses three wineglasses and places one to the side of each of our place settings. I get my own full bottle of Perrier.

"Ana, this is spectacular!" Russ assures her and sets his attention to the wine bottle.

"When you're married, Gaby will cook like this for you, you'll see."

Plates are filled. Laughter and light conversation visit the small dining space. Seconds, thirds, liberally washed down with Russ's wine. And my Perrier.

Ana fingers the rim of her wineglass. Reminds us that she will be leaving the following morning.

"My train leaves at eleven in the morning."

"Don't worry," I assure her. "We'll get you there in plenty of time."

Suddenly sad, I am in awe of my mother being like this. I know that asking will get me only *Like what?* and nowhere after that.

I let it drop and offer to make espresso and set dessert on the table. My mother nods, thinking aloud that she will shoulder the criticism and bring ravioli to Nani, who rarely eats anything except her own pastries.

We sit up late, Ana and Russ nursing limoncello and anisette. Discussing films they enjoy. Likes and dislikes for modes of travel. Shaking her head from side to side, Ana stresses that she does not like to fly.

"I feel like a sardine," she explains. "I'm always in the middle seat, and I always have to use those tiny bathrooms too many times. No. Give me a train."

I am yawning. If it had a sound, it would be loud. Linking his fingers, Russ is stretching his arms above his head. My mother is making moves to clean the tables.

"No, Ma," I tell her. "We will do it. It'll all be in order in the morning. Get yourself organized and get some sleep."

We hug and kiss all around, and my mother heads to her bedroom.

Ana cleans up as she cooks, so there's really not much to do. Russ and I play a favorite scene from the movie *The Big Chill*, bumping hips and guiding each other through a few easy dance steps, singing an off-key "Ain't Too Proud to Beg" as we complete our chore.

"It's been a great night," Russ says.

I agree. "Yeah, there are some nights I'd like to forget, but this one will be up at the top for favorite."

Holding on to each other by the waist, we head to our bedroom.

The next morning, I wake at 6 A.M., pull on my running tights and T-shirt. I hear nothing outside our bedroom as I tie my shoes. I open the door carefully and peek outside.

Then I hear it. The wooden spoon scraping against the bowl. The soft opening and closing of cabinets to find . . . what? Spices? Utensils? The vacuum of the refrigerator as my mother stands at the door searching for something to help her prepare breakfast.

She sees me come around the corner. I know her radar has been sensing me for some time. She continues mixing eggs into the batter as she orders, "Be quick. Breakfast is coming."

I head for the door. I realize we haven't even said good morning to each other. We're back to normal.

Russ and I are the first owners of our condo on Boston Common. Our house, similar to many of the others in our complex, is redbrick, constructed to resemble the eighteenth- and nineteenth-century homes on Beacon Hill. In this neighborhood, our cookie-cutter home is personalized, just as all of them are. Flower urns, door wreaths and door color the owners' signatures. Russ and I change our door wreaths with the seasons, hanging them against the bright lacquered red door.

Suddenly, my Boston landscape appears very different to me. Has my mother changed it just by being here for a few days? Or have I taken to seeing it through her eyes, comparing it to New York neighborhoods? Is everything just a quaint reproduction of a Manhattan brownstone filled with rabbit hole apartments?

My digestive system complains as I make my circuit around Boston Common, Beacon Hill, King's Chapel and into Chinatown. I have loved knowing this different mother. Happy, freer than I have seen her since Papa has been gone. I know my normal mother will return. I am enjoying this while I can.

I can almost hear her sigh of relief as I let myself into the house.

Conversing easily with my mother, Russ is sipping an espresso. She is checking the frying pan for heat. She wipes the pan down with waxed paper soaked in oil and begins spooning the batter. Drizzles a bit of oil onto each pancake and turns each one at exactly the right moment. Golden brown. Always perfect. Her skills amaze me—particularly this one. I can't manage to make pancakes like she does.

The kitchen produces a glorious tang of cinnamon and nutmeg. When she opens the oven, my mother releases the aroma of the bacon to the rest of the kitchen.

We linger over our meal, my mother repeatedly fingering her dog-eared train ticket.

Knowing the answer, I ask, "Ma, you all packed?"

"What? You think I'll wait till the last minute?"

"You want me to prepare some food for you?"

"It's okay. I wrapped pork and cheese for lunch, and ravioli for Nani and Zia. I made plenty. I left lots for you and Russ too."

She is anxious, so we leave her to her bedroom while we clean up. I know we'll be leaving here at 8:30 A.M. to get to North Station for an 11:00 A.M. departure even though it's only about fifteen minutes from our place to North Station.

She emerges at 8:20 A.M., purse resting on the crook of her left elbow, with her traveling cape draped across her shoulders—I covet this cape, though it would hit me in the ankles. Russ retrieves her bags from the bedroom. I pull on my running jacket and head for the front door.

"Ma, you've got your food and some water to drink?"

"Of course!" She adjusts her cape and leads us out the front door. I wait for Russ and lock the door behind us.

We don't talk on the way to the train station. My mother is already home, I know, planning to see Nani and Zia. Her default mood is on display. I look at Russ, hoping for validation. His left eyebrow rises in agreement.

I sigh inwardly in exasperation. Her transformation while she was with us has disappeared. She's back. I find myself rehearsing conversations as we take the last steps onto the neighborhood train.

The train rocking gently from side to side, we travel with her to North Station. The scraping on the rails accompanies us on our short trip.

As we approach our destination, we make small talk. Silently, I contemplate my two lives, the life in my mother's home and my life here in Boston. Living in two places has me disoriented, unsure. Which is my real world? How does my mother fit into our world here?

We reach the station quickly and join the fray. I reach for my mother's arm as we exit the train. She smiles, hikes her cape, and links her arm with mine. I fight getting choked up as Russ stands aside to give us a moment.

In good time, we hear the announcement for her New York train. We walk her to the gate, Russ handing over her suitcase and her carry-on bag. I kiss her again, hold her close, tell her I'll see her soon.

"When?" she asks, knowing I cannot give her an answer. My wanting desperately to be an independent adult holds me back. The distance in my head is much greater than the distance between Boston and the Bronx. The conflict is in my heart.

Russ saves me by stepping in with a broad smile as he grasps my mother's shoulders. She beams up at him as he plants kisses on her cheeks.

"Ana. Thank you for everything; for being with us and for all you've done. It's been wonderful to spend time with you."

Shyly, she dips her chin and casts her eyes up at him.

Almost joking, she admonishes him. "You take good care of her, okay?" She wags a finger in his face. "I'll know if you don't."

He laughs. "Don't worry. I'll never do anything but take great care of her. And you know she'd put me in my place."

Permitted to go only as far as we have, we remain at the top of the escalator and wait for her to turn around and wave before she approaches the train down below.

I yell down that she should call me when she gets home. I see the back of her head promise that she will.

Just like that, she's on her way.

Russ and I reverse our trip, quietly at first. My heart feels heavy, tired, and then, oddly, giddy and relieved.

"It was a great visit," Russ says.

Silently, I agree, and follow up with, "I will have to see Nani to hear about my sisters who are gone."

"What do you need to know?" Russ knows better than to hint that I should let it go.

I shrug off the question. "I need to hear it from Nani. She was there. I'm sure she took care of my mother when it happened."

He waits for me to keep going, but I'm done for now—too much emotion.

We drop each other's hands as Russ climbs the stairs to unlock the red door to our world. I follow him, making myself ready for the emptiness, her absence.

I hang my fanny pack on the coatrack. Russ sets out two cups for the espresso he's brewing and waits for me at the kitchen island bar.

"You know she's harsh with you because she's afraid," he says.

"This is the second time you've said that she's afraid. What could possibly scare my mother?"

He returns to the island with the espresso pot. "Well." He pours for us and sets the pot down. "She lost your father young. Maybe she's worried about losing you."

"I hate when people say they 'lost' someone when a person dies. What did we do? Mis*place* them?"

"Stay on point, okay." He knows me too well.

I encourage him to continue.

"Well, I think that was so painful for her, she can't invest her love like that again. So she dampens it just in case. And to predisaster herself."

"Predisaster? You're saying she's afraid I'm gonna die."

"I'm saying I don't think she knows this is what she does. But how else do you explain her taking a vacation from being afraid while she was with us. Seeing for herself that you're happy and secure." He adds, "Thanks to *me*, of course."

I laugh and throw my napkin at him across the island.

Over the next two days, we get back to our routines quickly. I speak to my mother twice, once when she confirms that she's home and once, after an unsettling dream, when I call to learn how Nani is doing.

After I tell Russ, I start making plans to travel to the Bronx in a month's time. I call Zia and let her know, mostly because she's always the last to know any news. My mother is next, unpleasantly surprised that Zia was my first choice.

"Okay, I'll tell Zia."

"I already called her." Long pause.

Wary. Wondering. Capitulating. "Oh? Okay, then."

My last call is to Claire. I exhale when she agrees to meet me in the Bronx.

CHAPTER 16

Three Sisters

With two weeks to go, I call Zia again to find out the best day to have lunch with Nani. I can hear that she is a bit stunned. And, as always, nosy.

"What's wrong?" she tries, hoping I will include her in my pilgrimage.

"Really, Zia, everything is great!"

"It's about the wedding? You need something? I can help maybe?"

In the course of speaking with her, I realize I've become an expert at deflection and evasion. Also, keenly aware of her need, I feel guilty that I can't offer her a sense of importance.

"No, no! Thanks, though. I just want to surprise Nani with lunch, so please don't tell her or my mother, okay?" She is bruised but reluctantly agrees to my request.

Having thanked her and ready to end our conversation, I bear the uncomfortable pregnant pause over the line. Right. She's waiting to be invited to lunch. I assure her I am looking forward to seeing her and hang up, silently praying she doesn't show up at Nani's.

As always, my mother is at the door to greet me when I drive up. She gathers me into a hug.

I confess to her. "I was missing you after you left us in Boston. I want to see Nani too. I want to bring lunch to her at her apartment."

"So when will you see her?" Her question is steeped in Zia's betrayal.

"Oh, I'm not sure yet."

"Hmmm . . ."

She orders me to sit at the kitchen table and serves a double espresso and fresh biscotti to both of us. As we sip and eat, she roots about in the freezer, searching for a dinner target.

"Why don't we go out tonight? I'm treating. Ask Zia—we'll go to Paolo's." I'm a genius for finding a way to soothe Zia's rejection.

"Let me think about it." Ma really doesn't like to eat in restaurants. Paolo's is the only one she'll go to.

As I bounce up the steps to my bedroom, I overhear my mother speaking with Zia.

"What do you mean, you're busy. You're never busy, I know this. What? You're mad at Gaby for something—what did she do? I'll talk to her."

Oh, the Sicilian custom of living in each other's pants.

I can hear my mother listening. "Okay. We'll pick you up at six thirty. See you then." A long pause. "Yes, I'll talk to my daughter."

Less than ten seconds after she hangs up, my mother launches my name up the stairs.

Catapulting me back to my seventeenth year, she shouts up, "Come down." I comply.

"Zia says you were rude to her. What did you do?"

Sighing and rolling my eyes, I provide a summary of my telephone conversation with Zia.

My mother delivers her harshest look and scolds me. "So you couldn't invite her to lunch at Nani's when you go?" Who said anything about lunch at Nani's? Right, Zia.

"No, Ma. She can go to Nani's anytime for lunch. I just want to spend some time alone with my grandmother—is that okay? *You're* not insulted, are you?!"

"No. But I'm not sensitive like Maria. You'll have to apologize to Zia when we see her later."

"Ma." Both her eyebrows are raised in tight V-shaped arcs.

"Never mind! You'll apologize."

Resistance is futile. "But I'm not inviting her to lunch with Nani."

"I don't know what all this secret stuff is. But you do what you have to do. Just remember that Zia is very insecure, especially when it comes to Nani."

Well I know it. Claire and I have been walking on those eggshells our entire lives. I realize, suddenly, that I don't respect Zia. I feel ashamed and unrepentant at the same time.

"Ma, I asked Zia not to tell you about lunch with Nani. And she turned right around and told you about it."

"What's so terrible? She's my mother, and Zia's too, no?"

I get some work done at the kitchen table while my mother cleans her spotless house. She serves me more espresso before going upstairs to change.

I decide to remain in my traveling clothes: pencil-thin twill charcoal pants, light patterned white collarless man-tailored long-sleeved shirt and lightweight black leather jacket with cuffs and lapels.

I check the time on my computer and head to the powder room to wash my face and train my hair into submission. By the time I am back, my mother has returned, her hair freshly styled and held in place. Subtle makeup. Lipstick. A beige silk blouse with pearl buttons and a tie closure. Tweed jacket paired with a solid brown A-line skirt, neutral stockings, brown-and-tan pumps. The earrings my father gave her for their fifth wedding anniversary, Italian-gold crucifix and chain.

She appraises me with her characteristic raised eyebrow.

"You going like that?" Suddenly, I feel like my mother's version of a biker chick.

"I thought I would. It's Zia and us and, uh, Paolo. Do we count him?"

A smile brushes her lips. "Okay, let's go get Zia. And remember, apologize and be nice. She's very sensitive about Nani—you know this. Behave."

I'm thirty-five and my mother is telling me to behave. Is this just a Sicilian thing?

Zia is poised behind the storm door in her tweed cape and patent leather pumps. She carries her matching purse and wears a soft gray beret.

I leave the engine running and sprint up the stairs to kiss her. She smiles as I link my arm in hers.

"Zia! It's wonderful to see you!" She squeezes my arm in response and treats me to another smile.

My mother nods her approval and pats my thigh, and we set off. I chastise myself for feeling like a good girl.

Paolo's fronts onto Tremont Avenue, the main thoroughfare through our neighborhood. A business first owned and run by Paolo's father, the aged brick building stands between a liquor store and a bakery. The scripted neon sign in the window spells out the restaurant name. It has been here for decades.

Paolo rubs his hands together as he reaches for my mother. Smiling broadly, he plants kisses on her cheeks and turns to Zia.

"Signoras! Benarrivata! Gaby, welcome!"

Paolo and my mother exchange current news, my mother visibly pleased to hear that Paolo's youngest daughter is expecting her first child in a few months. To my experienced ear, I know she ensures her delight is not lost on me. Paolo asks if we need menus. Both women encourage him to serve us a dinner of his own design.

Paolo first brings us an antipasto of cheeses, olives, eggplant and roasted red peppers. Accompanied by crusty Italian bread and a dip of herbed olive oil. We talk about Claire and Josh. I tell Zia how much I miss Claire. She wells up, letting me know how much she misses her too.

My mother raises her left eyebrow in my direction as Paolo returns to our table. I use my napkin and look straight at Zia.

"I am so sorry if I was disrespectful to you over the phone. I have no excuse. I will not let it happen again."

She caresses my hand and grants me absolution with a nod. I take a sip of Sanpellegrino and smile.

The two sisters, satisfied, nod in synchrony, and we tuck into Paolo's not-on-the-menu thinly sliced pancetta charcuterie. Insalata mista—mixed salad—is next, followed by stracciatella—Italian egg-drop soup—and then ravioli. I promise myself I will never leave this table.

I pour more wine for Zia and my mother. Another glass of water for me.

When Zia laughs at a story my mother is telling, I realize how rarely I have seen her happy. Zio Salvatore's death leached her capacity for joy. After that, she was terminally wary, always waiting for the other shoe to drop. Straining to shield Claire and herself from life. I feel unaccustomed compassion, seeing life through her eyes.

After supper, Paolo delivers a small platter of cookies and plates of ricotta cake drizzled with honey. Espresso. Petite delicate crystal glasses filled with Strega. I pass my glass to my mother, trusting her to share it with Zia when the time comes.

If I eat anything else, I won't be able to slide myself from my seat. I excuse myself to the ladies' room and find Paolo, thanking him for the extraordinary meal and handing him my credit card. He bows slightly, smiles and tells me he's happy.

Repeating the hospitality ritual at the front door as we prepare to leave, Paolo thanks us and invites us to return soon. The women are lighthearted as we head home. Zia is actually laughing, a sound I have not heard in some time. I'm already composing my end of a phone call to Claire. I will always be amazed at Claire's having imposed a moratorium on worrying about her mother.

Zia retires to her home, leaving my mother and me to share the living room. She offers me cannoli "made yesterday—they're still good." She knows well my weakness for cannoli. I put her offer aside until morning. She pours a thimble-sized glass of anisette for herself and a wineglass of Perrier for me.

As Ana places the delicate glass on an end table, I prepare for her interrogation.

"So why all this mystery about seeing Nani alone." It's not a question.

"No mystery, Ma, I just want to have lunch with her one-on-one."

She tries guilt. "And you expect me to make lunch so you can take it over."

"I didn't ask you to do that." I feel my hot-headed Sicilian taking over and order myself to maintain control.

She pins me down with her eyebrow. "Oh, and you'll prepare lunch for her?"

"I have a plan," I say simply. Holding her gaze, I'm treated to another eyebrow.

She turns down another alley. "Is it about the wedding?"

I don't respond. I take our glasses to the kitchen, wash them and rejoin her in the living room.

"What, then? Her health? She's good, you know. I would tell you."

I smile and hug her around the back of her neck. Plant a kiss on her cheek and let her know I'm going up to bed.

"Well, I don't care. It's your business."

"Sleep well, Ma. See you in the morning."

I wake earlier than usual, check email and organize instructions for lab people. Press send, dress for a run and sneak down the stairs. Too late.

"Don't be long. I've got breakfast."

I walk back to the kitchen, land a kiss on her forehead and promise her I'll be quick. The aroma of espresso is almost enough to turn me around.

On this gray day, my Bronx neighborhood wears a decidedly shabby veneer. Swaths of peeling paint, front-yard abandoned bicycles, left-behind garden tools stuck in flower beds. A pink tricycle sporting faded rainbow streamers. Sagging vintage 1950s bicolor aluminum awnings.

I swing around sooner than I would like. The pressure of her waiting for me is as familiar as my own breath. The practiced rise of anxiety is as predictable as it is unwelcome.

She hears me close the door. I remove my running shoes, gritty from the damp day, and meet her in the kitchen.

"Oh, good!" she says. "The frittata is ready. There's ham and Calabrese toast with butter. Espresso?"

What a question.

We sit together, no vibe from the previous night. I decide to stay calm. It's outside our playbook.

"So, you going over today? Let me know. I have a tablecloth and some napkins for her. She'll like them."

"I'll go tomorrow, Ma. I won't forget about the linens."

She nods and treats herself to a sip of espresso.

"So what happens today?"

I smile and bend toward her over the table.

"I'd love to visit Arthur Avenue. You game?"

"Game? You mean do I want to?"

She spears a chunk of ham and considers carefully.

"You know, it's filthy there. It smells and it's always full of people. Besides, what you want to get there? But we'll go if you want. I haven't been there, well, let's see. It's at least fifteen years."

"I want to look around the cheese shops. And get some sausage and bread to bring home."

"Okay! Be ready in an hour. I don't want to be late getting home."

For my mother, five in the afternoon is late.

Following my shower, I select a different T-shirt, but the same pants and jacket as the previous night.

My mother is puttering in the kitchen. Dressed in her favorite light wool gray dress. The one with the broad shawl collar. I'm reminded of how pleased she was when she completed this piece.

She has been waiting for me, her antennae primed. She rinses her hands, uses her apron and removes it, folding the fabric—she always tucks the waist ties—and places it on the counter.

"Good!" she says, looking me over, a subtle scowl playing at her mouth. "We're driving, right?"

"Yes, of course!"

"What about parking?"

"Don't worry, we only need one spot." I'm treated to a rare grin and we set off.

Arthur Avenue is less than five miles from my mother's house. If traffic and deliveries are against you, it can take a long time to arrive. Today, it takes us forty minutes. As we turn onto the street famous as Little Italy in the Bronx, we make progress slowly. There is no speed possible on this street crammed with merchants, shoppers and neighborhood kids chasing each other and their favorite lost playthings into the street.

I try to ignore my mother's backseat driving commentary. "Yah! Watch out! Kids will run after that ball in the street. Oh! Look at those shopping bags. Be ready. They could break. People will run out after their groceries. Ugh, that man and woman, flirting while they cross the street. Gaby. I told you parking would be a problem."

She doesn't get that I've been trying to give her a walk down memory lane. Or maybe she does, and I hadn't figured that it's painful for her to go there.

I finally find the one spot I've been looking for. Liberate my mother from the passenger side after ensuring I'm not guiding her into a puddle. Or worse.

Arm in arm, we negotiate sidewalks littered with vegetable greens, fruit peels, pizza crusts, glassine wrappings and paper bags stamped with the logos of local merchants.

We swing into the wide doors of the market, greeted by a cacophony of shoppers and merchants. While claustrophobic, the place is warm and welcoming. My senses drink in the melded aromas of bread fresh from the ovens, cured meats, cheeses, ripe red tomatoes.

My mother points out the many changes from her day. She is animated and chatty. Points to a huge barrel full of fresh mozzarella.

"You want some," she suggests hopefully.

"Oh, sure! I'll get some for Nani and for you too! Zia?"

"Sounds good, but I'll get my own."

I shoot a mock-stern look in her direction. "Whose idea was this anyway?"

She backs off and we walk away with a bagful of fresh mozzarella. I then find some "beautiful provolone"—my mother's description.

I know I'm going to overbuy, but I can't resist. These merchants bring in the very best of everything. And I love the show they put on selling it.

Next stop cured meats and sausage—sweet and hot for Russ and me. Genoa salami. I buy my mother and Zia two nice pork roasts. For Nani's lunch, cured olives, sun-dried tomatoes, stuffed olives, roasted red peppers. Prosciutto, bresaola—thinly sliced beef slathered in spices and grated cheese, rolled, tied and then simmered in tomato sauce at low heat for hours.

Intoxicated, I gently test the bread, selecting four warm sesame-encrusted loaves. Then, small prepared trays of lasagna—one headed for Boston. Finally, torrone and sfogliatella—a clam-shaped pastry made of crispy layers of thin dough, stuffed with lemon-and-orange-infused ricotta.

"Gaby!" my mother scolds. "This is all very expensive; who will eat all this?! Let me buy at least!"

"No, Ma, this is on me. For Nani and for you and Zia."

"We get good grocery all the time! You're bringing to Russ, too, right?"

"Of course! But you forget the North End . . . we get good food, but this, from Arthur Avenue, is a special treat."

She's in a much better mood as we exit the market, wondering if I want to see her old neighborhood. The one she and Papa moved into with Giuseppe and Concetta.

"Streets were always noisy," she explains, "but not so dirty. We didn't leave food waste on the sidewalks or in the streets. It smelled of food. Good food, not rotten. Mothers called their kids, sat together on apartment building stoops to catch up and gossip. It was friendly.

"I worked in the deli, so I met a lot of people. Concetta was strict about how I behaved. These people are looking for a reason to believe you're less than they are—only because you've just arrived. I was very careful. I didn't want to be the reason they'd be mean to Nani and Nonno."

The delicatessen is still here. It announces itself as Manni's, a brash neon sign buzzing us inside, the proprietor greeting us. My mother buys tiramisu, and we continue our stroll.

We pass the cyclone fence paddocks of her grade school—big facelift over the years—and her high school. Not so much face-lifted here.

We stand in front of the high school. "We both went here, your father and me, you know. I was a freshman when he was a senior. We would meet in the halls, spend a few minutes. He would go off, I would go off. It always made me feel like I belonged, like he knew who I really was."

"He did, Ma."

She shakes her reverie, squeezes my arm. "Espresso?" I ask.

She nods and we find an outside table at Esposito's. Espresso. Grilled eggplant panini with provolone. Pepperoncini and hot Italian peppers. Gelato.

We struggle the parcels back to the car. After helping my mother, I haul myself into the driver's seat, glad for my abbreviated run this morning. I'd repeat my passion in the morning before seeing Nani.

Respecting Ana's unofficial 5 P.M. curfew, we arrive home at 4:45 P.M.

Too full for a meal, I suggest that leftover cannoli will complete my day's feed. She straps on her apron and sets about cooking spaghetti Bolognese.

"You gotta eat," she says.

Resistance is futile. Paired with the fresh bread, accompanied by olive oil and balsamic dip, the result is divine.

We watch *What Ever Happened to Baby Jane?*, gradually moving toward each other on the sofa as we crack through a bag of salted sunflower seeds.

"I hate this part," I whisper as Bette Davis serves Joan Crawford's feathered lunch.

"It's only a movie," my mother reminds me. I'm seven years old again, for just a moment. And she, I notice, is spellbound.

I head up after kissing my mother good night and fall asleep almost immediately. I realize, in my early slumbered state, how much I am looking forward to seeing Nani tomorrow.

The next morning, I hear my mother in the kitchen when I return from my run.

"Nani needs a few things—take them to her. I told her I would bring them, so I won't ruin your 'surprise.' When you going?"

"I figure around eleven thirty, but I'll leave earlier to pick up what she needs."

We breakfast on pancakes and bacon, my mother reminding me not to gain weight before the wedding. I almost roll my eyes but control myself.

I spend most of the morning online and on email. I text Russ and feel relieved and grateful to hear his voice when he calls me back.

"My mother really turned up the heat when we got back from Paolo's the other night. Tried hard to get me to cough up why I want to see Nani alone."

"Did you give in?"

"No, I did not."

"Sweet."

I ruin the surprise present of sausages and lasagna that will travel home with me. "Just don't eat any of it on the way home, okay?" I can see him smile and miss him. We hang up after I promise I'll call after the visit with Nani.

The tablecloth and napkins are wrapped in clean brown paper. My mother places them into a large shopping bag with stern instructions to keep everything clean. "And don't rip the paper."

I place lunch for Nani and me in another of my mother's endless supply of repurposed brown paper shopping bags and kiss her at the door.

"Have a good lunch. And kiss your grandmother for me. Tell her I'll come by tomorrow afternoon."

As always, she waits by the door while I start the car and pull away from the tar-washed curb. I wave and navigate the short distance to Nani's house, wondering how I'm going to ask her about my unborn siblings.

Another door stalker, my grandmother would be waiting if she knew I was coming. When I knock, she ventures a strong-sounding "Who there? Chi è?" from behind the door.

"Nani! It's me, Gaby."

"Cosa c'è che non va—what's the matter? You mothah? She okay?" By now the door is swung as wide as her eyes and she is holding me close for the ritual cheek kissing.

"No, no, Nani. Everything's fine. I came in the other night and wanted to surprise you with lunch. And some groceries my mother told me you need."

She produces her best fake scowl followed by a huge smile that begs a few back teeth. "I cook for us, no?"

"No, not today." I heft the left-hand shopping bag as I walk into her tiny kitchen. I explain what's in the right-hand bag and she nods her approval. "Ah'm-a like-a this tovaglia—tablecloth. Ah, where this come from?" She points to the food bag.

"Arthur Avenue. I went with Ma yesterday."

"Okay." She starts laying the table—with her good dinner dishes—while I organize the food.

I serve the antipasti and the olive oil/balsamic vinegar dip for the bread first. Then the lasagna. The aroma is wonderful, but I find myself pushing the food around on my plate.

My grandmother interrupts me while I spar with a crust of bread. I assure her I like everything, but I know I'm procrastinating. And so does she. My anxiety mounts as I realize I'm about to ask her about my sisters.

"Wha'? Che cosa—what is it?"

I fiddle with a slice of Genoa salami. "You know when my mother came to visit us in Boston."

"Sure. Wha' happen?" I have her full attention.

"Well . . ." I take a drink of water. More procrastination. Nani is uncannily patient with me. She nods her head in my direction, her face flushed with expectation.

I plunge in, wincing. "I found out my mother lost two babies before I came along. I wanted to ask you about what happened."

"Why you no ask you mama?" She places her napkin on the table and walks to the kitchen to make espresso.

"Well. She didn't tell me about it."

"So how you find out?"

"Russ. She told Russ when they thought I'd gone to bed."

"But you listen, no? And they no see you."

I feel ridiculous revealing myself as a common eavesdropper to my grandmother. I shrug in her direction and she chuckles.

"I learn lots of things when I listen like that! It's good!"

I'm expecting she'll fall into storytelling mode as only she can. I ready myself to learn.

Suddenly, her face turns serious as she returns from the kitchen carrying a tray with espresso and cups.

"This you mama story, no la mia. You tell Russ you hear them?"

"Sure! I was jealous she told him and not me."

"Why you jealous? She tell him—she know he tell you. Maybe she scared to tell you."

"Scared of what? Ma is never scared."

She shrugs. "If she tell you, maybe she go back there an' cry to you. You mama, she got to show you she strong. How many times you see her cry when you papa pass?"

"Never. I heard her in her bedroom, but I never saw her. Still, it broke my heart."

"Sure. See her cry, maybe two, three time. No like Maria."

"Nani, can't you tell me?"

"Sure, I can tell. I remember everything. I tell you my storia only after you talk to you mama."

"But then I've got to tell her I was listening."

"Wha'? You think you mama stupida? She know you know. Maybe she wait for you to ask."

Twirling the espresso cup between both palms, I slump into my chair. Nani delivers a short laugh in my direction.

"Maybe you learn the hard side of listen like this?"

I laugh too. "Yeah, Nani! I think so."

"Not so bad. Here, more espresso and sfogliatelle, no?"

Yes.

We clean up together, Nani laughing as she recounts the absurdity of her best friend Luisa's behavior. Luisa doesn't speak to her grandson because she doesn't like his girlfriend. "Wha'? He gonna marry the girlfriend? Wha' happen when the babies, they come? She no gonna be there? Pah, stupida!

"She no say nothing. She just stay quiet with a dark face." My grandmother draws a wide circle around her own face. "Like wha'? That volcano we got at home."

"Vesuvius."

"Yeah: smart-a girl."

She tells me about the comings and goings of the clerks at her favorite A&P. The ones she likes—they bend over backward to help her—and the ones she doesn't like—they stare at her like they don't understand what she's saying. I don't have the heart to tell her they actually might not understand her.

It's time for me to go. I steel myself to talk to my mother.

With Nani waving at her front door, I fire up my CRV, blow a last kiss out the window, and make the short distance to my mother's by 3:30 P.M. A reliable guardian, my mother is already stationed at her screen door, waiting for me to mount the concrete stairs.

"Hold the rail," she orders, a blast command from my past. I wonder why I obey, but I do.

"How's Nani?" she queries, planting her first kiss on my right cheek.

"She's good, Ma. We had a great lunch together."

She searches my face as I walk through the vestibule. "You're staying tonight," she says. No argument. No negotiation. "Zia is coming for supper. We have to talk about where your wedding will be. We have to reserve. Better call Russ."

I had planned to be in the car by six, home by ten. Inwardly, I'm groaning. But, I reason, *This is good.* Not only a command performance supper, but enough time to come clean and ask my mother about my sisters.

"Oh! I wondered when this would happen!" Russ is already laughing when I ask if he wants to be part of the summit. "Oh, I wouldn't be there for the world. Just hang tough when they want to do something or not do something that we want."

"But, for sure, you have preferences that you want to talk about."

"Yeah. I just want us to get married."

"Me too," I tell him. And I promise that there will be a chuppah as well as a Catholic altar.

The great confrontation is not what I thought it would be. However, Ana did raise both eyebrows in alarm when I confessed to eavesdropping.

My mother understands human nature, especially her mother's and her daughter's. "So you went to see Nani to ask her about it." Not a question.

"What did she tell you?"

"Nothing." My mother flashes her best skeptical look my way. Lets it sink in.

"No, really. She said I have to ask you, Then she'll talk to me about it."

"Miscarriages are bad, don't get me wrong, but missed milestones are worse. First birthdays—your father and I had two that we couldn't celebrate. First days of school. Graduations. Career choices. Weddings, maybe grandchildren." She floats a meaningful look my way.

I am quietly enthralled by the persistence of her loss, altered with each passing year. I had no idea. When a baby dies in utero, I had always imagined that the event dies. I had not imagined that my mother's babies, my sisters, had unlived lives, kept alive by my mother with each passing year.

She relives how painful it was to try a second time. And how the first weeks of carrying me were like a dream from which she was afraid to awaken. "Wake me," she said to Papa, "when we know I will deliver our baby this time."

She tells me she became more and more terrified, then more and more hopeful as her pregnancy continued beyond the duration of the first two. Traumatized, her eyes take on a hooded appearance. She is, I realize, staring into the past, coming out of her reverie sporadically to look at me.

She confirms what she said to Russ about not telling me. She wants, she says, for me to live for myself, not for two sisters who never came into our family alive. Nevertheless, these two sisters shaped our family more than we could have realized.

"Ma, do you still think about them?"

"You'll know one day. Once you conceive a child, that child is yours. Always. You wake thinking they are with you. That it's time for school. Or a graduation. Or meeting their first boyfriend—I always knew they were girls."

Smiling, she pats my arm. "He saved me the best for last. You're my wine at Cana.

"I thought if Russ would tell you, it would be gentle that way. You have a good man, Gaby. I'm not happy that you live together now—before you're married." She waves her hand in a gesture of submission and goes on, "As it is, you are asking me about the babies." She rubs the nail of her index finger with her thumb. "I am glad." My mother. Always in control. Always planning several moves ahead in the chess game that is our lives.

"Ma, is this why you always, you know, hover?"

She tips her head in my direction and chuckles. "Oh," she says, "maybe some. I think most of it is being an Italian mother. You'll see one day. You and Russ want children, yes? Work isn't everything—you'll see this one day too."

I skirt the question of children for Russ and me. We do want them, but I want to start the clock on our time.

"What about Papa? How was he?"

She's back in the past again. "Very sad. But he was hopeful for both of us. He wouldn't let go of trying again, and then again. I knew he was scared, but he never told me about that. When my pregnancy with you was sure, we both breathed. When we were in bed, he would come close to my stomach, singing to you. He was sure you could hear him." She smiles at this memory of my dad. "He was just like when you grew up with him. He was wonderful."

Rising from her chair, she places both hands on the table, signaling the end of our talk. "Time to start supper. Zia will be here at six thirty. Ach! It's already five. I'll make pizza. Okay?"

My mother makes the absolute best pizza in the city; I could already smell it. I follow her into the kitchen, where she is removing the kitchen towel shroud from the dough. I draw in the scent of yeast and flour. Watch as my mother flours her hands and punches, then kneads the dough into submission.

I find her homemade tomato sauce in the fridge and turn on the oven. Pull out the mozzarella and shred it. Grate the Parmesan and ready the oregano and pepper.

"Olives, Ma?"

"If you want. I have Sicilian and Kalamata. Use what you like."

I slice several Kalamata olives and some roasted red peppers, just for good measure.

I root around for fixings and assemble a loaded arugula salad. Lay the kitchen table, complete with wineglasses. I know Zia will bring her homemade cannoli. Our feast for three is set with the addition of dessert plates and espresso cups.

My mother is just placing the pizzas into the oven when I ask if there's anything else she needs. She waves me away and I disappear to check my phone and emails.

I reach the last step as Ma greets her sister at the door. I rush to Zia with my best imitation of a bear hug and cheek pecks. She is smiling and ebullient. She is happy Ma asked her to join this planning session that both women believe to be the cornerstone of Russ's and my wedding.

The tantalizing aroma of pizza fills the house. My mother graces the table with sun-dried tomatoes, olives, chunks of provolone, oil and vinegar dip and crusty bread. We sit around, pecking at the antipasti, laughing and waiting for my mother to signal a start to the business of the evening. Half of me wants to dial Russ into the meeting. He and I know what we want, but I have to be patient. Let them go through their planning. Then get on my diplomatic hat, little worn and much dusty, and bring them around to Russ's and my vision.

Looking at and listening to the two women, I see they have discussed this and that they are in agreement. When she returns from rotating the pizza, my mother starts.

"So, we're thinking you need two ceremonies—ours and Russ's, right?" It's my mother's nod to Russ being Jewish. "Ours is easy—the church with Father Bernadin. What about the other? You need a, uh, clergyman, right?"

"A rabbi. Russ and I are wondering if Father Bernadin will let us have the chuppah in the church basement. Russ has talked with a rabbi he knows. He is saving the date for us."

"Chuppah?" This is the first—but, I know, not the last—word from Zia.

Eager to demonstrate her knowledge, Ana informs her sister, "It's the canopy. The couple stand under the canopy while the rabbi reads the marriage rite. Then, at the end, Russ will stomp on a light bulb—it should be a glass, but these days it's a light bulb—covered with a napkin that signals the couple are married by Jewish custom and law." My mother's clearly done her homework. Zia is impressed.

"I'll speak with Father Bernadin," I assure them, and I'm sure I hear them exhale.

Ana gestures an outstretched palm in Zia's direction.

"I know the receptions at Toscana Banquet Hall on Tremont are very good. The place is beautiful and the food is great. I think we should go and have a look."

I have the place up on my laptop. Tulle curtains. Sequins adorning pink chiffon upholstered throne-sized chairs. Huge tables. An expansive dance floor below a large stage. I turn my laptop around so the women can have a look.

"See?" Zia gushes. "It's gorgeous, right?" Not what Russ and I want. I keep that information to myself.

My mother pats her sister's hand. "What else, Maria? We want to see every place you found."

"Villa Amerigo. Also on Tremont. A very special dance floor. Also reports of great food. Around here, every place has great food."

Villa Amerigo boasts a dance floor chandelier reminiscent of a spaceship. The piece is a set of nested circles illuminated by muted blue and bright yellow-white lighting. Huge tables are dressed in pastel colors. The light gray fake stone wall is meant to be the perfect wedding photo backdrop.

After I once again display my computer screen, my mother signals that it's time for espresso and "Zia's prize cannoli." She motions me to the kitchen with a nod, and, as I leave the table, my antennae are way up and fine-tuned.

Ana faces Maria and delivers her commentary. "These are wonderful. You've done so much work here. But Gaby and Russ are simple. They don't like fancy."

"What? You saying they don't like these? How can they not like these? You like them."

"It's not what I like. It's what they want." My mother, the other diplomat in our family.

"Listen, there's one on City Island. Arnie's. Gaby will show us."

That's my cue. I lay the serving tray on the tablecloth and pour three espressos. Place the cannoli where we can all reach the platter.

The women begin serving themselves and sipping espresso. I click on Arnie's website and sit back.

There he is. Rotund, balding, tattooed arms crossed in front of an impressive gut. He sports a wide smile as he shows off his restaurant, looking like a facsimile of something in Italy. The restaurant sits on the City Island pier. Weathered wood, boat-and-oar decor. Fake fish mounted wherever they'll fit. Small tables. No dance floor. Fantastic photos of menu offerings. An upscale pub, almost a restaurant, not a banquet hall.

The women ooh and aah through the website, Zia trying to recover from her rejection as she basks in Ana's approval.

"What do you think, Gaby?" I know exactly what I think.

"I like it, Ma. But tell me, how long have we all been going to Paolo's?"

"Paolo's? Well, over thirty years, I think. You want to go to Paolo's?"

"Paolo is a friend to this family." Zia starts to object, but Ana stays her with the palm of her hand.

"Russ and I are thinking fifty people," I begin.

Zia draws a dramatic breath. "*Fifty?* Who you gonna have with only—"

My mother interrupts. Places her hand firmly on her sister's arm in an effort to quiet her. "Let her finish, Maria."

"But Claire had a big wedding, and it wasn't nearly enough!" She is both horrified and scandalized. Almost wild-eyed, she appeals to both of us in turn.

"Zia, we want people who are closest to us."

"What about the booster? The money the guests will bring to the wedding. It'll be so small!"

I resist laughing. "Russ and I are older, Zia. We've both been working for a long time. We don't need a booster.

"So, here's what Russ and I want: fifty people. Our list is on my computer. I'll print it out for you. You two and Nani can fill out the rest. We already have Russ's side. Catholic Mass upstairs in the church with Father Bernadin; Jewish rite downstairs under the chuppah with Russ's rabbi if Father Bernadin agrees. Reception at Paolo's. That's what we would really like to have."

Zia has built up a head of steam. She explodes. Slaps her palms on the table. "So why am I here? You don't want anything I found; you both toss me aside, like—"

Like Nani does.

I do my best to calm her. My mother finds her voice.

"Listen, Maria. I don't like the pantsuit, but I sewed it. Of course I'd be happy with only our Catholic Mass. I don't know anything about Jewish wedding ceremonies. I also want a bigger wedding at a hall, but this is what Gaby and Russ want. You really think anyone in this family would 'toss you aside'?"

"Zia, you and Ma are in charge of the menu. I know you'll consult with Nani. Russ and I would love a family-style meal—big platters of food that Paolo does so well—that everyone shares. And Russ and I are paying for everything."

"No," my mother insists. "Your father looked forward to paying for your wedding, and I have this money that I've added to since he died. No. I will pay."

"Russ won't like that," I say.

She sets her espresso cup in its saucer. Bayonets me with one of her high-eyebrow looks. "Too bad."

I exhale loudly, tell her it's not fair to take this away from us. I remind her again that we are older. We want to treat everyone and thank everyone for coming.

"Sure. Thank them—send thank-you notes. You never do, you know. It's very rude. The dinner is mine."

I try to negotiate. "You said, 'The dinner is mine.' So how about if the wine and liquor is ours. Open bar."

Zia squirms. "Oh, that's so expensive."

"Not when we're not paying for dinner."

My mother hasn't weighed in. A good sign.

"Ah," she says, "there's still more cannoli. Gaby, make fresh espresso, will you?

"Okay," my mother says as I serve the coffee. She's indisputably the five-star general in this army of women. "I'll speak to Paolo. Maria, you and Ma and me, we'll go see Paolo about the menu. Gaby, you and Russ line up Russ's rabbi. And, Gaby, you get in touch very soon with Father Bernadin about the chuppah. I have no idea where to rent a chuppah, so you'll have to do that too. And call Paolo about the wine and liquor, when I tell you that we've seen him."

Wait. Did I just win the liquor battle?

Yes, I am taking notes. I promise them I will send them each a copy "so we can keep everything straight."

"What's to keep straight?" my mother queries. "You think we won't remember?" I let it slide.

The following morning, I've checked and responded to email, sent the requisite instructions to the lab, had a good run, have eaten breakfast and cleaned up the kitchen. I'm ready to get home.

My mother wrings her hands into her apron, looks me square in the eye. "You know to go easy on Zia, right? She's very sensitive."

"She has no self-esteem, Ma."

"Wha'? Everyone whines about 'self-esteem' these days. We just got on with things. Our husbands died. We did what we needed to do. For us, for our kids. We never worried about what we were worth. Never."

"Was she like this as a kid?"

"She started out knowing who she was. She was proud of herself—smart in school. Even very young, she knew all she wanted was to get married, have a nice house and children. She was always taking scraps from Nani's sewing, making wedding dresses over and over again. She brought one to school one day—changed into it before going to class. Nani had to go get her. Lots of crying. Long punishment, no access to her favorite magazine—*Girls' Fun and Fashion*.

"My mother had no patience for Zia. She and my father taught us to fit into America, but to stay Italian. It was a full-time job. And my mother always gave Zia failing grades. She just wanted to fit in with all the other girls in her class. Of course, that never happened."

"But she's still so—"

"What? Fragile? Unsure? Needy? Yes, she's all those things, and very loving too. She needs our mother to accept her. To love her. Nani loves her but has trouble accepting her."

Signaling an end to our conversation, she shrugs, gesturing to my overnight bag and the shopping bag packed with pizza for Russ.

Stopped at a light, I call Russ, let him know I'm on my way. A little over four hours later, I'm home.

Over leftover pizza, I bring Russ up to speed on what will happen.

He pronounces success. "Hey! Sounds like it went great."

I smile back. "Betcha life, Cowboy. Stick with me, we'll make this our wedding yet!"

He kisses me lightly. "Betcha life I will stick with you."

"So, what about a rabbi? Anyone in mind?"

"As a matter of fact, yes. Rabbi Rosen. He's in the Bronx. My father—and our family—were part of his congregation. We grew up in the Bronx, so I know some of your haunts. I contacted the rabbi. He's agreed to officiate our Jewish ceremony."

"You know, I never thought you were religious, are you?"

"Not sure. It's just that I'm Jewish. I feel, well, connected. I might want to get better at that. My family escaped from Poland just before Hitler invaded."

"Wait a minute—you booked Rabbi Rosen! We just have to find a chuppah and a crystal glass. I don't like the whole light bulb thing."

I pop a final square of pizza into my mouth and focus on the computer screen as Russ types in *chuppah.*

We spend about an hour online, checking out ceremonial canopies. I pretend to favor pink Chantilly, but I get busted. Light gauzy beige linen mounted on a thin wooden frame is much more our speed. Oh, and we find a glass we like, but we have to buy a set of six.

"They'll come in handy, in case you miss," I tell Russ. He pretends to punch my left deltoid.

"Where're we gonna do this?" Russ asks. "Not a good idea to have a Jewish wedding ceremony up front in a Catholic church."

"I thought we—well, I—would ask Father Bernadin to let us have our Jewish ceremony in the church basement. No spiders, I promise. It's a really nice space; wedding receptions are held there. But ours won't be one of them."

Next morning, I take a break and place a call to Father Bernadin. The parish receptionist informs me he's on a hospital call. I leave a message, click off, noting my sweaty palms.

I'm setting up an experiment when my phone chirps. I ask one of the graduate students, Alex, to take over for me and greet Father Bernadin over the phone.

After our hellos, I am nervous as I state my business. The silence on the line lasts for what feels like hours.

"What does your mother think?" he asks.

I tell him and he summarizes. "So, you want to have our Catholic ceremony before our altar, and the Jewish rite downstairs in the reception hall."

"Yes, Father."

More deafening silence. "You're in Boston? Yes, I remember that when we booked your wedding. For this, I do need to see you and your mother, and your young man, before I decide. So you and your groom need to clear your schedules and get back to me with a date when you can come. Tuesdays or Thursdays are best."

I know Father Bernadin. He's unhappy, therefore icy. My wheels are already turning for an alternate site.

I've violated my good Catholic girl persona. I haven't played by the rules. I have arrogantly exhausted Father Bernadin's goodwill. Never married. Living a loose life, living with Russ, a Jewish man. Defying my mother's rules for me. Mass when it suits me—when I'm with her and I don't want to argue. If I ever go to confession again, it'll start like this: "Bless me, Father, for I am sin."

I have humiliated myself. What right do I possibly have to ask for favors from a priest who hasn't seen me in his church by my own choice in decades. I have humiliated my mother. In my mind's eye, I see her clenching her teeth and pinching my arm. Whose idea was this, anyway?

My face is hot, my palms sticky when we finish. I promise to get back to him soon.

I can't go to Russ with this yet. Certainly can't bring this to my mother.

I come back to Alex, ready to take the experiment back into my hands. Something in my face has him stare for a few seconds and offer to finish up. "Almost done, anyway. Go take a breather."

He turns his attention back to his work as I head for my office. I stare at my computer screen, deliberately ignoring the ping of new messages homing to my inbox.

Three weeks later, Russ and I are bouncing along the highway to the Bronx.

"Why so quiet?"

"What if Father Bernadin refuses the chuppah? I mean, what do we do then?"

Averting his eyes from the road for a second, Russ looks at me quizzically. This is a nonsensical question. I'm embarrassed.

He reaches across the stick shift to hold my hand. "So the church is the only place we can have our Jewish ceremony?"

"Yes, no, I mean my mother will be furious. It'll be my fault if he refuses."

"Let me ask you: Is any of this happening right now?"

"Well, no."

"So let's see what does happen. Anyhow, what do you think Paolo might say if we asked to set up a chuppah in the restaurant?"

"Paolo? He has no idea what a chuppah is!"

"Good thing I'm Jewish, huh? Maybe I can explain it to him? What do you think?"

I nod slowly in tacit agreement. *A plan.* A plan is always good, and always what I need. Russ knows this.

My mother's home is infused with the comforting aromas of pane di spinaci—spinach bread—and hot Italian sausage. Olives, sun-dried tomatoes, insalata—salad—wait for us at the table. My mother tells me to set up the espresso. "We don't have much time before our visit with Father Bernadin." Visit. Summons. Whatever.

She warns us how to approach the priest with our request. "You want to get him to say yes, okay? You, Gaby, you apologize for being a bad Catholic all these years; promise to do better."

Wondering how I can possibly apologize for my un-Catholic lifestyle, I strap on my bag and my running shoes. Russ stands beside me and drapes my mother's cape around her shoulders. Ana sits up front with Russ, quiet and thoughtful. I work on calming my gut. Slip a mint into my mouth; offer them up front. Both Russ and my mother take one.

Father Bernadin keeps us waiting ten minutes. I expected worse, but I know he has a soft spot for my mother. As we rise to enter the priest's office, my mother fixes her eyebrow on me. Silently she warns, *Don't embarrass me.*

The pastor kisses my mother's cheek and shakes Russ's hand as Ana introduces the two men. He motions to the seats across from his desk. He nods toward me silently as we settle ourselves. Still annoyed, he's making it clear that there's no soft spot for me.

"You are booked for a Catholic wedding ceremony here at St. Benedict's. I have asked you here to discuss your auxiliary request." He nods and begins with Russ.

He asks a textbook set of questions about Russ's family, his upbringing. His religious observances. These have been confined to bar mitzvahs, bat mitzvahs, weddings of Jewish family members and friends. Passover, Hanukkah, and childhood Shabbat observances.

"Shul?" asks the priest.

"After my bar mitzvah, on and off till I was about twenty."

"Why did you stop respecting God?"

"I never stopped respecting God."

Inviting him to continue, Father Bernadin inclines his palm toward Russ. My peripheral vision sees my mother wincing in despair.

"So what are you asking of me and our parish?" He knows exactly what we're asking. He wants to hear Russ confirm the request. Which he does.

"And you, Gaby, you are asking this as well?"

I echo Russ's statement. The priest inquires, "And you are a good Catholic, Gaby?" I have no idea what this has to do with asking permission for a chuppah in the church basement. Worse, I feel my Sicilian rising. He knows I am not a good Catholic. Glancing at my mother, I see she has set her lips in a tight line above her chin, her eyes boring a serious warning my way.

"I could be better. Both wedding ceremonies mean a lot to me. Same God, and we Catholics come from Judaism."

He nods and turns toward my mother. "So, Ana, what do you think of this request? Is it reasonable?"

"Father," she begins carefully, "you are the one who will decide if it is reasonable. For me, I would like to see the chuppah and the Jewish ceremony in the church—not at the altar, of course—because I think both ceremonies link Gaby and Russ. Their differences as they marry."

"Hmm." The priest rises from his chair, opens the door to his office and embraces my mother as she walks over the threshold. He squeezes my shoulder, shakes Russ's hand again, and, smiling, thanks us for coming.

"I will call you tomorrow, Ana, with my decision." It doesn't escape my attention that while Russ and I are making the request, the priest will contact my mother.

Ana thanks him and we head in silence back to the car. We remain silent as my mother's key unlocks the front door.

Later, over dinner, Russ asks my mother what she thinks. I bury my face in my bowl of pasta fagioli—pasta with peas—and dip a torn slice of bread into my bowl. It's Russ's question, but her answer is clearly for me.

"I think the pastor likes faithful people. He has a problem when people expect the faith to do for them, but they don't do anything to commit to the faith."

"No, Ma," I begin, but Russ pats my thigh in a signal that allows her to finish.

I am graced with a high-eyebrow stare and explicit interpretation of the meeting.

"He is angry. With you, Gaby, because you never made an effort. And now you want a favor. A Jewish wedding in his church! Really, why should he agree? Russ?"

My partner clears his throat. "Ana, I do get it. But we're asking because it means a lot to us. Otherwise, we could go for a civil marriage, right? And believe it or not, I've always intended to exchange vows under the chuppah."

"But you're not religious."

"No, Ana, but I have lived my whole life believing in God. Gaby, too, I know. But you're right, we're not religious."

"But you've agreed that my grandchildren will be Catholic, yes?"

"By Jewish law, children can be Jewish only if their mother is."

I've got to have my say. "Ma, Father Bernadin is more interested in religion than faith, adhering to dogma. You know this."

My mother nods and passes the salad bowl. We've all had enough of faith and religion for today.

The following morning, my run is early, fast and sweaty. No worries about waking Russ. My mother has ordered us into separate sleeping quarters. "You're not married yet," she explains, shooting me one of her most meaningful looks.

I hear Russ stirring as I complete my morning email tour and lab instructions. Still sweaty, I open the bedroom door to disheveled hair, bare feet and worn-out sweatpants. He hands me a crooked smile and ignores my protests as he draws me close. "I've never hugged you sweaty?"

We make ourselves human and migrate to the kitchen where my mother has espresso ready. A plate of prosciutto sits on the table, patiently waiting for eggs-in-the-bread to finish frying.

She uses her spatula to direct us to the table, wrings her hands into her apron, and addresses us without preamble.

"You need to think about where you want the chuppah. I don't think Father will allow it."

I twirl the tiny cup between my palms. "Did he call you already?"

"No, I know he's angry, though." I wonder, between them, who is angrier.

I wait for her to sip from her cup. Russ shifts his gaze between us. Expectant.

"You did a miserable job, Gaby. Not humble. Not asking. Behaving like you have a right. You don't. Why should he recognize two separate wedding ceremonies from different religions in his church? What? Now you have something to say?"

Impaled on her punishing eyebrow, I clear my throat searching for my voice. I hold my hand toward him when Russ starts to speak. This is clearly my problem, with the priest and my mother. She is furious.

"He can decide however he wants." I give her a casual I-don't-care shrug. "But I didn't sign on to be browbeaten and scolded. No, I'm not the Catholic girl poster child. That's clear. But Russ and I are asking for the celebration that will start our marriage. In the way that's best for us. If he won't provide it in his church, we'll move along."

My mother's mouth twitches, her eyes burn through me and her head swivels from side to side.

"Move on, to where? I don't think I've ever been so embarrassed. What will you do? Russ, how will your family feel if we can't have your ceremony in the church?"

"I think," he begins carefully, "my family might feel more comfortable with a chuppah that *isn't* in a Catholic church."

My mother acknowledges an insight she had not settled on by herself.

"So what will you do?"

I extend my palm in Russ's direction.

He explains that we will approach Paolo to ask about having the Jewish ceremony in the restaurant. Ana's eyes go wide as she listens.

"So what if that makes Father angry at Paolo? Paolo gets a fair amount of business through the priest."

Russ faces me, his jaw clenched, his eyes flashing.

Now that it's looking a lot better than plan A, I'm ready to introduce plan B. "Let's call Rabbi Rosen. We will organize this."

Russ's family has known the rabbi for many years. He is, as always, calm and cheerful. Rabbi Rosen behaves as if we are the only people who matter to him.

He sighs thoughtfully at Father Bernadin's suspected verdict. "It's better," he assures us. "Not too many of us feel comfortable in a Catholic church." Rabbi Rosen asks a few questions about our considering Paolo's for the chuppah. "Let me know what happens. If you have trouble, get back to me. I've still got a few friends, you know."

We decide to see Paolo in person. Utterly nervous, he dry washes his hands repeatedly, licks his lips and sprouts a crop of droplets along his hairline.

"Look. It's okay with me. But I worry about Father. He will be angry with me. And he sends me weddings, engagements, first Communions. I don't know."

Russ explains that we will speak with the priest ahead of time. And he stresses that the ceremony won't start before everyone is there.

We can almost see Paolo's calculations. Bar proceeds.

Paolo shakes Russ's hand. "You'll remember to speak with Father, right?"

Russ reassures him, places his hand at the small of my back and steers me toward the door.

"Is that it?" I ask, incredulous at the ease of our agreement.

"Look, he's scared of the priest, but more interested in his profit. More profit if folks are standing around waiting for everyone to arrive. It'll work. You'll see." He gently snubs my nose and tightens his grip around my waist.

"I'll have to come back soon, you know."

Wearing a look of surprise, he holds me away from him and asks, "Because the wedding's closer?"

"No. Nani said she'll tell me about my sisters after I speak to my mother. I spoke to my mother, and now I need to hear Nani's story."

"Okay."

"You think I should leave it, right?"

"Just don't know what you're hoping to get from it."

I'm ready for this. "A piece of my story." I shrug, knowing he'll understand.

He nods and gathers me close to him again.

The day we leave, my mother tables a huge breakfast. Zia joins us.

I am painfully aware that Maria knows the humiliating truth of how our meeting with Father Bernadin turned out, but she insists on asking detailed questions.

I have always resented my family's digging for information. They like to bathe in bad news, comparing misfortune to their own situations. They always come through, but it's the thinly disguised gloating that gets my anger up. Zia is a master at this.

I provide generalized answers to her questions.

My mother reminds her sister, "You'll take away what you don't eat now." No argument.

I tell her about the restaurant and that we'll stop to see the priest at the church. My mother nods. "He won't like it, you know. Father Bernadin. It challenges his authority." I agree but say nothing.

Zia shoos us away, assuring us she'll help my mother clean up. I hear her say to her sister: "This wouldn't happen if he was, wasn't, well . . ."

"Jewish," my mother reminds her. "Russ is Jewish. So what else do you want to say?"

"No, well, I didn't mean . . ."

Zia. Yes, you did "mean." In my mind's eye is Claire, dropping her head in her hands hearing her mother's allusion to Russ's background.

When we reappear downstairs, my mother is frowning but remains silent, offering her cheeks to both of us in turn. She hands me an olive oil–stained paper sack stuffed with food. Pancetta, roasted pepper and frittata sandwiches on crusty Bronx Italian bread. Biscotti. Zia's cannoli. A thermos full of espresso with two cups. Oranges and apples. Almonds. I can't possibly be hungry, but my mouth is watering.

Obligatory kisses from Zia as we share take-care-on-the-road small talk. I am furious at her but hold my temper in check.

I'm in no mood for Bernadin, but we promised Paolo. No guarantee the priest won't penalize him in some way somewhere down the road.

Anxiously, I ask Russ: "You think this is the right thing to do? I mean, telling Father Bernadin?"

"Paolo agreed that we should tell the priest in person. Yes, I think it's the right thing to do."

Father Bernadin smiles as he greets us, ushers us in, and sits behind his desk, elbows propped, fingers tenting his top lip. He asks what he can do for us.

Russ thanks him for seeing us and I launch in, telling him our plan for the Jewish ceremony.

His eyes turn to steel. "Paolo agrees to this." Not a question.

We take turns explaining that we've seen Paolo and that the agreement is made if he is on board.

"You are welcome, Father," Russ asserts, the tinge of humor not lost on me, "to attend the ceremony. It'll happen just before dinner starts."

Soundlessly, his mouth opens and closes as he thinks better of speaking. He recovers quickly and clears his throat, asking questions about Russ's family.

"Will they come?"

"Yes, they will. My brother, his family, my sister and her husband. Cousins, nieces and nephews."

"I'm happy to hear it. You have to have family there. Your mother and father?"

"My mother is deceased. My father will be with us."

The priest nods. "Well," he says, "I'm glad that you have reached a solution to your dilemma." I think he's not glad.

Now he is transparently in a hurry to move us along. He strides to the door, opens it wide and shuts it carefully after our goodbyes.

"I'll bet he's calling Ana," Russ says, and I release a short, low laugh in response. We're finally on our way home. Our home.

But home brings me no relief from my mother's unspoken mood as we left the Bronx. When I call her on our return, she is still testy. She reveals, as Russ had predicted, that she spoke with Father Bernadin who summarized his version of our meeting.

"Ma, why are you angry at me?"

"Me? Angry? I'm not angry. I am very disappointed in you, Gabriela."

I wince. My mother always uses my proper name like a slap.

"I am sorry for that." Against my better judgment I venture to ask, "Why?"

"When you disrespect Father Bernadin, you disrespect me. And Zia. And your father."

This is a literal slap. Since when have I ever disrespected either of my parents? Or the priest, for that matter?

This inclination of us Sicilians has always made me crazy. Coupled with Zia's unsubtle ploy to express her opinion about Russ's Jewish heritage, this sets my teeth on edge. I struggle to keep it together while I'm on the phone. I respond to an imaginary shout-out from Russ, tell my mother we're almost ready for dinner.

"You can't hide from this, Gaby. Mind yourself."

Hardwired Sicilian trait. You know what someone else is thinking. There's no expectation that they will tell you. Experience has taught me that my mother will give me the silent treatment for the next few days. Then she'll call, demanding an account of my silence. The Sicilian dance. After a lifetime of learning the steps, I still trip over my feet.

That night, I am quiet. Russ doesn't push. He knows somehow that being with the pastor and my mother and aunt have rattled me. My thoughts turn to the subtleties my family has always used to gather information.

* * *

I was fifteen years old. I told my mother I was meeting my friend Elena. We would walk to Mass together. I had planned this carefully. I knew Elena would go along with me. My mother would never know that we would skip Mass. I had my allowance of the past three weeks in my jacket pocket. We headed to the candy store and the bakery. From there, we found a bench in Elena's neighborhood and sat out our time at "Mass."

When I arrived home, my mother greeted me with a too-cheery, "You must be hungry. Sit down." I was anything but hungry, but I was careful not to argue.

"How was Mass?" she queried, the same displaced smile on her face.

"It was great." I forced a forkful of egg-in-the-bread into my mouth, inspected my plate so she wouldn't see my face.

"You went with Elena?"

"Yes."

"Lots of people at Mass?" Her eyes had begun to harden, the barometric eyebrow creeping up her forehead. "How about Father's homily. Good?"

Half a slice of bacon dangling from my fork, I finally looked at her.

She pressed on. "And what was the Gospel about today?" Her arms were crossed. She was cross.

I focused my eyes back on my plate, mumbled, "How did you know?"

"Mrs. Rossi phoned. She didn't see you. She hoped you weren't sick."

I knew the worry about my health was fiction. Mrs. Rossi was a coconspirator in the Sicilian game of Gotcha! and the president of the neighborhood Busybody Club. If we could, all us kids avoided her.

"Finish your breakfast," my mother ordered. "Then, go to your room. Write a letter to Father Pietro, telling him why you missed Mass."

I was shaken to my core. What would he tell the nuns to do to me? Didn't my own mother care about me? Death by humiliation at my tender age. I would simply not survive.

"But, Ma," I whined, only to stare into the palm of her hand.

"No," she insisted, turning up the volume for the first time. "You've lost your telephone privileges and your pleasure activities for two weeks. No TV, and you're grounded. Do you understand? And I want to see the letter you will deliver to Father Pietro. Repeat all this so I know you understand."

"Deliver it? I have to go there? What if he sees me?" I tried my protest again. "It's so unfair! He doesn't even know I wasn't there."

"Oh, so that makes it okay? And you convinced that poor girl Elena to go with you. She would never do such a thing on her own.

And you will never do it again. That's it. Upstairs. Letter. And don't you dare try to pin it on that poor girl. Now."

The first draft of my letter was a washout. I pretended I set out to go to Mass and got hungry. With a one-hour fast before Mass, everybody got hungry. And, I explained, when I finished eating, it was too late to go.

"So this is your idea of a good letter to Father Pietro? A lie, on top of what you did. Throw this out and write the truth. One more chance before your penalty goes up to three weeks. Go. Now."

This wouldn't be happening if my father were alive. He would ask me why what I'd done was wrong, tell me not to do it again, plant a kiss on my forehead and smooth the hair on the back of my head. My mother was a shrew, plain and simple. And she hated me. Papa would never have allowed her to get away with it.

Under my mother's eye, I wrote a letter of truth to Father Pietro. She ordered me to get to confession as soon as I could. *Why? I've just ripped my soul out telling what I did!* My stomach churning, I slipped on my shoes and headed for the door.

From the kitchen. "You're delivering the letter on Tuesday—two days from now," my mother commanded. "Not now. I have to get in touch with Sister Margaret Mary tomorrow. And you're punished, so find a book to bury yourself in."

Busted. So much for shooting the letter through the mail slot today, Sunday, and making a clean getaway.

Monday night, I complained of being nauseated and afraid. She jabbed the spatula in my direction as she continued frying the scallopini. "You brought this on yourself. So next time you'll think twice."

Scaloppini was normally one of my favorites, but I poked at it, finished my homework and went to bed early. I couldn't sleep. I imagined what the ruler would feel like on my knuckles. Would it leave marks? That would teach my mother. A horrifying thought that I might cry crept in. In the end, I thought I probably would not cry, not in his office, at least. And what would it be like with Sister Margaret Mary when I go back to class? Would she tell everyone? I saw myself in a corner of the classroom, a cardboard dunce cap on my head, my classmates laughing as they passed me by. Nobody talking to me. My once-friends ignoring me. The possibilities were mercilessly humiliating.

Tuesday morning, I dressed carefully. Clean white uniform blouse, perfectly starched and ironed. Tie perfectly placed. Clean knee socks. The smock on my uniform jumper placed exactly in the middle of my chest. The hated Scottish Glengarry tartan cap cocked exactly as it should be. Shoes shined and buffed.

My mother said little, her mouth fixed in a taut line across her face. She handed me a brown bag with, I knew, a potato-and-egg sandwich on Italian bread. My mouth threatened to water, but I was too nauseated. And I was too angry to say anything to her.

After I delivered the letter to the rectory, Father Pietro summoned me out of class and to his office together with Sister Margaret Mary. My mother, a true traitor, had let Sister know what I'd done and how disappointed she was in me. She had promised the nun that it would not happen again.

I waited outside the priest's office. It smelled of wax, incense and burnt matches. Sister finally came out to get me, her eyes stern, her lips tightly pressed. She tucked her hands beneath her scapular and nodded for me to follow her. Once inside, she found her seat as Father Pietro pointed to the remaining chair across from his desk. My nausea was now mixed with mild dizziness. For once happy that I had not had breakfast, I decided to keep my humiliation to a minimum and get my stomach and my head under control. I dug my fingernails into my palms to keep myself focused.

Father perched his glasses on the tip of his nose and examined my testimonial. Sister provided her opinion. *Disgraceful, hooligan behavior.* Then she shot the ultimate insult, labeling me a "bona fide bold article." Out of the nuns' line of sight, the phrase always made me laugh. But there was nothing funny about being the bold article in the crosshairs.

My hands were a sweaty, slimy mess. I was in danger of drawing blood from my palms, and my back was slick and cold with a steady drip of unwanted perspiration. Removing his glasses, Father Pietro reminded me that deliberately missing Mass is a mortal sin.

"I expect to see you in the confessional on Friday, young lady." I nodded my assent. This was only Tuesday. If I died before Friday, I was going to hell.

Then Father asked me if I had anything else to say. I assured them that I was sorry. And that I wouldn't do it again.

Sister communicated the sentence, "You will write a 450-word essay on why you will go to Mass every Sunday. This you will give to me in three days. And you will help clean up the lunchroom each day for two weeks, starting tomorrow."

My rage was private and complete. *What?* I couldn't go home for lunch? I couldn't possibly eat in the cafeteria. It smelled of half-eaten bananas, rotting apple cores and potato peelings.

In the end, of course, I did everything forced on me. I knew better than to complain to my mother. So I confided in Claire, who agreed that my punishment was cruel and unusual. And that my mother *had* betrayed me. We had great fun putting together a mock over-the-phone play featuring Father Pietro and Sister Margaret Mary.

I never again skipped Mass while I lived with my mother.

* * *

I ran far and early each morning, organizing my trip to see Nani about my mother's lost daughters, my lost sisters. Russ didn't want me to go so soon after our return. But he supported my need to do it.

I wasn't really sure how I would approach my grandmother this time. I didn't tell her or my mother that I was coming. Telling my mother why I wanted to visit my grandmother would be like slogging through quicksand in hiking boots. And Nani would just be glad to see me, after she was sure "nothing wrong, heh?"

When I pull up, my mother is already at the door, worry stamped on her features. She embraces me. "What's wrong? What's happened?"

"Nothing, Ma, really."

"You gonna tell me you were in the neighborhood?"

I laugh. "Noooo. Just wanted to see you. And Nani."

"Oh. Why do you need to see Nani?"

She makes way as I step into the house.

"I'll tell you in a bit. Just want to get settled right now, okay?"

"Sure, nobody's forcing you. I'll make some espresso."

Over biscotti and coffee, I try disarming her by asking about her cottage dressmaking business. Proudly, she shows off a few of her recent works-in-progress. A mother-daughter combo of dresses for the daughter's wedding. "You see? A *dress* for the bride!" A cinch-waist dove-gray chiffon three-quarter-length mother-of-the-bride dress complete with an as-yet-unfinished beaded bodice. For the bride, an ivory raw silk below-the-knee fitted shift dress with a muted shawl collar and a long tunic sporting wide silk lapels. She shows me a few more of her projects, but these stick with me. My mother is an artist.

"So, tell me about Nani. Why you're really here." Sensing that I will need a minute, she heads to the kitchen. Carries back more espresso and biscotti ai pinoli—biscotti with pignoli nuts.

"Don't pick off the nuts. Eat properly, like I taught you."

Enough stalling. We are both dangerously close to bursting. "About Nani. Don't get mad," I start.

"Since when do I get mad at you? Just tell me. I don't want to worry."

"Oh, no, Ma, there's nothing to worry about."

She studies my face carefully. Sits back in her chair and adopts a triumphant air.

Then, leaning forward, she folds her hands on the table. "I know," she announces casually. "It's about when I lost the first two babies—your sisters."

"How did you know?"

"What? You're so mysterious all of a sudden? But I already told you about this. Why don't you trust me?" The flash of her eyes tells me that she is hurt more than angry. I'd prefer to spark her anger.

"Last time I looked, this was my story to tell. So is this right—you go off to discuss with Nani something that is part of my life." She is not asking a question.

She is reasonably calm when I leave for Nani's, letting me exercise the kissing ritual, but her arms remain stolidly crossed in front of her.

Halfway down the stairs I hear the rasp of the screen door. "Bring lunch. She might not have a lot. She does her shopping tomorrow."

Ana has read my mind. I pick up pizza at Giancarlo's—the best in the Bronx. Medium Sicilian for Nani, so she'll have leftovers, and a small cheese for me. Except for Sicilian, all non-artisanal pizza in New York is delightfully thin-crusted. To eat it, you fold the slice into a V and let the oil drip off before you bite into it. I miss that in Boston.

In the short distance between the "best pizza in the Bronx" and my grandmother's house, I am thoroughly intoxicated by the aroma permeating the car. True to form, my mother has alerted Nani, who stands holding the screen door open, an enormous grin on her face.

"Oh! You bring the pizza! You know I no like cheese, right?"

I reassure her that her pizza is Sicilian. No cheese.

Nani is pure joy for me. Advice without judgment. No fear of my failure in her eyes.

We settle into catching up as we eat, my grandmother offering her critique of Giancarlo's pizza. "Ach! Not so great. Ah'm-a make better!" I could only agree.

She brews a pot of espresso and points to the counter, motioning to me to carry the plate of biscotti Regina—small flat-bottomed oval cookies encrusted in sesame seeds.

Naturally, she knows why we're having lunch together. She sips her coffee and plucks a sesame seed from her lip. "You mama. You already talk with her, no?"

I explain that I haven't gotten very much from my mother about her miscarriages. That she insisted I had heard the story when I'd eavesdropped on her conversation with Russ.

"I know, I promise I tell you after you speak with her." She sighs heavily as she dives into her memory.

She painted a picture of my mother I had never seen. As she speaks, I feel I've been treated, all my years, to the version ripened in Dorian Gray's closet. Not this cheerful, mischievous, funny Ana. Happy and endlessly flirtatious with my father. Creative, always painting, quilting, sewing clothes for herself and her friends. Redecorating, going dancing with Arturo. And dreaming of the children who refused to come.

* * *

"So her friends, they start having babies. I see she worry. But she no talk to me. I wait. I know it's about having a baby. So I no say nothing."

I nod, a silent prompt for her to continue. She passes me the plate of cookies and refills my cup.

"One day, she come. So excite! She tell me she pregnant. Ah'm-a excite too. She tell me she feel real good. No sickness. I say that's good, but I remember at home, no sickness, these ladies no get a baby. I no tell her this.

"They already pick a name. She very sure this baby a girl. Course, I ask, 'What about a boy? You nevvah know this,' I tell her. She laugh, too happy with her news. Already, she rub her belly. She only two months.

"'You wait till you tell everyone, right?' She say yes."

My grandmother peers into the tiny cup she caresses with both hands. Shakes her head from side to side.

"These the worst days. We make hope these days. We make plans. She 'Mama,' me 'Nonna,' Arturo 'Papa.' Ah'm-a ready. I buy the wool. To knit."

A month later, Nani was in her flannel nightdress and bathrobe when, barefoot and frightened, she opened her front door to an insistent knock.

"Ah'm-a see you papa at the door. He frantic. He tell me, 'Ana in operation. We go to hospital. Our baby gone.'

"I go, dress quick and we leave. In the car, we quiet. Ah'm-a say the Rosary.

"At the hospital you mama, she still have the operation. Arturo e me, we tired, afraid. We wait.

"When the doctor, he come, Arturo jump up. The baby gone, but Ana okay. She lose one 'tubes'? The doctor say Ana still be able to have a baby. He tell Arturo wait three month before they try again."

Arturo shook the surgeon's hand.

"He want to cry. I pray for you mama and the baby."

An hour later, the nurse admitted Arturo to his wife's recovery area.

"Arturo take me to Ana's bed. Lots of beeping, lots of nurses in Ana's room. Ana very pale, she so sad. I pat her hair, kiss her. We wait for her to talk. She just look at you papa. He take her hand and she say, 'Mi dispiace—I'm sorry.' Ana so sad. My heart break.

"I go home to Arturo and Ana's. She stay in the hospital one week.

"We go every day. Zia come too some days. Third day, when we come in, she walk in the hallway. Ah'm-a sure she have pain, she hold her stomach and she very slow. Underneath her eyes very dark. Arturo, he take her arm in his. She smile a little. My heart break when I see her, but I know she gonna get better."

Arturo and Nunzia agreed that Nunzia would be with them when his wife returned home.

"We go with Ana in the wheelchair to the hospital door. She say she a little dizzy, but no pain.

"When we come home, Arturo e me, we call the people to tell them what's happen. Ana need a lot of care. Her food not right—she not hungry—but Ah'm-a make pastina, rice, little bit of chicken. Everything with no spice. She eat. Bread with olive oil and basil. I start to add a little Parmesan to her pastina and rice. She like.

"These days they still so sad. Arturo and me, so worry. Zia too. You mama want to see her, so she come."

According to Nani, time moved more quickly than my mother's recovery. Arturo spent a lot of time with her, but she was slow to allow herself to be around people outside of him, Nani and Zia.

A gathering of close friends was planned to welcome Concetta and Giuseppe's visit to the city from their home in Spring Valley in upstate New York. Ana looked forward to going.

"You mama, she come in with you papa. She so happy to see Concetta. They go to the living room together. Arturo e me, with Zia, we come behind.

"You mama, she see all the kids in the room, playing, laughing, yelling. One new mama show her baby to everyone. They all take turns holding and rocking. Ana get a bad look on her face. I think she panic.

"Concetta e me. We get Arturo, who grab you mama and get her out.

"Ana, she no cry until we sit in the car. Then she cry so hard, she almost no breathe. I hold her from the back but she no stop. We get home an' Arturo tuck her into bed. He stay in the bedroom on a chair with her.

"Next day, she apologize. Arturo e me, we ask, 'What for?'

"Slow, but she get better. Zia, she say she need a new dress. You mama sew this. Ah'm-a teach her make pizzelle cookies, you know, the ones they look like lace? You mama love these.

"Arturo, he quiet, but he watch Ana very close. People not thinking, they say bad things. They want her to be Ana again, but they nosy too. *Well, you over this by now, right? You gonna try again? It happens a lot—be careful if you try again.* I ask them, 'What you know about this? How many kids you got? Five, right?' And Zia Maria ask, 'Over? What you think—it's an airplane flying over?'

"You mama count three months for the days her baby was gone. Then, the next month, I see Ana smooth her stomach. She ask Arturo to take her to her friend baby shower. I ask why she do this. She tell me she prove for Arturo and her that she okay.

"But she not okay. Once we in the grocery store. I need the baby powder. She walk me to the, you know, the top of the row. But she no come down with me. I see all the baby things. And smell the baby smell.

"She no talk about the baby. She just stay quiet.

"I worry, but Ana no talk. And Arturo he no speak about what Ana feel.

"One Sunday supper, Arturo, he tell us Ana expecting again. Ah'm-a happy. I pray everything go good. She scare the whole time. She lose this baby too.

"This time, more sad, she speak only with Arturo.

"Inside, Ah'm-a know they gonna have a baby. It take one year. She come home, tell Arturo she pregnant. She tell me she scare, but happy too.

"When she reach seven month, she believe she have you. She rub her tummy in the mirror. She laugh. We all know you come.

"I knit a lot. You mama sew for you, for her. She like to show Arturo and Zia and me what she make. She so happy, an' Ah'm-a so happy. Arturo an' you mama dance in the kitchen."

I asked Nani about my mother's labor with me.

"She never yell," Nani told me. "She just grab Arturo hand. He give her ice and wipe her face."

After twenty-six painful, writhing, sweat-drenched hours of labor I did come. From all reports I announced my arrival by screaming loudly. I would, everyone agreed, always be mouthy.

Nani told me, "She cry—so happy! She show Arturo an' me every part of you. We no stop to touch you. Arturo say, 'She ours for sure.'"

CHAPTER 17

Ana, Explained

I relive my conversation with Nani as I head back to my mother's house. I stop at the Italian deli on Tremont, indulge my food mood, and score fresh mozzarella, crusty Calabrese bread and fresh figs that I hope will suit Ana's mood.

Holding the door wide, she hugs me with her free arm and kisses me.

"What did you buy?" she asks, pulling back the edge of the bag. "Oh, figs! These will be great on the Calabrese with olives."

My mother and I do not discuss my visit with Nani. We share our appetizers and her spectacular veal and polenta. We laugh about my behavior as a child, always decisive and vocal. Forever calling for ham and chicken soup. And, naturally, bread and pasta.

I remember my father laughing at my stubbornness. Even at a young age. "I'm sure," he always said, "you got this from your mother."

When I was young, I heard my mother tell him: "She has a very strong will. If she wants to do something, it's done. If not, it will never happen." I remember my father's laughter and her eyes, a flash of light in his direction.

We spend a great night together, comparing favorite films and favorite books. Discussing how we prepare favorite foods. I rarely feel this close to Ana. Why don't I invite this mother to join me more frequently?

Tomorrow is Tuesday. The lab waits for me. I am ready to leave by six o'clock. I regret having no time for a run. But I do have breakfast with my mother.

Nani's account of Ana's disappointment and sorrow is more than I can bear. Mustering new respect for my mother's determination, I wonder how she and my father found the courage to keep trying.

I am almost heartbroken when I leave her at the front door, hugging herself, smiling and waving. I blow her another kiss and head down the concrete steps. My father's death always looms large. As always, I am nagged by uncertainty that I will see her again.

Knowing my mother's story leaves me selfishly disquieted. What if the same thing happens to Russ and me? Would we keep trying? Would I *want* to keep trying? Or would I retreat into work and turn the page? If I didn't have a child, would I always be sad? Would we adopt? How would I feel about a child who wasn't genetically ours?

The scientist supplants these thoughts. Reasonably, I remind myself that we don't know the cause of my mother's issues. Medicine has advanced since my mother's reproductive years. If it was hormonal, it could be supplemented and corrected.

I settle my rump into the seat and wrap my hands around the steering wheel. I drive convincing myself that there is no use thinking up disasters that aren't happening. Save energy, I tell myself, for the ones that will inevitably happen.

I call Russ when I get to the lab, happy that I will see him in a few hours. Until then, my time belongs to the lab. One by one, everyone appears at my door with the same lure and hook. *Got a minute?*

I review lab results and redo part of a lecture I will deliver in a few days. Time runs away from me. It is eight o'clock when I check my watch.

I call Russ, who greets me with a chuckle and, "Let me guess, you'll be late?"

"Need anything?"

"Just you, before dinner goes bad and we have to order out."

I assure him I'm on my way, grab my computer and briefcase and lock my office door.

When I arrive home, I toss my overnight case past the vestibule and run into Russ's hug. He brushes the errant hair back from my forehead, gently grazes my cheek with his and asks if I'm tired.

"Not anymore." We join each other on the sofa, enjoying the moment until Russ gives his thigh a decisive slap.

"You've got to be as hungry as me," he announces.

"I'll go wash up," I say as I sprint to the bathroom and reappear a few minutes later in our dining area.

"Wow, this is fancy; anyone else coming?"

"Tonight, no room for anyone but you and me." He pulls me into a gentle hug. We linger that way.

Russ is a great cook. Roast chicken stuffed with barley seasoned with lemon, thyme and rosemary. Spinach and arugula salad, fennel and red wine vinaigrette. Eggplant pureed with tomatoes and garlic, fresh salad with olive oil and balsamic vinegar. The aroma is intoxicating.

Over dinner, I finish describing Nani's version of my mother's reproductive history. Shaking his head in disbelief, Russ pushes a tablespoon full of barley toward the edge of his plate.

"Explains a lot about her strictness with you, don't you think?"

I crunch on salad and fennel between words.

"How do you mean?"

"Well . . ." He pauses, treating the corners of his mouth to one of our best linen napkins. "Think about it. Even after her lost pregnancies, she was, from the sound of things, very carefree with your dad—really happy, never thinking that things would change for years at least. So she could afford never to be critical; just let things flow. Until your father died."

Russ has a knack for spot-on accuracy.

I pick up on his insight. "So, she's protecting herself and me by controlling everything and being critical of me? Her insurance against bad things happening?"

"For sure, it's just speculation, but I think it's got some teeth." He tips more water into my glass and goes back to his chicken. I continue with my salad.

I am always looking over my shoulder, disapproval sticking to me like cheap dime-store perfume. I thought I'd given up caring. I have not. When I see her in my mind's eye, Ana's square jaw is set, listening to me as she reinvents what I speak and waits for what she needs me to say and do. All to protect both of us.

The next morning, I turn this over in my mind on the way to the lab.

CHAPTER 18

Zia's Confession

A rare phone call from my grandmother. "Call you mothah," Nani commands. "She want you call, but she no ask."

My mother is cheerful. Too cheerful. There's something underneath that she's keeping to herself.

"Ma, you okay?"

"Sure. What would be wrong?"

Yeah. I wouldn't know, would I?

"You would tell me, right?"

"So"—she ignores the question—"what about the wedding?"

"Everything's ready, Ma."

"You come home. You have to try on your clothes."

"Okay. I'll check with Russ. We'll come together."

"But he shouldn't see you, you know."

"Ma, he's seen my birthday suit, my wedding suit won't shock him."

She scolds, "Oh! Watch your language with me!"

She presses on. "Sure you don't want a dress just to get married in? Then wear the suit after. I saw some beautiful material last week at Matteo's."

I find myself enjoying her light small talk. But there's something she's not telling me.

The feeling nags me for the next week. When we talk about visiting the Bronx, I tell Russ about my latest anxiety.

Skepticism and a trace of worry write themselves across his face. "So what do you think she's holding back?"

"I have no idea, but I think I know how to find out."

Zia can't keep a secret. I hate to manipulate her. I've done it in the past, but she's easy to trap into letting loose what she knows.

She's surprised to hear from me. I endure the numbing small talk with my aunt that only she can engage in. In less than five minutes, I learn the baking secrets that get her invited to all the scopa games among her friends. "They don't play if I can't come. I always bring biscotti and my cannoli." One-sided laughter. "I'm famous!"

I assure her that she is.

I tell her I've just spoken to my mom. "Oh, yeah?! Me too." There's something forced about her admission. My gut begins to clench.

"Great to hear her sounding so good."

My insides lurch at the endless pause.

"Oh, yeah," she assures me. A little too enthusiastically. Another pause. My aunt is the queen of embellishment. This is where she should go on and on about all her outings with her sister. She adores my mother, and my heart hurts because Nani does not favor her second daughter.

Surprisingly, she changes the subject. "You call Claire? She'd love to talk to you."

"I need to do that, Zia. I miss her a lot!" I feel her sigh of satisfaction over the phone.

"So, what's up with you and my mom? What have you been doing? Gone anywhere good?"

This time, her sigh is charged with worry.

"Listen, Gaby. Don't tell your mother—she'll be angry at me for sure—but she's seeing a couple doctors. For her lungs, she get short of breath sometimes and she cough. But she say she okay. So don't worry."

Really? How can I not worry? My mother is the only living member of my immediate family. I caress my forehead, close my eyes.

"Gaby? Maybe not a good idea to tell you. She still need to see the doctors."

"Who is she seeing?"

"Dr. Miller, I think, for her breathing, and Dr. Fleming. Lung doctor and cancer doctor."

Cancer doctor. "When?"

"Next month. Maybe soon—I forget. She'll tell me, I go with her. She got to have blood tests and I think X-rays? Before she go."

Next *month*? I imagine Zia squirming in her chair when they see the doctors.

I need to get off the phone.

I tell her I will speak with my mother about coming to the Bronx for her appointments. "Zia," I tell her, "I'm so glad to talk to you. Thank you for telling me what's going on. I will speak with Claire before I come."

Zia finishes our call with: "She doesn't tell you because she wants that you don't worry."

Right. My palms are sweaty, my emotions a runaway train. I'm in a no-thinking tunnel.

Could she really be sick? Will she need the oncologist? Maybe it's nothing a week's worth or even an intravenous course of antibiotics wouldn't take care of. I have a distinctly bad feeling about this. And I want my mother to spill the beans. Find out how long she's been symptomatic.

But I have to get myself under control. Mixing anger and fear is a suffocating cocktail of chlorine bleach and ammonia. If I call Ana like this, not only will I lose my breath, she'll eat me for breakfast. With espresso.

The thought of her as anything but Herculean is anathema. I realize, in a rush, that my tenacity, my determination, is hers. I wonder, selfishly, how quickly those will disappear if she is no longer here. I can barely formulate the thought.

Woozy and unsure of my footing, I rush to the study to find Russ. Forced into abandoning his glasses and his computer screen, he jumps from his seat and hurries toward me.

Alarm prompts Russ's "*What?*" I start blubbering in response and he grabs for me, holding my head against his chest.

He rescues me by handing over his handkerchief. I catch my breath and choke on the words.

"I think my mother has cancer."

"You spoke to her?"

"No. Zia."

He smooths my hair. "Zia! How many times a day does your aunt get things wrong? Leo 'missing' on a camping trip out west? And then he wanders in with a walking stick he found on his hike. Lorna can't walk anymore—up and around two weeks later, recovered from a sprained ankle."

"No. This is different. Zia knew the doctors' names. And my mother has appointments after her tests."

"So what made your mother go to the doctor?"

"Shortness of breath, coughing 'sometimes,' Zia says. Something tells me a lot more than *sometimes*."

"So what do you want to do?"

"I've got to get her to tell me what's going on. She'll be her usual stubborn self. Then I've got to be there when she's tested and when she gets her results. I want to talk to the respirologist and the oncologist myself. She'll do everything she can to keep me from doing that."

Russ nods. Gentles the strands of my hair and holds me at arms' length. "I'm coming with you."

I ask myself if this is really happening. Evidently, it is. Me, the scientist, concluding without evidence that this is bad. But I am very sure.

With Russ's help I calm down, adopt a cheerful affect and call my mother.

We ask about each other, and then she asks, "How's Russ?"

I can feel her smiling when I say, "Chomping at the bit to be your son-in-law."

"Of course he is!"

"Listen, Ma, I want to ask . . . Zia says you have some doctors' appointments coming up? Who are you seeing?"

"Oh, it's nothing. I'm coughing some."

"Your breathing?"

"I have to catch my breath when I carry too many groceries. Oh, I get gorgeous fresh mozzarella and provolone, like Papa used to sell on Arthur Avenue! Remember?"

Nice try, Ma. "When are your tests? And don't say you don't know."

I get my pencil and paper ready and write down two dates three weeks in the future.

"And the doctors' appointments? I want both of them."

"Who are you? Another one of my doctors? Why do you ask all this? It's very rude!"

"Okay, so I'm rude. Let me ask you one more question: If you found out I couldn't breathe and had a lingering cough, what would you do?"

"You crazy! What'd Nani tell you? I breathe just fine!"

"Answer the question, Ma."

After we wait each other out through the silence, I hear her riffle through some papers, no doubt on the kitchen counter. She literally coughs up the appointment dates, scheduled for the week after her tests. I tell her I'm coming.

She sighs and starts digging into her protest. I stop her and tell her when we're coming. I have no idea what to do about the lab. Or how it will affect Russ's work. But we'll figure it out.

I tell Russ what's going on and he agrees to block the time off.

If she wasn't scared, she would have blamed Zia for telling me, not Nani, and for my overreacting. If she wasn't scared, she wouldn't have agreed to our visit so quickly. If she wasn't as scared as I am, there would not have been that strong note of relief in her voice when I confirmed the dates.

I see my chair, who has a soft spot for my family affairs because my father died so young. Then I turn attention to the experiments and the writing coming up in the lab. I divide the manuscripts among myself and two senior postdocs. Trent, I decide, will supervise the lab while I'm gone.

Russ and I don't ask each other the what-if question about our wedding. To my mind, the after-party is dispensable frolicking. If need arises, city hall will be fine with me. Either way, I will be dressed in my mother's suit.

Time evaporates like droplets off a freshly watered lawn. Each morning, I eye the calendar with suspicion and a dollop of dread. Everything is in slow motion, surreal. I adopt bad statistical thinking. Fifty-fifty odds. She's really sick or she's not. Nothing in between.

I try my don't-go-through-that-door technique for keeping doom at bay. I have no confidence that it will work this time.

On our way to the Bronx, I find myself choking on my words when I try to speak. Russ keeps me in his peripheral vision, quietly piloting us south. I have too much time to think. I am too anxious. How do I keep my anxiety under control as I face the reality of my mother's health, whatever state it's in?

Two specialists. One pulmonary. One oncologic. This can't be good. When we stop for a bathroom break, I rest my forehead against the inside of the stall door. I shake with worry and long to cry. Try to convince myself nothing is really wrong.

When we arrive, Claire greets us at the door to my mother's house. I'm glad it's not Zia wringing her handkerchief into a spitball. Claire hugs and kisses us both, tries a happy smile that falls short. "How's my mother?" I ask.

"She gets winded real easy; can't walk too far. She'll be glad you're both here."

I don't wonder where Ana is. I try casually to waltz into her sanctuary. She's sitting at the kitchen table, spotless apron in her lap, sharing espresso with Nani and Zia. Claire's abandoned cup wears the spongy evidence of the crema halo that sat on top of the espresso.

I am shocked at Zia's calm. Her gentle hand keeps my mother in her seat. I rush to Ana, trying to keep my wobbly legs in check. Nani balances on the back of Ma's chair, wipes her hands on her apron and meets me at my mother's side.

I hug Nani and Zia and bend to eye level over my mother. Russ starts, then thinks better of joining me.

"What?" she demands. "Why did you come? It's nothing!" But there's relief in her eyes. By the time we're finished sharing hugs, Russ is beside me, embracing her, asking how she is.

"It's just age," she tries, lamely. "I'm a little tired; can't carry so much, can't walk so far." Her voice is just the wrong side of hoarse. I can tell she is doing her best to mask a need to draw breath with every other word.

"You let Zia help?" I ask. Maria nods, proud to do for her sister. Claire stands over Zia's chair, caressing her mother's shoulders. Zia turns briefly toward her daughter. Pats her hand. So far, Nani is silent, her mouth tight and pale, her head almost imperceptibly rocking from side to side. For me, so far, this is the scariest part.

She pats her lap with both hands, stands, and announces, "Ah'm-a make supper." Rising from her chair, she motions Zia to stay put and points my way. "You, Gaby, come with me." An order. I exchange raised eyebrows with Russ. Zia obediently reclaims her seat.

In the kitchen. "Nani," I start, but she raises her hand in a show of silence.

"No," she orders. "You mama, she sick. I no like. She no breathe good. She no walk right. She no wanna cook o shop. She try to laugh—she only cough. Bad. What you think?"

"Nani, I can't tell. Only the doctors can tell us."

"You think it's the cancer?"

Seeing my grandmother scared is, so far, worse than anything I have imagined. "Let's not think anything until we hear from the doctors." I'm exerting a Herculean effort to be calm, but my insides are caught in the hurricane worrying the stone I've swallowed since Russ and I left Boston.

My grandmother has already started preparing a stracciatella—the Italian egg-drop soup that is one of my mother's favorites. I see chicken marinating in lemon and capers for us. She points to one of the cabinets. "Water for the pasta. Make the ditalini. It's small."

I'm quiet, running on autopilot as I carry out Nani's directives. Neither of us is making conversation.

Almost finished preparing, my grandmother commands me to go "fresh up." A sigh of relief treats me to one of her knowing looks and permission to go. Zia and Claire have set the table, their eyes searching me as if I know more than I did when I followed Nani into the kitchen.

"Go," says Zia. "Take a shower if you need. Your mother is lying down. Russ took her up." Claire concentrates on the table as she continues arranging serving pieces.

"Listen," I say, more for my benefit than for anyone else's. "We won't know anything until the end of the week, after the doctors meet with us. Pray for the best and we'll be able to deal with what comes. Okay?"

Claire looks down at the table and nods. Zia is quivering. But she controls herself.

Struggling for calm, I head upstairs.

Russ is reading, gently rocking in my mother's bedside chair to Ana's light snoring. He hugs my arm as I slip it around his shoulders from behind.

I burrow into his neck and raise my head to focus on my mother.

Her bluish lips accent an exhausted, gray, otherworldly expression. Solitary steel hairs wind their way through thick damp black curls. A sheen of clamminess oils her face. One hand grasps the blanket to her neck. Breath comes with effort, but she is peaceful.

Russ pats his lap and, like a five-year-old, I climb on. "What will we find out when she sees the doctor?" I ask. He places his book on Ana's nightstand.

"What's already been decided," he tells me, speaking truth. I know we both suspect that there is no comfort in this truth.

I must have truth. Truth rooted in reality. To bear it, I must also separate myself from the reality. It's important for me to be dispassionate so I can face the consequences of the truth.

We sit together, quietly watching her. When I was a girl, feverish, coughing, she did this for me. I'd ask for more tissues and ginger ale. She'd hold the straw for me so I wouldn't spill, and I wouldn't have to sit up. She served me saltine crackers with grape jelly on one of her good china plates. I would lick my finger to pick up grains of salt and shards of cracker stuck to damp sheets, and to me.

When we finally emerge downstairs, I tell everyone we shouldn't wait for Ana to have dinner.

Claire heats the soup, ladles it into the tureen. I lay the bread on the cutting board with the good knife. Mix olive oil and balsamic vinegar into the small porcelain saucer, crush some oregano into it and place the saucer next to the knife.

In my guilt, I realize that I can breathe freely only down here, away from my mother. When I'm with her, minute by minute I fear that the hesitant rise and fall of her chest will cease and that I will be there to witness it.

Downstairs, we eat to the sound of spoons scraping bowls. We speak in low, polite tones. Pass bread and salad. Make the chicken slowly disappear under Nani's stern unspoken instruction to fill our plates. "No worry," she says, "I save everything for Ana." Zia keeps her eye on the staircase, a silent voice willing her sister to join us.

Zia retreats to the kitchen. Water pours. The refrigerator opens and closes. The cabinets offer up plates, the drawers cutlery and serving utensils. My aunt carries a tray with everything onto the dining table. Anticipating the hiss of the espresso maker, she returns to the kitchen. As she waits, she stacks the cups. She passes Russ as he buses the table. He caresses my shoulder as he makes it past the back of my chair.

Nani is lost in her thoughts. I wonder if she is imagining my mother as her younger self. On the ship? At her wedding to Carlo? At the birth of her only surviving daughter? At Carlo's death? Arturo's?

I am restless. Claire and I catch up quietly through the distraction of my mother's condition and her absence. We have both adopted a fascination with the empty staircase. I am torn between wanting to stay downstairs and wanting to go up. I want to force her to wake up, to be healthy and managing everything. I envy Zia, who is knitting, pulling out her ruler every so often, inspecting the tightness of her stitches. She is lost in her work. For once, I wish I could knit.

Installed on the living room chairs and exhausted by tiramisu and espresso, Claire and I pull out our computers and pretend to work as we wait for Ana to show signs that she will join us. Nani has set her hook to a new crochet project. Zia forces her eyes on her knitting. Russ tucks his legs beneath him and sits near me, reading his latest novel. Each of us recognizes the staircase as the fulcrum of our attention.

My email response is interrupted by the sound of flushing, then of running water from upstairs. I jump from my seat.

"No!" my grandmother orders. "Let her come down slow, herself. She feel better this way. I go get the soup. Gaby, come. You bring the bread and make more espresso."

I fear Ana will simply return to bed. What if she's not able to handle the stairs? What if she starts coughing and she falls? What if she doesn't start coughing and she falls?

I follow my grandmother's instructions, tabling the place setting for my mother, water, bread and olive oil / balsamic vinegar. I feel like I will wait forever to hear her footfalls on the steps, the squeak of the fourth step.

She arrives. When she is seated at the table, Ana is under Nani's protection. She has warned us not to crowd her. We obey without question.

"You sleep, Ana?"

"Sì, Mama."

Mama. My mother uses this address most sparingly.

Nani nods. Places the shallow dish of soup in front of her daughter, points at the steaming surface,

"You eat everything, okay? We got lots more. An' chicken too, if you want."

"I'm good for now, Ma. Grazie." She tries a pale smile and begins coughing. Russ tops her glass of water. She nods her thanks and picks up her shovel-sized spoon.

Lightly massaging my mother's shoulders, Zia stands behind my mother's chair and swallows hard.

Ana manages four spoonfuls of soup and mashes a wedge of bread into the broth. Pronounces herself fed and sated. Tries smiling again. "It's good, Ma."

Nani nods. "Yeah. You want more later, we got plenty."

Ana asks, "What time do we go tomorrow?"

As if sharing a single neck, all heads swivel in my direction. "Our appointment's at nine. I figure we should leave at seven thirty. Russ?"

"Sounds good. That's what we'll do."

I pick up my mother's bowl and utensils. "Ma, you have your insurance and papers?"

She touches her napkin to her mouth and nods. "Gaby, I have everything."

She always does.

After she eats and we share the plan for tomorrow's doctor visit, Russ helps Ana to negotiate a slow climb up the stairs. The contrast with her accustomed energetic step, full of purpose, breaks my heart.

Nani watches worriedly until her daughter is out of sight. I bite the inside of my cheek. I am afraid of what I will learn tomorrow.

I clear my throat and incline my head in Maria's direction. "Zia? You'll get here by seven thirty? Claire, I hope you're coming, but I get it if you can't."

Claire nods vigorously. "Yes, of course. I'm staying with Ma tonight." Claire turns to Zia. "We'll be ready to go, Ma, at seven o'clock, okay? Then we'll pick Nani up."

Zia plucks her handkerchief out of her pocket. "I'll be ready."

"Nani? Seven fifteen okay?"

"Sure. Sure."

Russ rejoins us. Assuring us that Ana is settled in bed and already asleep, he rests for a moment at the dining table and retreats to the kitchen. We hear the sounds of his cleaning up the dregs of a meal with too many unspoken issues, too many questions. Too much anxiety.

Zia starts. She directs her question at me. "What will we find out?"

I know we've covered this before, but I understand why the question is being asked again. "She's not okay. We just have to wait to find out what's going on."

We spend a restless night. I depend on being in Russ's arms as he strokes my hair and my shoulders. When I come down the next morning, my mother is at the table, offering me coffee and biscotti. The dress she's wearing is familiar to me. But it hangs on a new, too-small frame.

"Did you sleep, Ma?"

She's become a careful liar. Her eyes are rimmed in rust, her cheeks have lost their color. I hug her and pour myself an espresso as Russ makes his way into the room.

"Great," he says. "We've got lots of time." He pours himself a coffee and grabs a cookie from the tray. Kisses Ana on the cheek.

"You want some eggs or something, Russ?"

He smiles at her.

"Only if I can make some for you, too, Ana." She smiles back, nods.

Russ looks my way. "Gaby?"

Well, if they're having eggs, I'll have eggs. I nod in Russ's direction.

Russ extends his hand in my direction as I sit down.

Ana's eyes are resigned, not worried. She knows already what the news will be. She's tired but she won't give in. I indulge her luxury of small talk.

Russ delivers three plates of cheesy scrambled eggs and buttered toast to the kitchen table.

Ana places her fork on her plate. "This is good, Russ. Gaby, I think you should marry him."

Russ's laughter is contagious.

Ana actually eats most of what's on her plate. I wonder if she realizes she needs to fortify herself for the day ahead. I know I do.

I hear my grandmother's firm footsteps in the front hallway, along with uncharacteristically muted conversation between Nani and Zia. I sense Nani is dispensing instructions. Followed by Claire's calm assurance. "Everyone will be fine, Nani. We'll all behave."

Looking back toward Maria and Claire, Nani starts toward the kitchen and responds, "Yeah. I know everyone behave."

As they enter the room, we stand and share kisses all around. We're anxious to go.

Russ clears the table. My mother offers espresso and biscotti to the latecomers. As expected, no takers.

Russ wipes his hands, grabs his keys, and zips down the concrete stairs to make sure the car is ready.

We have all gathered at the front door. I hand my mother her purse. She opens it carefully, pulls out her insurance card and other documents and flashes them at me.

I support her arm in mine. Hand the keys to Claire to lock the front door.

My mother moves slowly, but her gait is as determined as ever. When we reach the car, Russ tucks Ana into the passenger seat. Smiles between them, my mother patting his hand as he secures her seat belt.

I sit behind her, straining my own seat belt as she reaches for my hands on her shoulders.

Allowing for Bronx traffic, the hospital is thirty minutes away. We arrive at the hospital lobby with fifteen minutes to spare.

"Listen, Ma. We shouldn't crowd the doctor's office. Only two of us, besides you, should go in. Who do you want?" I hate to put her on the spot, but I don't want her to agonize over this, especially knowing her sensitivity to Zia's feelings.

She surprises me by answering immediately. She has thought this through. "You, Gaby, you and Nani come."

Nani nods. "Sure. Okay."

Russ takes note of Claire's arm tightening around Zia's shoulder.

I check my mother in and we all sit. I bring my mother a plastic cup full of water. She takes a sip, begins coughing as I rescue the cup from her hand. I offer to guide her to the washroom. When she recovers her voice, she tells me to stop fussing. "I'm okay," she insists.

We wait a ten-minute eternity. I feel myself fidgeting but can't seem to get it under control. Looking straight ahead, Nani sits to the left of my mother. She links her arm through Ana's elbow and rests her free hand on Ana's arm. She shakes her head when I ask if she needs anything.

Finally, Dr. Miller's resident is at the door. "Mrs. Pecorero, Ana?"

My mother rises from her chair, followed by Nani and me. "My daughter and my mother are coming, okay?"

"Yes, of course. Follow me, please."

We follow.

Dr. Miller rises and walks toward our side of the wide mahogany desk. His walls advertise his degrees and awards, the American Thoracic Society Edward Livingston Trudeau Medal and the American Thoracic Society Outstanding Clinician Award among them. Medical school—Columbia University, New York. Residency—Cedars-Sinai, New York. We are in NewYork-Presbyterian/Weill Cornell Hospital Center, the site of his practice.

On his desk stands a pull-apart puzzle of a set of lungs attached to vessels and airways. He smiles and greets my mother, who introduces us. We accept his invitation to have a seat, my mother smoothing the seat of her dress as she sits. And coughs.

Dr. Miller invites my mother to describe how she's been feeling.

"I'm really okay."

My grandmother chimes in. "No. She not okay. No."

"Is this true, Ana? If it is, you must tell me what you have been feeling."

My mother shoots her annoyance in Nani's direction. And begins to tell her story.

Coughing. Chest pain. Not a lot of breath. Tiredness. Voice changes. Can't get to sleep.

"How is your appetite?"

"Good," my mother lies again.

"No," Nani says, "she no eat hardly nothing."

"Do you usually eat well?"

Nani fills him in. "Dottore, we Italian. We always eat good."

The doctor smiles and returns his attention to his patient. He asks us to step out while he examines her.

"Ah'm-a gonna tell him she lose a lot of weight. She so skinny."

"Nani, I'm so glad because you've seen everything."

"But I no like what I see."

Ten minutes pass before he calls us back.

He explains that the physical findings and the imaging he ordered a few weeks before are consistent. He's glad we are seeing the oncologist in a few days.

Holding my breath, I ask, "Do you suspect lung cancer?"

"Let's see what Dr. Fleming says. Right now, we can rule out infection. But her lung function is compromised, and her stamina is taking a beating."

Once again, Nani contributes. "An' she too skinny, no?"

"How much weight have you lost in the past two months, Ana?"

"Oh, not much, maybe five pounds."

"No. Like twenty—this dress fall off her now. Before, it fit nice. She make it, so it fit nice before."

Our visit is winding down.

"I will communicate with your family doctor and with Dr. Fleming."

He tells my mother to rest and to drink a liquid diet supplement.

"It will help, Ana, to stall your weight loss, but you have to drink it."

I am taking notes.

"Sleep propped up on pillows. It will help your coughing and breathing."

He smiles and ushers us from his office. Comes to the door and calls me back inside.

Dr. Miller asks, "How long has it been since you've seen your mother?"

I notice for the first time how relatively young he is. Clear, kind brown eyes, shiny auburn hair, straight, parted on the left, shaggy on the right side of his forehead. A prominent dimple on his left cheek. Evenly white teeth and large, soft, self-manicured hands.

"About three months. I live in Boston."

"What changes have you noticed?"

"She has no energy—very odd for her—and no breath. Every conversation brings on coughing. I haven't seen blood, but I wouldn't be surprised to hear that she has had blood in her sputum. And my grandmother's right—last time I saw my mother she was, well, robust. Now we can barely see her when she stands sideways, and she is hardly eating. Also not like her."

His eyes lock on to mine. "I see. The imaging looks suspicious, but we'll know more after we hear from Dr. Fleming. For now, let's make sure she's comfortable. And get some nutrition in her. Ensure or Boost is okay, but if there's food she really likes, go for it."

I want to ask what *suspicious* means, but he's used the word together with the oncologist's name. That answers my question.

We settle into the car, Nani announcing that we're going back to her apartment. "Ah'm-a make the lunch this morning before we leave. We eat. You too, Ana."

Nani, she who must be obeyed.

"How are you, Ma?"

"Okay. Tired a little."

"What do you think about what Dr. Miller had to say?"

"We wait on Dr. Fleming, right? So I think it's probably cancer."

A sharp intake of breath from Zia. She clutches Claire's hand. Challenging her daughter's self-control, Nani throws a menacing look Zia's way.

I lamely offer that we don't know anything yet for sure, but we'll deal with whatever it is.

Russ eyes my mother in the passenger seat. "Ana, you need to stop off for anything?"

"No, Russ. I'm good."

Nani pipes up. "Ah'm-a need good bread from Tremont. We go, Russ."

"Sure, Nani." He bleeds onto Tremont traffic, parks with hazard lights flashing and runs across to the bakery. He comes back with the points of two crusty loaves poking out of a paper bag and a greasy-bottomed box wrapped in string. I'm sure it's my mother's favorite tiramisu.

At Nani's, Russ hangs back to help my mother out of the car. Nani has her slippers on, and her apron tied by the time they get to the door.

Lemon. Chicken. Roasted potatoes with Italian herbs. Green beans with olive oil. Fresh garlic, the staple of every meal. Click of the gas pilot as my grandmother sets the pans to heat. As I watch her wrap the dish towel around the pot handles, I wonder again how she manages to avoid a kitchen fire.

Claire and I slice bread and set the table, place olive-oil-balsamic-and-herb saucers out, and get the espresso maker ready. Sanpellegrino for everyone. Ice. We're ready as Nani ushers in the first platter of food and instructs me to "bring the insalata—salad."

Ana takes her place next to Nani, across from me. She manages a smile, says grace, and Nani commands us to "mangiare—eat."

We don't discuss the doctor's visit. I know now, without a doubt, that my mother is suffering from lung cancer. Discussing it, especially with her smiling and eating, is not on the menu.

Nani nods in Maria's direction. Maria rises. In a quick minute, we hear the espresso maker being charged with coffee and the sound of the refrigerator door.

Zia emerges with the tiramisu, plates, cups and cutlery. She heads back to the kitchen for the espresso. When she returns, I pour and Claire leaves to make another pot. My mother, happy, chuckles with Russ, who squeezes her shoulder. My heart breaks but soars for the first time in days even as my mind wanders to the coming appointment with Dr. Fleming.

Somewhat breathlessly, Ana speaks with everyone with more energy than I've seen on this visit. She carries her fatigue in sunken eyes and in her shoulders, but she's not giving in.

Russ shuttles plates of tiramisu round the table. Places the knife in the pan, rounds his eyes and treats my mother to a huge smile when her hand motions *more*.

We stay only a short time after lunch. My mother, I know, needs to sleep, and I need to research Dr. Fleming.

Day after tomorrow. I remind myself that we can move only forward, wherever it leads. We cannot change what is already happening.

At the front door, my grandmother leans into me and whispers, "She eat better when you here." I draw her in for a hug and cheek kisses.

My mother dozes on the short ride from Nani's to her home. Russ supports her climb to the front door. But she is winded and wheezing by the time I unlock it.

"Upstairs, Ana?" Russ queries. "No, no, the sofa," she insists.

"Ma, I'll get you a pillow and a comforter."

"Okay." I can't remember when I have seen my mother sleep on the sofa. Ever.

I prop her up on three pillows, drape the comforter around her and kiss her cheek.

Three o'clock. I wonder if she will wake later this day or if she'll sleep through the night.

From the wing chair, Russ maintains a bird's-eye view on my mother. I let him know I'm heading upstairs to check out Dr. Fleming. He nods, returns his attention to his book. And to Ana.

Dr. Fleming is also top drawer. Undergraduate medical training at the University of Michigan–Ann Arbor—second in his graduating class. Respirology and oncology training at the Mayo Clinic, Rochester. Chief resident at Memorial Sloan Kettering, his current professional home.

Distinguished Service Award from the International Association for the Study of Lung Cancer, Lifetime Achievement Award from the American Thoracic Society, among others. I review his publications, learn that he specializes in the management of late-stage metastatic lung cancers. Especially non-small cell lung cancer. I decide I'll let him treat my mother.

I check my lab email, deciding that responses can wait until tomorrow. Five-year survival for advanced non-small cell lung cancer is a bleak 8 percent. Immunotherapy, from a potential menu of monoclonal antibodies—pembrolizumab, nivolumab, durvalumab, atezolizumab—is indicated for some patients. Tomorrow's research for me.

After a restless hour in the living room, Ana wakes briefly and allows Russ to guide her upstairs. They walk slowly and deliberately, at my mother's pace.

The next morning, she has espresso, a biscuit and jam and a few spoonfuls of yogurt. Her face takes on a gray hue at the offer of an egg.

"Gaby, the appointment's tomorrow, right? Not today?"

"Not today, Ma. Tomorrow. You still have your insurance and papers in your purse? What about any special papers Dr. Fleming asked you to bring?"

"Gaby, I have all my papers."

I nod and start clearing the table. Russ motions me from the kitchen, plants an index finger across his lips. Through his smile, he points toward my mother, rummaging in her purse and pulling at papers. I can hear her "Hmpf!" as she replaces everything.

Tired, she snoozes on the sofa, between showings of some of her favorite movies: *All About Eve*, *Rear Window*, *Strangers on a Train*. Her taste in films is simple: old Hollywood; film noir; Hitchcock; anything with Gregory Peck, Bing Crosby, Cary Grant, Bette Davis, Joan Crawford, Grace Kelly. Nothing with Victor Mature.

I eat popcorn and crack sunflower seeds while we watch movies. We shoot looks of surprise, fear, amusement, suspicion at all the right scenes, at the same time. These movies are a great joy to share with my mother. She refuses lunch. "I had a big breakfast," she says.

We take a break while I make supper. Russ escorts my mother up the stairs. I hear her laugh as he calls her Your Majesty.

"You go! Make yourself useful downstairs." And he's dismissed.

For supper, I prepare Italian wedding soup, paired with good crusty bread that Russ runs out to buy.

"Tiramisu?" he asks me, just before he leaves.

"Definitely. That she will always eat."

I ask him to stop at the drugstore to buy two cans of Boost and two cans of Ensure.

Exercising her unfailing sixth sense, Ana emerges just as the table is set, and just as the door announces Russ's return.

"You put out the good china." She tries to be annoyed—it's only for special occasions or special guests—but she can't quite fake it.

At supper, she decides to try the soup. Even in the face of this mostly liquid meal, she often pauses for breath. The fine sheen on her forehead advertises her discomfort.

Finishing three small meatballs and about half of the broth, she soaks a slice of bread in her bowl, signaling the end of her meal. Folds her napkin and places it next to her place setting.

"Done, Ma?"

"Yeah. It's good, Gaby. I'll have more later."

Russ rises to arrange the tiramisu and plates with forks. He starts the espresso maker and, facing us, rests both hands on the counter.

"Ready for some dessert, Ana?"

"Tiramisu, I hope," she says. When he nods his response, she says, "Ah, yes," and waits for him to serve her.

We all have some. I ask Russ to portion two slices for my mother as I pour her a small glass of Boost.

"What kind of milk is this?" she asks. "It tastes like chalk. Want me to make some espresso?"

"No, Ma, we already made some. You want?"

"Yes. And what's the milk?"

"A drink called Boost. It will help you to stop losing weight, okay?"

"I was expecting milk. And I'm not losing weight."

We watch an episode of *The Naked City* while Russ cleans up and my mother struggles to keep her eyes open.

I kiss her good night. "Sweet dreams, Ma."

"I pray to dream of your papa," she says as she rises and Russ supports her arm. He ushers her toward the staircase and upstairs.

Has she been reliving her life with my father a lot these days?

Too early the next morning, we're all ready to go. I fix breakfast for all of us, happy to see Nani smile as she shares a story with my mother. Claire is funny and lighthearted. She keeps close to Zia, who is anxious and unsettled. Nani moves around the table, whispers something in her ear, finishes with a rare look of compassion for her daughter and finds her seat.

My mother eats a single small pancake with a smear of strawberry preserves. No ham. One cantuccino—a small biscotto-like cookie—with her espresso. Dabs her mouth, lets us know she's headed to the sofa to relax. Russ pilots her into the living room. I hear him ask her if she wants the television or music. "No, grazie, figlio mio." My pleasure takes me by surprise. It's the first time I have heard Ana call Russ "son." Nani smiles meaningfully in my direction. Zia is busy controlling herself. Claire is busy controlling her mother.

I'm relieved when it's time to leave. We repeat the car routine from two days ago, everyone quiet, Russ focused on navigating my mother down the steps and into the passenger seat before he tackles Manhattan traffic. We're at Memorial Sloan Kettering with a half hour to spare.

The oncology suite of offices is, like all of Memorial, modern, high-tech, populated with busy professionals and waiting patients, many of the women without facial hair, wearing chemotherapy turbans. A melting pot of weary, happy, resigned, restless, scared faces.

We take our seats in Dr. Fleming's waiting area. I check my watch and wonder if he's running on time. No way to know. Anyway, it makes no difference. We're not going anywhere.

He comes into the waiting area right on time. He is in his late forties or early fifties, fit and slim with short-cropped dark brown hair, except for his sideburns, which have a shot of silver. A neatly knotted tie reveals itself from the V in the collar of his lab coat, bearing the Memorial Sloan Kettering logo. His name is embroidered above the logo. Advertising his profession, his hands are soft and well manicured. He greets my mother first, then offers his hand to each of us in turn.

Introductions complete, Dr. Fleming gestures toward his office door with the palm of his hand. I stand, asking if my grandmother and I can accompany Ana.

"Certainly," he assures us and ushers the three of us through the door across the corridor.

His office is airy and bright. Floor-to-ceiling windows with inside-glass shades. Spartan furniture, decoration limited to wall-mounted degrees and awards. Large-screen computer on his desk accompanied by an even larger screen set up on the wall directly behind his desk and chair.

He invites us to sit and, taking his place behind a modern blond wood desk, swivels in his chair. He tells us he is about to project my mother's latest imaging results onto the computer screens. Her lungs look like a snowscape. My gut tightens.

He asks my mother how she is feeling. Nani corrects her several times. About her breathing, her fatigue, her appetite. Same routine as with Dr. Miller.

We're asked, once again, to allow the doctor to examine my mother alone.

Nani and I spend a tense ten minutes waiting. I watch my grandmother's left hand move systematically inside the pocket of her dress. Silently, I join her in the Rosary. But I'm not praying for good news. I'm praying for the strength to take bad news.

Dr. Fleming calls us back in, re-invites us to take a seat. He compares a normal lung image side by side with Ana's. Blessedly clear, blessedly displaying a black background. Not my mother's result.

Dr. Fleming explains that we do have a diagnosis and that my mother's condition is serious. Sweat is beginning to trickle down my back. I already feel clammy.

Tapping a key on his computer, he advances to an image of what looks like brain tissue. Bingo. This, he explains, is a site to which the disease has spread.

"So this is metastatic lung cancer," I lamely offer.

"Yes," responds Dr. Fleming. "Yes, it is."

Saying nothing, my mother nods sagely. Nani focuses on her daughter and assumes a straight-backed position in her chair.

"Ana, you have a non-small cell lung cancer—the most frequent kind—stage 4A, meaning that you have cancer in your lungs and also a small tumor in your brain. This is not a brain tumor, though it is in your brain. It's part of the lung tumor that has traveled to your brain."

My mother asks what can be done.

"Well, I don't recommend surgery. The lung tumor is very dispersed. I do recommend we try immunotherapy. Do you know what that is?"

My mother informs the doctor that I'm an immunologist.

Looking my way, he says, "You can explain thoroughly to your mom why that therapy has a chance of working." He describes the main features, including the side effects.

"What are my chances?" my mother asks calmly. Her strength amazes me.

"Approximately eight percent of patients with this type of lung cancer survive to five years."

He goes on to recommend starting the treatment as soon as possible; within the next week. He explains that he will admit her to Memorial so he can supervise her treatment and monitor her response.

"The rooms and the nurses here are wonderful, and the food's not bad, either." He smiles. And goes on to explain that he understands that our news is very difficult. But that he treats and manages this type of disease every day, and my mother has her baseline good health and relative youth on her side. "And you've never smoked," he reminds her.

My mother agrees she will try the therapy. "Nothing to lose," she says.

Dr. Fleming tells us he will get back to us when the hospital arrangements have been made with the hospital administration.

After he escorts us back to the waiting area, I tell my mother we will speak about the treatment and side effects in detail at home. For now, we have a lot to digest.

When we return to the waiting area, Russ, Claire and Zia bolt from their chairs. Russ's eyes search my face. I shake my head ever so slightly, producing the characteristic furrow across his brow.

My mother beats me to the punch.

"I have lung cancer," she announces. "It's advanced. No surgery." Zia clutches her chest and finally breathes. Claire supports her mother and returns her to her seat.

"We'll see what happens," Ana continues. "I'll get some fancy immune medication. Gaby will tell us about that later. For now, I'm sick. But I'm still here. No hysteria." She fixes Maria in her sights and smiles.

Nani looks into my mother's eyes, nods sagely and pulls herself up to her full height. Exhales broadly and closes the space between herself and Ana. Touches her arm gently and reaches for me at the same time.

"Take me home," my mother commands. "They'll call with the hospital plan when they're ready."

My anxiety spikes as I wonder if and how much she'll be able to tolerate. Selfishly, how much will *I* be able to tolerate?

"Keep Gaby calm," Ana confides to Russ on the ride home. "She'll be upset." I already am. My mother is actually dying. Now.

Back at the house, exhausted, we all retreat to our corners after I get my mother settled on her sofa. I stroke her head as she closes her eyes. Her skin is clammy after climbing the stairs to the front door. I wonder if they make those mechanical stair-climbers for outside and if we should get her more permanently moved into the house, downstairs.

My mother is dying. I know almost nothing about her life. Her own life. Uselessly, I am too embarrassed to admit this to her now. I know she keeps a storage box in the linen closet. Surely I will find something. Some evidence of her secrets. I am panicked. I have to do this now. She is dying.

Well concealed on the top shelf of the linen closet, I find a worn box, its top fixed with yellowed once-transparent heavy-duty tape. Brazenly, I open the box to find two letters written to her old Bronx friend Francesca. Francesca had sent the letters back to Ana with a note that read: "These are precious. I have loved them, and I know you will want to save them."

Before this, I had not realized my mother liked to write. I had not realized she *could* write.

I tuck into the first letter.

* * *

Dear Francesca,

After we married, Arturo was committed to visiting his mother in Sicily. His father had died the year before, and his mother wailed that Arturo cared more about a wedding than his own father. Enlisting the help of the entire village, Arturo had done his best to calm her.

Giulia, his mother, was never able to forgive Arturo's father, Fantino, for leaving her so soon. Collapsed in the fields, his heart had caught up with him where he lay for the better part of a day before some of his workers went searching for him.

Giulia had been abandoned by the two men in her life too soon. She set no value on Arturo's constant communication over the years. Or on his American-sent goods and financial support across the ocean. Photos. Long letters. The offer of tickets to visit their home in New York. "No," she responded each time. Once, she returned his generosity with "I don't want to see this life you live." She believed our marriage was a disgrace because we had been raised in the same family. For her, we were brother and sister.

When we visited her in Sicily, even though we were married, Giulia would not allow Arturo and me to stay in the same bed or under the same roof. She insisted it was an abomination.

So Arturo stayed with his mother, and I stayed with Giulia's sister Graciela. Graciela was completely different from Giulia. She was a beautiful spirit, full of love and compassion for everyone. I survived that visit because of Graciela.

One night, Graciela told me Fantino's story.

Fantino was a good man, but not a very smart man. He made lots of bad decisions. All the farms were going through hard times. The village women banded together to branch out. They traveled to neighboring villages to sell their eggs and cheese and baked goods at local markets. They made quilts, dresses and other household goods and sold them. They entered contests and shared the winnings. Giulia wasn't allowed to take part. Fantino insisted that he alone should provide for his family.

And then, Graciela explained, one day, Fantino did have money. He spent money on equipment, different sources of seed, and people to help work his fields. Graciela said that the whole village was afraid it was too good to be true.

Apparently, it was. Fantino spent too much too fast. It was clear he had borrowed money, and the farm wasn't profitable enough fast enough for him to keep up with the payments.

One night, three men came to the farm looking for Fantino. Giulia made a show of not knowing where her husband was. But she knew that they would find him.

As soon as they walked away, Giulia ordered her son upstairs and out of sight. She watched as Fantino came out of the shed and got pushed around by all three men one after the other. The leader slapped his face with the butt of his pistol.

Before the men left, they took turns beating Fantino. Then, they set fire to the tinder-dry shed, which caught fire immediately. Giulia was worried they might burn the house, but they left.

I hope all is well with you. Let me know what goes on.

I have to stop for now, but I'll tell more later,

Love,

Ana

Dear Francesca,

After Fantino's visit by the thugs, he became afraid for his son Arturo. He made the decision to ask my father, Carlo, to take his boy to New York. But he didn't ask Giulia. The rest you know.

We were very close on the ship, Arturo and me. We spent every minute together. We spent time in English classes given on the ship, but I was sure I would never learn. Compared to our Sicilian dialect, it was confusing and complicated.

I was anxious as we approached New York. Arturo stayed close to me, reassuring me and giving me courage. He would always do this for me.

The night before we left Sicily, Giulia called me aside. From her apron pocket, she handed me a worn leather-bound box.

"Arturo's father gave this to me on our wedding day."

She told me, "It's yours now. Open it."

Inside there was a brooch of fine Italian gold. Two peach-faced lovebirds, their beaks touching. I was amazed she gave this to me. I thanked her, but I couldn't find real words. She was a very sad woman with a very sad history.

Well, I'm back here in my own life! Feeling much better for telling you this story of ours.

Let me know what's going on with you.

Have to go for now. Talk soon.

Love,

Ana

* * *

I refold the letters carefully and return them to the box.

I'm not sure how long I've been in my mother's memories of Sicily and coming to America. I use the bathroom and splash water on my face. I smooth my blouse and try my expression in the mirror. Worry consumes me.

My mother sleeps on the sofa. From the kitchen, I hear Claire ask, "Where do we start? What are her chances? How long will she survive?" Russ draws my attention to the raft of eyes focused my way.

In this nightmare, I am at once unbelieving and praying for wakefulness. I want to cry, but knowing it will do no good, I decide to abort my mission to remain upstairs and take a seat in the living room with my family. I crave being alone to think about what will happen next, but I remind myself that I don't really know. I know she will die. Having no handle on how exactly it will happen is derailing me. I always need to know. In this crisis, I am overwhelmed by an unsure ill-defined immediate future. A very unnerving and frightening place to be.

I assume a confident posture, one I don't feel, when I respond to Claire. As always, I lean on the science.

"It's serious. She's at the most advanced stage of lung cancer, and we have no idea if she'll tolerate the treatment or if it will work. If it does, it won't cure her. It will just give her, at best, a few more months. That's what 'working' means here. Not great. But we'll take it, as long as she's not in pain or too uncomfortable. If she does have pain or is uncomfortable, she will decide if she wants to continue."

"But surgery! Remove it, no?" My aunt's eyes beg agreement from each of us.

"Afraid not, Zia," I tell her. "The cancer in her lungs is painted all over. It's not in a ball or even a few balls that can be removed." My aunt tugs Claire's shoulder.

The rest of the day features the anticipation of Nani's meatballs and the numbness of knowledge I cannot absorb. I finally do run upstairs, retrieve my laptop, come down again and prop my legs on the wing chair ottoman in the living room. I sneak peeks at my mother on the sofa while she sleeps. I pretend to read lab email.

I'm staring across the room when Russ walks around the corner. "Nani needs you in the kitchen. You up for it?"

I unwind my legs, snap the computer shut and follow him.

"Gaby. Ah'm-a need you make the gravy. You know where you mama keep everything, sì?"

She peppers me with questions as we work side by side. I repeat what I've already told Claire and Zia, but I know we all want different information. We want a rosy crystal ball. But I know we're in for the Wicked Witch version of what we'll see when we look in.

"How we take care her here?" She searches my face carefully, willing me to move in and care for my mother. "Ah'm-a help you. Okay?"

There's no way I can entertain moving here during my mother's illness, but I can't find the words to deny her.

"Let's get her treatment started and decide from there."

Nani is not impressed.

My mother emerges from the living room, makes her way into the kitchen, pointing to the bathroom on the right.

I approach, asking if she needs help. "I can still go to the bathroom on my own."

Hopefully, Nani asks my mother, "You hungry?"

"Yeah, soon," she says and I know food is the last thing she wants. Nani shoots me a knowing look.

"I make some pastina an' chicken broth for her."

"Sounds good, Nani." I give her shoulder a tight squeeze and get a hug in return.

Waiting for the gravy to simmer, I head to my computer to check lab email again. Claire and I do a ships-in-the-night rite of passage on her way to set the table. I move to reposition my mother's pillows on the sofa. "No, no," she tells me, "I want to sit up."

"More pillows, Ma? You'll breathe easier."

"Yeah, okay, please."

I carry an additional pair of pillows from upstairs and place them at her neck and back. She nods to the television. I set the channel she selects.

My computer in tow, I head for the stairs. "I'm off to check some lab stuff. I'll be down soon."

"I'll have some tea when you come back down."

When I get upstairs, Russ tells me he's going to sit with Ana. I grab his arm and plant a real kiss. He smiles, smooths my hair, and heads down.

I am revisited by the familiar feeling of guilt on both ends of a hopeless divide. I am uncomfortable leaving my mother on the sofa.

What if this is the last opportunity I have to see her alone, when she is sensible and communicating? What if the lab is upside down, in the middle of a crisis I have to solve? What if I have to go back to Boston? What if I absolutely have to stay in the Bronx right now? What if I really can't handle any of this?

As I always do in a crisis, I immerse myself in work. An hour later, I emerge from a sea of petty problems and, thankfully, easy fixes.

When I return downstairs, I find my grandmother hauling a huge plate of meatballs, steam from the sauce curling wisps of salt-and-pepper hair to her forehead and threatening to weaken the tight bun at the nape of her neck.

Zia follows with the pasta, arranged in my mother's favorite shallow white bowl. The one with the embossed tomatoes around the rim. It's my favorite bowl too.

Claire ushers in the covered casserole guarding my mother's pastina. Russ delivers my grandmother's garlic bread on the ancient wood cutting board with the worn depression along its length.

Zia urges my mother to the table. Ana lies about being hungry. She sighs in relief when she spies the simple child's soup at her place setting.

Nani says grace to start our meal. Asks Ana if she needs anything.

My mother gestures toward the Parmesan cheese. Grabs Russ's arm, asking if there's any plain bread in the kitchen.

"Garlic doesn't sound good right now," she explains. Russ returns quickly with a plate of plain Italian bread. She leans into his arm and treats him to a warm smile.

Our conversation is light, garbled by the frequent intrusion of Ana's coughing. We try not to notice. We try not to make her laugh. I push away wondering how debilitated she will become. I have never envisioned my mother weakened or losing control of any situation in her life. I've had trouble envisioning her losing control of any situation in *my* life.

Ana enjoys the gelato Russ has brought. "It's very soothing. I love lemon. Thank you, Russ." She turns to me. "He will always know what you need—do the same for him."

I realize, uncomfortably, that my mother is trying to teach me everything on a short timetable. I know that she will be with me for less time than I thought she might.

We get her settled upstairs—a three-person job: Russ, Claire and me. I am glad she can sleep in her own bed. So is she. Gentle snores usher us out of her room.

In her sitting position, propped with several pillows, my mother passes a relatively comfortable night. She sputters and coughs gently in her sleep, but it does not wake her.

I stroke her cheek gently, wondering how I will continue without her. Is it possible for me to be without her? Against my will, I play back the doctor's news. Each time, my breath catches in my lungs, and I am taken by a wave of hopelessness. I cannot feel. I cannot react. My breath shudders. Abject helplessness replaces my bodily functions. I want to go back to last year when I didn't know.

Russ pads into the room and, standing behind me, gently hooks his arm around my neck. The touch of him, the smell of him, spell normal and safe.

Russ has come to be with Ana. I indulge in a short nap while we watch her. I am mesmerized by the rising and falling of her chest. Is this the last? When will the last come? Do I want to be here for the last? Will I be?

Taking both my hands in his, Russ leans into my sharp intake of breath. "She's here. She's had a good night. Just stay here and be with her as she is right now."

"But you know it's not really her." I had never imagined Ana vulnerable. Without strength. She has, before my eyes, become a victim, someone I don't recognize.

Russ brushes my hair behind my ears and holds my face between his hands. "Just stay here—in this present place. You can do this."

"I don't like this present." As soon as I say it, I realize I am in for future realities that I will like even less.

It doesn't take long for us to get the call that her hospital stay is arranged. Russ guides us there again and the medical staff begin her immunotherapy immediately. Over the next two days, we learn that she is not responding well. Her prognosis is poor.

She is now susceptible to infection. Lung infection being most troubling. With the appetite of a gnat and the antibiotics for her infections, she melts into her hospital bed.

CHAPTER 19

A Fever Pitch

I have been here two weeks, grateful that Russ can remain with me and work remotely. I am forcing myself to work on manuscripts, review theses. But my absence from the lab is a slab of concrete falling from a Manhattan skyscraper.

I steel myself when I open the door to my mother's room. Nani is here every day; Zia most days. My grandmother struggles to fit food to Ana's tastes and tolerance. Polenta or pastina in chicken broth seems to work. Cannellini—the white beans she used to love—not so much.

I am empty. I breathe deeply to fill the emptiness. When Russ encourages me to go for a run, I go. In fact, I want to run away, but, eventually, I round the corner and my childhood home appears. Even when Ana and I were warring, the sight of the house always said Comfort. Safety. Love. Now it is a place where anxiety blooms. A place of discomfort and sickness. Death. The only uncertainty is when death will visit.

Nani takes control of the kitchen. Zia follows her mother's orders. Two suppers. One for us, one for my Ma. For some reason, my mother craves my grandmother's bonata—her spinach pie baked in a soft phyllo shell. Ana has been avoiding garlic, but she loves Nunzia's spinach-garlic-olive-oil concoction. This, eggs, mild broths, thin slices of pork or beef, Italian bread, preferably soaked in chicken broth, make up my mother's diet. We all notice how little she actually eats.

Claire and I walk together, remembering the forgotten antics of two childhood friends who always found a way to defy their mothers. With their mothers never the wiser. Or so we thought.

When we were kids, I was jealous of Claire's hair, her clothes—always fashionable—her thin figure. The way her mother was so obviously proud of her.

Claire is astounded. "What are you talking about? Your mother was always bragging about you—in that way she has—you know, she never really said, 'I'm so proud,' but she would talk about what you'd done lately and finish with how you were so humble about it. I always rolled my eyes when she did that."

I stare at my cousin in genuine disbelief. "*You?* Jealous of me?"

We stop at the bakery and pick out our favorite pastries to eat on the way home. We buy bread for dinner and, guessing what might spark Ana's appetite, dessert.

Russ meets me at the door, darkness defining his features. My heart skips.

"What?" I demand. I am latched to his wrists.

"Your mom is running a fever. Not sure how high, but to me, she feels like she's burning up."

I take the stairs in four strides. Close and insistent, the air in her bedroom swaddles her, betraying her illness. I plaster a smile on my face and take a seat on the bed next to her.

Her eyes refuse to focus. She points them toward the ceiling and grasps my hand. "Where's your father?" she asks.

She *is* burning and she is delirious. Cancer can be associated with fever when it invades the liver. I swallow hard, slammed yet again by the seriousness of her condition.

To answer her question, without thinking, I reassure her that "Papa will be up soon."

As expected, Russ is at the door, accompanied by my grandmother. The remainder of my mother's entourage—Claire and Zia—stand at a stunned distance behind them.

I whisper to Russ and Nani, "We need to get her to the hospital."

Russ nods and skips down the stairs.

With Nani's help, I change my mother into fresh underwear, a dry shift dress and socks. I grab a sweater from her dresser drawer while Nani brushes her hair and does her best to answer her questions.

Ana continues her soliloquy. "What should I make for Arturo tonight? Is Gaby home from school yet? Ma, when do you want to go food shopping this week?"

Claire supports Zia down the stairs. "Ma, come on. We can't do anything here. They'll know what to do at the hospital."

"*Ospedale?*" Zia moans. "No."

Claire is firm but kind. "Ma, don't make it worse for Gaby and Nani and Russ."

At her bedside, Claire and I coax my mother into slip-on shoes.

"I'm cold," she complains. I fix a fresh blanket around her shoulders. We shuffle to the top of the stairs and Russ gathers her in his arms. I am behind them, caressing the back of her neck, stiff, I'm sure, with pain and fever.

Outside the front door, the concrete staircase is a challenge of a higher order. Again, Russ takes firm hold of my mother and, obeying her signal, stops halfway down.

"Oh," she asks, "do I have my car keys?"

"Yes, Ma," I lie. "But you won't need them. Russ will drive, okay?"

"He's a great driver. But what about your father? Why isn't he driving?"

I pray she doesn't expect a response. Russ places her gently in the passenger seat, straps her in and wraps her in the blanket.

Blessedly, she begins to doze as the car starts to move.

Through our collective anxiety, we exhale a sigh of gratitude and measure the miles to the hospital.

I call my mother's oncologist en route. He agrees to meet us at the emergency room.

"Ana," he asks when we arrive, "do you know where you are?"

"Sure," she responds, "Arthur Avenue. I'm near the delicatessen."

He fills me in with his observations and planned course of action. "She's febrile, of course—a high fever—which I believe is responsible for her delirium. We'll draw some blood and get her fever under control before we start running any other tests."

My body language alerts him that I'm about to launch a barrage of questions.

The doctor holds his ground. "One thing at a time. Okay, Gaby?" He rushes past me through the doors of the emergency room inner sanctum.

We wait. Babies squirm in their mothers' arms. They arch their backs, whining and screaming in tandem. Older siblings beg for vending machine change.

A boy of about five years old waves a Snickers bar in his mother's face. "I got this, but I don't like it. I want a Butterfinger."

Too exhausted to argue, the mom hands over another fistful of quarters, assuring her son that this is his "last chance—no more!"

Her face streaked with tears, a young girl caresses her arm while her mother smooths her hair, encouraging her to hang on. I watch the mother approach the triage station. She returns with a small white pleated paper cup and one larger one. Her daughter throws the two pills to the back of her throat and gulps the water in one draft. She places the paper cups inside one another, crushes them with her good hand and returns them to her mom.

I turn my attention to a construction worker, still wearing his high-visibility vest as he maintains pressure on his hand swaddled in a bloody shop towel. I hear him trying to pressure the triage nurse to hurry. Without looking at him, she hands him a clip chart and a pen, suggesting he get somebody to help him complete the form. "You've got insurance, right?"

He snorts, turns his back on her and joins his colleague in the sea of chairs.

We stand as one person when Dr. Fleming emerges.

"We're stabilizing her," he tells us. "She's on a mild sedative, so she's sleeping. I'm admitting her."

Dread and relief fill my heart in equal measure. Leaving just enough room for a side order of guilt.

We all decide on a timed schedule to sit with Ana until she wakes. Nani insists on taking the first shift, followed by me, then Zia, Claire and Russ. I pray she will be lucid when she rejoins us.

Ever prepared, Nani pulls her needles and yarn out of the Sicily bag her cousin in Camastra sent her years ago. I can't think of my grandmother without that bag.

"You need anything, Nani? Something to eat? Drink?"

Already counting stitches, she dismisses me with a wave of her knitting needles.

I stroke my mother's forehead, downgraded from furnace status, but still hot. I bend, kiss her dry, papery cheek and join the others waiting at her door.

Glad she is being cared for, we spend a few minutes watching Ana sleep. The road to dying is full of twists and turns. Infection. Delirium. Exhaustion and low energy.

Claire asks if anyone needs anything. I tell her I could go for coffee.

"It's a cliché, isn't it?" she says. "Hospital cafeteria coffee."

"Only game in town," I say. And then I realize, "We can wander outside the hospital and find coffee, right? Ma will sleep for a while, I'm sure." Nani nods her approval.

There's got to be an Italian café around here. We'll all feel much better if we can score some espresso.

In the end we find a small café around the block from the hospital entrance. We order cannoli with our espresso, assuring Zia that her pastries are head and shoulders above these. But they disappear instantly.

I check my watch as we finish our coffee. It is 2 P.M. when we set out to return to the hospital.

Russ has brought a small box tied with string back to my mother's floor. "Tiramisu—for Ana, if she can."

In the nurses' break room, Russ leaves the box of doughnuts he bought on our way back to the hospital.

My mother is awake when we return, her back propped up with four pillows, a nasal canula strapped across her cheeks. Her body language spells exhaustion, her face a whiter shade of pale. Dark circles punctuate the area between her cheeks and her eyes. She smiles weakly and reports that she ate a late lunch of salty elbow macaroni. She makes a point of telling us she enjoyed it.

Russ steps up to hand me the box. I redirect him to my mother.

Russ begins, "Ana, we brought you some—"

I cut him off. "Ma, Russ brought this for you—the rest of us approve of it, but we didn't do it."

"Tiramisu," Russ continues. "You can save it or—"

"I don't want to save it," she assures him. "Can I get a plate and a real fork? Oh, and a cup of water with ice." She points to the swivel table hovering over the foot of her bed.

Russ nods and heads to the nursing station to satisfy her requests. Nani pours water from the plastic pitcher. Claire places the cup on the table. I activate the electronic hum of the bed that raises her backrest to a full sitting position.

Russ carries Ana's dessert on a chunky hospital issue melamine plate with a stainless-steel fork to her bedside table. A plastic cup holds the ice. Unconvinced that she will actually eat the dessert, Nani watches her daughter closely. I find myself swallowing for her, willing her to eat and enjoy.

Four bites in, she pushes the plate aside. Asks Russ to make sure the rest is saved for her. A weary hand prompts me to lower her headrest. She is asleep within a minute.

Dr. Fleming marches into the room with an entourage of medical students. Rounds. A mixture of curiosity and dread on each of the trainees' faces.

Dr. Fleming nods at us, introduces his patient, greets Nani, then me.

He accesses my mother's chart on his iPad and begins peppering the students with questions. He evaluates their answers, greeting each incorrect one with a nod, then calling on one of the other students.

"Since our patient, Mrs. Pecorero, is sleeping, we will come back to see her at the end of rounds, hoping she will be awake."

The doctor invites me outside the room, reporting that her infection and fever appear to be under control "for now." I report that she has been lucid, and that she has snacked on a bit of tiramisu. He smiles. "How could she possibly resist?" he asks.

He taps his way through her chart. Touches my arm lightly. "She will not get better, but we will treat her again tomorrow."

"Why do that?" I ask, my tone more testy than I had intended.

"Your mother has told me that she wants to be treated. She also told me that she did discuss her preference with you? Please tell me if you have other information."

I feel my head moving from side to side. "No," I assure him. "I know that it won't really give her anything." I shrug. "But she does want the treatment. I am just feeling helpless."

He touches my arm lightly. "I have seen many patients in your mother's condition achieve calm, even though they realize that the treatment is very limited. I will advise you to live by the minute. I know you honor what your mother wants. So make sure you keep asking her. We will adjust if her preferences change."

He spends a moment searching my face. "Yes, this is very difficult. I'll advise you to let her speak, express her desires." With that, he extends his hand and tucks his iPad under his arm, and I watch the back of his white coat billow behind him.

Very little in my mother's life has been easy. She always organized everything so I would have it easy. I realize this for the first time, it seems, as gratitude and guilt rise in me in equal measure. Not for the first time, I pine for a sister to talk to. Claire. I'll speak with Claire.

My mother is snoring lightly when I check on her. Nani is propped on the chair near the head of Ana's bed. Arms crossed, Russ is leaning against the broad windowsill, beside Claire. He straightens when I walk in. Zia stands behind Nani's chair, mopping her eyes with a selection from her embroidered linen handkerchiefs.

I link arms with Zia and walk her to the seating area near my mother's room. I try to distract her by asking how she and my mother played together when they were girls.

She dabs her nose and offers a weak smile. "Oh," she begins, "we were so different! She liked climbing trees, dodgeball, racing around the block with her friends. Later, badminton, basketball." Her eyes light up as she continues. "Me? I wasn't any good at those things. I never did that."

"So what did you do, Zia?"

"Me? Hah! I played dolls with my friends. Made clothes for my dolls—and my friends' dolls, too—with Nani's scraps. Of course, your mother was already an expert seamstress when she was about twelve."

"Zia, you ever wonder why she's so impatient with you? Nani, I mean."

Zia inspects her hands, smooths her skirt. When she raises her head, her eyes tell me she wonders about it all the time.

Shrugging lightly, she tells me, "Nani thinks I'm weak."

"But, Zia, you've had a lot of sorrow."

"Yes, this is true. But I think she's angry because she raised a weak daughter. She has never told me, but she compares me to Ana, who is very strong."

"Does it make you angry?"

Inclining her head slightly to the left, she considers this. "No. I can't be angry with Ana, ever. And being angry at Nani would only make things worse. I love them both a lot."

She continues, "You know, she hates the weak most when something bad happen."

I hug my aunt. Surprisingly, I can't think of anything to say. I realize a new appreciation for Claire. I can't imagine being my mother's parent. And, unbelievably, for the first time, I wonder how my mother has managed good relationships with both Nani and Zia, always the target of Nani's frustration and ire.

Doesn't bode well, I think, for Zia, as we all enter this phase, which will pass with Ana's passing.

Back in my mother's room, I deliver Zia back to Nani's chair. She squeezes her mother's shoulder lightly. She smiles when Nani meets her eyes.

Nani pats her—other—daughter's hand and pauses to scrutinize Ana's sleeping face.

Ana wakes herself with a fit of coughing. Disoriented, she takes a good look around the room, settling on Russ.

"Where is Gaby?" she asks.

Russ encourages me toward my mother's bed. I hold her hand and smooth the hair back from her forehead. She is cool to the touch and making sense. She chats lightly, assures us through charcoal-rimmed eyes that she's had a good rest. I encourage small sips of water through the straw in her cup.

"It's too warm," she complains. Oddly, Ana drinks nothing without ice except espresso, tea and hot chocolate.

"It's good for you to drink. We'll get you some ice, okay?" Russ is off to the nurses' station.

"Why? Will it save me?"

I ignore her sarcasm and ask her if she's hungry.

"Can I get some applesauce? And bread. Good bread."

Applesauce and bread? Okay!

My anxiety rises steadily over the next few days. My mother adopts the color of gray sheets and her breath labors over words. As determined as she is, Ana cannot make it to the bathroom alone. She wants only Nani or me to guide her. The nurse's aides sponge bathe and feed her when she can't manage.

On the fifth day, still in the hospital, she begins coughing non-stop. She refuses food, even good bread, and fluids are just as likely to travel up as down. I worry about her nutrition as the color beneath her eyes intensifies. She gives up conversing, spends most of her day trying to sleep between coughing fits.

Before we head to the hospital each day, Russ and Claire conspire to keep me running.

"It always gives you energy," Claire urges. "And God knows this takes all the energy you can find."

Both Russ and Claire keep a careful eye on me. I'm not teary. I'm angry. And anger is just a form of energy.

I run. I am blind to the familiar streets, buildings, businesses. Early in the day, my shoe stomping leads me to the aromas of the bakery. Fresh warm rolls, cornetti—Nani's favorite croissant cousin—and fresh sesame Italian bread.

Russ is busy, always, at the stove when I finish my run. He's preparing eggs and pancetta, cheese and roasted red peppers. He's also placed pickled eggplant on the table. Along with a pot of espresso, jars of tangerine and prickly pear jam. Nutella and butter. A spot is reserved for the bread and cornetti.

Nani walks into the kitchen tying her apron around her waist.

"Good job, Russ," she assures him, her critical eye taking in every detail.

Russ smiles. "Grazie, signora!" He's rewarded with an approving nod of her head.

"An' you?" She waves her hand over my running clothes. "You eat th' brekkfas' like this?" She waves a hand over my running outfit.

"Yes, Nani. Then I'll go shower."

"Good, go shower aftah."

I don't dare glance at Russ.

"You call th' ospedale this mornin'?"

"No, Nani. They will call if there is anything new."

"Hmpf."

She finishes placing a cup of espresso at each setting just as Zia's and Claire's footsteps sound on the stairs.

Russ takes his cue to deliver the platter of eggs and pancetta to the table. Meanwhile, Nani instructs Zia and Claire to bring everything else.

We begin with the scraping of chairs and grace.

We scrutinize each other, waiting for one of us to speak.

Nani raises a critical eyebrow and starts.

"Ah'm-a stay with her first." None of us dares to argue.

"Oh," says Zia, her voice catching in her throat, "I hope she can talk today."

We finish and clear quickly, anxious to get going. Dreading the visit, but drawn like moths to a flame.

After greeting the nurses and doctor at the nursing station, I reach her room first. I stand back and let Nani lead us. We step in, single file, to find my mother awake, sporting an oxygen mask. She lifts it, smiles, lets us know she's happy to see us.

Nani takes her seat as we file up to greet my mother. When I kiss her, she grasps my hand and smiles. Guides me to her ear and orders me, gently, "Don't be afraid, okay?"

I nod and rest her hand at her side. The oxygen mask has given me an even more serious dose of reality. At least, I think, she can speak if she lifts it.

Russ rubs my shoulder as he hugs me and I let him in on Ana's message.

I'm heartbroken, but I know a heart can easily be broken in more than one place, in more ways than one.

I offer to relieve Nani, but she shakes her head and continues knitting. She does not look at me. Claire guides her mother into the hallway as Zia begins crying.

Russ stands next to me, his hand on my shoulder, as I fix a smile to my face and take a seat on Ana's bed. Miming a cup lifted to his lips, he motions a question about coffee. I nod my thanks with a smile, motioning toward Nani. I know she won't drink hospital coffee. As expected, she declines.

Starting to doze off, my mother squeezes my hand and smiles back at me as she loses herself in sleep.

My grandmother does not speak. She sighs in my mother's direction, squeezes her shoulder. Continues knitting, her mouth wrinkled into a fixed frown.

Russ returns, armed with espresso for Nani, American coffee for himself and me, and a box of cookies and pastries. The small box, I know, is for my mother. I suspected he would forgo the hospital cafeteria for the café down the street. I smile and pat my thanks across my heart. I'm treated to his return smile and a strong hug across my shoulders.

Nani is happily surprised. "Grazie," she whispers, rooting through the box for two biscotti. She sets aside her yarn for the first time since we arrived and sighs at her first sip of espresso.

On their return, Claire and Zia settle themselves outside my mother's room. Russ goes out to greet them. I hear Claire thank Russ. She tells him they're "all coffeed out," but they'd love some Italian cookies and pastry.

We begin our conversations when we realize through her gentle snoring that my mother will be asleep for a while. She squirms a bit and delivers short, staccato coughs that wrinkle her brow. Each of these feels like a blow.

Quietly, Claire sidles up to me and points to the door.

Calmly, she asks, "Who should I call? Lots of people will want to see her."

"I know, Claire, but how do we control the number of people who go in? She's obviously very tired."

"I can control the number of people who visit at once. She will want to see them as much as they want to see her, don't you think?"

I tell her I do think so. Claire nods and says, "I will put together a draft list with my mother and Nani. Then you can have a look and I'll start calling."

"I'll give you a list too?"

"Good," she replies.

We return to my mother's room and, pulling out my computer, I start working on my list. As gracious as she has been to everyone in her life, many people will want to see her. I know who she will want to see, so I've prioritized the groups.

Uncomplicated arithmetic tells me that given three visitation periods a day, it will take about two weeks for everyone to visit. As long as I stay on the list, I don't care who else is there.

Will she last for two weeks? Will we?

When we return to my mother's house, I am struck by how we have always coalesced around her. Like the proverbial set of theater masks, Nani's face mirroring comedy when she's around my mother and tragedy when she's with Zia. Now, my grandmother is damaged and worn, and I am sure I have witnessed the birth of a dramatic number of new wrinkles around her mouth.

Zia is simply lost. She has never had the support of her mother, but she has always enjoyed the support of mine. I swear I can read her thoughts: *Who will love me when she's gone? Who will I depend on?*

Claire will teach her mother to adjust her outlook and to accept a harsh reality. And she will suffer. My mother always encouraged Claire, taught her to realize that Zia's problems were Zia's. Not hers, and mostly of Zia's invention.

Claire tells me how my mother coached her through her first year of college. Zia was at turns angry and petulant. She wanted

Claire to go to college. But she did not want to be without her daughter.

Claire told me that my mother explained Zia's insecurities and the impact of a mother who wanted her to be something, someone else. It still hurts my heart to witness how hard Zia always tries.

I find myself dreadfully expectant over the following few days. The sound of my mother's home phone jangles my bones and finds me fighting for self-control. Claire appoints herself phone attendant and chief dispatcher. I am grateful to her and cannot imagine being mindful enough to identify the faces on the other end of the line, or to connect with them.

As expected, over the next few days, my mother sleeps more and more and eats less and less. All told, we get about three hours a day when she is awake and communicating. Once, when she wakes briefly, her battered eyelids open and shut, and she asks weakly but with a smile on her face, "Russ, where's my tiramisu?"

Delighted, he makes his way to the nurses' break room and returns to the head of her bed. "Right here, Ana." I bring him a spoon and gently coax the head of the bed into a sitting position.

She eats half the pastry from Russ's spoon. And signals her need for more sleep.

I feed her short sips of water through a straw, and when she waves me away, I kiss her on her brow. She is sweating and clammy. She is going, I know. Soon.

But not yet, I pray. It is torture to watch her go in stages, but I simply cannot imagine being in the world without her.

We try to engage in normal activities. Russ and I work remotely. I run. Claire returns to work, tethered to her phone, with my mother's forwarded to hers. Her husband joins us when he can. Zia shops to supply Nani-mandated ingredients for our meals. Nani knits both in and away from the hospital and prepares her spectacular meals. "You mothah, she love this!"

Despite Nani's wizardry, eating is no more than a quiet diversion. We ask each other to pass the bread. Pasta. Another ladle of soup. Listen to flatware scraping and to each other chewing. We don't converse much, except to tell Nani how good her food is.

None of us wants to air our questions or feelings. When will she go? Is she in pain? Will I speak with her again before she dies? She never smoked. How did this happen to her? What will we do with her furniture? Her clothes? Her sewing studio and fabrics? Her house?

The weight of Ana's end-of-life drama and of the necessities of what will remain after her death press on me. My breath shudders and my head aches. When I run, my mind cannot wander away from my mother's hospital bed. For the first time in my running life, I simply want any run to be finished.

My mother was admitted to the hospital two weeks ago today. Russ greets me inside the front door as I untie my running shoes. I arrange them on the mat, afraid to meet Russ's eyes.

"We have to go," he says simply. "Here, I've got some fresh clothes for you. You'll want to just sponge off."

"She's worse."

Russ nods, his brow furrowed, his mouth drawn.

Nani and Zia emerge, apron-free, in their best shoes, handbags clutched in their arms.

I accept the clothes and the washcloth from Russ and fit my feet into slides.

Zia has called Claire. She and her husband Josh will meet us.

And so will Dr. Fleming.

When I finished my run, I thought I was hungry. Now, I taste bile. My mother is really dying.

My heart beats a steady thrum of dread as we head to the hospital. Russ has my hand. Zia fixes her gaze out the window, a handkerchief absorbing soft sobs and tears. Nani looks straight ahead, determined and composed. I wonder briefly if all the tragedy in her life has prepared her for this. The death of her favorite child.

None of us speaks. Russ deposits us at the hospital front entrance, promising he'll meet us upstairs. I link arms with my aunt on my left and my grandmother on my right as we head up to my mother's floor. In the elevator, we all fix our eyes on the ceiling, waiting for the ding that sounds our destination.

I check in at the nursing station. "I will get your mother's nurse. She'll have the best information for you."

It is the worst information. "Overnight, she was very restless. Her breathing was more labored. The doctor ordered midazolam to calm her. It helped. Right now, she's going in and out of consciousness. She does know where she is, and she has been asking for you all. Go on in." The nurse peeks around the door. "She's dozing, but I think she'll wake up when she senses you're all here. Dr. Fleming will be here shortly to talk to you."

As Nani steps across the threshold, my mother's eyelids flutter. She lifts the oxygen mask an inch or so and says, simply, "Ma." She reaffixes the mask and smiles. An exhausted smile for each of us. Dying, I suddenly realize, is hard work.

She motions for me with her free hand—Nani is mistress of the other—and I grab on, determined to smile, and determined not to cry.

"Where is Russ?" she asks me.

"Parking the car, Ma. He'll be right here."

As if on cue, Russ enters the room. She looks at him as he joins me, his smile bathing warmth on my mother, his arm circling my shoulder.

Claire has gone to the waiting area to manage would-be visitors. I hear low sighs, one almost-complaint, "But I came so far! I'll only stay a minute!" The Sicilian minute—a lifetime. And I'm afraid it just might be the rest of my mother's lifetime. Now, I hear Claire's even, understanding voice as she talks people down, knowing that many will stay awhile, hoping, after all, to see Ana. A no-win proposition.

I invite Zia in. She plants an agonized kiss on her sister's forehead and, careful to avoid her oxygen line and intravenous tube, squeezes her upper arm.

The mask lifts for a second time. Ana musters flagging energy to announce that she wants to see each of us, one at a time, beginning with Claire. I motion Zia ahead of me and, in single file, we make it back to the waiting area. I summon Claire and let her husband Josh know what is happening.

Claire emerges with both tears and a smile on her face. She embraces Josh and then guides her mother back to Ana's door. Zia clenches her handkerchief as, desperate to be delivered from her sister's death, she searches her daughter's face.

Zia is in with my mother for a longer time. I am sure Ana is calming her, reminding her of all the grief she has come through. Assuring her that she will come through this too. I can feel my mother's strength, muted though it is by illness and near-death, on the other side of the door.

Zia emerges sobbing, clutching her heart, finally falling into Claire's arms. Claire finds them chairs. Ready with a fresh handkerchief, Claire lovingly dries Zia's tears and strokes her mother's tortured face. In many ways, these weeks have taken the worst toll on Maria. My invisible Aunt Maria, visible only to her sister Ana.

Nani is, of course, next. She smooths the lap of her dress and clutches her handbag beneath her breasts. As she approaches the door, Nani lifts her head and straightens her back. She steps lightly toward the door and closes it carefully behind her.

Wandering to the nursing station, my attention is drawn to Dr. Fleming, flipping through an electronic chart and querying one of the nurses. His eyes are serious, concerned. He nods, and, seeing us outside Ana's room, singles me out. "Is your grandmother with her?" I tell him she is, and that my mother has asked to see each of us in turn. A compassionate smile. "I'll just nip in when your grandmother comes out, okay?"

What am I going to say, "No"? I wonder if my nerves will survive this waiting game. If my mother will still be there when it's my turn to see her.

Finally, Nani comes out. She tips her chin in my direction, smooths the skirt of her dress and repositions her handbag. She returns Dr. Fleming's greeting and sits with Claire and Zia, dry-eyed, straight-backed and stoic.

Dr. Fleming drapes his stethoscope around his neck, tucks the nursing notes under his arm and disappears behind the door.

Just before the door soft closes and just after his greeting to my mother, I hear him ask her if she is in pain. My heart sinks, and then immediately rises to hear her say, "No, Doctor." The rest is between Dr. Fleming and his patient.

He doesn't stay long. He allows the door to close as we gather around.

"She is dying," he informs us.

"Oh, we know," I protest, incredulous that he should tell us this.

"No. I mean, she is dying now."

Shocked and stunned, I say, "Oh." And leave it at that. Unbelieving, but knowing it is true, I hear my brain repeating *Now* over and over again. My mother is dying *now*.

Dr. Fleming describes what is happening medically, and that he has ordered medication for her that will calm any agitation. "She is not in pain, which, of course, is good."

"How long?" I hear myself ask.

"It's hard to say. Right now, she's lucid and communicating. But it won't be long," he responds.

"She is a lovely woman. I am sorry this is happening." He hugs me and shakes hands with everyone except Nani. He invites her into open arms. She moves toward him, and, squeezing his shoulders, keeps herself at a respectful arm's length.

Zia begins to recite the Memorare in Italian. Nani joins her.

Dr. Fleming briskly retraces his steps back to the nursing station and signs a few papers before we watch him exit the floor.

His leaving feels like the captain has abandoned a sinking ship. We are cold and wet, casting about for hope. And life.

I've never watched my mother die before. I feel only tremendous weight in my chest and belly. I vacillate between unsatisfied ravenous hunger and crippling nausea at the thought of food.

It's time for me to go in. Russ, ever by my side, smiles and kisses me on both cheeks. "For your mother," he says, and I smile back.

The room is warm, but my mother is swathed in blankets.

I sit near the head of the bed and caress her hand. Gentle her damp hair from her forehead and kiss her on both cheeks.

"That's from Russ," I say, and she smiles as she moistens dry lips. I bring a wet washcloth for her face and mouth. She asks for ice and settles down.

"You know I'm going now."

I nod, my eyes dry, my heart like lead.

"Don't forget, I'll always be with you. Your father and me, we love you more than our own lives."

I nod again, ready to speak. "No," she says. "I have things to say. I know many times"—she stops to cough—"you're angry with me because I'm strict."

"Ma."

"Let me speak."

I adjust the blanket around her ice-cold feet.

She is nearly breathless. "I am sorry I didn't get your wrist fixed. I should have found the money. I know it hurts you and you never complain."

I try again. "Ma, you really worried about my wrist right now?"

"It's bothering me. Always has."

Another bout of coughing lasts longer than the last.

She recovers and drinks in a large dose of oxygen.

She says, "Claire is calling Father Bernadin to come to me."

"I'm sure he'll be here soon."

She adjusts the oxygen mask around her mouth and nose and rests her eyes. I panic. Oh no. She's not going now?

"I love you, Ma. Even if I disagree with you a lot. I love you."

She smiles behind the mask and sets it aside.

"I know. I need you to take care of Nani. She makes like she's strong, but inside she hurts very much. And Zia, show her special love. Nani can't help how she is with her, but it hurts Zia to her soul. I am glad you and Claire have always been friends. I pray you get closer." I tell her I will fulfill all her requests.

"Get Russ."

I open the door and signal to him. He walks softly toward the bed, and I release my mother's hand to his care. He treats her to his best smile. She squeezes his hand and smiles back, fogging her mask. She lifts her hand in a stop sign gesture, commanding that he should not speak.

"Hold hands with Gaby," she says.

He takes my hand.

"You won't see me at your wedding. I know you young people write your own vows. I want to hear your vows now."

We haven't written our vows yet, but in this final moment, I find a way to share some version of them with her.

At Russ's signal, I speak first.

"To my partner, the love of my life. My life is everything fulfilled because of you. I will always honor you as we move forward in time and love."

Russ clears his throat. "You are my challenge to be better, to strive, to achieve. As we make our lives, I will always hold you close as we move ahead together."

To Ana's obvious approval, we hold each other after we present our vows. I am swaddled in comfort and a soft duvet of trust. Russ kisses me lightly and strokes my hair.

My mother advises us. "Always take care of each other. Don't listen to anything anyone else tells you to do. Just listen to each other. And have a wonderful wedding. Better, have the kind of marriage Arturo and I had. Promise me."

We promise her.

"Gaby, you say five Hail Marys with me. Now. Then Father Bernadin can come in to confess me and give me last rites and Communion."

To my great surprise, Russ joins me in the Hail Marys. I hand him a quizzical look and receive a shy smile in response.

In her exhaustion, my mother makes a sound close to laughter followed by another coughing fit.

She swallows hard and reaches for Russ's hand. "You sneaky. You know the Hail Mary."

"Sure," he responds, "and the Our Father too. We're having a wedding Mass, aren't we?"

We gather more closely to her. Russ says his goodbyes, promises he'll get Father Bernadin "on deck," kisses me, squeezes my hand and heads out the door.

I hold my mother's face in both hands, totally unaware of how I will ever let her go.

"You are a spectacular mother. I don't know how I will let you go."

She studies me over her oxygen mask.

I tell her, "I am overwhelmingly proud to be your daughter."

She lifts the mask and says, "You make me proud every day. Remember that I am always with you."

I see Father Bernadin try the door and, noticing me, softly close it again. I don't want to leave. In a fit of desperation, I adopt the thought that she can't possibly die as long as I'm in the room. But, finally, I turn to leave, her eyes resting closed, the gray paper color of her face following me out.

My brain knows I won't see her alive again. I will not speak to her again. I will be without her. Always. My heart is wrenched. I have known for weeks, but I could never be ready.

Father Bernadin enters and grasps my hand as he steps toward my mother, his prayer book and sacramental kit secured in his left hand and a purple stole hung around the neck of his white floor-length gown—the alb. As the door closes, I watch him caress my mother's shoulder as he adjusts his stole. She offers him a weak smile.

Outside Ana's room, none of us speak. Claire kneads Zia's shoulder, bracing her mother's head in the crook of her neck. Zia sobs softly, for all of us.

I think about my mother's wishes. She started telling me what she wants in small doses when she was diagnosed. A funeral Mass, naturally. Her burial clothes, including shoes. Of course, she wants to be buried next to my father.

"She's sleeping peacefully," Father Bernadin announces when he exits my mother's room. His sacramentals stowed safely, he kisses both edges of his stole, folds it carefully and places it in his case. I know he will unfold the stole again when he offers us confession and consultation. One at a time. Nani opts for first audience. Russ leans in and asks me if it's okay to ask for consultation. I assure him it is, and I suggest he ask for a blessing. I realize for the first time how much he has been through with me. And with my mother.

Nani emerges from the room with Father Bernadin making the sign of the cross. I pass her across the threshold, wondering what I will say.

I sit across from the priest avoiding his eyes while I examine my feet.

"I am numb," I tell him. "My time with my mother has been a roller coaster."

"Why?" he asks simply. "How do you mean, a 'roller coaster'? Just now, because she's dying?"

"Her dying is bad, but she has never really approved of me or my choices. Always criticizing."

"And how are you with her?"

"Wanting her to accept me. And to tell me I've done well. She can't do that."

"So," asks Father, "what is your confession?"

I look into his eyes as he smooths the ends of the purple stole across his lap.

"I need absolution for wanting her to be someone else. I haven't recognized who she actually is. I have hardly ever told her that I love her."

"*Do* you love her?"

"With all my heart, yes."

"Why haven't you told her more often?"

I am afraid to admit this, but this is the priest and this is the Sacrament of Confession. "Because I've wanted to punish her."

"For what?" he asks simply.

"For making me angry."

Father Bernadin rests his chin in the seat made by his thumb, index and third fingers.

"So, what's your first emotion right now?" he asks.

"Guilt, Father."

"Do you think other daughters experience guilt over the course of their relationships with their mothers?"

"Yes, but I don't care about them. I only care about my guilt with my mother. And now I can't do anything about it."

Father Bernadin nods sagely; I finish my confession relieved to have absolution, but I remain riddled with guilt and regret.

Russ is last in. He emerges with a muted air of surprise.

"He was pretty shocked to see me."

"Did he help?"

"Some. I think I'm going to see Rabbi Rosen too."

I tell him it's a good plan. I wrap both arms around his back. I caress his neck and kiss him on both cheeks. He cups my face in his hands and kisses me.

My mother's nurse exits Ana's room with an update on her vitals.

"She is slowing down," he reports. "She is going. Give me a phone number and I will call when things change."

We sneak looks at each other, silently sharing a group decision.

"We'll stay," I say. Everyone nods agreement.

Rosary in hand, Nani heads back into Ana's room.

Russ goes on an espresso run. Claire takes Zia for a walk.

I join Nani in the Rosary. She nods her approval as I take a seat on the edge of my mother's bed.

Her breathing is increasingly labored, the mask fogging with each short exhalation. There is a thin pocket of mucus in the corners of each of her eyes. Her lips are dry and cracked. I wonder briefly if I should administer Vaseline. In the end, afraid of disturbing her, I decide against it.

As Nani and I continue praying, I squirt a dollop of Keri lotion into my hand and rub her legs and feet. I graduate to hands and arms, mindful of her medical devices. Emboldened by her continued sleep, I wonder if she is unconscious as I change my mind, lifting her mask briefly and applying Vaseline to her lips.

She is deathly gray, but the moisture gives her a shallow illusion of life.

We finish our Rosary, Nani in Italian, me in English. Nani smooths her dress, black as always for those who have gone before and now for her daughter. She nods silently to me and squeezes my shoulder as she leaves.

Alone again with my mother, I feel the urge to speak to her out loud. I assume that even in her state she can hear and understand me.

I hold her hand. I will her to wake, but she does not. I start speaking, without knowing what I will say.

"Ma," I say, "I have every memory of all the times I slighted you. Hurt you. Disappointed you. I need to tell you about them.

"In third grade, I wouldn't introduce you to my best friend Elizabeth. I don't know if I was being independent or just being a brat. I lied to you about my part in jumping on my bed with Claire, producing Claire's epic nosebleed. I threw up after eating the drippy red berries with the black pit from the bush in the front yard—the ones that look just like little cherries. Telling you that lunch made me sick.

"Staying at the park after school until past suppertime. Watching you inside the front door, panicked, arms crossed, lips tight, grabbing my arm as I got to the door, demanding to know if I realized how poor my behavior was. Me, responding with anger, letting you know how suffocating you were.

"You, stunned that I could speak to you that way. I couldn't believe you didn't say anything back. You just rushed me into the house.

"Abandoning you when Papa died. Angry that you weren't paying enough attention to me. Leaving Nani and Zia to be with you.

"Feeling disappointed and useless when you didn't congratulate me on my spectacular grades. 'What's this? A ninety-nine in math? Where's the other point?' I'd roll my eyes, grab my report card, and you'd say, 'Wait! I have to sign it.' And I'd turn away, flop onto my bed, and stare at the ceiling, wishing for a different mother.

"Remember the high school prom dress I wanted from Macy's that you vetoed? Your magic sewing machine produced a much-superior product. Sullen, annoyed, I wore it without telling you how much I loved it. I loved it.

"For my prom, you bought me a beautiful corsage. I refused to wear it. I felt your hurt as I returned it to the fridge. Feeling guilty, I wore it the next day on my regular clothes.

"I'm sorry I didn't come home from college more often. I even missed Christmas a few times. I felt good, somehow, that you missed me. Feeling my heart explode when you reached your arms out in anticipation of one another's hugs.

"You were exasperated when I had not been home for two months. 'Why aren't you coming home? When are you coming home?' you demanded.

"'Ma! I'm busy,' I said.

"'What are you busy with?' you wanted to know.

"I told you, 'I'm making a life.'

"When you broke the momentary deafening silence, I heard you say, 'You making a life!' I didn't try to backpedal. I just blamed you for being mean.

"I waited so long to bring Russ home to meet you. I told myself you wouldn't approve because he's Jewish. You didn't say much when you first met him, which made me anxious and suspicious. I figured you were saving it up for a surprise salvo, when you'd be angry at me for something un-Russ. Which didn't happen. Much later, on the phone, you asked when Russ and I were coming home again. You invited us both.

"If I had it to do again, I'd behave the same way, I'm sure. Because I am stubborn. But now, I am sorry."

I rest my head on Ana's chest, listening to her irregular respirations and to her heart. Her good heart.

"I wonder if you ever can forgive me. I wonder if I ever can forgive myself for being afraid of you. For not letting you in. I was very smart at not letting you in. So smart."

This is my first time tasting this kind of sad, but I can't cry. I have wasted the chances that were mine. I am out of time. Crying is a relief I haven't earned.

I feel your spirit rising beyond me with every breath. I want to come with you. No. I want you to stay here with me. Neither is an option.

"My heart tumbled when I first found out your diagnosis. It was happening to you, and we could only live it with you, each in our own way. Nani, controlled in her grief, Zia, emotional and dependent in hers. Claire devoted to her mother as well as to you, Russ a steel pillar."

Exhausted, but reluctant to leave, we finally head home at 10 P.M. We aren't hungry. We sit up in the living room and compare notes. Everyone's account confirms that this is our death watch. We wait for the call from the hospital.

At 11:30 P.M., we begin making noises about sleep—maybe not tonight?—when my phone jangles our nerves. I do not want to answer. Nani focuses on me, one sharply raised eyebrow pinning me to the phone and to my duty. Zia mewls like a wounded kitten. Claire wraps her arm around her mother's shoulders. Russ positions himself behind my spot on the sofa, his hands already kneading my arms.

I look around the room as I answer the phone. "Yes," is all I can manage to say. "That was Ma's nurse. We need to go."

Zia clutches Claire's arm. Russ stabilizes Nani as she heads toward the door. He carefully navigates the stairs with her, then, fixing Nani's seat belt in the passenger seat of the car, he opens the back doors. We usher ourselves in.

Before we get to the hospital, I fantasize that I will bolt into her room, but standing outside the door I feel scared and small.

How will I handle being around her, so close to death. How will it smell inside her room? Will she already be gone? Will that be better than more waiting? Will there be any sound? My mother's nurse squeaks down the hall, placing herself in front of us.

"I'm so sorry. She went about ten minutes ago. I was with her. She did not wake up." Claire guides Zia to a hallway chair. Nani and Russ stand with me. The nurse nods toward the door. "You can go in."

I go in with Russ. The room is unfamiliar, the woman in the bed someone I do not recognize. The room is antiseptic. There is no noise.

I can't bear to look at her. *What am I doing here if I won't look at my own mother?* Her hair is brushed in a side part, the way she likes it. How do they know this is the way she wears her hair? Gray strands accent the edges around her cheeks and forehead. Her eyes are closed, her arms at her sides.

"Is that a smile?" I ask.

Russ nods. "Yeah, it is."

In an obituary-worthy cliché, all I can think is, *She died peacefully.*

I thought Nani would be next, but she insisted Maria and Claire go in. They do not stay long. Claire supports my aunt as she emerges from the room, clutching her rosary and struggling to control herself. With a worried frown, Claire shakes her head as she passes me.

Nani goes back in with Ana. She says nothing, simply kisses her daughter's forehead and motions me toward the door. She remains alone with Ana for several minutes, emerging dry-eyed. She nods toward the exit.

Russ has spoken to the nurse about arrangements to collect Ana. I can't process attending my mother's funeral before she's attended our wedding.

The hospital room is unfamiliar to me. My mother, deceased, is unfamiliar to me. But I am not prepared for the difference in my mother's house. My house.

I finger the BLESS OUR HOME plate hanging inside the front door. The crucifix hanging beneath. Nothing looks right. I open the closet just inside the front door and inhale my mother's scent. Her soap and shampoo and hairspray.

On the shelf, I find her shaggy red wool beret and hold it to my face. Gloves, the fingers shaped to her own. One double-breasted navy-blue jacket. One red coat with a faux fur collar. An assortment of sweaters. These I also hold to my face. Two pairs of her favorite pumps, one brown, one black, on the closet floor.

I walk back to the kitchen. The floors are immaculate, but suddenly no longer level. The oven, the stovetop and the refrigerator are alien. The only familiar sight is Ana's painted brick backsplash behind the stovetop.

I run upstairs. The favored, familiar and ancient chenille bedspread is in place on her bed. Her hairbrush is in its usual spot on the dresser mirror. I run it through my hair as I remember the careful pre-Mass rituals with her hair and mine.

I open her bedroom closet, but have to shut it quickly, reminding myself that I am nowhere near ready for this cut-to-the-quick change all at once. It isn't the sight of my mother's clothes. It is their scent—surely she has just stepped out of her tweed suit and her favorite blouse. Quick flashback to Matteo's fabric store. And to Ana, bent over the ancient Necchi sewing machine, inspecting her work at the turn of each seam. Rarely reaching for the seam ripper, nodding her approval and moving on to the next step.

Opening her nightstand drawer, I find an unframed photo of my parents, my mother's smile inclined Papa's way, my father arranging a lock of her hair behind her ear. Young. I wondered if they were married. Probably.

A journal. I read those two brief letters so I could know more about my mother. I am curious about who and what I will find in the journal's pages.

Next to the journal sits a Bible and a rosary. One of Gloria Steinem's feminist books is tucked nearby. How is it I never knew she had read Gloria Steinem? I found two carefully folded scarves and half a dozen embroidered handkerchiefs with crocheted edges, Zia's work. Holy cards from my father's funeral, and from Salvatore's and friends of my parents who had died.

I pull myself away from my mother's belongings. I have to make a list of what I need to do for Ma's funeral. Zia can be counted on to source the holy cards. I decide to ask Claire about it, and to see if Zia can work with the funeral home. I hope to inject some status into Zia's position in our family and to give her an outlet for her grief.

Claire and I will work the phones. We will endure earfuls of *Mama Mias*, sobs and over-the-phone keening. I can see the women wearing black dresses and veils with opaque black stockings rolled down to their knees. Sturdy black oxfords, immaculately embroidered handkerchiefs, and sensible black purses. These signore will sit in the second row at my mother's funeral Mass. When the Mass is completed, their skirts will be worn, shiny, and wrinkled in a pattern of uneven pleats. They will try to iron them out with their hands.

At the viewing in the funeral home, younger women, dressed in more stylish black, will urge their children toward my mother's casket and her lifeless form. Burying themselves in their mothers' legs, some will cry. Their mothers will hush them along, returning alone later to kneel and pray at Ana's casket.

I want to pray, but I cannot decide what I want to pray for. She is gone. What I really want is for her to come back. There is no prayer for that. I want to go to Nani for advice, but I can't intrude on her own grief. I know I will talk to Russ, but I'm not ready. Patient and sure, he anticipates what I need. And waits.

Claire cares for her inconsolable mother. Exhausted but stalwart, Claire helps Maria to organize the holy cards, the funeral Mass and the reception. I know my cousin is quietly doing most of the work, anxious to give Zia credit for loving her sister, for providing for her.

I can't turn forward the blank pages of my life. I want desperately to go back, to right some of the wrongs. To feel her draw me to her, her hand stroking the back of my head. To greet her at the door, her smile everything I ever needed.

I am shocked that I am not sad or grieving. I am empty.

Right now, Nani and I do not talk much. I know this will come after Ana's funeral. For the time being, my grandmother is in advice mode.

"You no need take away you mothah clothes right away. Va bene? You no go back to Boston so quick. Russ an' you stay here. E no worry for the house. Plenty time."

Three days after my mother dies, still unable to cry, I grind my teeth to powder while I sleep, waking each morning disoriented and with a sore head. In the morning, I am always momentarily convinced that my mother is downstairs preparing breakfast. But it is always Nani.

This morning, I force myself into my running gear. I find Russ for a kiss, and head down. I hug my grandmother and tell her I'll be back soon. She nods and gestures toward the front door. "Go, cara," she says.

This is it. The Day of Dread is finally here. I am grateful that my father's funeral is so far in the past. It changed me, but I survived it without knowing how. I have no idea what survival will look like with my mother's passing.

Unanchored, floating on an unknown current in an unknown sea, I am headed for a port never seen. Or maybe I'm moving in circles? Maybe I split my time between one and the other? I can't tell which.

The world is different without my mother in it. Our neighborhood is muted, tired and gray. No visible clouds, but no direct sunlight. I walk my last quarter mile and stand outside my childhood home.

The drapes and curtains are drawn open, but for me the windows are shrouded and closed. In the small garden the flowers are bowed in tribute. I make a mental note to water them, but I know it is not water they want. As I survey what was once so familiar, Nani appears at the door, scrubbing her fingers with the edge of her apron.

"You come, Gaby! Get ready," she calls. I take the steps quickly and we exchange hugs.

"Come, breakfast. You got to eat. We afraid to be late."

Nani is also showing the strain. It is now 9 A.M. My mother's funeral is at 3 P.M.

I splash water on my face in the downstairs bathroom and run upstairs to change my running shirt.

We drink more coffee than we eat of Nani's spread. Zia clutches Claire's hand on the table. Her face is swollen, her eyes red-rimmed circles. We talk, starting with how we slept. Claire reviews the arrangements Zia has made for the day.

"My sister," Zia tells us, "is the only one besides my husband who really knew me. To her I was a person. Not only emotional and worried. She was always here for me. I will always love her. I will be calm today, because I know she loves me too."

Looking into her mother's eyes, Claire squeezes her hand and smooths the back of her head. It isn't often I have seen Zia so composed.

After breakfast, Claire and I clean up. Ready to go, Russ has already showered. Nani and Zia use the bathroom. Claire and Josh are next. I opt for the rear.

I fish my plain black pants and gray striped shirt out of my small case. I will layer my black vest over my shirt.

Claire and I pass each other to and from the bathroom.

"Hot water?" I ask.

Adjusting the towel around her wet head, she responds, "Plenty," and continues to her room.

With all our last-minute needs cared for, we assemble at the front door. Russ is our chauffeur, refusing to let a stranger drive us to the church for Mass and the cemetery.

We arrive at the church to find Father Bernadin in glowing white vestments. He greets each of us as the church slowly fills. When I look behind me, I am amazed at the number of people gathered to honor Ana. Did I ever respect her this much?

I am distracted during Mass. Claire nudges me; points to the altar, a reminder to receive Communion. Nani leads all of us out of the pews. Russ walks with Nani on one arm, me on the other. As we approach the altar, Russ crosses his arms to receive a blessing. Zia walks straight-backed and dry-eyed, supported by the arms of her daughter and her son-in-law.

When Mass ends, we procession after the casket; I am stunned that I cannot capture a single thought. My legs are lead; the rest of me trudges out of the church, watching the pallbearers place my mother into the hearse. Ana's face, as it was in her last hours, leads me on.

Afterward, I get through a tasteless meal at Paolo's. Paolo is unfalteringly solicitous. I tell him all the food is great. I don't tell him I just can't taste it. I'm offered sad condolences from people who share laughter and wine as they turn away, content that this is not their story. I am not shocked at my own cynicism. I just want my mother here with me.

After the interment, at my mother's home, Russ stays beside me, stroking my arm gently, asking if I need anything. "Yes," I mumble, "my mother. Alive." I feel him nod into the back of my neck and we settle back. Numb and unbelieving, I realize: *At the age of thirty-five, I am an orphan.*

Russ and I have to get back to Boston. On no sleep, we make it through the next morning. I am dreading the time to think as we navigate the highway.

Haunted by my mother's death mask, I doze intermittently, uncomfortably. Powerless to help, I hear her coughing and sputtering. I witness Maria by her sister's side, Claire gently clawing at her mother's arm to draw her away. Nani's knitting needles slicing into yarn, her mouth a stern slash across her face.

Everything has changed since my mother's illness and death. On my face I am sure I wear a perpetual look of surprised disbelief. My thoughts, my feelings are host to the great void that is the loss of my mother. Nothing is predictable.

When I try to think about our wedding, I am consumed by useless stress and exhaustion. What is the point? I start to wonder if I am entertaining marriage only for my mother's sake. Russ and I are good without being married. If it isn't for my mother, is there a point?

CHAPTER 20

Bronx Bombshell

Two days later, I look around at our home. It feels like an abandoned landscape. It's 3 P.M. I am desperate for my back to find the sofa but resist, knowing the migraine that will be waiting if I fall asleep in the afternoon.

I make tea for Russ and me. He lets me know he's going out for groceries and I settle into email.

I thank everyone at the university for their condolences, confirm that I'll see them in two days. I dig into additional mail but find myself on the university's human resources administrative portal.

Since my mother's hospitalization, I realize how attached I am to my family home. It is both nature and nurture, my cocoon, the death of my childhood and the birth of my adulthood. The first and last place my family was whole. The place where all of us, Nani, Zia, Claire, friends and relatives outside the inner sanctum, gather.

In my chasm of loss, I cannot fathom being without my childhood home. Slowly, I realize I have been hatching a plan to keep my home, my mother, close to me.

The Precision Immunology Unit at Mount Sinai in New York has been on my radar for a while now. I know the director, and, on spec, I message her.

I want to talk to Russ about this. I want to go live in New York, in my mother's house. Work in New York. Regrow my roots and live near Nani and Zia. Convince Claire to visit often.

I hear the door shut and Russ's keys slide onto the front table. I come out and kiss my good man. He circles my waist with one strong arm as he places the grocery bag onto the table.

"Got something I need to talk to you about."

"Well, you look calmer than I've seen you in a while, so that's good, right?"

I follow him into the kitchen, retrieve plates, utensils, glasses, napkins.

Unpacking the bag, he displays the first carton from our favorite Thai restaurant. For the first time in forever, I am hungry.

I tell him I don't want to sell my mother's house. My house in the Bronx.

"So, what, you want to rent it?"

"No."

He hands me an almost amused, quizzical look.

"Other options?" he asks, but I can see he's worked it out. Smart man. "You want to live in your house."

"Yes."

"Tell me how this works, because our home is here, and your house is, well, in the Bronx. You want to move?"

"Not right away, no. I've got sabbatical time. I want to take it in New York."

"Anything in your sight?"

"Mount Sinai. I know the director of the Precision Immunology Unit there."

"So you've already reached out?"

"Not really; just messaged her to see if she gets back to me."

We talk beyond dinner. How I'll cover the Boston lab while I'm away. My status if I'm offered a position at Mount Sinai.

Russ gets it. "So you're thinking of permanency."

"Building the lab again."

Russ sits back slowly, watchful, grave.

His head makes a gradual circuit from side to side. "It's risky, you know. We're both pretty well established here. Not sure how many clients will stick with me if I move."

"And I don't know if I'll be able to stand up to the Mount Sinai culture and colleagues. If I'll want to be there. If they'll want me to be there. It's an adventure."

He reminds me, "You always use 'adventure' for complication. And you're treating me like an 'adventure'—a complication."

I pick at the edge of my placemat as he continues, "What about our wedding?"

He reads that I am guilty of not having thought about him or about our wedding.

"I'm not treating you like a 'complication.' And our wedding *is* in New York. We can do it anytime."

My suggestion that celebrating our lifelong union as a movable feast isn't lost on him.

He buses the table. The espresso machine hisses in the kitchen. He comes back in with a tray bearing espresso and two plates of tiramisu.

"To say 'welcome home' to Ana," he explains.

I walk over, try to stroke his hair.

He avoids my hand. "You know, let's just leave this for now, okay?"

I agree and we abandon it for the night. Share a huge bowl of popcorn while we watch *Goodfellas*. Again.

In the morning, I know Russ didn't sleep well. I couldn't ignore tossing and turning punctuated by cycles of deep sighing.

I try to convince myself that I've hatched a world-class hare-brained scheme. And should let it go. It's just a house, after all. But to me it isn't.

I have to be there. Live there, closest to where my mother had been, at least for a while. And I have no idea how long I will need that space. The irony of my not wanting to be there as desperately while she was there is not lost on me.

My run doesn't do much to order my thoughts or emotions. I just want to set things in motion. How can I do this without dismissing Russ? How could he possibly want to live in New York, with all his clients and friends here and without any mental preparation? How can I possibly ask this of him? And yet, I am asking. More than that, I'm expecting.

When I finish my run, I line up my runners at the door and wander into the kitchen. Russ's absence screams volumes. Will I have to get used to this? For now, I register running water followed by Russ's strong footfalls. I am anxious.

Do I try this again? Do I wait for him to bring it up? What if he says no? Do I go by myself and force us to launch long-distance living? Will Russ agree to that? What if it doesn't work?

My mind, my heart, will not calm. Our wedding has suddenly become a major, sad adventure—a complication—in our lives. In my life. I can scarcely bear to form the thought that my mother will not be there.

Russ pecks me on the cheek, hands me a cup of espresso.

"Look," he begins, "I can't talk about this right now. Sitting with it overnight, I'm not happy. I feel ignored and—"

"Oh!" I object, "I don't want—"

"No. Just listen."

"You've been thinking about this the whole time your mom was dying. And you should have told me. And you seem to have forgotten about our wedding."

I can only nod. He's right.

"So I'm pretty pissed. And very confused, now, about when we'll marry. I'm not even sure if you want to get married anymore, or where we'll live."

My mouth has gone dry.

"So," he says, "we need to prioritize. And I need to think about my work and friends we have here. I've got to tell you, right now, I really don't like this idea."

I gulp a mouthful of air and clear my throat.

"You know I want to marry you. I am just exhausted and sad," I respond to his raised eyebrow.

"This is too big to think about when you're 'exhausted and sad.'"

I try to backpedal. "Maybe I'm like a little kid, the I-want-my-mommy kind. And I just have to let it pass, y'know?"

"I know your mother is larger than life for you. I just hope I am too."

"Russ, I wasn't thinking; I'm not sure that I am thinking now."

"I know. Not thinking about us, about me, mostly."

He heads into the kitchen. I'm left alone, chewing my cuticles with a bellyful of regret.

By now, I'm pretty sure that in a revised reality I'll survive my mother's death. This, though? I'm not sure how to think or feel about it. It's the first time we've ever really been out of sync. Before this, our dance has always been in step with the same music.

I can't apologize for this. It's too big. And my reality is the same. I want to move into my mother's house. Make it our home.

We retreat to separate corners to work online. About a half hour in, I start to concentrate. I'm glad for the diversion even if I am struggling to find my normal breathing rhythm.

I take a break to make fresh espresso.

"Thanks," Russ says as I hand him a cup.

I surface just after noon. "Hungry yet?"

"Yeah," he says, "what do you want?"

I tell him this one's on me and head to the fridge.

Genoa salami. Provolone. Olives and artichoke hearts. Italian bread with sesame seeds. More coffee. I call to Russ that it's ready.

He rubs his hands together when he sees the table.

Are we normal now? I wonder.

We're not.

"After supper tonight I'm going to Jack's. Stay there for a few nights."

My stomach folds in on itself. I narrowly avoid choking.

Russ explains, "I need to think."

"You can't think here?"

"I need some other air, Gaby. I won't stay away long."

"But you can't know that, right?"

Time drops a beat before he answers. "It'll give you some time too."

I don't need time. Numb, I form the thought that we might be breaking up. Could that be true?

Everything that has happened over the past month is illuminated, suddenly, in my own self-absorbance. I can't consciously remember considering Russ at all. Only myself, my mother, Nani, Zia and Gaby. My childhood inner sanctum.

He never deserved that, but I can't take it back. I know I have to step away and let him have space. I pray his space is circular and walks him back to me.

I like Jack—great sense of humor, great friend to Russ. A great guy as far as I can tell. Jack is a good person to confide in. But I don't know him well enough to know how he will react to this event in Russ's life. And I really haven't seen much beyond his great-guy veneer.

For the remainder of the day, everything is normal. Except that in a few short hours I'll climb into an empty bed. And I have no idea what tomorrow will bring.

I tune into my escape, the lab, and fall onto the sofa with my computer until Russ steps into the room.

It's dinnertime when I surface. Russ nudges my foot. "Starting dinner. Okay?"

He's so normal. Feeling anything but normal, I answer in kind.

We make small talk while he cooks—steak and fries, green beans, carrots and salad. I play sous-chef and set the table. How can this feel just like any other night? Maybe he's changed his mind? Changing his mind I can live with. Changing his heart is something I can't face.

After we clean up, he heads upstairs. Carries a small suitcase back down. I allow myself the encouragement that this is a signal that he will stay with Jack a short time. Overnight?

He slips on his shoes, comes to me. Holds me by the shoulders and lifts my head until I look at him in the eye.

"Be okay with this. It's only for a little while. I need some space to think."

"I'm not okay with it, but I'm glad you're taking what you need. I never meant to broadside you. And I am sorry I have not considered you more over this time. Right now, mostly, I'm afraid you might not want to come back."

He strokes my face and smiles. "That's not happening. And I know you didn't diss me purposely, but it still hurts."

I kiss him and ask, "So, what about Jack—will he be good to talk to about this stuff?"

"Yeah. I think so." He smiles again. "But he has a short attention span."

I nod. I had suspected as much.

"You'll call me, right?"

"Count on it."

He tells me he loves me. I return my love, and he's through the door. I wait until he starts the car, wave, careful to wear my cosmetic smile, and close myself to the weight of silence.

I am empty space, angry at myself, seeing my sleights and missed opportunities, my impotence in helping my mother to die well. My failure to be closer to Nani. And to comfort Zia.

The silence gives way to my connecting with Claire.

I tell her.

"What?" she says simply.

I repeat the news. After an eternity of flat white noise, the line comes alive again.

I cough up the backstory.

"Wait," she interrupts. "You want to live in your mother's house? How long you been thinking about this?"

I tell her.

"And you figured you'd just spring it on Russ? Did you say anything to him along the way?"

"Well, no."

"So now the penny drops. Are you pissed at all at yourself?"

"Yes, of course."

Claire gets us back to discussing Russ's absence.

I tell her, "Our day was insanely normal. We're not angry. Well, yeah, I'm angry at me but he's infuriatingly normal and I'm just drained inside out."

She reminds me that Russ is a man of his word, and that he has told me he will be back soon. "How big was his suitcase?" she asks.

"His smallest carry-on."

"That's encouraging," she says.

Over the longest seven nights of my life, Russ and I connect many times. I'm happy for the rush attached to his name display each time his ringtone interrupts me.

We don't discuss when he's coming back.

I am grateful for the activity in the lab. Results to sort. New questions; new experiments. Two articles to prepare. I watch the calendar closely.

The eighth day, suppertime. A key slips into the lock, and, before the piece of luggage and the bag of groceries hit the floor, Russ is grabbing me, kissing me, and I erupt into laughter. My first real laughter in what is a very long time for me.

"Salmon," he informs me, pointing to the grocery bag. Neither of us lets the other go.

We settle onto the sofa, Russ with a beer, me with a wineglass full of seltzer. I hold up a finger and sprint back to the kitchen. Olives. Prosciutto. Good bread. Provolone.

Yes, he is hungry. And so am I.

Over this week, I have missed laughter. And light. I am suddenly not tired.

A man of his word. He is back.

But there is a change between us. For the first week, the effort to put him first more often costs. I've been, I realize, very selfish, caught up in the royal me. I have no idea how to make it up to him. He watches me closely. I think he is waiting for me to open door number one. Our wedding.

So we go on circling each other in good spirits, enjoying each other's company, talking about everything except door number one. And door number two, a move to New York. Or not.

Some nights, sleep does not visit. Other nights, I wake, knowing I've dreamed unrecognized sights and sounds. I am anxious. Unrested. But I am relieved knowing we are together. Will we stay together?

I eventually pull up the calendar on my computer to find myself targeting dates six to nine months in the future. It's the earliest I see our wedding. The earliest I see my mother inviting us to open door number one. Door number two crowds me. How do I talk about it without the penance of another stay at Jack's, or worse?

We carry on with my silence for a full month. Russ is definitely waiting for me.

When I decide I am about to burst, I get cagey, leaving Russ to decide. "Let me know when you want to talk."

He shuts his computer. Raises an eyebrow in my direction. "Been waiting for you."

I look at him straight on. "I've got to know you'll stay here. Will you?"

"Yeah. Been doing a lot of thinking."

"Good. Me too." I know he'll tell me when he's ready.

So I lay out door number one and door number two. Stressing that I'll need to start with door number two.

We weigh the options for each of us.

"Sinai's a great institution. But I don't know yet if I can negotiate what I want, so I'll have to investigate."

"If you don't get what you want?"

"There are other immunology units in New York."

He nods. "So you'd try other universities?"

"Yes."

He considers for a moment and reveals that he has been doing some investigation of his own.

"My three biggest clients will come with me. Not sure yet if any others will join. I am in touch with Boston people to help me target New York clients."

"That's all we can do for the moment on New York," I say.

"I think so. How about getting married?"

"Funny you should ask. I've been looking at the calendar."

"I don't really care how long the date is as long as we've got a wedding date," he says.

I bring up the calendar, and we decide on a date seven months from this day. I make notes to contact Father Bernadin and Rabbi Rosen. Paolo. Nani, Claire, Zia. Russ's family. We will get on the phone together to call all the principal people.

I am both calm and highly excited. I realize, suddenly, how important it is to me that we are married. When I tell him this, Russ grabs me by the waist and expresses his agreement.

"Okay," I announce. "A good night's work!"

"Only work?" he asks. We stop working.

CHAPTER 21

The Wedding Dress

I am burning to discuss it, but I avoid the Bronx as a subject of conversation. I'll know when Russ is ready.

Three weeks later, he is.

He looks up from his bowl of Cheerios. Bobs his spoon around in milk and multigrains. "So what do you want to do about your house in the Bronx?"

"You know what I want. The bigger question is, What you want to do?"

"I've been thinking that my life is here. Really, though, it's with you. And I'm pretty sure yours is with me. Am I wrong about that?"

"I'd say you're dead right. You know that." I ask my question a second time. "So what do you want to do?"

"If you go, I'm going too."

"What about your work? Clients?"

"In addition to my top three, a handful more tell me they will stay with me. Maybe I'll need to spend some time as a kept man?"

"You know, my mother's house is paid for."

He grins. "You don't say. What's up with the New York lab?"

I dig back into my oatmeal and blueberries. Swallow, put my napkin to work.

"Susan Cox, the immunology director at Mount Sinai, messaged me last week and asked if I'm still interested. Told her I am, but you and I need to talk. She gets that."

Russ says, "Good. If we do this, it will take some time to put together."

I tap his hand. "Right. We'll start a project list."

Russ asks, "So does this mean we're doing this?"

Being reasonable, I answer, "Let's make the list first and see what it will take. We've got a wedding list too."

The next four weeks disappear in working on our lists. I breathe life into my Mount Sinai aspiration every couple of days to keep Susan interested as I scrutinize my lab for what has to be done. First, I will have to set up a regular travel schedule to shuttle between Boston and New York. I think Russ will have to do the same for a while. Items for the list.

Some days, my mind races with the lists. A road trip to see Nani and Zia and Claire. Visits to Father Bernadin and Rabbi Rosen. Invitations. Deadlines. Securing Mount Sinai. Boston lab people to invite to New York in the event I'm welcome at Mount Sinai. Coverage for Boston courses.

What am I thinking? Russ would be much happier to stay in Boston. Married in New York, okay. But continue to live in our city. Our home. Not just my home.

But I now think of my mother's house, New York, as our home, Russ's and mine. Sitting at the dining room table, espresso steaming into the pot, studying the leaves on the huge maple tree down the block swaying as they greet us. This place roots me in time to who I am, to all I have become. And overcome.

When did I start to define this house in the Bronx as home? Was it before she died? Before she became ill? Me, always with one foot in two separate worlds. To dampen the sting of old, young feelings. To keep alive the dream of what I wished my young life had been. To have my mother there, always. And to have her drift away, her life so much sand between my fingers.

Where to start? How to talk about all this with Russ without going too fast? It is my reality, not his. I want to be in my childhood home because I want the chance to rewrite the painful parts of my childhood and the conflict of my adulthood with Ana. I could not settle in with her while she was alive. I was too angry, expecting and avoiding conflict and playing defense.

My nightmare is the event that Russ will not want to or will not be able to endure the upheaval I am causing. Just in case, I nurture a plan to commute between Boston and New York on a regular basis. A long-distance relationship, a long-distance marriage. How will Russ feel about making this work? One thing is certain. I cannot be without him, my great love.

Once I start, the list pours out of my computer. Even minus the details, I can feel the enormity of it standing my hair on end. It is a potential wrecking ball, maybe on par with Ana's death.

I print the list for Russ. Knowing him, I realize he has prepared his own list, and we will have a meeting of the minds.

I break my activity by satisfying a point of curiosity. Access our bank website. Click on the evaluation of our home here in Boston. Stunned, I realize that even if the evaluation is exaggerated to twice its actual value, we will be okay to move. I share both the evaluation and the list with Russ.

We make tacos for supper. As we sit at the table, Russ asks, "So, when do you want to go to New York?"

I stall mid-bite, re-deposit my taco to the plate. "Anytime. What do you think?"

"Call Nani—find out what's good. Then you can get in touch with the priest. I'll contact Rabbi Rosen. Oh, we want to go see Paolo, too, right?"

"And Claire and Zia too."

"Okay. Let's get the show on the road. We'll visit your house. See what we might want to do."

An amazing surge of energy takes me. I make a note to set up an appointment with Susan at Mount Sinai.

Is this happening?

"Do you want to do this?" I ask. Tentative. I am holding my breath.

"To tell you the truth, I'm not totally sure. But I want to investigate. And I want to be together."

"Okay."

We're on the road again six weeks after my mother's funeral. Nani and Zia and my cousin meet us at my mother's, our house. Kisses and hugs. Through wet eyes. Zia is smiling.

Everything is exactly where it was before, but it couldn't be more different.

The hall closet is almost empty. Claire explains, "Your mother's things are in boxes. We haven't taken anything away."

I start to tear up. Claire would have known that I couldn't bear to see my mother's clothes abandoned, cold, untouched.

"Come," says Zia, grabbing my arm and leading me to the dining room. Nani claims Russ. Claire brings up the rear.

An Italian delight waits at the table. Our favorite antipasti. The aroma of Italian wedding soup and roast lamb from the kitchen.

Russ announces our new wedding date. I let Nani know that I need to go shopping, and I need her with me. She nods. "Where we go?"

"Manhattan. Garment district."

She nods again, understanding where we're headed. "You want the wedding dress, no?"

"Yes."

"Good. You mama, she like this." My turn to nod.

I let my family in on our plans. "We'll see Father Bernadin and Rabbi Rosen while we're here. And visit Paolo."

I fold my napkin next to my plate. "Listen," I say.

Three concerned faces swivel in my direction. Russ's eyes are fixed on my grandmother. Her back, worn by years bent over a sewing machine, goes stiff.

I continue. "We're thinking of moving back here. To live in my mother's house. Our house now. It's not for sure yet—we have to organize a lot of things—but we're investigating. Seriously."

Zia clasps prayerful hands to her breast as joyful tears trickle down her cheeks. Claire wraps her arm around her mother's shoulder, pats her back and hands her a pristine linen handkerchief.

"It's good," says Nani. "You be near us." A smile and a nod of approval to Russ. "You no think too hard. You just come."

"Oh, Nani," he says, "I *want* to come."

The next few days sees us making all our promised visits. We're getting organized. We discuss my potential move to Mount Sinai and Russ's client requirements. The dock may still be remote, but from this small Boston boat it is in view for both of us.

At the end of a productive day, Zia and Josh join us. We take everyone to Paolo's for his signature homemade ravioli followed by veal stuffed with polenta. Tiramisu for dessert. "For you mama," Paolo whispers as he sets my plate in front of me. Plenty of espresso. Paolo leaves us with the bottle of amaretto.

The next day, we all head into Manhattan. Josh and Russ splinter off to Madison Square Garden to score basketball tickets. We women find the Garment District just next door.

I've decided where we're going, what I want and how much I'm spending. Mostly, I want Nani's approval.

The oversolicitous attendant rubs her hands together as we approach. Listens as I summarize who we are and what I want. She asks for coffee/tea orders as her assistant shuttles a tray of small sandwiches and pastries in our direction.

The attendant ushers me behind a screen to take measurements and to find out what sort of dress I'm looking for. Then she invites me to the coffee and snack area and asks for a few minutes.

Fifteen minutes later, we see she has been paying attention. Five different dresses, variations on a theme. Beige. Crossover bodice. A-line skirt, mid-calf. Various fabrics: chiffon, taffeta, satin, tulle. Plain. No lace. For good measure, she carries four cowl-neck styles, just in case. These have full-length or three-quarter-length sleeves.

"You try," Nani orders. "This one first." She points to a cross-bodiced dress with an impressively full flowing skirt while my cousin and aunt nod their agreement. No one dares to disagree with Nani when she's this emphatic.

I am not enjoying having a wedding dress. Nani and Zia are all in favor. Knowing this is against my grain, Claire is watching me closely. I promise myself I will make amends by changing into my wedding suit when we sit down to dinner during the reception.

Everyone approves. I insist on trying a cowl-necked dress. I like it better and decide to buy it. Almost. I am reminded of the reason for this outing.

"Nani, which one does my mother like?"

"This one you just try. Ah'm-a know."

She doesn't tell me this is the dress Ana would have sewn for me.

Wrapping them in a napkin, Zia selects a parting pastry and tea sandwich from the tray.

We're done.

The next morning, we visit Father Bernadin at St. Benedict's. Good thing I've steeled myself for his mood.

"I expected to hear from you before now." His bushy eyebrows scold us as he waits for an explanation.

I stammer through Canon authority. Russ comes to my rescue.

"We can't explain, Father. We have no excuse. Ana's death has hit us hard." Russ lets this sink in and adds, "We hope you will marry us."

I'm sure the priest doesn't really get it, but there's a subtle promise. If he doesn't marry us, we will find a priest who will.

"Oh," he says, "of *course* I'll marry you. To honor your mother."

We're both happy to leave.

We have enough time for pizza before we head to our appointment with Rabbi Rosen. In the four years Russ and I have been together, I have met the rabbi three times during gatherings for Russ's siblings. With his long gray beard, his yarmulke and his tallit, he is like a comfortable armchair for me. His eyes hold a warm smile as he searches for the eyes of the person he's greeting.

He kisses Russ on both cheeks, holds both my hands in his and gently kneads my shoulders.

"I hope this is to ask me to schedule your wedding," he starts, indicating the two guest chairs across from his desk.

Russ nods and smiles.

The rabbi produces a leather-bound calendar from his desk drawer and chooses a fountain pen. His thick gray eyebrows ask for the wedding date, and he scratches our event into his planner. He sits back, ready to listen.

Russ asks about the ceremony. We are still planning to have it in the restaurant following the Mass. The rabbi waves his hand. We both know he's not pleased with the venue for a holy event, but he will not try to talk us out of it. Again.

I am starting to hatch a plan to request having our Jewish ceremony in shul. I say nothing because I haven't yet brought this to Russ.

Balancing his weight from side to side, the rabbi begins swiveling gently as he focuses his attention on us.

"Russ, who will walk with you and accompany you under the chuppah?"

"My father and Noah," Russ answers. He and his elder brother have always been close. Rabbi Rosen officiated at Noah's and Rebecca's weddings and is fond of all Russ's siblings.

The rabbi rises from his chair and escorts us to the door. Tells us he is glad we have come to him.

I tell him, "It's complicated, Rabbi. Joining two different faiths, no?"

Smiling, he assures us, "I do know something about it."

Russ has told me about the rabbi's childhood experience in Poland. His father hid him with a Polish Catholic family before he disappeared in the murder of the Final Solution. His mother had also been taken. Neither of his parents had returned.

Russ assures the rabbi that we will be in touch soon, and we leave, skipping down the steps of the synagogue.

"Two big things down," I chirp on the way home. "Only a thousand to go."

Russ smiles at me.

He turns serious. "What's next?" he asks.

"Jobs?"

Russ summarizes for us. "Yeah, I think I'm easier than you—being mostly online."

"I think so. I have to get applications and seminars in order. See if they'll offer me a position. Then I'll get the Boston lab organized and that'll be an even better start."

"Plan B if there's no position?"

"I'll look into working with members of the unit."

His eyes abandon the road for what seems like a whole minute.

"Now I know how badly you want to make this move. You'll be okay if you have to work for someone? You do spell *independence* in all caps."

"Wouldn't be working for them. Think extended sabbatical. A guest in their labs."

The next morning, before espresso, I message Susan at Mount Sinai and ask if I can come in.

That afternoon, just as I'm starting to turn over plan B alternatives, my computer chirps with her reply. She suggests I present a seminar to faculty in the unit the day after tomorrow. This is great news. The seminar will be a formal presentation of my work to the Mount Sinai immunology faculty. It means she's vetted my curriculum vitae to her faculty, and they are interested in my research. I try not to get excited.

I begin organizing my seminar right away. Susan's told me to present only the science. The financing, the grant money I would bring with me to the unit will be a separate discussion. No need to review money if they think the work will not fit. I know my research would add another dimension to the unit's studies. If they want to stretch the unit's expertise, it will be fine. If not, I'll be searching for plan B.

I message my lab in Boston asking for the most recent results on two of our projects and spend the rest of the day putting together the presentation.

It is 9 P.M. when I call Nani. She slows down at this time of day. I imagine her holding the phone to her ear with both hands, her long white flannel nightgown buttoned to her throat, the pleats stiff to her waist. I am concerned it might be too late for her, so I am happy that she brightens when she hears my voice. I tell her what Russ and I have achieved with Father Bernadin and Rabbi Rosen.

"Ah'm-a glad!" she says. "Now we know there's a wedding."

I tell her I have some work to get done in Manhattan for a few days and ask her if we can have everyone at my mother's house for dinner five days from now. Anticipating an inquisition, I wince and wait.

"Oh," she begins cautiously. "Everything okay?"

"Yes, Nani. We just really want to see everyone."

Over the next day, Russ works the phone with clients while I polish my presentation to the unit. I have to admit I am excited as I review the work and how it organizes itself so easily. I am looking forward to presenting it.

I message Claire, who assures me that Nani has already contacted her and Zia. And that she and Josh will be there too.

During a break in his action, Russ comes in and rubs my shoulders. "I want to ask Rabbi Rosen to have the chuppah in shul instead of at Paolo's. What do you think?"

I turn from my computer, a wide smile, I know, on my face.

"Well," I say, "great minds do think alike. I've been thinking about that since we saw Rabbi Rosen. I would love to have that happen. Should we make another appointment to see him?"

"I'll call him today," he says, kisses me, and heads out to buy dinner.

I've always been, as my dissertation supervisor would often say, *good on your—my feet.* So I had learned long ago that speaking to the listeners' point of view is the most important ingredient of a good presentation.

I spend a portion of my time researching the work of the unit's faculty. I am pretty sure that I am ready to push at least some of the right buttons.

The next day, I head to Mount Sinai for my presentation. I learn that some of the buttons are indeed the right ones.

Great questions from the unit, ending with Susan's "Please tell us how much grant money you are prepared to provide coming to Mount Sinai, and the sources of funding." This surprises me. I realize her asking is a further step forward.

I am prepared. I flash the money slide I prepared just in case and explain the funding sources.

Susan calls the following morning, just after my run, wanting to know how I feel about acting as scientific support for the unit for six months to a year before taking on a tenured position. She explains I'd be paid at a tenured rate.

I hold the phone away from my ear and take a breath before I find my voice.

"Negative feedback to the work discussed yesterday?"

"No, no! It's just that it's a stretch to bring your focus of work into the unit; everybody wants more time to evaluate."

"Susan, six months to a year sounds like the unit needs some high-priced labor without hiring another scientist, don't you think? I certainly understand if faculty aren't interested, but *I'm* not interested in being brought on as junior staff. Can we work this out?"

I have Susan on speaker. My palms are sweaty. I wonder if I'm blowing it. After all, I had made the first move.

She returns quickly, "What do you have in mind?"

"As we've discussed, I'd like to come into the unit, with my grant money, tenured, with trainees and staff from the Boston lab, with space and access to communal equipment. Ready to work. As we also discussed, there is some equipment I can bring with me. I'll apply for grants to replace stuff I can't bring—and hope to share the group's equipment in the meantime."

"I'll go back to the unit's faculty and tell them what you want. Send me an email with the points we just discussed. I'll deliver it to the faculty and set up a meeting in the next few days. I'll be back in touch."

The labs in the Mount Sinai unit are carved out of communal square footage. I am told there is space for the Boston group to spread out. Susan wants some expertise to ease the unit's academic load. I am anxious to discuss this with Russ. I am ready to agree to the scientific assistant position, Susan's proposal, but only if saying no is a deal-breaker.

I'm put out by Susan's proposal, but grateful that Russ has been at the door, listening to the conversation. No need to thrash it out.

"So," I ask, "what do you think?"

As I expected, he shoots his own question back at me.

"What do *you* think?"

He has come armed with fresh espresso and a plate of biscotti. He grabs a cookie from the plate before he sets it down and takes a seat to my left in my mother's wing chair.

"I want to come on as tenured faculty. I've earned it."

"Yes, you have. But they didn't advertise a position. You asked for the job, right?"

"Yeah, but I've got lots of grant money and good people. And a really good track record."

Depositing an army of crumbs on the plate, I crunch a length of my cookie and consider. I need to think this through. Russ is right. I approached Mount Sinai. They did not have an advertised position.

Russ plants a kiss on my forehead and announces that he is ready to make breakfast for us.

Suddenly, I am starving.

Later in the day, we call on Rabbi Rosen.

He invites us into his office. "Come," he says. "Sit."

Always straightforward, right after he thanks the teacher for seeing us, Russ put his question to the rabbi.

"Rabbi. We've gotten, you know, a second chance at getting married. And, of course, it's complicated by our Jewish-Catholic dynamics."

We wait. Rabbi Rosen shifts in his seat, his left hand cradling his cheek.

"You know I will encourage you to seek the blessings of both faiths in your wedding celebrations. And in your marriage."

"Yes, Rabbi," I assure him, "we want this too."

Russ picks up the thread of our conversation.

"Rabbi, we want to marry in shul, after the Catholic Mass, on the same day. The chuppah does not belong in a restaurant."

The rabbi considers us before he responds.

"Why do you want this? You know it's not for the Jewish community, right? You won't be the first Jew who moves away from our faith. Don't throw it a bone. Decide if you want to start practicing our way of life. Your children, HaShem willing to bless you, will be Catholic. That's not a choice you can make. Your choice is to be a Jew. Or not. And to teach your children. Or not. You have to decide. Either way I will marry you under the chuppah in shul."

We thank him, Russ promising that he will review his commitment to his faith. Rabbi Rosen agrees that he will meet with Russ to discuss his decision. The teacher leans toward us again.

"About the shul ceremony. Your Catholic guests?"

I shrug. "They are all welcome. We will not pressure them to attend," I say simply.

Russ closes the parenthesis. "We feel the same way for Jewish guests at the Catholic Mass."

Rabbi Rosen nods and with his ancient fountain pen he amends the event in his synagogue calendar to confirm that the synagogue will host the Jewish rite. Supporting himself on the desktop with his hands, he rises from his sunken leather chair.

We thank him again. He embraces us both, walks us to the door, and holds it open for us.

When we return home, I get started on our family dinner. After antipasti, stracciatella, two varieties of insalata mista—mixed salad—and caprese; the pasta course will feature ziti in tomato sauce with eggplant and ricotta. For the main course, we will have bistecca fiorentina, the way my mother used to marinate it. I know Zia will bring her cannoli. And Russ is already out buying the tiramisu from Ana's favorite bakery.

Lost in my mother's routines, I feel her guiding my hands and my mind, as I time the preparation of the dishes. Marinate the beef. Prepare the soup. Then, eggplant for the pasta. As I work, I feel her smiling at how well she has trained me.

Russ returns, places the bakery box on the counter and circles me from behind. "Smells fantastic. Sure you're using enough garlic?"

I slap his hand and he moves along the counter to grind beans for espresso.

He points to the pastry box. "You want some now?" he asks.

I steal a look at the clock. Two hours. Enough time for sure.

"Hey," I say. Russ invites me to continue.

"The Italian part of our wedding dinner is in Paolo's hands. What do we want to do for the Jewish part?"

By the time we discuss kneidlach—matzo ball—soup, challah—the tender braided egg bread—the egg-and-tomato shakshuka, roast chicken, blintzes and latkes, my mouth is watering.

"Oh," I remind us. "Lox."

"And brisket," Russ puts in.

"We won't run out of food! D'ya know who you want to cater it?"

Russ shakes his head. "I don't, but Noah will." Noah now lives with his family in the Catskills north of the Bronx, so he knows the area and the businesses.

"I'll clear it with Paolo," I say.

My family arrives greeted by antipasti from the living room and the aromas of the kitchen.

After kissing us, Nani makes her way to the kitchen. She ties one of my mother's aprons about her waist, lifts pot covers, peers inside the oven. Wraps the long loaf of garlic bread in aluminum foil.

"Looks good," she assures me. "The fiorentina like you mama, no?" I nod, and she rubs my back.

We join everyone in the living room.

Zia hugs and kisses me for a second time, caressing my cheek with her well-worked hands.

She hands over a platter. "Ah," she says, "some dessert."

"Oh, Zia, it just wouldn't be dinner without your cannoli."

Claire has settled herself next to Josh on the sofa. I go to her for an exchange of hugs.

For the first time in forever, I am laughing with my family around the table. Claire, Russ and Josh take turns serving and clearing. Scraping her chair behind her, Nani disappears into the kitchen, carrying back wafts of espresso steam, demitasse cups, plates and forks. Zia folds her napkin and leaves the table to prepare the cannoli. Russ rescues the tiramisu from the kitchen.

A chorus of *aah*s greets Zia's cannoli.

Over dessert, Russ summarizes our meeting with Rabbi Rosen.

"This is good," Nani assures us. "Russ needs the synagogue. You too, Gaby."

Over the next four months, professional and wedding arrangements start to fall into place.

My Mount Sinai plans are shaping up too. I will come to Mount Sinai with tenure at New York University. Over each academic year, I will teach two courses that I will introduce and two that the university requires. Four students/postdoctoral fellows and one technician will follow me from Boston, supported by NYU. I am invited to ask two additional trainees, supported by my grants.

Susan and I negotiate the scientific support position, essentially a junior faculty watchdog job, keeping faculty on track with deadlines and plans for grants and course offerings. Things faculty normally do for themselves. Susan hasn't mentioned it, but I am sure she has created this position to free up faculty research and teaching time. For me, this function is in addition to the responsibilities of my tenured position and my own research and teaching.

Sue insists on a year fulfilling this position—a prison sentence of sorts—with an additional stipend for doing it. I agree, of course, but I am already dreading it. Academics hate people looking over our shoulders.

Our wedding plans progress. Paolo books us for our wedding dinner, and, after sampling their wares, we take Noah's advice and invite Rabinovitch's Catering to provide our Jewish menu.

CHAPTER 22

The Other Wedding Dress

Before Russ and I head back to face our Boston music, I fix a date with Nani for me to come back a month in the future.

Russ is satisfied with his client following to New York. He is confident he can build it. The official Mount Sinai offer arrives two weeks after we return to Boston, launching us into departure mode. After meeting with me about the people in my lab, and lamenting the loss of my grant funds, my chair sends me to the dean, who tries to talk me out of moving to New York.

The dean tells me, "I need someone to coordinate all of Immunology—lots of departments doing immunology research and teaching, but there's no coordination. You'd have an office and a staff."

He's offering a huge headache with too many academic prima donnas and another full-time job. The only thing worse than looking over an academic's shoulder is herding a bunch of them. We are, after all, like cats.

I thank him and politely decline his offer. I explain again why I want to make the move.

A quizzical look on his face, he says, "I don't really understand." Inviting me to explain, he extends his palm and relaxes into his chair. "I mean, your mother is not there anymore."

"But my history is." He nods, we talk a bit more, and he rises from his chair, the green light nudging me out of his office. He shakes my hand and wishes me well, and I am gone.

Getting back to the lab, I call everyone together and tell them what I've decided to do. Jaws drop. Some lab members elbow each other and nod *I-told-you-sos* in each other's directions.

"I know you have lots of questions. I'll start answering them tomorrow. For now, I need to see everyone's progress over the last four weeks. Organize yourselves into a roster. Fifteen minutes each. Let me know who wants to go first. We start in an hour. Okay?"

I know I'm pushing them, but I know they'll comply. They have no choice. I have intentionally fast-tracked the meetings. Whoever is really on top of their work will be ready.

This done, I get ready to invite selected lab members to New York. The when-where-rank-salary offers.

I've already picked my dream team. This is a final check. I have a backup plan in case my intentions fall short of lab members' plans.

In the end, three of my four dream team members agree to a future in New York. I invite an additional trainee from our roster. I wonder briefly how everyone will react to the city. I hope they will love it.

The month goes quickly. When I arrive back in the Bronx, I lure Nani into coming shopping with me for her dress for the wedding by telling her we're shopping for me.

When we're halfway there, Nani asks, "Why we go Man-hatt?"

"I thought it'd be nice. We can go to lunch after."

"Hmm. Where we go?" At the news of Little Italy, she says, "Okay."

My plan is to work our way toward Little Italy. In Macy's on Thirty-Fourth Street, I tell her we're shopping for her. She shakes her head firmly, first left, then right. "Ah'm-a no buy for me."

"You're right," I say. "I'm buying for you."

"No, my dear," she insists. Her mouth is set, arms crossed.

Time to pull out the heavy artillery. "Nani, do it for Ana."

She takes a minute to pull herself together. And falls into step with me.

"What color?" I ask, knowing that my grandmother has worn only black from the time my grandfather died years ago. I guide her toward the fancier dresses for women of her size and age. I am not surprised when she gravitates toward black.

"Ah'm-a wear black with you mama no here."

I offer her first a black suit, the skirt just below the knees, with wide lapels on the jacket sporting silver piping.

She examines it critically and responds to my selection with "What else?"

I offer a longer dress with black sequins sewn onto the bodice. Sheer chiffon long sleeves. A slit in the skirt, showing off the same chiffon lining.

Her head bobs hopefully from side to side.

Finally, a black-accented pearl-gray dress, three-quarter length sleeves, mid-calf length. "Bee-*yack*," she says, forcing me to place it back on the rack.

"Any more, Nani?"

"No," she says. "Ah'm-a like this one." She points to the black dress with the sequin bling.

"Here," I encourage her. "Try it on."

This is the first time I remember seeing my grandmother's waist. The fit is perfect. With her hair piled into a bun, she will look beautiful, especially showing off her wedding earrings from Grandpa.

Shyly, she turns to me after I help her into the dress. "Ah, you like?"

I do like it, but I need to hear it from her. "What do you think?"

She almost giggles. "Ah'm-a like!"

"Good! You look absolutely beautiful!"

She blushes. "We done," she decides.

"No, Nani. We need shoes and a jacket."

She tries to wiggle out of it, but she's finally convinced. "We don't have to come again if we do it now, right?" Sturdy sensible black raw silk shoes. Black raw silk jacket. Black silk shawl shot with silver thread. We're set.

She complains about the expense. I reassure her that it is part of our wedding budget. Besides, my mother will haunt me if I let her pay for any of it.

We make our way to Little Italy and sit down to lunch. The air in the restaurant, circulated by large ceiling fans, is infused with garlic and onions. We start with Italian wedding soup and antipasti followed by Lombardi's legendary pizza.

With a look, I offer my grandmother a silent question halfway through the pizza.

"It's okay, but we make better, no? And the zuppa—soup—not so much flavor."

Behind my napkin, I smile at her critique, classifying it as high praise.

The cannoli really does not measure up to Zia's, but it's good. And the espresso is great.

By the end of our meal, I know that Nani is tired. I pay the bill, usher her to the restroom and link arms with her as we approach the exit.

We head back to the car arm in arm. She breathes in the streets and the shops. As we stop at a deli that catches her eye, she's suddenly energized. Fresh mozzarella, fat bread, Italian sesame baguettes, hot peppers, pepperoncini and Genoa salami. Some for her, some for me.

She dozes on the way home. My heart skips a beat thinking how much longer I will have her. I know I cannot possibly prepare for her being gone. Looking over at her, content in the passenger seat, I push the torment away.

When we arrive at her home, she tells me, “Come in. Ah’m-a call you aunt to come see.”

Which she does, invoking all the appropriate accolades during my grandmother’s fashion show. I am delighted that she is so happy with her choices.

Nani insists we stay for supper. She pulls baked marinated chicken and stuffed artichokes from her fridge as she secures her apron around her waist.

Insalata caprese with the mozzarella from the Manhattan deli and her forever stash of fresh basil.

I slice bread. Zia arranges our deli lode on a platter, and we sit down to my grandmother’s lemon-garlic chicken and artichokes stuffed with seasoned breadcrumbs, drizzled with olive oil and balsamic vinegar. Good thing Nani prepared enough of them for a party.

I am calm and validated that Russ and I are making a good decision by coming back to my birthplace.

Starting our marriage is the only thing left to do.

Which we do.

CHAPTER 23

Pomp and Ceremony

Russ and I begin our married lives under Father Bernadin's celebration of the Mass. My family participates from the front pew. Physically missing my mother, I make a mental space that sees her between Nani and Zia. I wear the dress I bought to honor Ana as I approach the altar. I feel elegant as Russ and I walk with our arms linked. He kisses me and Father Bernadin begins.

Russ's family, including his brother Noah, his sisters and his dad, take their cue from my family, rising and sitting and kneeling at all the right times. They are relaxed and smiling. I wonder if they are at all uncomfortable. They do not appear to be.

Some of Russ's cousins and friends occupy the pews behind his family. They look uncomfortable.

We greet everyone after Mass, reminding them with the help of Claire's printed cards that we will meet at shul in thirty minutes. We head out as a convoy.

Russ and I drive with Nani and Zia. "Ah'm-a so happy," says Nani. "You mama, too, Gaby." She and Zia hold each other's hands as I stroke Russ's knee. His broad smile is contagious.

The rabbi greets us at the entrance to the synagogue. After he kisses each of us, he reaches for my hands. "Come," he says simply.

The chuppah, symbolizing the home we will make as a married couple, stands ready for us. Most of our guests, Jewish and Catholic, are present. We all listen to the moving words of the rabbi as he introduces us to our Jewish life together. Russ's brother Noah and their father are under the chuppah with us.

When Rabbi Rosen has completed the prayers in Hebrew and a summary in English, I walk around my husband seven times to symbolize our wholeness and the seven blessings of marriage.

Russ smashes the glass draped under the linen cloth on the ground. This symbolizes our commitment and a marriage that will last forever.

We are twice married. I am renewed, ready for this new life that is beyond what Russ and I have had before.

CHAPTER 24

Pomp and Aftermath

Russ and I have just celebrated our fifth wedding anniversary. Zia and Claire and Josh, Russ's brother Noah and his wife and a few friends shared our dinner starting with kneidlach soup and antipasti, followed by a huge assortment of foods from both sides of our aisle.

Afterward, I am seated in our dining room, watching my favorite maple tree gently wave its leaves at me. I cradle a cup of espresso as I nibble one of Zia's biscotti.

Nani died two years ago. She was content at her passing, happy she would see Nonno and Arturo and my mother again. I talk to my mother and my grandmother every day, to my father a little less frequently. I am grateful for their continued presence in my life and for their wise advice.

Russ and I enjoy New York. Often, when I've finished work in the lab for the day, we meet in Manhattan. The lab goes well. I'm well pleased when my indentured servitude as a scientific advisor is complete.

To treat ourselves, we sometimes visit Boston, staying at one of the hotels near Boston Common, where we lived. I am always happy to relive my mother's visit with us.

We have tried for children twice. Both times I suffered abrupt, life-threatening ectopic pregnancies, losing one fallopian tube, the other remaining, intact but scarred by significant adhesions. I imagine it unmoored and floating around uselessly.

The first loss doubled me in cramps, forcing Russ to carry me up the concrete staircase. I fell into the vestibule, vacantly wondering if this was what labor was all about. I knew in my heart I would not experience the event. Surgery removed both the child and my fallopian tube at nine weeks of gestation.

The second event was nearly as dramatic, but without surgery. The pregnancy was already terminated, again in the ninth week. The medical team treated the remaining tube with medication. After this, neither Russ nor I had the heart to try again.

We are growing into our family of two. It helps that we see Claire's family often and delight in her twins, Evan and Gertie.

Now in my forties, I consider myself learned in some important ways. Grief, I have learned, is lived in layers. And peeling back each layer comes with pain and tears. I have learned love served to me and, I hope, how to return a helping or two. I am learning the damage of judgment to others and to myself. Though I still practice it, I am learning to temper it.

I have learned the importance of the big picture—the main course—and am learning how to leave the "small stuff" as side dishes I can pass up.

In some ways, I have suffered Nani's loss more deeply than I have my mother's. Always happy with who I am and where my life led, Nani was my head cheerleader. Her advice was always sound, her smile always true. She was my moral compass. I always felt myself in her heart, as much as she lived in mine.

In my mother's lifetime, I feasted on bitterness and winning against her. Now, I feel her warmth and her wisdom as I sense her supervising my cooking and my sewing. As I play back her advice, I am able to admit how her experience and her good heart make her right in so many circumstances.

And, after all this time, I have learned how to love Ana.